A
Christmas

Are these bachelors Down Under about to propose?

By
Request™

Praise for three bestselling authors –
Miranda Lee, Emma Darcy and
Lindsay Armstrong

About Miranda Lee:
'Miranda Lee's talent for penning colourful
descriptions tantalizes the imagination…'
—www.thebestreviews.com

About THE MARRIAGE DECIDER:
'Emma Darcy creates a strong emotional
premise and sizzling sensuality…'
—Romantic Times

About MARRIED FOR REAL
'Lindsay Armstrong adds an interesting
twist to this marriage of convenience tale.'
—Romantic Times

An Australian Christmas

THE SEDUCTION PROJECT

by

Miranda Lee

THE MARRIAGE DECIDER

by

Emma Darcy

MARRIED FOR REAL

by

Lindsay Armstrong

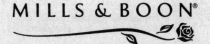

MILLS & BOON®

MILLS & BOON and MILLS & BOON with the Rose Device are registered trademarks of the publisher.
Harlequin Mills & Boon Limited,
Eton House, 18-24 Paradise Road, Richmond, Surrey, TW9 1SR

AN AUSTRALIAN CHRISTMAS
© by Harlequin Enterprises II B.V., 2002

The Seduction Project, The Marriage Decider and *Married for Real*
were first published in Great Britain by Harlequin Mills & Boon Limited
in separate, single volumes.

The Seduction Project © Miranda Lee 1998
The Marriage Decider © Emma Darcy 1999
Married for Real © Lindsay Armstrong 1996

ISBN 0 263 83163 9

05-1202

*Printed and bound in Spain
by Litografia Rosés S.A., Barcelona*

Miranda Lee is Australian, living near Sydney. Born and raised in the bush, she was boarding-school educated and briefly pursued a career in classical music, before moving to Sydney and embracing the world of computers. Happily married, with three daughters, she began writing when family commitments kept her at home. She likes to create stories that are believable, modern, fast-paced and sexy. Her interests include meaty sagas, doing word puzzles, gambling and going to the movies.

Look out for Miranda Lee's powerfully passionate office romance:
AT HER BOSS'S BIDDING
on sale next month in Modern Romance™

THE SEDUCTION PROJECT

by

Miranda Lee

CHAPTER ONE

TWENTY-FIVE today, Molly thought as she brushed her hair back from her high forehead and coiled its straight brown length on top of her head.

A quarter of a century.

Sighing, Molly inserted the first of six securing pins without having to look at what she was doing. She'd done her hair like this for the last few years. It was easy and practical and, above all, cheap. She needed every spare cent from her pay packet to make ends meet.

At last she glanced up into the vanity mirror and surveyed the finished product with a wry smile. There was no doubt she looked the stereotyped concept of a librarian through and through. Prim hairdo. Prissy blouse. Pleated skirt. All she needed was horn-rimmed glasses balancing on the end of her none too small nose to complete the staid image.

Molly had twenty-twenty vision, however. Which was unfortunate in some respects. How much kinder it would be, she imagined, to have a fuzzier reflection first thing every morning.

She suddenly saw herself looking in the bathroom mirror on her fiftieth birthday and nothing would have changed much, not even her hairstyle.

She would still be living at home with her mother. She would still be plain.

And she would still be madly in love with Liam.

Her shudder was part despair, part self-disgust. For loving Liam was such a waste of time; such a waste of her life.

Molly knew he would *never* love her back.

She no longer clung to the teenage fantasy where Liam woke up one day and saw that his feelings for the girl next door had somehow miraculously changed overnight from platonic friendship to an all-consuming passion. By the time she turned twenty-one, Molly had graduated from romantic to realist. Difficult to hold onto such a futile dream in the face of the type of girl Liam brought home with regular monotony.

'Plain' did not describe them. Neither did blue-stocking, nor bookworm, as Molly had been labelled all her life. Liam's girlfriends were better known for their bodies than their brains. He liked them tall and tanned, with long legs, lush breasts and hair which shimmered.

Molly told herself she had the right breasts, but nothing short of the rack was going to add four inches to her average height. And, while her hair was always clean and healthy, mousy brown just never seemed to shimmer.

So Molly had long since abandoned any romantic schoolgirl dreams when it came to Liam. Common sense told her he was a lost cause. Yet still she clung to the emotion of loving him, clung to it as a drowning man clung to the most tenuous lifeline. Why else was she living in this house which was far too big for just two people, and far too expensive?

Because Liam's family lived next door, that was why. If Molly and her mother moved, she would never see him again. Never feel the joy—as bittersweet as it was—of having him drop in for a drink and a chat, as he did every once in a while.

Liam called her his best friend, but Molly knew she wasn't really that. She was simply *there*, a convenience, a ready ear to listen and give him feedback on his latest computer game or graphic design idea.

A deep dismay momentarily filled her soul before it was abruptly banished by a surprising burst of anger. How could Liam be so blind? And so darned insensitive? And why did *she* have to go on wallowing in his lukewarm and highly one-sided version of their being 'best friends'?

Best friends were supposed to share things, weren't they? Where was the give and take in their relationship? Today was her birthday, damn it. But would he remember? Not on your nelly! The dynamic head of Ideas and Effects Pty Ltd couldn't be expected to remember such trivia. He was far too busy running his excitingly successful business. Heck, he hardly had time to come home any more! She hadn't sighted him since Christmas, a full two months back.

There would be no phone call. No card, let alone a present. Yet she'd shopped for hours to find him the right gift for *his* birthday last year. She'd even cooked him a cake!

'Molly,' her mother called out through the bathroom door. 'What's taking you so long in there? Your breakfast's been on the table for a full five minutes.'

'Coming!'

Breakfast that morning was a small glass of orange juice, one boiled egg, one thin slice of wholemeal toast, one teaspoon of margarine and black coffee. A big improvement on the minute bowl of cereal Molly usually ate.

Ever since her father had died of a heart attack two years before at the relatively young age of fifty-one, her mother had become obsessed with health and dietary matters. Nothing passed their lips these days that exceeded the strict fat and calorie limits which were now Ruth McCrae's culinary bible.

This meant mealtimes held little joy for Molly, who had a chronically sweet tooth. She found it all a bit trying, yet could not deny that her once plump curves had benefited from this change of eating habits. She'd dropped two dress sizes and would now not shrink from going to the beach—if she hadn't freckled like mad.

'Wow!' she exclaimed as she sat down at the kitchen table. 'This looks really good.'

'Well, it *is* your birthday, love,' Ruth said. 'I'm going to cook you a special dinner tonight as well.'

Molly could not help wondering what a 'special' dinner constituted these days. She'd bet it wasn't baked pork with crackling and crispy roast potatoes, followed by a big chocolate cake and coffee with cream in it. 'That'll be nice, Mum,' she said, and picked up her knife, ready to attack the boiled egg.

'Aren't you going to open your card?' Ruth asked plaintively.

Molly could have kicked herself. She put down her knife and picked up the long white envelope propped against the fruit bowl. Inside was a sweetly sentimental card and a couple of lottery tickets which promised first prize of half a million dollars.

'I'm sorry I couldn't afford more,' her mother said apologetically.

Molly glanced up with a bright smile. 'Don't be silly. This is great. I might win a fortune and then we could both go for a trip around the world.'

'Oh, I wouldn't want to do that. I like my home too much. But you could go, I suppose,' she added hesitantly.

Molly could see that this idea did not sit well with her mother. Perhaps she was already regretting giving her daughter the chance—however slim—of becoming rich and possibly flying the nest.

Ruth McCrae was a naturally shy woman, who'd become even more reserved and reclusive since her husband's death. She rarely left the house except to go shopping, and that was only down to the small local shopping centre which also housed the library branch where Molly worked. She had no close friends and lived for her house, her garden and her daughter.

Once in a while, Molly found her mother's dependence on her stifling. But on the whole she accepted her fate without undue distress. She was, after all, her mother's daughter, which meant she was a quiet, undemanding girl with few unsettling yearnings.

The only yearning which could disturb her dreams—as well as her equilibrium—was Liam. Even then, she'd learned to control her unrequited passion for him. Clearly, he'd never guessed what smouldered behind her cool green eyes whenever they looked upon his handsome face.

And he never would.

This realisation suddenly brought another stab of anger. But this time none of it was directed at Liam. All of it was channelled straight at herself.

You're a fool, Molly! If it was one of your girlfriends pining after some man who was way out of their reach, you'd tell her to forget him and move on. It's about time you took your own advice.

Forget Liam. Move on!

Molly picked her knife up again and sliced the top off her egg with one decisive stroke. That was going to be her from now on. Decisive.

And her first decision was to stop fantasising about Liam and move on!

CHAPTER TWO

MOLLY was standing at the library computer, running the wand over the first of the huge pile of returned books, when something caught her eye. Something bright and red.

She glanced up through the glass doors to see a shiny red car turning its brand-new nose into the empty parking space right outside the library.

It brought no flash of recognition, despite being a very memorable model. Not quite a sports car, it was still stylish and expensive-looking. A newcomer to the area, no doubt, not knowing that this particular library branch was closed to the public on a Wednesday morning.

Molly was about to return to the job at hand when the driver's door opened and a heart-joltingly familiar head of hair came into view, gleaming golden under the summer sun.

Liam.

Her heart leapt. So he *had* remembered her birthday. He'd even come in person. She could hardly believe it!

Her happiness knew no bounds as she watched him close the car door and stride up onto the pavement and across to the front doors. He smiled at her through the glass as he tap-tapped on the wooden frame.

'Can't they see we're closed?' Joan complained from where she was sitting at her desk, flipping through one of the new publisher catalogues. She could not see who was knocking. If she had, she would not be so anxious to send the unwanted visitor away. Joan might be a happily married thirty-three-year-old woman with three children, but she still had an eye for a good-looking man.

Liam was just that—and more. At thirty, he was in his physical prime, his elegant body in perfect tune with his equally elegant face. Six feet two inches tall, his lean frame made him look even taller, as did his choice of clothing. He had this thing for jackets, wearing them all year round.

In winter they ranged from soft suede numbers to tweedy sports coats. In summer he chose linen or lightweight wool in neutral colours, and teamed them with cool T-shirts during the day and silk shirts at night. Ties rarely graced his neck. In fact, Molly had never seen Liam dressed formally.

Today he was wearing stonewashed blue jeans, a navy T-shirt and a loose cream linen jacket with sleeves pushed up to the elbows. His streaky blond hair was longer than when she'd seen him last, falling to his ears from its side parting and flopping with its usual rakish charm across his high forehead. He looked slightly wind-blown and utterly gorgeous.

Molly immediately put her 'moving on' decision

on hold for a good five years. Thirty, she decided anew, was soon enough to give up all hope.

The fact that Liam was standing where he was at this very moment *had* to give her some hope. Fancy him abandoning his precious business on a working day to drive the fifty miles from Sydney to Gosford, just to see her on her birthday.

'For pity's sake!' Joan snapped when Liam knocked a second time. 'Can't they read? The library times are on the darned door!'

'It's someone I know,' Molly said. 'I'll just go let him in.'

Joan jumped up from her desk. 'But it's almost…' The sight of Liam's handsome self stopped her in her tracks. 'Mmm. Yes, by all means let him in,' she murmured, primping her glossy black waves as Molly hurried out from behind the reception desk and across the functional grey carpet.

Molly wasn't worried that Liam would find Joan attractive. As pretty as she was, she was a married woman.

Liam believed in keeping his sex life simple.

'One girl at a time,' he'd once confided in Molly. 'And never anyone else's.'

It was a surprisingly conservative attitude in this day and age, especially coming from a man who looked like Liam, who had women throwing themselves at him all the time.

He had a similarly strict attitude to marriage. Only one per lifetime, which was why he'd always said he would not bother with marriage till he was in his thirties and financially secure. He didn't want to make a mistake in finding his perfect partner.

'In the meantime,' he'd joked to her one day, 'I'm having a lot of fun auditioning possible future candidates for the position of Mrs Liam Delaney.'

It had always terrified Molly that one of those future candidates might capture Liam's love as well as his lust. Fortunately, that hadn't happened, and Molly had taken heart from the failure of his various very beautiful girlfriends to last more than a few months.

But his latest was a bit of a worry. A statuesque blonde who went by the name of Roxy, she'd already lasted six months—a record for Liam. He'd even brought her home with him for the Christmas break, during which time Molly had had many opportunities to see Roxy's physical assets. What she could do for a bikini was incomparable!

But I'm not going to think about Roxy right now, Molly told herself as she turned the key and swept open the door. Today is my birthday and my very best friend has come to celebrate it with me.

'Liam!' she exclaimed, smiling up into his dancing blue eyes.

'Hi there, Moll. Sorry to interrupt. I know you're working but I simply had to show you my new car. Picked it up this morning at one of those dealerships just the other side of Hornsby and couldn't resist taking it for a spin. Before I knew it I was on the expressway and heading north. I was over the

Hawkesbury Bridge before you could say boo, and was about to turn round when I thought, What the hell, Liam? You haven't had a day off in ages. Drive up to Gosford and visit your mum.'

He smiled a rueful smile, showing perfect teeth and a charming dimple. 'It wasn't till I pulled into the driveway that I remembered today is her golf day. Took all the wind out of my sails, I can tell you. But no way was I going back to Sydney without showing someone. Naturally, I thought of you. So what do you think of it?' And he waved in the direction of the car. 'It's one of the new Mazda Eunos 800s. The Miller Cycle version. Great red, isn't it?' he finished.

Every drop of joy drained out of Molly. Liam hadn't come for her birthday. He'd come to show her a pathetic car. Worse, she hadn't even been his first choice of viewer. She'd run a very poor second. As usual!

Something hard curled around her heart, setting it in concrete and trapping her love for him deep inside. Molly determined it would never see the light of day again. She glanced coldly over at the offending car and shrugged dismissively.

'If you've seen one red car, Liam,' she said coolly, 'you've seen them all.'

There was no doubt he was taken aback by the icy indifference of her tone, for his eyebrows shot up and he stared at her with bewilderment in his beautiful blue eyes.

Molly was disgusted with herself for instantly feeling guilty. So much for her first foray into hating Liam! But she was determined not to weaken this time. Enough was enough.

'You know me, Liam,' she went on brusquely. 'I've never been a car person.'

'That's because you've never learned to drive, Moll. You'd appreciate cars much more if you were ever behind the wheel. Come on, come for a short spin with me.' He actually took her arm and began propelling her across the pavement.

'Liam!' she protested, wrenching her arm away from his hold and planting her sensible shoes firmly on the pavement. 'I *can't*. I'm at work.'

'But the library's not even open,' he argued. 'Surely they won't miss you for a couple of minutes?'

'That's beside the point,' she said sternly. 'You might be your own boss, Liam, and can come and go as you please, but most people can't, me included. Besides, it's almost morning tea and I have to be here for that.'

The rest of the staff had all chipped in to buy her a cake. It was a tradition in the library whenever one of them had a birthday. No way was she going to run out on her real friends to indulge Liam's ego.

'I don't see why,' he said stubbornly.

No, you wouldn't, Molly thought mutinously, and toyed with telling him, just so he could feel terrible for a full ten seconds.

The decision was taken out of her hands when Joan popped her head out the door.

'Come on, birthday girl. Greg's brought your cake along and all twenty-five candles are alight and waiting. So get in here and do the honours. You can bring your hunk of a friend, if you like,' she added, looking Liam up and down with saucily admiring eyes. 'We've more than enough cake for an extra mouth.'

Molly relished Liam's groan. To give him some credit he did look suitably apologetic once Joan disappeared.

'God, Moll, I had no idea it was your birthday. There I was, blathering away about my new car, and all that time you must have been thinking how damned selfish I was being.'

Frankly, she was enjoying his guilt. It had a deliciously soothing effect on her damaged pride. 'That's all right, Liam. I'm used to your not remembering my birthday.'

He winced anew. 'Don't make me feel any more rotten than I already do.'

Molly almost gave in. It was awfully hard to stay mad at Liam. He didn't *mean* to be selfish. He was, unfortunately, the product of a doting mother and far too many God-given talents. Brains *and* beauty did not make for a modest, self-effacing kind of guy. Liam could be generous and charming when he set his mind to it, but in the main he was a self-absorbed individual who rarely saw beyond the end of his own classically shaped nose.

God knows why I love him so much, Molly thought irritably.

But then her eyes travelled slowly from his perfect face down over his perfect body, and every female cell she owned clamoured to be noticed back.

But the only expression in *his* eyes when he looked down at her was remorse. When he forcibly linked arms with her, she glared her frustration up to him.

'Don't be mad at me, Moll,' he said with disarming softness.

'I'm not mad at you,' she returned stiffly.

'Oh, yes, you are. And you have every right to be. But I'll make it up to you tonight, if you'll let me.'

'Tonight?' she echoed far too weakly.

'Yes, tonight,' he said firmly. 'But for now I think your colleagues are waiting for you to blow out those twenty-five candles.'

With typical Liam confidence he steered her into the library and proceeded to charm everyone in the place. It annoyed Molly that he gave her openly curious workmates the impression he was a boyfriend of sorts. He even extracted her promise in Joan's goggle-eyed presence to go out with him later that evening. She initially refused dinner—no way was she going to disappoint her mother—but grudgingly agreed to after-dinner coffee somewhere.

Molly told herself afterwards that she would *never* have agreed to go out with him at all if she'd been alone with him. She would have sent him on his way with a flea in his ear! She didn't need his pity, or his guilt.

The moment his new red Mazda roared off up the

road back in the direction of Sydney, Joan settled drily knowing eyes on her.

'Well, you're a dark horse, Molly, aren't you?' she said as they walked together back into the library. 'I've always thought of you as a quiet little thing and all this time you had something like *that* on the side.'

Molly silently cursed Liam to hell. All he ever caused her was trouble and heartache. 'Liam's mother lives next door,' she explained with more calm than she was feeling. 'I've known Liam for years. We're just good friends.'

'Oh, *sure*. He drove all the way up from Sydney to wish you a happy birthday because you're just *good friends*. You know what? I'll bet you're one of those girls who go home from the office at night, and perform one of those ten-second transformations. You know the type. Off come the glasses and the strait-laced clothes. Down comes the hair. On goes the sexy gear, make-up and perfume, and—whammo!—instant heat!'

Molly had to laugh. It would take more than ten seconds to transform *her*!

'You can laugh,' Joan scoffed. 'But I'm no one's fool. And you're far prettier than you pretend to be. I always did wonder why you never seemed to be on the lookout for a fella. I was beginning to think all sorts of things till glamour boy arrived on the scene today. He gave *me* a case of instant heat, I can tell you. And I saw the way *you* looked at him when you didn't think anyone was noticing. You've got it bad,

Molly. I know the signs. So why haven't I heard of this paragon of perfection before? Why all the mystery and secrecy? Is he married? A womaniser? A bad boy? Look, you can trust me with your deep dark secrets,' she whispered. 'I won't tell anyone.'

Molly laughed a second time. 'There's nothing deep *or* dark to tell. I repeat…we're just good friends. As I said before, Liam used to live next door. We went to school together, though not in the same class. He was doing his HSC when I was only in my first year.'

'Well, there's nothing remotely boy-next-door about him any more,' came Joan's dry remark. 'He has city written all over him. Not to mention success.'

'I'm well aware of that, believe me. I'm not blind. But there's never been any romance between us, and there never will be. He has a steady girlfriend. Goes by the name of Roxy.'

'Roxy,' Joan repeated, her nose wrinkling. 'Don't tell me. She's a stunning blonde with boobs to die for, hair down to her waist and legs up to her armpits.'

Molly was startled. 'You know her?'

'Nope. Just guessed. Men like your Liam always seem to have girls like that on their arm.'

'He isn't my Liam,' Molly said tightly.

'But you'd like him to be, wouldn't you?'

Molly opened her mouth to deny it. But her tongue failed her when a thickness claimed it. Tears pricked at the back of her eyes.

Her Liam.

What a concept. What an improbable, impossible, inconceivable, unachievable concept! To keep clinging to it was not only demeaning to her personally, but depressing in the extreme.

'There was a time when I did,' she said at last, her tone clipped and cold. 'But not any more. I have better things to do with my life than pine for the impossible.'

'Impossible? Why do you say it's impossible?'

'For pity's sake, Joan, you've seen him. You yourself said men like Liam go for girls like Roxy, not mousy little things like me.'

'You'd be far from mousy if you made the best of yourself. To be frank, Molly, a little make-up wouldn't go astray. And an occasional visit to the hairdresser.'

Molly stiffened, despite the criticism striking home. 'I wouldn't want a man who didn't love me for myself,' she said sharply.

'That's rubbish and you know it! I'm an old married lady and I still have to work hard to keep my man. Now you listen to me, Molly. When Liam comes to take you out tonight, surprise him.'

'Surprise him?'

'Yes. Leave your hair down. Slap some make-up on. Use a sexy perfume. Wear something which shows off that great little figure of yours.'

For a split second, Molly was buoyed up by Joan's compliment on her figure. But then she thought of

Roxy's tall, voluptuous, sex-bomb body...and her momentary high was totally deflated.

'I don't have any sexy perfume,' she muttered dispiritedly. She didn't own much make-up either. But she wasn't about to admit that.

Joan gave her an exasperated glare. 'Then buy some at the chemist during your lunch-hour!'

Their library was in a small regional centre which boasted quite a few shops, a well-stocked chemist shop included.

Molly declined telling Joan that she only had five dollars in her purse. Sexy perfume was expensive, and she'd rather wear nothing than douse herself in a cheap scent.

Molly was actually contemplating asking Joan to lend her some money when reality returned with a rush. She could wear more make-up than a Japanese geisha and drown herself in the most exotic expensive perfume in the world and it would not make Liam fall in love with her. To think otherwise was ludicrous in the extreme, and belittling to his intelligence.

'Thank you for your advice, Joan,' she said with a return to common sense, 'but I'd really rather just be myself. Now I'd better get back to these books.'

Molly resumed checking in the returns, blocking her mind to everything but the thought that at least she would not have to starve to death tonight after her mother's special birthday meal. Liam could buy her something delicious and creamy to go with her after-dinner coffee.

She gave no more thought to Joan's advice about make-up and perfume, till she arrived home late that afternoon and opened her carryall to find a paper parcel sitting on top of her house keys.

It contained a small but expensive-looking spray bottle of perfume.

And a note.

'Happy birthday, darls!' Joan had written in her usual extravagant hand. 'This always works for me. Well…sometimes. Still, what have you got to lose? Go for it!'

Molly sprayed a tiny burst of perfume onto her wrist and lifted it to her nose. It was a wonderfully sensual smell, its heavy musk perfume bringing images of satin sheets and naked bodies and untold unknown delights.

Molly shook her head. To wear such a scent in Liam's presence would be the ultimate self-torture.

And let's face it, Molly, she told herself, wearing perfume—no matter how sensual—isn't about to turn Liam into some kind of sex-crazed lunatic. With a girl like Roxy in tow, no doubt he has all the sex he can handle.

Molly glanced at the perfume's name and almost laughed. Seductress, it was called. Good Lord. It would have to be a powerful potion to turn her into that!

It was a nice thought of Joan's, but a total waste of time and money.

So was her advice. For Molly believed she *did* have

something to lose. Her self-respect. And possibly Liam's friendship. She would not risk her relationship with him—such as it was—by acting differently or provocatively. He was an intelligent man and would surely notice if she climbed into his car wearing such an overpoweringly sexy scent.

No. She would not do it. Neither would she change her hairstyle, or put on more make-up, or scrounge through her limited wardrobe in some vain attempt to find something more figure-revealing.

Molly had her pride.

She shoved the perfume back in her bag and extracted her house key.

'Is that you, dear?' her mother called out as she pushed open the front door.

'Yes, Mum.'

The smell of a roast dinner teased Molly's nostrils as she made her way along the hall and into the kitchen. Not a pork smell. Chicken.

Naturally, came the rueful thought. Chicken carried the least fat and calorie count, provided the skin was removed. Which it would certainly be. She almost sighed when she also spied her mother wrapping the hoped-for crispy baked potatoes in foil.

Ruth glanced up and smiled at her daughter. 'Have a good day, dear?'

'Pretty good. Joan and the others bought me a birthday cake for morning tea.'

'I hope you only had a small slice,' her mother said, frowning. 'I was going to get you a cake tonight but

I thought it an extravagance when we can't eat all of it.'

Molly suddenly felt like screaming. She turned away to hook her navy carryall over a chair, schooling her face into a more pleasant expression before turning back. 'You'll never guess who dropped in to see me this morning,' she said brightly.

'I can't think. Who?'

'Liam.'

'Liam? You mean Liam Delaney?'

'The one and the same.' Molly declined telling her mother about the fiasco of his new car. 'He was up this way today and asked me out tonight for my birthday.'

'But I'm cooking you a special dinner tonight!'

'I'll be here for dinner, Mum. Liam isn't picking me up till around eight.'

Ruth gave her daughter a sharp look. 'You do realise he already has a girlfriend? A very beautiful one too, if I recall rightly.'

Molly controlled her growing irritation with difficulty. 'I'm well aware of that, Mum, but we're only going somewhere for coffee. Don't forget Liam and I were friends long before Roxy came along.'

Ruth began to frown. 'I still don't know about this. I have an awful feeling it's not a good idea.'

Molly came forward to give her mother a hug. 'Mum, stop worrying. I'm a big girl now and quite capable of looking after myself. Besides, it's not as though Liam is engaged or anything.'

Ruth's head jerked back and she looked at her daughter with worried eyes. 'You...you're not going to do anything you shouldn't do, Molly, are you?'

Molly was quite startled, and more than a little annoyed. 'Such as what?' It wasn't as though she was about to leap into bed with the man. Not that she wouldn't, if she ever had the chance. Making love with Liam was at the top of the list where her secret sexual fantasies were concerned. She was pretty sure, however, that she wasn't even *on* Liam's list.

'I...I don't know exactly,' her mother murmured. 'You seem different tonight...'

Molly now thanked her lucky stars that she wasn't attempting any kind of pathetic make-over tonight. She could just imagine what her mother would have said if she'd waltzed downstairs all dolled up and doused in Seductress.

'Liam and I are just good friends, Mum,' she repeated for what felt like the umpteenth time that day.

Molly was shocked when her mother looked at her the same way Joan had. 'Come now, Molly,' she said. 'I'm your mother. I know exactly how you feel about that man.'

'Yes...well, he doesn't feel the same way about me, does he?' came her taut reply.

'No. And neither will he. *Ever*.'

Molly could not believe the pain her mother's words brought her. It was one thing to tell herself there was no hope. Quite another to hear the futility of her dreams spoken aloud and with such crushing finality.

'I realise that,' she countered, her throat thick with hurt. 'You don't have to tell me.'

Molly just managed to sweep from the room before she burst into tears.

CHAPTER THREE

AT FIVE to eight, Molly was standing at her bedroom window, watching for Liam's car. She doubted he would be late. Surprisingly, punctuality was now one of his virtues.

He hadn't always been like that. When Molly had first met Liam, and he'd been a computer-mad adolescent of seventeen, she could not count the number of times he'd been late for things. Back then, he'd always been working on some computer-based project, becoming totally absorbed as soon as he sat down in front of the screen. Time had had little meaning for him once his concentration was focused on his latest game, or graphic design.

Every morning, Molly would wait anxiously outside his house for him to accompany her to school—a job he'd volunteered for when some bullies had started hassling her on the walk to school. Barely minutes before the school bell was due to ring, Liam would come dashing out, yelling for her to start running.

How she kept up with his long legs she would never know. But hero-worship made you do things your body was incapable of, although in that final year she was to share school with Liam she hadn't yet reached puberty—or her fat phase—being only twelve. Somehow, she'd managed to stick to his shadow like glue all the way, down the hill then along the flat beside the railway, over the railway bridge, across the highway then up another hill to school, usually arriving in time but in a totally breathless state.

She would have to run home too, so that Liam could be sitting back down to his all-consuming hobby all the quicker. Although never interested in sport, Liam had been very fit in those days from running to and from school at full pelt. He still ran every day, jogging to and from work, apparently. He'd told her once that his best inspirations and ideas came while he was running.

Molly was about to turn away from the window when Liam's bright red car came up the hill and turned into their driveway. Right on time! She shook her head in rueful acceptance that Liam had changed in many ways. He was no longer the forgetful boy next door. He was an exceptionally sharp businessman. Ambitious. Brilliant. Successful.

Way out of your league, Molly.

Sighing, she bent to switch off her bedside lamp, and was about to leave the room when she hesitated, walking back to where she could watch Liam, unobserved, from the now darkened window.

He sat there for several seconds, combing his hair. Though not with undue vanity. He didn't even glance into the rear-vision or side-mirror, just swept the comb quickly through both sides and down the back before slipping it back into his jacket pocket.

At least in that Liam hadn't changed. He'd never been vain about his looks, and still wasn't. There was nothing of the peacock in him.

Yet, for all that, he did like to look good. Molly believed his sense of style came from his mother, who, though in her late fifties, was very young at heart and kept up to date with the latest trends and fashions. A writer and illustrator of children's books, Babs Delaney had ably supported herself and her only son after her husband was killed in a rock-climbing accident when Liam was only twelve.

It suddenly occurred to Molly how similar her and Liam's family backgrounds were. Both only children with widowed mothers.

But there the similarity ended. Babs Delaney was nothing like her own, timid mother. She was an outgoing personality with a wide range of friends and interests. She loved Liam to death but did not live her life through her son. She was encouraging, never clinging, a positive force, without a pessimistic or negative thought. She always said she wanted the best for her son, but that it was up to him to find what was best for himself.

It was no wonder Liam thought the world was his oyster; no wonder his business had been a great success. He'd even won an award a couple of years back as New South Wales Young Businessman of the Year and was often asked to be a motivating after-dinner speaker at various functions.

A quiver rippled down Molly's spine as she watched the object of her secret obsession unfold his elegant frame from behind the wheel. He was dressed in the same blue jeans, navy top and cream linen jacket he'd been wearing earlier. He stretched as he stood up, and another *deeper* quiver reverberated all through her.

For the first time it struck Molly just how intensely sexual her love for Liam had become with the passing of the years. Her more innocent schoolgirl crush had long since graduated to a full-on physical passion, filled with needs and yearnings which would not be denied. More and more she dreamt of making love with Liam, rather than just loving him. She would lie in bed at night and think about what it would be like to kiss him and touch him; how he would look, naked and erect; how he would *feel*, deep inside her.

She blushed in the darkness, her blood pounding through her body, her head whirling with a wild mixture of shame and excitement. Was she wicked to think about such things?

She didn't feel wicked. She felt driven and compelled, oblivious to everything but wanting Liam with a want that had no conscience, only the most merciless and agonising frustration. Oh, how she wished she were dazzlingly beautiful, with the sort of body no man could resist!

A bitter longing flooded Molly as she watched

Liam stride confidently towards her front door, his golden head gleaming under the street lights. Her grip on the curtains tightened and inevitably her thoughts turned to the dreaded Roxy.

How often did Liam sleep with her? she wondered enviously. Molly knew he didn't live with her, but that didn't mean they didn't share most of their nights either at his place or hers. Was she great in bed? came the added tormenting thought. Did she know all the tricks that a man would find irresistible? What was it she did to him that had kept Liam interested for six whole months?

Another awful possibility snuck into Molly's mind, twisting her heart and her stomach. Surely he couldn't *love* Roxy. Surely he wasn't going to *marry* her? Surely not.

The front doorbell rang, the sound jarring Molly's suddenly stretched nerves. She resisted rushing downstairs, her thoughts still simmering with resentment at the situation. She should not have agreed to go out with Liam tonight, not even for coffee. She was only torturing herself.

She heard her mother slide the door back from the family room then walk with small steps along the plastic strip which protected the hallway carpet. The front door creaked slightly on opening.

'Hello, Liam,' Ruth said with stiff politeness.

'Hello, Mrs McCrae. You're looking well.'

Molly listened to their small chat for a minute or two before gathering herself and coming downstairs, glad now that she hadn't made a superhuman effort with her appearance. Even so, her mother looked her up and down as though searching for some hint of secret decadence.

Molly doubted if even the most devious mind could find anything to criticise in her knee-length black skirt and simple white knitted top, even if the latter did have a lacy design and pretty pearl buttons down the front. Her choice of jewellery could hardly give rise to speculation, either. The string of pearls her own parents had given her for her twenty-first birthday was conservative and sedate, as were the matching pearl earrings.

The rest of her was equally sedate. Skin-coloured pantyhose, medium height black pumps, hair up in its usual knot and no make-up on except coral lipstick. Even her underwear was sedate. But only Superman with his X-ray vision could see that. Not that the sight of her modest white crossover bra and cotton briefs would send any man's heart aflutter.

Molly was at a loss to understand, then, why Liam himself frowned up at her as she came down the stairs. She had no illusions that he was struck by some previously untapped appreciation of her beauty. So why was he giving her the once-over with that slightly surprised look in his eyes?

Her curiosity was not satisfied till they were alone and walking along the curving front path towards his parked car.

'You know, Moll,' he said, 'you've lost quite a bit of weight lately, haven't you?'

Molly clenched her teeth down hard in her jaw. She'd been losing weight steadily for two years, and had been this size for at least three months. Hadn't he even noticed before this moment? What about at Christmas, or earlier today, at the library?

No, of course not. For the last six months his eyes had all been for Roxy. And this morning he'd been all wrapped up in his stupid new car.

'Not lately I haven't,' she replied coolly. 'I've been this weight for quite a while.'

'Oh? I didn't notice.'

Tell me something new, Molly thought tartly. She felt piqued that there wasn't the smallest change in him that *she* didn't notice. She knew whenever he'd had his hair cut; when he'd bought a new jacket; when he'd changed women.

'Are you sure Roxy won't mind your taking me out tonight?' she was driven to ask, barely controlling the lemony flavour in her voice.

'Roxy and I are having a trial separation,' he bit out.

'Oh?' Molly battled to look perfectly normal. Difficult when your stomach had just done a back-flip. 'You have a fight or something?'

'Or something,' he muttered.

'You don't want to tell me about it?'

His smile was wry as he wrenched open the passenger door. 'Not tonight, Moll. I don't want to spoil my mood by thinking about women.'

'But *I'm* a woman, Liam!' she pointed out archly.

'Yeah, but you're different. I don't really think of you like that. You're my friend. Come on. Get in. I'm going to drive us out to Terrigal. It's a lovely night for a walk along the beach.'

Which it was. Clear and warm, with stars sparkling in the night sky. A night for lovers.

Molly tried not to think about that. Masochism was not one of her vices.

Or maybe it was?

'But I'm not dressed for the beach,' she protested when Liam climbed in behind the wheel. 'I have high heels and stockings on for one thing.'

'You can take them off in the car,' he suggested without turning a hair.

His indifference to her undressing in front of him was depressing in the extreme. She could just imagine what would happen if Roxy started stripping in the passenger seat, wriggling her pouty bottom while she unpeeled her stockings down those long, tanned legs of hers. Liam wouldn't concentrate on his driving for long. Molly had an awful feeling that *she* could sit there stark naked in front of Liam and all he would do was ask her if she was cold!

Molly was saved from terminal depression by the lovely thought that dear Roxy seemed close to receiving her walking papers. Molly had hated her more than all of Liam's other women. Perhaps because she was the most beautiful. And the most confident in her position as Liam's girlfriend.

Molly's mood lightened considerably just thinking about Roxy's failure to be promoted to fiancée.

'I hope you don't think you're going to worm your way out of buying me coffee!' she told him while he reversed out of the driveway. 'I was going to order a big rich slice of cake with it. You've no idea, Liam, what food Mum has been feeding me ever since Dad died. She's become a ''fat-free for ever'' nutcase!'

'No worse than having a mother who wants to feed you up,' he countered drily. 'Every time I come home, Mum says I'm getting too thin, then out come the chips and the pastries and God knows what else.'

'You're not too thin,' Molly said. 'You're just right.'

He smiled over at her and her heart lurched. God, but he was heart-stoppingly handsome when he smiled.

'You know, you're good for me, Moll. You always say the right thing. And you always *do* the right thing,' he added meaningfully. 'You put me to shame today. I never remember your birthday and you always remember mine. So if you open the glove box in front of you there's a little something there which I hope will make up for all those other forgotten occasions.

'And don't tell me I shouldn't have,' he went on before she could open her mouth. 'And don't tell me it's too expensive. I can afford it. Fact is, I can afford pretty well whatever I want these days. That computer game I told you about some time back has just gone on the worldwide market and it's going to make me a multimillionaire.'

'Oh, Liam, that's wonderful!'

'Maybe,' he said drily. 'I'm beginning to find out being rich and successful isn't all it's cracked up to be. Except when it comes to buying my best friend something really nice,' he added with a warm smile. 'Go on. Rip the paper off and open it up. I'm dying to see what you think of it.'

Molly did just that, and gasped. 'Oh, Liam! You shouldn't have.'

'I thought I told you not to say that,' he said ruefully. 'Now, are you sure you like it? There were so many designs to choose from. I was in the jewellery shop for hours this afternoon trying to decide. In the end I settled for something simple, but solid. Like you.'

Molly tried to take his words as a compliment, but somehow some of the pleasure of his gift dissolved at that point. She lifted the heavy gold chain necklace from its green velvet bed, laying it across one palm while she slowly traced the heavy oval links with the index finger of her right hand.

Simple, but solid. Like me.

'You don't like it.'

Molly heard the disappointment in his voice and forced herself to throw him a bright smile. 'Don't be silly. I love it.' When his attention returned to the oncoming traffic, her eyes continued to secretly caress him for several moments. How could I not love it? was the heart-catching reality. It's from you, my darling. I will treasure it for the rest of my life.

Liam was frowning. 'I hope you're not just saying that.'

Molly found everything about the situation rather ironic. What would happen if she told him how she really felt about him? Knowing Liam, he would be terribly embarrassed. He hated complications in his life. He was a simple man at heart.

'Would I lie to you?' she quipped, though unable to keep the sardonic edge out of her voice.

He slanted her a rather bewildered look as though he'd never associated her with sarcasm before.

'Hmm. I hope not. You were always a brutally honest kid. But right on the ball. Why else do you think I used to ask your opinion on things? Mum would just say everything I wanted to do was great. I needed someone who told me as it really was. Which you did. When I think of the time I might have wasted on some of those airy-fairy projects I came up with. You were always able to make me see what was worth working on, Moll; what would last.'

A pity you never asked my opinion on your lady-friends, Molly thought wryly. I could have told you all those females loved themselves too much to have much left over for anyone else. But then, it wasn't love you wanted from them, was it, Liam?

Still, old habits die hard. What's going to happen

when you want a girl to love you, and whom you can truly love in return? You'll never find the right wife, gravitating towards the wrong type of girl. The Roxys of this world are only out for what they can get. Whereas I...I would love you as no other woman could ever love you, my darling. Look at me, Liam. Can't you see the love I bear you? Can't you *feel* it?

'Anyway, Moll,' Liam went on, oblivious of Molly's thoughts and feelings. 'I hope that necklace goes some small way to making up for my thoughtlessness in the past. I know I'm a selfish bastard. But your friendship means a lot to me and I wouldn't want you to think I never give you a moment's thought, because I do.

'Trouble is...' He threw her a wry smile. 'It's usually only when I need your help. Or your advice. Or your opinion on a new car.'

She didn't know whether to laugh or cry at that point. Anger, however, came to the rescue. 'And is that all tonight is, Liam?' she snapped. 'A test drive? Are you taking me all the way out to Terrigal just so you can get my opinion on your new car?'

'God, no!' He looked and sounded appalled. 'No, that's not it at all! Far from it. The thing is, I realised today down at the library that I never ask you about you. It added to my guilt, I can tell you. All these years and all we ever talk about is me. So tonight I want to hear all about *you*, Moll.'

'Me?' she echoed weakly.

'Yes. *You*. I want to know what's going on in your

life these days. You could have knocked me over with a feather when that woman said you were twenty-five. It suddenly came to me that a girl as great as you should have been married by twenty-five. I began to wonder why you're not. I wanted to ask you then and there but it was hardly appropriate. So I'm asking you now, Moll. Why haven't you got a boyfriend?'

Molly was really stumped. What to say? What to tell him?

She busied herself putting the gold chain tidily into its case and slipping it into her purse, all the while trying to find the right lie to tell.

I just haven't met the right man yet…

I'm waiting till Mum gets over Dad's death…

I'd like to marry but the man I love doesn't even know I'm alive in that sense…

The awkward silence grew till finally Liam shot her a shocked look. 'Good God, Moll, you're not, are you?'

'Not what?'

'Not…gay?'

CHAPTER FOUR

MOLLY'S eyes rounded. And then she laughed. That was one excuse she'd never thought of.

'No, I'm not gay.'

'So what's the problem?'

'The problem...' She considered her answer at some length, then decided excuse three carried a perverse kind of truth. Yet Liam—dear, sweet, blind Liam—would never guess. 'The problem is...that I *am* in love with a man. But he just doesn't love me back. In fact, he doesn't know I'm even alive in a sexual sense.'

'Why not?' Liam demanded to know, apparently affronted by this mystery man's lack of passion for his best friend.

Molly almost felt soothed by Liam's chagrin on her behalf. 'I guess I'm not his type, physically speaking. I'm not pretty enough.'

'What rubbish! You're *very* pretty.'

'No, I'm not, Liam. But it's nice of you to say so.'

Molly was grateful that Liam dropped the subject of her beauty. He scowled all through Gosford, not opening his mouth till they were on the Entrance Road and approaching Erina.

'So who is this idiot?' he flung at her. 'Is he a local?'

'Yes, of course.'

'Do I know him?'

'I should hope so.'

'Did he go to our school?'

'Yes. But that's as much as I'm going to say.'

'Our school...' He frowned as he scoured his memory. 'I can't think who it could be. Still, there were over eight hundred kids in our school.' He shook his head in frustration. 'I've no idea. Look, just tell me who he is. Don't keep me in suspense!'

'Sorry, but I'm not telling you, or anyone else for that matter. I would find it embarrassing. Besides, it's quite pointless my telling you who he is. I've pretty well accepted he's not interested. Shortly, I aim to get on with my life, so you don't have to worry, Liam. I don't intend to suffer indefinitely.'

Liam mumbled and muttered all through Erina, swinging the car around the large roundabout and heading for Terrigal before he launched into another verbal attack against her mystery man. Molly found it amusing that he was railing against himself.

'So! Does this splendid advertisement for feminine taste have a girlfriend?'

'Actually, he's between women at the moment.'

'Had a lot of them, has he?'

'Oodles.'

'And you *love* this inveterate ladies' man?'

'He takes my breath away.'

Liam pulled a face. 'What is it about women that they always fall for the bad guys? He sounds positively awful!'

'I don't think he's at all awful. And he's been very successful, businesswise.'

Liam's top lip curled into a sneer. 'I suppose he's good-looking.'

'Drop-dead gorgeous,' she agreed.

'Handsome is as handsome does, you know,' he growled, then muttered some more under his breath all the way to Terrigal.

Molly sat next to him in a self-satisfied silence. She hadn't enjoyed herself so much in years. Perhaps she was playing with a double-edged sword, but if so it was worth the risk. She didn't think the penny would drop for Liam. Meanwhile, she was experiencing a heady exhilaration in toying with the truth in this manner.

They came round the sweeping hillside corner which brought Terrigal beach into view and Molly sighed her pleasure at the sight. It was a pretty place during the day, but even more so at night, especially when it was cloudless, and the moon sent ribbons of silver rippling across the dark waters.

Tonight, the moonlight was strong, and the waves extra gentle as they lapped up onto the golden curve of sand. Some people were still swimming in the peaceful water. Many couples were sitting on the warm sand, arms around each other, or strolling along the beach, hand in hand. As Molly had thought earlier, it was a night for lovers.

Liam drove past the public car park at the bottom of the hill and along the narrow main street which flanked the beach, tall pines on the sea side, shops on the other. He eased into a space under a pine at the far end.

He snapped off his engine and swivelled in his seat to face Molly, a scowl on his handsome face. 'It's not Dennis Taylor, is it?'

Dennis Taylor was the only boy in Liam's class who could rival him for looks and subsequent business acumen. As dark as Liam was fair, he had thick black wavy hair, heavy-lidded dark eyes and the body of a bouncer. He did not have Liam's super intelligence or creative flair but he was a born salesman who'd gone into real estate after leaving school and done very well. He'd opened his own agency on the Central Coast a couple of years back and had recently expanded. Unmarried, he was a swinging bachelor type who played the field without mercy. He'd recently bought an acreage not far from Terrigal beach and built an orgy palace of a house, the rumoured activities therein supplying plenty of fuel for the local gossips.

Molly only knew Dennis as well as she did because his folks lived two doors up. He came to visit them quite often, and, Dennis being Dennis, he always waved at Molly if she was out the front watering or weeding the garden.

A couple of months back, he'd also knocked on the door and asked if she and her mother wanted to sell the house. Even after they'd said no, he'd left his business card then stayed talking to Molly for ages. He was one of those males who could not go past a female without proving he was God's gift to women. His charm operated on automatic pilot.

Molly found him likeable enough, but shallow. It irked her that Liam should think she could be madly in love with him.

'Well?' he probed. 'Is it?'

'I'm sorry but I refuse to answer any such questions on the grounds they might incriminate me.'

Liam glowered at her. 'You're being damned difficult.'

'I don't think so. You might be my friend but there's a limit to what I will tell you. And I think my love life is my own private business, don't you? After all, when I asked *you* what had happened between you and Roxy, you wouldn't tell me.'

'Hmm. Fair enough. But if it *is* Dennis,' he growled, 'then I hope to hell you never get your heart's desire. His reputation with women is appalling.'

Molly rolled her eyes. As if Dennis Taylor would take any serious notice of her anyway. That was as far-fetched as Liam doing so! Suddenly, she tired of this game. 'If it will make you feel any better,' she said wearily, 'then it's not Dennis. But please don't come up with any more candidates. I'm not going to tell you and that's that!'

'You've really dug your heels in about this, haven't you?'

'You could say that,' she pronounced, and crossed her arms with finality over her chest.

'I had no idea you could be this stubborn.'

Her sideways glance carried a sardonic flavour. 'There are quite a lot of things about me you don't know, Liam.'

'Mmm…I'm beginning to see that's the case. And there I've been all these years, telling people what a sweet little thing you are. It seems Roxy might not have been altogether wrong.'

Molly bristled. 'Oh? And what, pray tell, did dear Roxy say about me?'

'She said you were a sly piece and she wouldn't trust you as far as she could throw you.'

Molly's blood pressure rose a few notches. 'Humph! That's the pot calling the kettle black!'

'I take it you don't like Roxy?'

'You take it correctly.'

'Why?'

Molly almost launched into a tirade about vanity and superficiality and naked ambition, but pulled herself up just in time. There was little point in being vicious, now that the girl was possibly on the way out. Besides, the truth might sound too much like jealousy.

She managed a light shrug. 'You can't like everyone in this world. Some people just rub you up the wrong way right from the start.'

'True. Okay, I won't be a pain and press for more. Neither will I ask you any more embarrassing questions about Mr X. I'm just relieved it's not Dennis. Come on, let's go for that walk.' He was out of the car before she could say Jack Robinson, bounding around the front to her side where he wrenched open the passenger door.

'Do…do you think we could have our coffee first?' she asked a little shakily when Liam took her hand and drew her upright out of the rather low-slung vehicle. Whilst she told herself it was sheer hunger causing her stomach to cramp suddenly, she rather suspected there was another cause, and extracted her hand from Liam's as soon as she could.

'I guess so,' he returned with a casual shrug. 'If you're dying for some.'

'It's not the coffee I'm dying for so much as something to eat.'

Liam frowned. 'Haven't you had dinner? You told me your mother was cooking dinner for you tonight.'

'Yes, she did, but dinner these days wouldn't feed a flea. I tell you, Liam, some nights I could just scream!'

Liam laughed. 'Don't complain. You're looking darned good on what your mother's been feeding you.'

Molly could not stop the flush of pleasure. 'You…you really think so?'

'I really do.' And his eyes were close to admiring as they swept over her new slender figure for the second time that night.

After that, Molly knew she would not eat a morsel.

Fifteen minutes later she was sitting opposite Liam in a booth in one of the cafés along the esplanade and had been fiddling with a large slice of iced carrot cake for a full ten minutes when he finally burst forth.

'I thought you said you were hungry!'

Molly bit her bottom lip and put down the fork. 'I thought I was too. Do you want it?'

He sighed. 'Women! Here, give it to me.'

As she sheepishly handed it over, his exasperation dissolved into a cheeky grin. Molly grinned back, then sat in contented silence to watch Liam eat.

It wasn't long before this innocent enough activity had a less than innocent effect on Molly. Liam's mouth, unfortunately, was incredibly sexy, wide and curving, his full lips saved from outright femininity by the masculine set of his jawline below, and the strong straight nose above. It was also a very mobile mouth, with a very mobile tongue.

Molly's concentration was soon totally on that tongue, and the way its moist pink tip snaked out after every forkful of cake to sweep any crumbs back into his mouth, leaving Liam's lips wet and glistening. Her stomach twisted at the thought of having that tongue-tip do the same to *her* lips, of having it dart between those same lips and slide deep into her waiting, wanting mouth.

Molly smothered a tortured groan and pressed her parched lips firmly together. What she would not give to have that experience…just once.

Regret that she hadn't taken Joan's advice and gone for broke tonight with her appearance rose up to haunt her. Maybe, if she'd left her hair down and worn that perfume, Liam might have found more to admire than her slimmer body. Maybe, if she'd used make-up and worn a sexy scarlet lipstick, he might have been tempted to give her a goodnight kiss.

'Go for it!' Joan had commanded. And what had she done? She'd wimped out. There she'd been, asked out by the man of her dreams, and she'd presented herself to him in clothes her mother would have worn. She was hopeless, absolutely hopeless!

'What's the matter?' Liam asked as he placed his fork across the now empty plate.

Molly was beyond pretending. The eyes she lifted to him were sad eyes. Eyes without hope. She was seeing the end of her dream here.

Liam reached across the table and picked up her left hand. 'Loving this Mr X is making you terribly unhappy, Moll, isn't it?'

Not till today, she accepted with a degree of surprise. Before today, it had been quite a lovely dream. And she *had* had his friendship to sustain her. How many girls did she know who loved lesser men? Unworthy individuals. Creeps, even.

Liam was a man amongst men. He was handsome and clever and essentially good. He loved life, and his mother, and he loved *her,* in a lukewarm brotherly kind of way. Molly could see that now.

'Is there anything I can do to help?' he asked gently, stroking his thumb along the top of her hand all the while.

Molly stiffened under the tinglingly electric feelings it was sending through her. 'I don't think so,' she said tautly. 'It's my problem, and as I said I've decided to move on soon.'

'I think that would be for the best, Moll. Forget this idiot. He doesn't know a good thing when he sees it.'

Molly merely smiled and finally extracted her hand from under his. Liam straightened and studied her with still worried eyes.

'Why don't you do what my mother does when she's down and wants a lift? Go get yourself a new hairstyle. New clothes. New look altogether.'

A bit late for that, she thought, even if I had the money.

But Liam's saying as much piqued her curiosity. 'And what would you suggest?' she asked him. 'I mean, what do you think would suit me?'

Liam laughed. 'Good God, Moll, don't go asking *me*. I have no idea.'

'Liam, you just asked me if you could help, but as soon as I ask something of you you opt out. Look, you're a trained artist, with an eye for design, shape and colour. Think of me as one of your graphic design projects. Pretend you have me up on the screen of your computer, and then make me over to your personal taste and liking.'

'*My* personal taste and liking? Wouldn't it be better if I made you over to Mr X's personal taste and liking?'

'You and he are similar types,' she invented, warming to the game again with each passing moment. Not only that, she was going to take his advice. Whatever Liam suggested she would do, and to hell with the money. She would beg, borrow or steal some, if she had to.

His smile was wry. 'I thought you just said you were moving on.'

'It's a woman's privilege to change her mind.'

Liam shook his head, his eyes wry. 'Somehow I pity this Mr X. He might not know it yet but he's not going to get away easily, is he?'

'Do stop quibbling, Liam. Just give me the once-over and tell me what to change.' She sat up straight and smiled encouragingly at him.

Liam frowned as he looked her over, then shook his head. 'Honestly, Moll, I don't feel at all comfortable with this. You're not a graphic design project. You're a female…with feelings.'

Molly's eyebrows arched. 'Goodness, Liam, that's observant of you. But I shall bravely put aside my feminine sensitivity long enough to hear your unqualified opinion. You said you always admired *my* honesty when I gave you *my* opinion. Now I'm asking for yours.'

He stared at her, still frowning, then shook his head again. 'I'm sorry, Moll, but I really must decline. I suggest you get an expert's opinion.'

'I don't *want* an expert's opinion. I want *yours*. Okay, if you won't tell me straight out, how about we play tick one of the boxes?'

'Tick one of the boxes?'

'Yes. I will suggest a change, then give three possible courses of action. You tell me which one you think will suit me best.'

Liam shrugged. 'If you must. But I won't give any promises or guarantees.'

Molly smiled. 'All care and no responsibility?'

He smiled back. 'Something like that.'

'Fair enough. First thing on the agenda is my hair. I'm going to have it cut. Should I go shoulder-length, jaw-length or really short?'

He tipped his head on one side to consider his answer. 'Really short,' he said at last. 'You have an elegant neck. It's a shame ever to hide it.'

Molly's hand automatically fluttered up to her throat, her stomach curling over at the compliment. She would have to have a good look at her neck when she got home.

'What…what about colour?' she finally went on, hoping she wasn't blushing. 'What do you think would suit me best? Blonde, brunette or redhead?'

'Why don't you just leave it the colour it is?'

'No way! I've lived with mousy brown long enough, thank you very much. There's going to be nothing mousy about me from now on, I can tell you! Now choose!'

Liam sighed. 'Okay, but be it on your head.'

'Well, it will be, won't it?'

He shook his head at her. 'First sarcasm. Now a savage wit. What next?'

Molly crossed her arms on the table. 'Blonde? Brunette? Or redhead?'

'Hmm. Well, you have that fair delicate skin usually associated with redheads, but please...not one of those harsh reds. A rich copper colour would be nice.'

'A rich copper colour,' she repeated, swallowing nervously. Somehow she just couldn't see herself with short red hair. Good God, this was going to take some courage, but she was determined.

Molly opened her mouth to ask Liam about make-up, then shut it again. A man wouldn't know much about that. She would have to consult an expert, maybe in the cosmetics section of a department store.

She began totting-up the cost so far. A top hairdresser. A dye job, which would need retouching every six to eight weeks. New make-up. Not to mention a new wardrobe. Goodness, the mind boggled!

'What about clothes?' she continued. 'I mean...what kind of clothes do you like a girl to wear? Of course I do realise I don't have a spectacular figure like Roxy, but I'm not too bad these days.'

'Don't underestimate yourself, Moll,' he said brusquely. 'I've been noticing tonight what a good little figure you have—one which you seem to have hidden successfully for years. You have a more than adequate bust, a shapely bottom and a nice little waist. You also have remarkably good legs for such a short girl.'

A shocked delight rippled through Molly. Joan had said she had a good figure, but hearing Liam say so was wonderful! And to think all he could find to criticise was her height.

'Unfortunately, Liam,' she said, 'there's nothing I can do about being short. I would dearly love to be taller, believe me.'

'Your Mr X is tall, then?'

'Fairly. And he really likes tall girls.'

'Stupid man. Doesn't he know good things come in small parcels?' He sounded decidedly irritable. 'I suppose you could always wear higher heels than what you have on. You could also give the illusion of further height by shortening your skirts.'

'I have no intention of going to work every day in five-inch heels and minis!'

He gave her a long, hard look. 'You see this Mr X at work, do you?'

'Er...not very often.'

'Then what you wear to work is irrelevant. What you wear when he's around is another thing entirely.'

'If I go to the trouble and expense of all these changes, Liam,' she said firmly, 'then it won't be for Mr X. It will be for me.'

'Sure, Moll, sure. By the way, I don't like stripes,

checks or floral prints. I like my women in figure-hugging clothes in strong block colours.'

When Molly gave him a blank look, he smiled a drily amused smile. 'You said Mr X would have similar tastes to me. Please don't go on pretending this isn't for him. It insults my intelligence.'

'All right. I won't insult your intelligence. Go on. What else don't you like?'

'I don't like girls to wear pants.'

Molly gaped at him. 'If you think I'm going to swan around without my underwear on, then you have another think coming!'

His expression was droll. 'Pants, Moll. Not panties. I'm talking about slack suits, or trousers, if you will.'

'Oh…'

'I don't mind tights. Or jeans, provided they fit well. Men are attracted to a woman's shape. They like to see it.'

'You're a sexist, do you know that?'

The corner of his mouth lifted in a wickedly attractive smile. 'Yes. I like sex. Very much. Is that what you mean by sexist?'

'No. And you darned well know it!'

He looked at her for a long time before speaking.

'Do you like sex, Moll?'

She went bright red. 'I think that's a very personal question.'

'Not really. It's just a general one. I'm not asking for a blow-by-blow description of every sexual experience you've had.'

'Well, if you did, it would be a mighty short conversation,' she snapped. 'In fact, I wouldn't have to say a word!'

He just stared at her. 'Are you saying what I think you're saying?' he asked at last in hushed tones.

His obvious shock infuriated her, as did her having blurted out the awful truth. But she wasn't about to go all shy and embarrassed on him. Pride demanded she hold her head high.

'Really, Liam, there's no need to whisper,' she said coolly. 'I'm not ashamed of my virginity.'

'But you're twenty-*five*, Moll!'

'So what? Is there a prescribed date for such dubious milestones? Where is it written in stone that a girl must lose her virginity before such and such a date? I happen to be waiting for someone special. I didn't want to throw it away on some fumbling boy down behind the school gym, or in the back of a car after a disco. And don't think I haven't had any offers,' she lied. 'Because I have!'

Liam's blue eyes darkened. 'You're waiting for this Mr X, aren't you?'

'And if I am? What's it to you?'

He seemed taken back, then almost outraged. 'You're my best friend, damn it. I don't want to see you hurt.'

Molly was touched, and terribly close to tears. It was a struggle to retain her composure and sense of proportion. If nothing else, she'd made up her mind tonight to do something about changing her dreary

appearance. On top of that, her friendship with Liam
had subtly shifted onto a deeper plane, more like that
of true best friends. There was something very intimate and bonding about sharing confidences.

So now he knew she was a virgin. It was not such
a disaster. How could the truth hurt?

'I'll be all right, Liam,' she said, and actually
reached out to touch *his* hand in a comforting gesture.
'Please don't worry about me and Mr X. Just promise
me you'll be there…when and if I need you.'

She looked deep into his eyes and was moved by
the sincerity of the affection for her she saw there. 'I
think you'd better take me home now,' she said softly.
'Tomorrow's a working day.'

CHAPTER FIVE

JOAN grabbed her the moment she walked into the library, and dragged her down to the privacy of the back room.

'I'm dying of curiosity,' she said, quite unnecessarily, since her whole body language reeked of a breathless tension. 'Did you doll yourself up like I told you to? Did you wear the perfume? Did you knock glamour boy for six when he came to pick you up?'

Molly had thought about what she would tell Joan this morning. She'd walked more slowly to work than usual, mulling over whether she should lie or not. Now the moment of truth was at hand, and despite Joan's eager face Molly could not bring herself to make up a story.

'No, I didn't doll myself up,' she confessed, with a wealth of apology in her voice. 'I didn't wear the perfume, either, though it was a lovely thought, Joan, and I do thank you for it. And as I'm sure you've guessed…no, I didn't knock Liam for six when he came to pick me up.'

Joan exhaled a huge sigh of disappointment. 'Oh, Molly! How many chances like that do you think you're going to get?'

'Actually, last night wasn't a total disaster. Liam did notice at last how much weight I'd lost. He also told me I had a nice figure and good legs...for someone so short.'

'He *did*? Wow! You must have been thrilled to bits.'

'It's not quite as good as it sounds,' Molly said ruefully, then went on to tell Joan exactly how the compliments had come about. She listened intently, her eyes rounding further with each new revelation.

'You mean he thinks you're in love with someone else? This chap he dubbed Mr X?'

'Uh-huh.'

'And he told you how to dress so that you would be more attractive for another man?'

Molly nodded.

'I'd like to strangle him with my bare hands!'

'Don't blame Liam. I forced him into it.'

'Rubbish. The man's a blind fool. Oh, poor Molly!'

'Not "poor Molly" at all, Joan,' she returned with a very firm resolve. 'Because I'm going to do it. Follow all of Liam's suggestions. But not for him. I'm going to do it for myself.'

'Go on with you! You're not!'

'Yes, I am.'

'You're going to cut your hair short and dye it red?'

'For starters. So do you happen to know a good hairdresser who doesn't cost the earth? Also where I might find a make-up expert who gives free advice and tuition?'

Joan's dark eyes twinkled with excitement. 'I certainly do. But gosh, Molly, whatever is your mother going to say?'

Molly wasn't sure. But she would find out that evening. To be honest, the prospect was a daunting one. It wasn't like her to make waves. Or to do something as bold as this.

But she was determined to change herself, and her life…whatever the cost.

Fortunately, she had three hundred dollars put away for emergencies—and which she would use for her first visit to the hairdresser, and some make-up. Still, if she was to find enough money from their tight budget for regular visits to the hairdresser and a whole new wardrobe, then some more changes would have to be made to their day-to-day lifestyle.

Her own salary was almost totally eaten up with the two mortgages her father had taken out shortly before he died, and her mother's pension barely covered their living expenses and other bills, with little left over for luxuries.

Molly waited till after dinner before she brought up her plans for her future, and was not really surprised when her mother reacted badly.

'But *why* do you want to change yourself so dramatically?' Ruth asked in a tremulous voice. 'I don't understand. This isn't like you at all!'

'Mum,' Molly returned patiently, 'I'm twenty-five and I have not had one single steady boyfriend in my life. I do not want to become an old maid. I want to get married one day and have a family of my own. To get married I need a man, and to get a man I need to do something about attracting one.'

'It's not *any* man you want to attract, missie,' came her waspish accusation. 'It's Liam Delaney. You were perfectly happy till you went out with him last night and now you've got all these silly ideas in your head.'

'They are not silly ideas,' Molly said more sternly. 'Yes, I do have feelings for Liam. I always have had. I won't deny it. But you were right when you said he'd never fall in love with me. He thinks of me as a kid sister. But that doesn't mean I'm going to spend the rest of my life pining for him. Since men don't exactly come flocking to my door, I aim to get out and about a bit more, and I aim to look darned good when I do so. Looking good costs money, which brings me to my first suggestion. What do you think about selling this house and buying something smaller? The mortgages are killing us.'

Her mother gave her a truly horrified look. 'Oh, no. No, no, no! I love this house. It's all I have. You can't ask that of me. You can't!'

Molly relented and moved straight on to plan B. To be honest she hadn't really wanted to sell. As much as she'd told both Joan and her mother that these radical changes were for herself, she still wanted to see Liam's reaction to the finished product. Silly of her perhaps, but a fact.

'Okay, forget selling,' she said briskly. 'My alternative suggestion is that we advertise for a boarder.'

'A boarder!'

'Yes. We have four bedrooms in this house, Mum, two of which are never used, the master bedroom being one of them. You could get good money for that room. It has an *en suite,* a dressing room and lots of space.'

'Oh, but I couldn't have some strange man living in your father's house and sleeping in his bed!'

Molly prayed for more patience. Her mother's devotion to her father had increased considerably since his death. Couldn't she remember what a selfish bastard he'd been? How he'd wasted all her inheritance from her parents on one of his stupid get-rich schemes? Worst of all, how he'd often come home late, smelling of booze and cheap perfume?

'You don't have to have a male boarder, Mum. I'm sure there are plenty of widows around your age who need accommodation. It would be company for you as well,' Molly pointed out. 'I'm not going to be at home quite as much as I used to be.'

Ruth opened her mouth to protest again, then closed it, her expression petulant. She looked like a sulky child sitting there. Molly felt sorry for her but knew she had to make a stand or her future would be as dull and dreary as she'd been fearing.

'Do I have your agreement to put an ad in next Wednesday's paper?'

'I won't have anyone I don't like.'

'Of course not.'

Ruth gave her daughter another resentful look. 'So how much money is it that you want to spend on yourself?'

'Not as much as I first estimated. Joan's put me on to a local lady who does hair from her home and is very reasonable. And she says the make-up department at the David Jones store at Tuggerah will give me good free advice on making up my face properly. Still, a reasonably good make-up range could run to a couple of hundred dollars. I have enough rainy-day money put by for that, but I will still need to save at least a hundred dollars a week for a while so that I can get together a decent wardrobe of both casual and dressy clothes. Luckily, I wear a uniform to work, so that's not a problem.'

'Next thing you'll be wanting to get a driving licence and buy a car!'

Molly accepted her mother's caustic outburst, disarming her with a sweet smile. 'I hadn't thought of it but that's a very good idea. Thank you for mentioning it, Mum. I'll definitely put that on my list for future projects, along with a South Seas cruise. Now I think I'll go upstairs and have a nice long bath. My legs are aching from standing up all day. Oh, and Mum, do you think I might have a bit more for dinner at night? I'm going to need a lot more energy in the not too distant future.' And she swept from the kitchen, leaving her mother to gape after her.

* * *

'I can't believe it's me!' Molly exclaimed delightedly. 'You're a genius, Leanne!'

The hairdresser's smile carried a delicious satisfaction. 'I must admit I have outdone myself this time.'

Molly beamed anew at this striking and sophisticated-looking creature who was staring back at her in the mirror. She turned her head from side to side and watched the smooth coppery cap shimmer and sway, then fall perfectly back into place.

'This particular cut will give your hair body and style,' Leanne had pronounced reassuringly while she proceeded to shape and shave Molly's hair around her ears and at the back, while layering the top in concentric circles from the crown.

Molly now had a stylish fringe right down to her eyebrows, the effect being to diminish the size of her nose and highlight her wide, deeply set green eyes. The new coppery colour, besides being eye-catching in itself, was a perfect foil for her pale skin, giving it a translucency and delicacy which had been lost against her mousy brown hair.

When Molly stood up she saw delightedly that the clean lines made her neck look longer and even more elegant.

'You really look different,' the hairdresser said, shaking her head admiringly. 'Taller, too.'

'Yes, I think you're right,' Molly agreed excitedly. 'Oh, Leanne, how can I ever thank you? And it was so kind of you to fit me in tonight.'

'It was my pleasure. Now, how are you going to

get home?' Leanne asked once Molly had handed over the money.

'Oh, I'll walk. It's not far.' Leanne lived less than a block from the library, which was only a fifteen-minute walk from her house.

Leanne frowned. 'Do you think that's wise? It's Friday night, you know.'

'What do you mean?'

'People let their hair down on a Friday night around here. You'll have to walk past the tavern on your way home, won't you?'

'Yes.'

'Then watch yourself. You're not exactly inconspicuous with that new red hair, you know.'

Leanne's warning startled Molly. She'd never been hassled by unwanted male attention in all her life and simply could not anticipate that a mere change in hair colour would create trouble for her, especially when she was still dressed in her library uniform.

But she was wrong.

She'd just passed the tavern and was halfway along the flat stretch which followed the railway line when a hotted-up Chevie full of some less than savoury individuals rumbled by.

'Hey, babe,' one of them called out.

Molly averted her eyes and crossed the road as soon as they passed by, then nearly died when she heard the tyres screech as the driver executed a U-turn. Before she could blink, the car was cruising along next to her and an obviously drunk, loud-mouthed lout was leaning out of the passenger window in her direction.

'Where's yuh goin', honey?' he said, breathing beer fumes her way. 'Wanna ride?'

She quickened her step and kept her eyes straight ahead.

'Whatsa matter? You think you're too good for us? She thinks she's too good for us, fellas. What do yuh reckon? Do yuh think we should teach Madam Muck a lesson or two?'

Her mouth dry with fear, Molly was just about to run for it when a sleek black car shot around the Chevie and pulled up dead. The driver of the Chevie had to brake hard to avoid a collision and the lout hanging out of the window almost tipped out onto the road. When a really big dark-haired man dressed in black jumped out from behind the wheel of the black car and began stalking back towards Molly's verbal assailant, the lout shouted something and scrambled back into the car. The Chevie reversed like mad, spun round and roared off.

Her saviour curved his big hands over her shaking shoulders and peered down into her ashen face. 'You all right, little lady?' he asked.

It was only then that Molly recognised the identity of her rescuer.

It was Dennis Taylor.

'Yes, I think so,' came her weakly breathless answer. 'Thanks so much for stopping, Dennis.'

His surprise at her knowing his name was obvious

in the jerking back of his head, and the widening of his dark eyes.

Molly would have been gratified if she hadn't still been shaking like a leaf. 'It's Molly,' she said. 'Molly McCrae.'

'Molly?' His startled gaze lifted to her hair, then swiftly ran down her body and up again. 'Good Lord, so it is. I didn't recognise you with that stunning hair. And you've lost weight too, haven't you?'

'A little.'

His smile took on a knowing edge as he looked her up and down again. 'More than a little. You're looking fantastic. Too fantastic to be walking around these streets at night on your own. No wonder you almost got yourself into trouble. Come on, I'll drive you home.'

After her frightening experience with those creeps, Molly wasn't about to refuse. She wouldn't have been human, either, if she hadn't been flattered by Dennis's compliments on her appearance, and by the way he kept looking at her.

His touch seemed gentle and solicitous as he helped her into the passenger side of his roomy black sedan, but when he sashed the seat belt into place for her Molly was quite sure his left hand deliberately brushed over the tips of her breasts. She stiffened inside but said nothing, ignoring his attempt to make eye contact at the same time.

Creeps came in various forms, she realised ruefully. Dennis wasn't much different from those louts. His approach was different, that was all. No doubt he didn't go in for outright rape. Silky smooth seductions and one-night stands would be more his forte. He would use his silver tongue to talk his way into a girl's bed. Molly decided not to get too carried away with Dennis's words of praise. She didn't doubt she looked better with her new hairdo, but she wasn't competition for Roxy just yet.

They were only a minute away from her home by car. But Dennis didn't waste a second, bombarding her with questions designed to elicit the only information from a female he would want to know. How old was she exactly? Where did she work these days? Did she have a boyfriend? Unfortunately, Molly didn't realise where Dennis was heading till she'd told him several truths with naive honesty.

As soon as he pulled up at the kerb outside her house, he turned and asked her if she'd like to come out with him for a drink later that night.

'I could pick you up at…say…around ten-thirty?'

Molly might have been inexperienced with men but she knew that to agree to such an invitation at that hour of the night was to agree to more than a drink. She didn't doubt she'd *get* a drink. Plenty of them. And all of them alcoholic. Then, when she was suitably plastered, Dennis would take her back to his orgy palace for a night of raw naked sex.

The very thought of Dennis naked made her want to retch. Facially he was quite handsome, if you liked Mediterranean-looking men with thick wiry black hair and a permanent five o'clock shadow. But his body was humungous in size. And hairy. Like a big gorilla.

No doubt a lot of women fancied his darkly macho appearance, but Molly preferred Liam's fairer, more elegant looks. Her favourite fantasy always included running her hands through his silky blond locks and over his smooth, hairless chest. It turned her on just to *imagine* touching his body, whereas the thought of touching Dennis made her skin crawl.

'Thank you, Dennis,' she said politely. 'For everything. But I'm sorry, I can't. Not tonight.'

To give him credit he took rejection well. Maybe, because of his salesman's training, he did not regard anyone saying no on a first occasion as rejection, but as merely a challenge, for his black eyes glittered with undeniable confidence as he smiled over at her.

'That's all right. Another time maybe?'

'Perhaps,' she replied, not wanting to be too rude after his kindness in rescuing her.

'I'll call you,' he said, and restarted the engine.

Molly could see she was expected to let herself out. Maybe Dennis didn't take rejection so well after all.

She waited till he had driven off, then turned to walk along the front path. An upward glance showed the light on in the bedroom her mother now occupied. Molly wasn't looking forward to showing her mother the result of the first stage of her make-over. But there was no getting around it. Better she get it over with tonight.

'I'm home!' she called out as she came into the house.

No answer.

Her heartbeat quickening with nerves, she locked the door behind her then trudged on up the stairs and tapped on her mother's door. 'Can I come in?'

A down-in-the-mouth 'I suppose so' finally filtered through the door.

Molly would always remember the look on her mother's face when she first entered the room.

'Well, you've really done it now, haven't you?' Ruth snapped. 'Gone and cut off all your lovely long hair and had it dyed a cheap brassy red. Don't expect me to say I like it, Molly, because I don't. I'm sorry, but I'm not going to lie.'

It saddened Molly that her mother was not only *not* sorry at all, but she *had* lied. For the truth had rocketed from her momentarily rounded eyes before she'd been able to hide it.

Her new hairstyle *was* fantastic, as both Leanne and Dennis had said. And so was the colour. Fantastic and flattering!

Molly generously put her mother's negative reaction down to insecurity over her daughter's belatedly spreading her wings. It could not be jealousy. Surely not!

'That's all right, Mum,' she said with determined cheerfulness. 'You don't have to like it. *I* do. And I'm pleased to announce it's already an unqualified success where the opposite sex is concerned, which is the name of the game, isn't it?'

'What?' Ruth sat up straighter against her pillows. 'You're saying Liam's seen you already? I didn't know he was home for the weekend. I didn't see his car outside.'

'Not Liam, Mum. Dennis.'

'Dennis? Dennis who?'

'Dennis Taylor. You know Dennis Taylor, Mum. Well, he saw me walking home and gave me a lift. He said my hair looked fantastic. He even asked me out.'

'Asked you out? Dennis Taylor asked you out?'

'That's what I said.'

'You…you didn't say you would go, did you, Molly?'

'Not this time,' came her airy reply. 'But that was because I was too tired. I'm sure he'll ask again. Meanwhile, I think I'll go to bed. I have a busy day tomorrow, what with make-up to buy and lots of lovely clothes to look at and try on. See you in the morning, Mum.' And, after giving her a goodnight peck, Molly whirled round and walked from the room.

CHAPTER SIX

MOLLY was practising her daytime make-up routine the following Sunday morning when the telephone rang.

'Can you answer that, Mum?' she called out.

There was no reply and the phone kept on ringing. Molly suddenly remembered that her mother had gone down to the corner store to buy the Sunday papers. Carefully, she put down her new mascara wand then hurried downstairs to sweep up the receiver.

'Hi there,' she said breezily.

'Molly? Is that you?'

Her heart caught at the sound of Liam's voice, reminding her forcibly how much she loved this man. The realisation wrenched her momentarily out of her newly found optimism, bringing her down to earth with a thud. But then she regathered herself, her spirits lifting with the thought that Liam was actually calling her. That was a first!

'It certainly is me, Liam. Don't I sound like me?'

'Actually no…you sound different, somehow.'

'Really?' I *look* different too, she was tempted to add, but didn't want to spoil the surprise when he eventually saw her in the flesh. 'Sorry. It's just the same little old me,' she went on, smiling to herself.

Her height was one thing she simply could not change. Though the four-inch heels she'd tried on yesterday and which she would buy shortly certainly gave her a taller view of the world. 'So to what do I owe the dubious honour of your call?'

'Are you being sarcastic?'

Molly chuckled at the shocked tone of his question. 'Who, me? Never!'

'Have you been drinking?'

Now he sounded almost churlish.

'*This* early on a Sunday morning?' It was five past ten. 'Which brings me to a repeat of *my* question. Why are you calling me?'

'What? Oh, I um…I'm on my way up to help Mum move some furniture around. She's decided she's bored with the layout in the living rooms. Actually, I think it's just an excuse to get me home and feed me up. Anyway, I thought of you saying the other night that you don't get fed properly at home, and I was wondering if you'd like to join us for lunch.'

'Join you for lunch,' she repeated, swallowing convulsively and immediately going blank.

'You don't have to sound so thrilled,' came his testy remark. 'I realise I'm not your Mr X but I've always thought you enjoyed my company.'

'Oh, but I do!' she hastened to assure him. 'I mean, I…I…'

'You have something else on? Is that it?'

Molly tried to pull herself together. It was the shock, that was all. She glanced in the wall mirror

above the telephone table and nerves immediately be-
sieged her. Would Liam think she looked fantastic
when he saw her? Might he be inspired to ask her out
on a date, like Dennis had? A *real* date?

'No, nothing else on,' she said at last. 'And I'd love
to join you and your mother for lunch. Would you
like me to help you move the furniture as well?'

'Would you?'

'Love to. Make-overs are my thing this week.'

'What?'

'Nothing,' she muttered, and wished she were more
confident of Liam's reaction to her own make-over.

'I'll see you in about fifteen minutes, then. Just
come over when you see my car.'

'But…but…'

'Look, I'm ringing from my mobile and I'd better
hang up before I get into trouble.'

He hung up and Molly groaned into the dead receiver. Fifteen minutes. Oh, God…

With a squawk, she dropped the receiver back into
place and dashed upstairs, throwing open her wardrobe and searching for something Liam might like.
No pants, she reminded herself, and passed over the
cheap tights and tracksuit pants she lived in around
the house. Her eyes went to the lime-green T-shirt
she'd bought the previous day, the only item of clothing she could afford with the fifteen dollars she'd had
left over after her skin-care and make-up splurge. It
was one of the 'in' colours of the season and suited
her new vibrant hair colour.

But she had nothing to go with it.

In despair, she pulled on a pair of cream Bermuda shorts which, though bought two years back when she'd been larger, had an elastic waistline and didn't look too bad. Didn't look too good either, but, darn it all, it was too hot for jeans and she didn't have enough time to find anything else. Ten minutes had flown by since Liam had called.

Shoving her feet into tan sandals, Molly spun round to the dressing-table to finish her make-up, but her hands were shaking so badly she had to abandon applying mascara. Fortunately, she'd already done her eyeshadow and eyeliner, adding enough depth and definition to her eyes for casual daytime wear. Her foundation, blusher and translucent powder were also in place, covering up the smattering of freckles across her nose and cheeks. All that was left to do was her lipstick.

She'd bought two new lipsticks the day before. Bronze and Flame, both in a stayfast brand. She hated lip-prints left on cups and glasses. Neither did she want to become one of those females who had to touch up their make-up all the time. All the make-up she'd purchased was supposed to stay all day—and all night if necessary.

This last thought sent Molly's pulse racing. There was only one man she'd want to wake up with in the morning, with her make-up still intact.

Somehow, the bronze-coloured lipstick found its proper place without wandering all over her face. A

quick brush of her hair, several deep, steadying
breaths and she was ready. Just in time, too, for when
she leant across her bed to glance through her bedroom window she was greeted by the sight of Liam's
new red car coming up the hill.

Her stomach tightened another notch, her heart
pounding. One last glance at her baggy shorts brought
a grimace and another flicker of doubt. The last thing
Molly needed at that moment was to come downstairs
and be met with her mother's open scorn.

Ruth walked in the front door just as Molly approached it. 'And where do you think you're off to
with your face all done up like a dog's dinner? No,
you don't have to tell me. I can guess. I saw his car
pass by as I walked up the hill, and you're running
straight over to parade yourself in front of him. Dear
heaven, but you're a fool, Molly McCrae. That girlfriend of his would still run rings around you for looks
and style. You can tart yourself up all you like and it
won't make a blind bit of difference. Not where *Liam*
is concerned. Of course there are *other* men around
here who aren't so particular. Not that they ever *marry*
the girls they ask out.'

For a few seconds, Molly's confidence in her appearance wavered. But she'd come too far to allow
anyone to undermine her newly found self-esteem.
Not that her mother's nasty comments hadn't hurt.

'Maybe I'm not in Roxy's league in the looks department, Mum,' she said, her voice shaking with
emotion. 'But I still think I look pretty good. And I'll

have you know I'm not running over there to parade myself in front of Liam. He rang me while you were out and asked me over for lunch. It seems he and Roxy have broken up. Maybe I don't stand a chance with him, Mum, but that's no excuse for your trying to put me down like that. It was mean.'

To give her credit, her mother looked shocked, then stricken with remorse. 'Oh, Molly... I... I... Oh, dear. Oh, I'm so sorry. I... I just don't want to see you hurt...'

'Then stop *hurting* me,' she countered, sweeping out of the house before her mother could say another word, anger propelling her down the front path. As she stalked out onto the roadway and turned right, Molly indulged in some none too ladylike mutterings.

'My, my,' drawled a male voice. 'Does that brand-new temper come with the brand-new hair?'

Molly scudded to a ragged halt, her eyes whipping up to see Liam leaning against his open car door, watching her. His eyes immediately narrowed on her newly made-up face, then lifted to once again take in her new crowning glory. She couldn't tell if he approved of her transformation or not.

'You...you don't like it?' she almost groaned after a few seconds' silence, one hand flying up to touch her hair in that age-old feminine gesture which invited more reassurance.

Liam straightened and slammed the car door before glaring back her way. 'Don't be ridiculous. What's not to like? You look fantastic. But I think you know that, don't you?'

Molly glared back at him. So much for Liam being bowled over by her sudden beauty!

'I only did what you suggested the other night,' she defended hotly.

'True. But I honestly never expected you to do it. I guess I underestimated the power of your Mr X. So…has he seen the new you yet?'

Molly bristled, then lifted her small chin to look Liam straight in the eye. 'Yes, he has, as a matter of a fact.'

'I suppose he said you looked fantastic.'

Once again, Molly was spurred on to play an ironic game with the truth. Somehow, it soothed the pain of Liam's ongoing blindness. How could he not guess? she agonised inside. Couldn't he see her love for him in her desperate desire for his approval? 'Actually, they were his exact words,' she tossed back coolly.

His frown was instant. 'Where is it that you see this…Don Juan?' he demanded to know.

Molly smiled a darkly devious smile. It amused her that Mr X didn't find favour with Liam. If only he knew!

'Oh, he lives nearby, and I run into him from time to time. But, as I said before, my love life is really none of your business, is it? Now, shouldn't we be going inside to help your mother with the furniture?' she went on with more forcefulness than was usually her nature. 'Time is a-wasting, you know, and I have to get back to practising my new make-up before the working week begins. I aim to knock their socks off tomorrow morning.'

He threw her an incredulous glance, then shook his head. 'They say women change their personalities when they change their hair colour. I'm beginning to believe it.'

'Oh? Did you know Roxy before she peroxided her hair? Was she a sweet little thing before she became a bottle-blonde?'

'We're not discussing Roxy here, Miss Sarcasm. Which is exactly the sort of thing I'm referring to. You were never one to be bitchy before. Neither did you go round swearing under your breath.'

'Maybe you just never heard me before. Maybe you don't know the real me at all, Liam. Maybe you've never stopped to smell the flowers.'

'Stopped to smell the flowers? What in hell has my stopping to smell the flowers got to do with your turning into a shrew?'

Molly laughed while Liam scowled. It was at that moment his mother opened her front door and came out onto the porch to stare over at both of them.

Babs Delaney was a handsome woman. Somewhere in her late fifties, she was tall and slender, with intelligent blue eyes and streaky ash-blonde hair which fell to her shoulders in a stylish bob. Unlike her son she obviously liked women in trousers for she lived in them. Today she was wearing a loose pair of fawn cotton trousers with a bright floral floaty overblouse.

A pair of reading glasses hung on a gold chain around her neck.

She lifted a hand to shade her eyes from the sunlight, squinting down at this strange young woman with her son. Molly smiled with satisfaction when she realised Liam's mother didn't recognise her.

'Hi there, Mum.' Liam waved. 'Be right with you. Moll here's going to help us.'

'Moll?' his mother repeated, frowning.

Liam sighed his exasperation. 'Oh, all right. I'll call her Molly in your presence, if you insist. I can't understand why you have such an aversion to nicknames when you go by the moniker of Babs. Come on, *Molly*.'

'Molly?' Babs stared as Liam guided her up his front steps. 'Oh, my goodness, it's *Molly*! From next door!'

'Yes, it's Molly from next door,' Liam said as he pecked his mother on the cheek, then threw Molly a dry look over his shoulder. 'In a fashion…'

'I'm so sorry, Molly, dear,' Liam's mother directed at Molly with an apologetic smile. 'I didn't recognise you with that stunning new hair colour and style. My, but it suits her, doesn't it, Liam? She looks a different girl entirely.'

'She does indeed,' Liam said in a tone which had his mother raising her eyebrows at him before turning to take Molly's arm.

'Who did it for you, dear?' she asked as she led

her inside. 'I'm always on the lookout for a good hair-dresser.'

They stopped together in the tiled foyer while Molly raved on about Leanne's abilities and moderate prices, till Liam finally interrupted. 'Have I come home to move furniture or not?'

'Don't be rude, dear,' Babs told him dismissively. 'The furniture can wait. It's not going anywhere. I'll just go put on the jug and catch up with Molly here for a bit. I haven't had a good talk to her in ages. Remember when she used to come over every Sunday, Liam, and you would make her sit in your room all afternoon while you showed her whatever game you were working on that week? I used to think she deserved a medal for how patient she was with you. And how kind. Not too many girls her age would have bothered being friends with an egocentric computer nut like you, dear.'

'I didn't mind, Mrs Delaney,' Molly confessed. 'Truth is I enjoyed it though I can't say I always understood everything. Liam's nothing short of a creative genius. I dare say he gets that from you.'

Babs smiled her pleasure at the compliment. 'What a nice girl you are,' she said. 'But my son is no genius. Not in the things which count, that is,' she muttered as she turned to walk down several steps into the sunken living areas of the house.

Liam's home was roomy, split-level and messy, Molly saw as she traipsed after Liam's mother. And it smelt like a tavern. Housework was clearly not a

priority with Mrs Delaney. Funny. Molly couldn't remember it being so unkempt in the old days.

She and Liam followed his mother through the
large family room into a kitchen which would have
given her own mother an instant nervous breakdown.
Molly had never seen so many piles of dirty dishes
in her life!

'Sorry about the mess,' Babs Delaney excused with
an unconcerned but elegant wave of her right hand.
'My cleaner had to quit through ill health a couple of
weeks back and I'm on a deadline for a book. I've
been meaning to advertise for a replacement but
haven't got around to it.'

An idea popped into Molly's mind. 'How much
does a cleaner earn?'

'What?'

Molly repeated the question.

'Oh, I'm not sure what the going rate is. I paid my
lady fifty dollars a day cash in hand,' Babs replied as
she angled the kettle under the tap. A difficult task,
under the circumstances, since the sink was full. 'She
used to come in on Mondays and Fridays for six hours
a time. Still, she did do all the washing and ironing
as well as the cleaning, and any extra jobs I needed
done, so she was well worth every penny. It left me
totally free to write, which meant I earned more
money in the long run.'

'I see,' Molly murmured thoughtfully.

Liam's mother slanted her a sharp look. 'Do you
know someone who might be interested?'

Molly hesitated. 'I might…'

'Your mother?' Babs guessed, turning to put the kettle on the counter and plug it in.

'Well…yes. Dad left her with a lot of debts, you see, and her pension doesn't go far. I suggested that we take in a boarder to help make ends meet better, but I don't think Mum liked that idea much.'

'Why don't I go ask her, then, right now?' Babs offered. 'And while I'm at it I'll ask her over to lunch with us. I've got plenty of food. Meanwhile, Liam, load up the dishwasher for me, like a good boy, will you? If Molly's mother's house is anything like her garden then she'll be horrified at the state of this place. Molly, love, would you mind collecting the dirty glasses from the living room? Oh, and the ashtrays as well? I had some visitors over last night who smoked like chimneys.'

Molly was happy to. What a nice lady Liam's mother was! As soon as Babs left, she whizzed around the living room, straightening it up a bit while Liam made clattering noises in the kitchen. When she came out at last with four dirty glasses and a stack of ashtrays to empty he had just closed the dishwasher door and started the cycle.

'I'll wash these up in the sink,' she said, and set to work straight way.

Liam leant against a nearby counter, his arms crossed and his eyes thoughtful upon her. 'When you say your father left debts behind, just how much debt do you mean?'

'A lot,' Molly admitted. 'The year before he died, he took out loans against the house to finance his latest business venture, which went bust like every other one of his get-rich-quick schemes. Unfortunately there was no life insurance to cover these loans. The repayments take nearly all my salary each week.'

Liam straightened, his expression appalled. 'But that's terrible! Why didn't you tell me about this sooner?'

'Why should I have? It's not your problem, Liam.'

'Some best friend you must think I am,' he said sharply.

Molly was astonished by his annoyance. 'But I… I…'

'I want you to tell me exactly who these loans are with and what interest you're paying.'

'Why?'

'Because I want to help you, that's why.'

'Help me how?'

'That depends.'

'On what?'

'On how much stupid pride you've got.'

Her chin shot up. 'I have quite a bit. And I don't think pride is at all stupid!'

'That's what I thought, so I could do one of two things. I could have my accountant look at these loans and see what is the best way to refinance them at the lowest possible interest. Men like your father always have to borrow at exorbitant interest rates because they're a credit risk. On top of that, interest rates have dropped lately. Alternatively, I could organise to pay off the debts myself by giving you an interest-free loan. We could draw up a legal document to satisfy your pride. Either way, your repayments would be substantially less than they are now.'

Molly's face lit up. 'An interest-free loan! Oh, Liam, that would be wonderful! Simply wonderful!' But then her face fell. 'But they're not my debts. In a legal sense, that is. They're Mum's. She would have to sign any documents. And I don't think she would agree to your last suggestion. I mean…she might think it was…funny.'

'What do you mean…funny?'

'She might think there were strings attached to such an arrangement.'

'Strings? What kind of strings?'

'Liam, don't be thick, please. Between you and me.'

Liam's shock was not altogether flattering. 'She thinks I would demand you sleep with me in exchange for money? Why in God's name would she think such a thing?'

Molly could hardly tell him the truth—that it was her daughter Ruth believed capable of bad things where Liam was concerned, not the other way around. Still, she had to say something. Liam was clearly offended by the implication that he was the type of man who would blackmail, or bribe, a girl into bed.

'Don't take it personally. Mum doesn't have a great opinion of men in general when it comes to sex,

Liam,' she said. 'Dad was an inveterate womaniser, you know.'

'No,' he said slowly, that frown still in place. 'I didn't know. You never told me. You never told me anything much about yourself or your family.' Now he was sounding frustrated.

'You never asked.'

'Well, I'm asking now!'

'Why?'

'*Why?*'

'Yes, why this sudden interest?'

Liam was taken aback, then thoroughly exasperated. 'Why must women make mountains out of molehills? There's no mystery to my interest. Neither is it *sudden*. I've always cared about you, Molly, but I guess I've been so wrapped up in myself and getting my business going that I haven't had much time to think of other people's problems. I suggest you put this change of heart down to my maturing at long last, if you have to put it down to anything. I did turn thirty this year.'

'Yes, I know,' she said drily. 'I bought *and* lit the candles on your cake.'

'You still haven't forgiven me for forgetting your birthday this week, have you?'

'I'll forgive you anything if you have your accountant get me some more money each week. I'm dying to buy myself some lovely new clothes to go with my new look. Believe me, Liam, if you can organise that refinancing business, I'll be your willing slave for ever.' And wasn't *that* the truth, she thought ruefully.

He gave her a decidedly disgruntled look. 'So I'm to be responsible for even *more* changes in my Molly. Your Mr X won't be able to resist you soon. Frankly, I'm not so sure I want to send you into the arms of some good-looking bastard who's had oodles of women and who didn't appreciate the lovely person you were *before* you became a fashion plate.'

Molly was startled, then flattered by the jealous edge in his words. It occurred to her that inventing the mythical Mr X was the best thing she'd ever done. She'd never had so much attention from Liam in her life. Suddenly, she was a reasonably attractive female, complete with a secret sexual obsession. The fact that that sexual obsession was Liam himself might have escaped him, but the concept of her being madly in love with some good-looking Casanova clearly bothered him. Surely that had to be reason to keep hoping?

'I don't think you're in love with this man at all,' Liam pronounced abruptly. 'From what I've heard, it's a simple case of infatuation. When and if he ever takes you to bed, you'll realise that. Men like him rarely live up to the romantic and sexual fantasies women weave around them. They're much too selfish to be good lovers.'

'That's a very interesting theory,' Molly said thoughtfully. 'And do you think you're a good lover, Liam?'

'*Me*? We're not talking about *me*!' he grumbled irritably. 'We're talking about lover boy here.'

'I was just wondering,' she said with feigned innocence. 'After all, you confessed the other day to being selfish. And you just said selfish men weren't good lovers.'

'Yes, well, there's selfish and there's selfish. I like to think I excel in anything I put my mind to. So yes, I think I'm a good lover. Are you going to argue the point, Miss Picky, or accept my word for it?'

Actually, I'd like a demonstration, Molly thought with a quickening of her heartbeat. She stared first into Liam's beautiful blue eyes, then down at his equally beautiful mouth before letting her hopefully unreadable gaze drift down his even more beautiful body.

Her own ached with longing for that body. It was a bittersweet ache, filled with a delicious sexual awareness, yet framed within a frustration so acute, she wanted to scream and shout and stamp her feet.

'I guess I'll have to accept your word for it,' she managed to say, though her words were clipped. 'I certainly won't be ringing Roxy and asking her, that's for sure. The best thing you ever did was to break up with *her*.'

'Break up with Roxy? I haven't broken up with Roxy. Wherever did you get *that* idea?'

'But the other night…you said…'

'I said we were having a trial separation. Actually, it was her idea. She had some bee in her bonnet about my taking her for granted, which was probably true. So she told me she wasn't going to see me for a month, during which we were to have no contact whatsoever, even by telephone.'

'I see.' Molly felt her brave and exciting new world tip out of kilter. 'So when is this month up?' she asked, her voice flat and heavy.

'Next Sunday.' He raked his hands agitatedly through his hair. 'And it can't come soon enough, I can tell you. This has been the longest, most frustrating four weeks in my life!'

CHAPTER SEVEN

AFTER that, nothing could have made Molly happy, not even when Babs returned with her still apologetic-looking mother in tow. Amazingly, Ruth was thrilled by the idea of becoming Mrs Delaney's cleaner, then ecstatic when Liam explained his refinancing offer.

'Isn't that wonderful news, Molly?' her mother exclaimed. 'Now we won't have to have a stranger in the house. And you'll have some money for yourself for a change.'

Molly smiled and said yes, it was wonderful. She smiled all through lunch and laughed when the four of them moved Babs's living-room furniture to new spots, then had to move everything back again to their original places when the end result did not please Babs's creative eye.

No one would have guessed how wretched Molly felt. She was a past master at hiding her feelings, especially around Liam. But her heart grew heavier as the hours passed. By afternoon tea, she was exhausted with the emotional strain of pretending to be bright and breezy when inside she was shattered. Liam's getting back with Roxy the following Sunday was the final straw.

His eagerness for their reconciliation had been palpable, his body language reeking of sexual frustration as he'd spoken of his time away from Roxy. He could not wait to jump back into bed with her. Molly could no longer fool herself. Any attention he'd been giving *her* had been the result of his boredom, not because of any suddenly selfless maturity.

'You won't forget about the refinancing,' she reminded him stiffly when it came time for them to leave.

'Not at all. In fact, Ruth's going to give me the relevant papers this very afternoon. I'll collect them shortly, Ruth, and have Nigel get onto it first thing this week, then I'll bring up whatever needs to be signed next Saturday.'

'You coming home next Saturday, are you?' Molly asked with a weary resignation. Normally, the thought of Liam being around thrilled her to pieces. Now there was no pleasure in the news, only the cynical thought that of course he was coming home. He had nothing better to do till Sunday, did he?

'Yes, I've been invited to speak at a local business awards dinner on Saturday night. I'm also presenting the prizes.'

'How nice,' Molly said blandly.

'Why don't you take Molly, Liam?' his mother suggested. 'The invitation says "and partner".'

Liam's instant frown was enough to turn Molly off the idea, despite her stupid heart giving one last feeble leap. His eyes turned her way then travelled slowly over her. She could actually see his brain ticking away. Dear old Moll doesn't look half bad now. She wouldn't be an embarrassment to take, not like she would have been a week ago.

'Would you like to go?' he asked her. 'It's black tie, so you'll need a dinner dress.'

Molly steeled herself to do the one thing she'd thought she would never do. Reject the man she loved.

'Thank you, Liam,' she said with superb indifference, 'but I have other plans for next Saturday night.'

His blue eyes instantly clouded and a small stab of triumph lifted her spirits momentarily, quickly followed by a much stronger stab of despair. Tears threatened and she just had to get out of there.

Panic had her glancing around for her mother. 'Ready to go home, Mum?' she asked, determined to keep up the false gaiety to the bitter end. 'I have quite a bit to do before the working week starts tomorrow.'

'My working week starts tomorrow too, doesn't it, Babs?' Ruth returned happily.

'Indeed it does.'

'Thank you so much,' Ruth went on, clasping her neighbour's hands with her own with rather touching gratitude. 'For the lunch. And…and everything.'

Babs smiled and patted Ruth's hands. 'It's I who's grateful. I've found myself a wonderful cleaner and a new friend as well. See you in the morning, Ruth.'

'And I'll be seeing you later, Mrs McCrae!' Liam called out as Molly shepherded her mother out of the house. 'To get those papers.'

'What nice people they are,' Ruth said on the short way home. 'And wasn't it kind of Liam to help us out with that money business?'

'Yes, it was,' Molly admitted, but tight-lipped.

A silence descended between the two women as they made their way inside, but Molly could feel her mother watching her.

'Why didn't you say yes when Liam asked you to go out with him?' Ruth asked once they were safely alone in the kitchen. 'It…it wasn't because of what I said earlier, was it? About your not being… well…pretty enough for him? Because that's not true, Molly. You're plenty pretty enough. And he really likes you. I can see that now. He could hardly take his eyes off you all over lunch, and then later when he…'

'Oh, Mum, *please*,' Molly begged. 'You don't have to lie. You were right the first time.'

'No, Molly, I wasn't. I was wrong. Very wrong. And I'm thoroughly ashamed of myself. I was feeling sorry for myself, and I was afraid. Yes, afraid,' she repeated when Molly's eyes widened. 'Afraid some man would snap you up, looking as you do now, and I'd be left all alone in this world.

'But today opened my eyes a lot. There's Babs Delaney, a widow like myself, but she doesn't sit around feeling sorry for herself. Besides her writing, she plays golf and bingo and bridge. And she doesn't try to tie that boy of hers to her apron-strings, either. I can see it's up to me to make something of my life for myself. I know becoming a cleaner isn't much, but at least I'm good at it, and it's a start. I might even go to that hairdresser of yours with some of my cleaning money and become a blonde!'

'Oh, Mum!' Molly exclaimed, a burst of very real joy dragging her heart back out of the doldrums. 'You've no idea how happy you've made me, hearing you say that!'

'Do…do you forgive me for saying those awful things to you, darling? I didn't mean them, you know…'

Molly could not help but relent. 'Of course I forgive you,' she said gently. 'I love you, Mum.'

'Oh, Molly,' her mother cried, and threw her arms around her daughter.

Unfortunately, it was not the best time for Molly to be hugged. Her mother's display of affection tipped her over the edge on which she'd been balancing for several hours, splintering the brittle control with which she'd been holding in her misery. Her shoulders began to shake as sobs racked her whole body.

'Oh, Molly,' her mother groaned, and hugged her daughter even more tightly. 'Don't cry, darling. Please don't cry. Oh, you make me feel terrible. If only I hadn't said those awful things, you would probably have gone out with Liam when he asked you. It's all my fault!'

'No, it isn't,' Molly sniffled when she at last pulled out of her mother's arms. 'Liam only asked me out because Roxy's trying to prove some point or other and she's refused to have anything to do with him for a month. But come next Sunday they'll be back together again, as thick as thieves. Who knows? If she plays her cards right, he might even ask her to marry him.'

'What rubbish!' her mother pronounced firmly, startling Molly. 'Liam's not in love with that flashy bit of goods. No man in love with one girl looks at another girl as he looked at you today.'

Molly was dumbfounded. 'But I...I didn't notice him looking at me in any special way...'

'Then you're as blind as he is, my girl. You made a big mistake refusing to go out with him next Saturday night. Now listen here; when he comes over to pick up those papers, you tell him you've changed your mind and you'd like to go with him after all.'

'But...but...'

'No buts. You said he's not getting back with that Roxy till Sunday. Make the most of what time you have!'

'I was just going to say I don't have anything to wear,' Molly said, smiling weakly.

'Well, that's easily fixed.'

'How? Liam's accountant can't get us any more money immediately. And I'm not taking the cleaning money you earn, Mum. No way. One hundred dollars wouldn't be nearly enough anyway,' she added with a sad sigh. 'A dinner dress, complete with shoes and bag, doesn't come cheap these days.'

'Would five hundred dollars do?'

'Five hundred! But where…? I mean…'

Ruth smiled her pleasure at her daughter's surprise. 'You're not the only one who has rainy-day money stashed away, my girl. Come this way.'

Molly followed, fascinated, while her mother led her upstairs and into the master bedroom where she proceeded to lift up the mattress and draw out a battered brown paper envelope. She opened the flap and tipped the contents out onto the patchwork quilt. Notes of all sizes fluttered down, mostly fives, tens and twenties.

'I used to hide this in an empty washing powder box in the laundry when your father was alive. But now it's safe enough here. I know there's at least five hundred dollars, maybe more.' She gathered the notes up and pressed them into Molly's hands. 'I want you to buy yourself a dress which will knock Liam's eyes out!'

Molly hated the wild rush of elation which flooded her heart, for she feared she was setting herself up for a disaster of monumental proportions. No matter what her mother said and no matter what dress she bought, how could she seriously compete with Roxy? It was like comparing a nice little house wine with a top-brand French champagne. Roxy's extravagant self fizzed and sparkled. She was a special-occasion lady whereas *she*, Molly, was the common, everyday, value-for-money variety.

When Liam looked at her he only ever saw a familiar face. And everyone knew what familiarity bred. Contempt. Never chemistry.

Or was that how he'd seen her in the past? Dared she hope that her new look *had* evoked a new appreciation? Molly had told the truth when she'd said she hadn't noticed Liam looking at her differently today. But after his news about Roxy she'd been too upset to notice anything, and had avoided Liam's eyes as much as possible.

Could her mother's observations possibly be correct, or was she just trying to make her daughter feel better? She'd been very guilty over her earlier less than generous remarks.

Molly didn't want to get her hopes up too much.

And yet…

Something was stirring within her soul. Something she'd never felt before. Something rather wicked.

Roxy had called her a sly little piece. Maybe she was right, Molly thought with a steeling of her spirit.

Because I am not going to go quietly, Roxy, darling. Neither am I going to let you have Liam back without a fight. Come Saturday night, I'm going to use every female trick in the book.

The only trouble was…she hadn't read that particular book yet. She would have to depend on her feminine instinct.

The front doorbell ringing startled both of them.

'That'll be Liam,' Ruth said urgently. 'Now drop that money and go down and talk to him while I get those papers he wants. Tell him you've changed your mind about Saturday night, and ask him what time he wants you ready by. Be cool, though. Not overly eager.'

'Mum, you sneaky thing.'

'Well, there's no point in being easy. Any girl who looks as good as you do can play a little hard to get. Besides, men never want what they think they can have, gratis. They like a bit of a challenge.'

Molly went downstairs, shaking her head. Who would have believed that within her own shy reserved mother lurked the makings of a *femme fatale*? Heaven knew what would happen if the McCrae widow ever became a blonde!

Molly summoned up a pleasant smile to answer the door, resolving to watch this time for any sign that Liam looked at her differently in any way.

'Hello there again,' she said. 'Mum won't be a minute with those papers. Look, about next Saturday night, Liam. That was rude of me to dismiss your very nice invitation out of hand. I know what it's like to go to these things all alone...'

She didn't actually, because she'd never been to an awards dinner. But Molly had never lacked an imagination. Just think of all those times Liam had made love to her in her mind!

Unfortunately, she began thinking of one of those times right at this moment. It was her favourite scenario where Liam was concerned. He would bring her home to this door after a serious date and there would be much kissing and panting on the front porch. When she finally unlocked the door, he would push her inside, then scoop her up into his arms and carry her upstairs to her room where a three-foot bed was no barrier to true love.

Her mouth dried as she thought of their naked bodies blended tightly, writhing together. Her green eyes glittered as they began unconsciously to rove over the object of her desire.

Before they reached his waist, Molly swallowed then cleared her throat. 'Er…could I possibly change my mind and say yes?'

He stiffened. He actually stiffened.

Why?

'Is there a problem with that?' she asked airily, even while her heart was thudding.

He just stood there, frowning at her. The atmosphere on that doorstep was suddenly charged with a quite alien tension. Molly didn't know what to make of it except that she found herself holding her breath.

'Liam?' she choked out.

He seemed to have to shake himself to answer. 'No,' he muttered. 'No problem. I'll look forward to it.'

Molly had to be careful not to let all the breath out of her lungs in a rush. 'Fine,' she said with a small smile. 'Well, where is this dinner and what time should I be ready?'

'It's being held down at the League's Club, upstairs in the Admiral's Quarters. The dinner starts at eight.

Pre-dinner drinks at seven-thirty. I'll pick you up at…say…seven-fifteen?'

'I'll be ready. And thanks again for helping us with the finance business.'

'My pleasure.'

But it didn't look as if it was his pleasure. Not at all. He hadn't smiled once since she'd opened the door. Molly could not make head or tail of his mood, except that it was obvious he had mixed feelings about taking her to that dinner.

She prayed his reluctance was because he'd begun to feel things for her which he found confusing, and not because he was worried Roxy might get jealous, if she ever found out.

Her mother's arrival at that point steered the conversation to less stressful grounds. Liam left a couple of minutes later and as Ruth closed the front door she threw Molly a questioning glance. 'Well? What happened? You both seemed a little tense when I came down.'

Molly shrugged. 'I don't rightly know. I told him I'd changed my mind about the dinner, and he agreed to take me, but not with any great enthusiasm. To be honest, I think it worried the heck out of him.'

'Well, that's better than indifference, Molly.'

'That's what I was thinking.'

'Only time will tell, I guess.'

'I suppose so. But by golly it's going to be a very long week.'

CHAPTER EIGHT

'Long' wasn't the word for it. 'Excruciating' was better.

Molly could not concentrate on her work. How could she, with Joan besieging her with suggestions from the moment she arrived at work on Monday morning and spied the newly made-over Molly?

Joan's main advice was directed at Molly's choice of clothing for the big night. The trouble was, she changed her mind every day. On Monday she insisted Molly buy black. Lace, preferably. Black lace was so-o-o sexy!

Molly didn't think she could carry off black lace and told Joan as much. So on Tuesday Joan moved to red satin…before she realised red would clash horribly with Molly's new hair colour. From Wednesday to Friday she went through every other colour in the rainbow, plus every possible style from strapless and sexy to tight and slinky, then finally to white and virginal.

This last, desperate idea was an attempt at reverse psychology, since Roxy would never dress in such a fashion.

Molly was glad to leave work on Friday afternoon, having informed her avid friend that she would simply buy something that suited and flattered her. Joan had pulled a face before pressing the solemn promise from Molly that she would finally wear the perfume she'd given her on her birthday.

'And buy yourself some drop earrings,' had been Joan's last hurrah. 'I was watching this body language expert on television the other day and he said dangling earrings projected highly sexual messages on some subtly primitive basis. It seems they bring attention to the earlobes, which was one of our earliest erogenous zones. Apparently there's this tribe in Africa where the women stretch their earlobes with heavy rings and weights. The ones with the longest earlobes are considered the sexiest, so the longer the earrings the better.'

Molly had sighed and agreed to wear long, dangling earrings as well as the perfume.

Saturday dawned slightly overcast but the sun came out during Molly's short train trip up to the shopping centre at Tuggerah. The forecast that morning had predicted twenty-eight degrees, average for the Central Coast in early March. Fortunately, the humidity was low so Molly would not have to worry about perspiration ruining whatever dress she bought.

She arrived just as the shops opened, her mother's gift of five hundred and forty-five dollars tucked safely in her purse. Four hours later her mission was finally accomplished, and her purse was pretty empty. Molly could hardly contain her excitement on the train ride home, hugging the parcels on her lap.

She would never have dreamt she could look so good. Or so sexy. Of course, it was to be seen what Liam would think of her, but she could never reproach herself for not pulling out all the stops.

She hurried home from the station, puffing a little as she struggled up the hill with her four plastic bags. It was just after one-thirty and Liam's red car was nowhere in sight. His mother was, though, Babs waving from where she was attending to her pot-plants on the front porch.

'Been shopping for tonight, dear?' she called out, her smile bright.

Molly was grateful to stop for a minute. 'Yes, Mrs Delaney. I've been very extravagant,' she confessed rather breathlessly. 'New dress. New shoes. New everything, actually.'

'Oh, you must come in and show me. I'd love to see them.'

Molly hesitated, then glanced back down the hill. She didn't want to be caught by Liam coming home. She didn't want him to see her today till she was ready.

'Don't worry,' Babs said. 'Liam's not due. He has to work all day today. He just rang to say he'd get ready down in Sydney and drive straight to your place. Come on. You can have a cool drink while you're at it. You look hot.'

Molly *was* hot. But it wasn't just from the shopping. Suddenly, tonight was all too real. It was also her last chance. If nothing came of tonight with Liam then she would have to give up all hope.

Total failure was less than a few hours away.

'What a lovely green!' Babs exclaimed when Molly drew the silk bit of nothing out of the bag. 'It reminds me of the colour of the water around the Great Barrier Reef. Hold it up against you,' she urged. 'Oh, yes, that's just the thing.' She chuckled delightedly. 'You're certainly going to make that boy of mine sit up and take notice in *that* dress, aren't you, my dear?'

Molly's eyes rounded at Liam's mother, who gave her a softly knowing smile in return. 'You think I haven't guessed all these years that you're in love with my son?'

'I... I...'

'You don't have to say a thing. Just listen. Liam does not love Roxy. She is, however, a beautiful and clever girl who panders to his not inconsiderable ego and knows exactly how to handle him.'

Molly was all ears as Liam's mother went on. She'd been riveted from the moment Babs had said Liam did not love Roxy.

'I know my son very well, Molly. I know his strengths and his weaknesses. Basically, he is a good, kind, loving boy, but he has an obsessive workaholic personality with a one-track mind. I'm sure you've seen evidence of this for yourself. I used to have to set an alarm clock next to his computer to get him to school reasonably on time. When he becomes absorbed in a project nothing can distract him, not even his male needs, which I might add are as strong as any other normal red-blooded man's.'

This wasn't any news to Molly. She'd seen the trail of girlfriends, all of them not exactly the types you just *talked* to on a date.

'You might think Liam has only ever been attracted to the most beautiful of girls,' his mother went on. 'That he's like a moth drawn only to the brightest of flames.'

'Well, his girlfriends have all been stunners, Mrs Delaney,' Molly pointed out.

'True. So I suppose if I said it was their personalities which won him you would be sceptical?'

Molly just laughed.

'I understand your cynicism. Nevertheless, what I am saying is true. The only girls who've attracted Liam have been the ones who had enough confidence in themselves to break through his absent-minded nature and force him to notice them. I have no doubt most of them approached him first, made none too subtle passes and flirted with him outrageously in order to win him away from his other, all-consuming passions.

'Naturally, the only girls who have such a degree of confidence are usually very beautiful ones which gives them that added edge. Once they have Liam's attention, they have the equipment to ensnare his sexual desire as well. Even so, he usually tires of them rather quickly. Either that or they themselves become frustrated with his tendency to forget dates, and they leave the relationship of their own accord.

'Roxy, however, has hung in there. I think she must be very good in bed. I also think she knows Liam's net worth and wants to hitch her wagon to a star. I suspect this so-called trial separation is supposed to frustrate Liam enough for him to agree to marry her. I don't know if it will work. I sincerely hope not, because she does not love my son and will make him miserable in the end. He does not believe in divorce, you see. Liam needs someone who truly loves and understands him. In short, Molly, he needs you.'

Molly was speechless.

'You have the perfect opportunity to put a spanner in Roxy's works tonight, my dear,' Babs continued in a conspiratorial voice. 'But you must be bold. And daring. Make him notice you, in more ways than one. Flirt with him. Let him know you want him. You *do* want him, don't you?'

All Molly could do was nod.

'Then go after him, with as much cunning and ruthlessness as Roxy did. In short, seduce him!'

Seduce him?

Molly went home with those daunting words ringing in her ears. How did an inexperienced virgin seduce a man like Liam? According to his own mother, he'd had countless sexy, beautiful women do just that and do it superbly! What chance did *she*, Molly McCrae, have? Made-over she might be, but that was only a skin-deep transformation. Inside, she was still a quiet, reserved kind of girl. Basically, she was not bold. Or daring.

Okay, so she'd spoken up for herself a few times recently, but only in private and with people she knew well. The thought of openly flirting with Liam in a very public place at a well-attended formal dinner sent frenetic butterflies fluttering around in her stomach.

Seven o'clock found those butterflies still in full flight. Yet her reflection in the dressing-table mirror went some way to boosting that confidence Liam's mother had insisted she find. Molly knew she had never looked better. Or sexier. Joan had certainly been right about those earrings. Outrageously long, the green crystal drops hung nearly to her shoulders, swaying seductively whenever she moved. They'd been worth every cent of the fifty dollars they'd cost.

'Oh, Molly, you look gorgeous!'

Molly swung round at her mother's voice, the A-line skirt of her green silk dress flaring out before settling into more discreet folds against her thighs. Not that a skirt that short could ever be really discreet. It ended a good five inches above her knees. When combined with the four-inch heels of her strappy, bronze-coloured Jane Debster shoes she looked all leg.

'Do you really think so, Mum?' Molly was desperate for reassurance, her own eyes not to be trusted.

Ruth's admiring gaze travelled from her daughter's shimmering hair, down over her perfectly made-up face, past the flamboyant earrings and finally to the

very sexy little dress which showed off Molly's recently reshaped curves to perfection. The low,
scooped neckline hinted at a very adequate and perfectly natural cleavage, the tight bodice and nipped-
in waistline showing that Molly could rival Scarlett
O'Hara in the hourglass figure department, and *without* the help of a corset.

'Turn around,' her mother said. 'Let me see the
back again.'

Molly did so a little tentatively. She knew the lace-
up back was daring, exposing a deep section of
creamy flesh right down her back to her waist. This
was part of the style of course, but it precluded the
wearing of a bra, even a strapless one. The only underwear Molly had on, in fact, was an expensive pair
of shiny skin-coloured Lycra tights which had built-
in tummy-control panties.

Molly turned back to find her mother frowning
slightly. 'What's wrong?' she asked, panicking. 'Do
you think the neckline is too bare? Should I wear a
necklace instead of these earrings?'

Ruth smiled reassuringly. 'Not at all. Those earrings are perfect. No, I was just hoping everything
turns out right for you tonight.'

Molly scooped in a steadying breath. 'I do too...'

Ruth came forward to take her daughter's hands in
hers. 'Whatever happens, you look lovely.'

'Thank you, Mum.'

'You smell lovely too. What's that perfume you're
wearing?'

'It's the one Joan gave me for my birthday. It's called…Seductress.'

Ruth's eyebrows shot up. Mother and daughter looked at each other, then laughed.

'Let's hope it has a secret ingredient,' Molly said, shaking her head ruefully, 'because I think I'm going to need it.'

'You'll do fine, love. Just be your sweet lovely self and Liam will be enchanted.'

Now Molly felt confused. She had Liam's mother telling her to be a vamp, her own advising the natural approach. She had an awful feeling neither would work. The only time she'd had a real response from Liam was when he'd been jealous of Mr X.

Maybe that was the way to go. Mr X had been very useful so far…

Molly was speculating on how she could use Mr X to further advantage tonight when the doorbell rang. Her stomach immediately cramped. Oh, dear heaven.

'That will be Liam,' her mother whispered. 'I won't come to the door. Say I'm in the bath or something. If he has those papers for me, just put them on the hall table. Oh, and don't worry about how late you get home. *I* won't. In fact I won't worry too much if you don't come home at all!'

Molly's green eyes rounded at this amazingly broad-minded mother she'd suddenly acquired. 'Mum,' she said. 'I'm shocked. But I love you for being so understanding. Still, I think you'll find I'll be home soon after midnight like a good little Cinderella.'

'I don't know about that,' Ruth said wryly with another glance at her striking-looking daughter. 'Now off you go,' she added when the doorbell rang a second time.

Molly picked up the bronze clutch purse which matched her shoes and made her way carefully downstairs, taking her time lest she trip over in her new high heels.

Be confident, she kept telling herself as she approached the front door. And bold. And daring.

Schooling her face into a cool smile, she swung open the door, prepared to accept Liam's surprised admiration as though it were the most natural thing in the world. Unfortunately, she hadn't prepared herself for being confronted with Liam standing there looking blisteringly handsome in a superbly tailored black dinner suit.

Most men looked good when dressed in a tux.

Liam was breathtaking.

She stood there in speechless admiration of *his* beauty and missed his initial reaction to her own appearance. By the time she'd recovered sufficiently to look into his eyes he was shaking his head at her with a mildly rueful reproach.

'I can see this is going to be a long and difficult night.'

Molly was taken aback. Did he like the way she looked, or not? 'What do you mean?'

'You know very well what I mean, you minx. My God, are you wearing any underwear at *all* under that excuse for a dress?'

Molly blushed and bristled at the same time. 'I'm only following *your* suggestions. You told me you don't like women who wear pants.'

His shocked blue eyes zoomed to where the hem of her skirt ended at mid-thigh. Molly rolled her own eyes. 'That's not what I meant. I *do* have pantyhose on with built-in panties,' she said drily. 'I was talking about my wearing a dress and not a pants suit.'

'Oh, that's a dress you're almost wearing, is it? I though it was a left-over from a lingerie party.'

'Very funny. Truly, Liam, you're acting like some over-protective big brother, though I don't know why. You never have before.'

'You've never looked like *this* before.'

'It that a compliment or an insult?'

'It could be a damned problem.'

'I don't see how,' she said airily. But she wasn't as thick as she was making out, and the reality of Liam's brooding reactions thrilled her to bits. He was perturbed by how she looked. And already jealous of any other man she might attract tonight.

His own mother's words popped into her mind. 'Go after him, with as much cunning and ruthlessness as Roxy did…

'So,' Molly went on, twirling around and merci-lessly pretending she had no idea of the effect the back of the dress would have on him. 'Will I knock 'em dead at the dinner?'

'I don't know about the others,' he growled, grabbing her wrist to stop her from twirling round again, 'but I'm in my grave already.'

She feigned a flustered frown. 'But I'm not talking about *you*, Liam. I was thinking of all those successful and possibly available businessmen at this dinner night.'

Liam glared at her. 'So that's why you changed your mind about partnering me tonight? Because you want to parade yourself for other men's eyes, like you're in some kind of meat market?'

'Well...I wouldn't put it quite so crudely. And I'm really only interested in *one* man's eyes.' Molly only meant she wasn't the sort of girl who played the field, but Liam immediately took it the wrong way.

'*One* man?' He frowned, then scowled. 'Oh, my God, don't tell me your infernal Mr X is going to be at this bloody dinner tonight!' he bit out.

Molly tried not to colour guiltily, but failed. For the first time, the use of Mr X had backfired on her.

'Damn and blast it, Molly!' Liam exploded. 'You should have told me.'

'Why? Would you have refused to take me if I'd said he was going to be there?' she asked, even while her mind raced. Mr X simply had to be disposed of once and for all, she decided. He'd been very useful up till now, but suddenly he was beginning to get in the way.

Liam opened his mouth to say something, then snapped it shut again.

'It's an irrelevant question anyway,' Molly went on swiftly. 'Because Mr X is *not* going to be there. Mr X has been wiped from the planet from this moment onwards. I've decided to take your advice, Liam, and move on. This is me moving on. Now, do you think *we* might move on and get going? Or do you want to be late and make a grand entrance?'

'With Moving-on-Molly by my side?' he mocked. 'Heck, no. I'd much prefer to slink in the back door.'

'There's no pleasing you tonight, is there?' she snapped as she stepped outside and banged the door shut behind her. 'I only did everything you told me to do. I happen to think I look very nice.'

Liam gripped her nearest elbow and began urging her along the front path. It set her crystal earrings swinging, along with her unfettered breasts. She kept her eyes straight ahead but had a feeling Liam was glaring daggers at her highly mobile bust. She hadn't realised till that moment what substantial movement did to braless breasts. Ones of her size, that was.

'"Nice" is a very ineffectual word to describe how you look tonight,' Liam muttered.

Molly extracted her arm from his grip once they reached the passenger door of his car. 'So how would *you* describe how I look?' she challenged.

His blue eyes blazed as he yanked open the door and waved her inside. Not a word passed his lips while she lowered herself into the seat, but his eyes spoke volumes when they dropped to take note of the way her skirt rode up dangerously high when she sat down.

'Provocative,' he snarled at last, then banged the door shut.

'Good,' she snapped back, once he'd settled himself behind the wheel. 'That's exactly the look I was looking for tonight.'

Molly dropped her purse into her lap, noting with some dismay that the smallish bag covered almost half of the minuscule skirt. Had she gone too far with the dress? She wanted to attract Liam, not revolt him. She'd had no idea he could be such a prude. He certainly wasn't around Roxy. Good God, some of the gear that girl wore was downright disgusting!

Still…at least she *did* have his attention. That was something.

Pulling the seat belt out, she was in the process of buckling herself into place when Liam's hand shot out and gripped her chin. She gasped when he wrenched her face round his way, then gasped again when his mouth was suddenly covering hers.

His lips pressed down hard, insistent in their demand for surrender. She yielded more from shock than any immediate passion. Her lips fell apart and his tongue plunged deep into her mouth.

Her whimpering moan seemed to snap him back to the reality of his quite savage kiss, for his head whipped back abruptly, his eyes widening. She just stared at him, the back of her left hand coming up to cover her still stunned mouth.

He groaned and shook his head, clearly appalled at himself. 'I'm sorry, Moll. Hell, I don't know what got into me.'

Molly didn't believe him. He knew darned well why he'd done what he'd done. But by adopting ignorance of his very male actions he was throwing the ball in her court. How she acted now would set the tone for the whole evening.

Her hand trembling slightly, she removed it from her mouth and reached out towards him, letting it come to a shaky rest against his cheek. She twisted and leant towards him till her mouth was only inches away from his. '*I'm* not,' she whispered, and made the momentous decision to close those inches.

His shock was even greater than hers had been. For a few excruciating moments his mouth froze under her kiss. Molly hesitated herself. Good God, if he wrenched his mouth away, what would she do? Impossible to laugh it off. She would be utterly crushed.

Don't be tentative, came the voice of desperation. Be bold! Be daring!

She lifted her mouth from his and smiled. 'What's the matter, Liam? Haven't you been kissed back by a girl before?'

He didn't say a word, just kept staring at her as if she were a stranger.

Sighing, she dropped her hand away from his face

and settled herself back in the passenger seat. If nothing else, she'd taken the initiative and salvaged her pride.

'It's not that,' he growled as he fired the engine. 'Let's be honest, Moll. It's not *me* you really want to be kissing anyway, is it? Look, I won't say you're not a temptation, looking as you look tonight. But might I also remind you that I'm supposed to be getting back with my girlfriend tomorrow? I don't like complications in my life, and if I don't watch myself you might become a complication. So let's just keep our old status quo going, if you don't mind. We're good friends. Nothing more. I'm sorry I kissed you just now. I promise you it won't happen again.'

Molly bit her bottom lip and turned her face away to stare through the passenger window. Her immediate response to Liam's words was to sink back into herself, and oblivion. Underneath, she'd expected failure, hadn't she? Game, set and match to Roxy!

But it seemed her new appearance had imbued her with more confidence in herself that she would ever have believed. Or maybe it was everyone else's confidence in her. Whatever, her mind gradually turned more positive, clinging to the fact that Liam hadn't mentioned Roxy as his first excuse for backing away. His initial withdrawal had been because he thought she didn't really want to be kissing *him*. He mistakenly thought he was just a substitute for Mr X.

Molly's frustration was acute. She heartily wished she'd never invented Liam's mysterious alter ego! She toyed with telling Liam the truth during the tensely silent drive down to Gosford. That *he* was Mr X, that she was crazy about him and would do anything for him.

But by the time Liam turned into the club car park ten short minutes later she'd abandoned that idea. It smacked too much of desperation and would send any man running in the opposite direction. No, her mission tonight was to seduce Liam, not openly declare her undying devotion.

Tomorrow was several hours away and she aimed to make the most of them.

Now, what had worked best for her this past week or so?

Jealousy.

But not over Mr X this time, she decided. Over some other man. Molly hoped and prayed there would be a suitable candidate at this dinner tonight, and that he would find her as provocative as Liam had.

CHAPTER NINE

THE League's Club had been the main social hub of the Central Coast area for some years. Membership was cheap, and not even necessary to gain entrance. Visitors and tourists were welcome to enjoy the many facilities and entertainments the club had to offer. There were poker machines galore, bingo nights, discos, variety shows, bars, lounges, snooker tables and even a TAB betting branch. The large bistro section provided inexpensive meals, with three other restaurants catering for patrons who wanted a more extensive menu and silver service.

Then there were the large rooms on the first floor set aside for conferences, weddings and award dinners.

It was understandable, then, that the club car park was almost full by seven-thirty on that Saturday night. Liam finally found a spot on the top level, his face showing irritation by the time he and Molly made their way over towards the lifts. When a black Jag sped around the corner from the level below and almost collected them, Liam could no longer contain his temper.

He swore, shaking his fist at the unseen driver.

The Jag screeched to a halt. The tinted window

purred down and Dennis Taylor's distinctive dark head leant out.

'Liam!' he exclaimed. 'I thought it was you I nearly killed. Pretty stupid of me since I gather you're presenting me with my award tonight. I was voted Young Businessman of the Year, would you believe?'

Dennis's deeply set dark eyes suddenly shifted to Molly, his heavy black brows shooting upwards. 'Good God, is that our little Molly you've got with you? Wow, girl, you're looking even better than you did the other night. Hold the lift for me, you two, will you? It won't take me a sec to park this old chariot.'

Liam's grip on her arm tightened as he steered her over to the lift. '*Our* little Molly?' he grated out. 'What did he mean by that? And where in God's name did he see you the other night?'

Molly thought all her Christmases had come at once. She could not have orchestrated things better herself. Fate had, for once, been on her side.

'Dennis drove by as I was walking home from the hairdresser Friday week ago,' she said truthfully. 'He stopped and gave me a lift home.'

Liam reached out with his free hand and jabbed the 'down' button before glowering down at her. '*And?*'

Molly had no trouble adopting an innocent expression. She *was* innocent. 'And what?'

'And he told you you looked fantastic, didn't he?'

Molly stiffened. Suddenly, she could see which way Liam's mind was working and it wasn't what she wanted at all. Damn that infernal Mr X!

'He did say something complimentary,' she hedged. 'I can't really remember his exact words.'

'Don't play games with me, Moll. You're not likely to have forgotten the exact words your precious Mr X said to you. Dennis Taylor *is* your Mr X, isn't he? You lied to me about that. And you lied to me about knowing he'd be here tonight.'

'Don't be silly, Liam.' She shrugged out of his bruising hold. 'Dennis is *not* my Mr X and I had no idea he would be here tonight. But now that he is I can't say I'm sorry. I've always liked Dennis. He's good fun.'

The lift doors slid open and they walked in, Molly and not Liam reaching for the 'hold' button.

'You do realise that he'll try to hit on you,' Liam pointed out scathingly.

'Will he? Well, why should that worry you?'

'Your even saying that shows your naivety,' he snapped. 'God, you're a bloody babe in the woods where men like Dennis Taylor are concerned. I wouldn't trust him with an eighty-year-old grand-mother, let alone a silly young thing like you who's set her sights on *moving on*.'

'I don't think Dennis is as bad as everyone makes him out to be,' she defended hotly, her face burning over Liam's calling her naive and silly.

'I wouldn't advise your putting that notion to the test,' he ground out.

An awkward silence fell between them, broken only when Dennis strode into the lift. He was wearing a dinner suit of similar ilk to Liam's, but somehow it just didn't look as good on him. Not as elegant. Or as impressive, in Molly's opinion. They said clothes maketh the man. In Liam's case it was the other way around.

'Thanks, babe,' Dennis said, pressing the ground-floor button while openly ogling Molly. 'So how come you two are out together tonight? Last time I saw you, Liam, you had a big blonde bombshell on your arm.'

'Liam and I are just good friends,' Molly piped up before Liam could say a word. 'His girlfriend couldn't make it so I'm here in her place.'

Dennis looked decidedly pleased at this news. 'So you're not on a real date?'

Molly laughed. 'Good heavens, no!'

'So what are you doing later, *after* the dinner?' he persisted.

Molly had to give Dennis his due. He didn't believe in wasting time.

'I'm taking her home,' Liam pronounced firmly.

'Come now, old chap, don't be a spoilsport,' Dennis said cajolingly. 'If you're not interested in this little lady, then I surely am.'

'Then I suggest you ask her out some other time,' Liam said politely, even though his eyes would have set low-calorie jelly in ten seconds flat. 'Contrary to Molly's opinion, I *do* consider this a real date. When I take a girl out for the night, I see her safely home.'

The subtle emphasis on the word 'safely' did not

escape Molly. Or Dennis, who rolled his eyes and snorted.

'I didn't realise you were so old-fashioned.'

'I don't consider myself old-fashioned. But I do have certain standards.'

Dennis guffawed. 'Yeah, I've seen some of them. And I must congratulate you on your standards. When you've finished with Blondie, you can give me her phone number.'

The lift doors opened, and Liam took Molly's arm. 'Find your own girlfriends,' he advised brusquely. 'And leave Molly alone.'

Dennis grinned. 'Them's fighting words, Liam.'

Molly was astonished by the look Liam sent Dennis. She'd always thought of Liam as a pacifist. Violence would never be his way. But there was violence in his eyes when he glared at his former classmate.

'Any time, Dennis,' he said in a voice reminiscent of Clint Eastwood at his tough-guy best. 'Anywhere.'

Doubt filled Dennis's face. He glanced from Liam to Molly to Liam again. In the end he shrugged and stalked off.

Molly couldn't make up her mind if she liked Liam's proprietorial manner or resented it. Whatever, her blood was up, and so was her temper.

'I don't understand your dog-in-the-manger attitude,' she hissed on their walk from the lift to the club entrance. 'You don't want me, but you don't want any other man to want me.'

'Who says I don't want you?' he hissed back.

Molly ground to a halt, her crystal earrings in pendulum mode as she gaped up at the man she loved. But his returning glance was rueful and not full of the out-of-control, smouldering passion she was hoping for.

'Any red-blooded man would have to be dead not to want you, the way you're looking tonight,' he ground out. 'You must have got some inkling of the effect you had on me when I kissed you earlier. I had to exercise considerable self-control to stop when I did.'

'No kidding,' Molly muttered. And she knew just how he'd found that self-control. He'd only had to think of Roxy tomorrow, she thought with savage despair. Why waste all that pent-up male sexuality on silly, naive, innocent Molly when you have a blonde sex-bomb just waiting in the wings?

Her green eyes flashed as they raked over his handsome face. 'Congratulations on your self-control,' she said caustically. 'But what good is that to me? I told you I wanted to move on, Liam.'

'Meaning what?'

Molly's laugh was dry. 'And you called *me* silly and naive. Do I have to spell it out for you? I'm sick and tired of waiting for the man I love to love me back. And I'm sick and tired of being a virgin. Everyone keeps telling me to move on, even you. Well, I've decided to do just that tonight in a way where there's no turning back. Since you won't oblige me, Liam, then I'll find someone who will.'

'You don't mean that, Molly,' he said in truly shocked tones.

'I do mean it.'

'Not Dennis, for pity's sake!'

'Why not Dennis? I'm not expecting him to love me. Just to *make* love to me! I hear he's pretty good at that.'

Liam groaned. 'I can't bear to think of it.'

I can't bear to think of you and Roxy tomorrow, Molly agonised. 'Well, you know what to do in that case,' she threw at him in one desperate, last-ditch attempt. 'Do the honours yourself. If you were really my best friend, you would.'

He just stared at her as though she were mad.

She whirled and began to stride on ahead, her skirt swishing angrily around her legs. She was mad all right, mad with herself. If she had any real guts she'd take Dennis up on his offer. Who knew? Maybe she would before the night was up.

Liam caught up with her just as she approached the floor-to-ceiling glass doors which led into the club's brightly lit foyer. His arm linked forcibly with hers, slowing her step before turning her to face him.

His blue eyes burned down at her with a darkly angry frustration.

'All right,' he bit out. 'I'll do it. But be it on your

head, Moll. God knows, I seem to have suddenly lost mine!' And, with that, he swing her round and swept her into the club.

CHAPTER TEN

MOLLY would be eternally grateful that other people pounced on Liam as soon as they entered the club, because she was in a state of shock. Good manners had her smiling and saying the right things on automatic pilot, but it was a real relief that she couldn't have a private conversation with Liam at that point. She needed time to assimilate what had just happened, what he'd just agreed to. She needed time to calm the panic within.

But time brought little calm, only the most debilitating cluster of nerves. Her mind whirled with a possibly inaccurate memory of a saying which was perversely apt for the occasion, and went something like this: Careful of what you might want, because one day you might get it.

Molly now appreciated that acting out a scenario in one's imagination—however endlessly—was no preparation for actually living it. One of her most persistent and dearest fantasies was going to come true tonight, and her only feeling was terror! Where was the heady excitement which permeated her dreams? Where was the wild elation? The ecstasy?

Nowhere in damned sight, that was where! In their place was a gut-twisting apprehension, a suffocating sense of disbelief and an overwhelming feeling of inadequacy.

Naturally, she could not eat any of the dinner placed in front of her. Not a bite. Liam, however, was not similarly stricken. He ate his food while chatting casually with the others seated at the official table, acting as if he had nothing untoward on *his* mind. Clearly, his agreeing to deflower his best friend after the dinner was over did not rate as a sufficient reason to go off his food. He might have lost his head but he hadn't lost his appetite!

Men, Molly decided with growing cynicism, were a different breed altogether. Their egos, never their feelings, dictated all their actions. Liam was only taking her to bed because he could not bear for Dennis to. It had nothing to do with desire for her and everything to do with male competitiveness.

She moved her food around the various plates, trying to make it look as if she'd eaten something. She found some comfort in continuously sipping her wine, an easy task since her glass was never empty. The very attentive waiter kept topping it up, perhaps because from his elevated position he could peer down her cleavage.

When he went to top it up again during dessert, Liam's hand suddenly appeared over the glass, barring the way. Not a word was spoken. But the waiter got the message. After he'd moved on to attend to others at the table, Liam leant towards her.

'Under the circumstances, a reasonable alcoholic

consumption could be beneficial,' he said quietly. 'Too much, however, would definitely be counter-productive.

'Unless, of course, you wish to be close to unconscious when I take you to bed,' he added on a dry note. 'I do realise I'm not your first choice for this honour, but I would like you to at least remember who was responsible the next morning.'

Molly felt totally miffed. So she'd been right! Liam's decision to be her first lover *was* just a matter of ego. She vowed to find something cutting to say in return, but floundered abysmally.

The Master of Ceremonies' introduction of the night's guest speaker put Molly out of her misery. Liam rose from his chair to walk up onto the stage which had been set up at one end of the long rectangular room, standing to one side of the podium while the MC ran through a praise-filled résumé of Liam's achievements in business. Molly wasn't really listening. She was too busy staring at Liam, at this absolutely gorgeous man whom she'd adored for years and who, in a couple of hours' time, would hopefully do what she'd always wanted him to do.

And she'd been stupidly sitting there, finding fault with him and indulging in all sorts of insecure female rubbish.

Good God, what was wrong with her? This was the stuff romantic dreams were made of. She'd accused Liam once of never stopping and smelling the flowers yet here she was, letting panic and pride spoil what should be the happiest night of her life.

Well, from this moment on tonight, she was going to stop and smell the flowers. She would not question Liam's motivations for making love to her. She would not worry about tomorrow. She would simply enjoy each moment for what it was and let the rest of the world go by.

Her eyes softened as they watched Liam step up to the podium, looking so sophisticated and impressive. With her silly anger gone, she listened to every word he said, quickly rapt in the power and sincerity of his speech. He spoke of achievement in terms of faith in one's own ability and that unswerving tunnel vision which refused to accept defeat and called every seeming failure a learning experience. He did not gloss over the necessity of hard work, nor the difficulties of the present economic climate. He was passionate and inspiring. You could have heard a pin drop in the room. Molly felt so proud.

That's the man I love, she wanted to call out to everyone.

But of course she did not. She sat there silently, vowing that tonight she would show Liam that love, in every touch, every caress. She might not have Roxy's expertise in bed, but she would give him something the other woman could not. True love. And true passion. Nothing feigned or faked.

When Liam finished his speech, the room erupted

with applause, Molly clapping as enthusiastically as everyone else.

After that, it was time to get on with the award-giving, Dennis coming lucky last. When he strode up onto the stage to accept the award, Molly tensed a little. But no one would have guessed the two men were anything but the best of friends, both of them smiling broadly while the photographer snapped them together.

But Dennis whispered something after the photographer had finished, something which had Liam frowning momentarily over at Molly. He said something back to Dennis, who made another remark then laughed and clapped Liam on the shoulder. By the time Liam sat back down next to Molly, she could not contain her curiosity.

'What did Dennis say to you just then?' she asked tautly.

'When?'

'Just then!' she repeated, frustrated.

'Dennis never says anything of importance.'

'But you frowned at me afterwards.'

'Did I?'

'You know you did.'

'It was nothing. Just Dennis being Dennis. He's always been a bad loser. Come on. Let's go.'

When he stood up abruptly, Molly gaped up at him. 'Now? You want to go *now*?'

'Yes. Why not? Surely you don't want to stay here and make meaningless chit-chat? It's already ten-thirty. It'll be nearly midnight by the time we make it to my place. If I'm to deliver you back home before the dawn I think we should shake a leg, don't you?'

'Well, I… I…' To tell him that her mother would not worry if she didn't make it home before the dawn would have been met with much scepticism. 'Fine,' she finally said, her voice not much more than a squeak.

Swallowing, she stood up and let Liam propel her shaky legs from the room, and the club.

'Where exactly *is* your place?' Molly queried on their way to the car. She knew if she didn't talk she would simply die of tension. 'I mean, I know you jog to your office in North Sydney every morning, but I'm not sure where you live.'

'My old place was in St Leonards, but I bought a new apartment in one of those new inner-city high-rises a couple of months back. I only moved in this last week, though.'

'A new car, and now a new place,' Molly remarked casually, though her heart was singing with the thought that if he'd only moved in this last week he'd never spent time alone with Roxy there, never slept with her in that particular bedroom. Who knew, maybe even the bed was a new one?

Thinking about bedrooms and beds brought a re-surgence of nerves which reminded her forcibly of her empty stomach. Maybe she should have tried to eat something. The last thing she wanted was her hunger pains making embarrassing noises when Liam made love to her.

They reached the car and Liam opened the passenger door for her. Their eyes met and Liam's were irritatingly unreadable. If he was nervous about the rest of the evening, he certainly wasn't showing it.

'You're not the only one who's decided to make changes in their life,' he said matter-of-factly. 'Turning thirty made me realise time was moving on.'

Oh, my God, she thought. He *is* thinking about marrying Roxy. 'Thirty's not that old, Liam,' she said hastily. 'I mean, not for a man. Now, it might be for a woman because she has to have the babies, but in a man's case there's no need for him to rush into marriage.'

'Marriage! I wasn't talking about marriage. I was talking about enjoying some of the money I've worked so hard to make. Oh, do just get in. And don't, for pity's sake, gabble at me all the way to Sydney. I like to listen to music when I drive. And I like to concentrate. That excuse for an expressway doesn't suffer fools behind the wheel.'

Liam slotted an Enya CD into the built-in player before easing out of his parking space. Maybe *he* found her music relaxing, but Molly discovered a disturbing eroticism in several of the numbers, especially the ones with a repetitive and very rhythmic beat.

The next hour seemed eternal. Molly stared through the passenger window, first into the blackness of the countryside, then later at the city lights. She tried every method known to mankind to still her churning stomach. Deep, even breathing. Meditation. More common-sense reasoning of the type she'd soothed herself with at the dinner.

This is what you've always wanted. Stop being such a silly ninny. Liam knows what he's doing. He's an experienced lover. It won't hurt. It's going to be wonderful. Simply wonderful!

These last thoughts had a small measure of success till they drew close to the Harbour Bridge, after which the butterflies in Molly's stomach reached plague proportions. When Liam slowed to join the toll queue on the other side of the bridge, creeping along at a snail's pace, her pressure-cooker tension simply had to find an outlet.

'You know you don't have to do this if you don't want to,' she blurted out.

His sideways glance carried total exasperation. 'If you think for one moment I'm going to let you back out now, then you have another think coming!'

'Yes, but if you don't really *want* to…'

'Don't *want* to?' he grated out. 'Are you mad? I'm sitting here in bloody agony, I want to so much. Hell, I've thought of nothing else all night!'

'Oh.' Molly was stunned, then thrilled by the dark frustration in his voice. She would certainly never have guessed by his manner. Maybe he wasn't doing this just because of ego after all. Maybe he really *wanted* her, Molly McCrae.

Or maybe any attractive female would have done

as well, came the added dampening thought. Clearly, he'd been celibate since his separation from Roxy started over four weeks ago. Maybe he was just dying for some sex, and she'd tipped him over the edge tonight with her provocative dress and flirty manner. Hadn't he said when he'd agreed to sleep with her that he'd lost his head?

'Look, just in case you're languishing under a misapprehension here,' Liam went on quite irritably, 'I am not sacrificing myself on the altar of friendship tonight. It's passion that sends men to bed with women, not compassion. I wanted you the moment I saw you tonight.'

Molly took little comfort from this confession. It sounded like a classic case of uncontrollable male frustration to her.

'So you can stop sitting there worrying I might stop this time,' Liam informed her with a savage sideways glance. 'My conscience is well and truly routed. And you can stop acting like a nervous bride on her wedding night. You knew exactly what you were doing tonight, you wicked little minx. I finally realised that. No one comes out on a date dressed like *that* without a preconceived game plan. You were determined to seduce some poor, unsuspecting male tonight no matter what, weren't you?'

'Something like that.'

It was finally their turn at the toll gate. Liam dropped the fee into the basket, then surged off as soon as the green light blinked on. They followed the

Cahill Expressway over the top of Circular Quay and around the back of the Domain where Liam turned right at a set of lights, heading back towards the city proper. Molly gasped when he did an abrupt left-hand turn, zooming across the pavement and down a dimly lit ramp into an underground car park. He braked hard at a barrier at the base where he leant out and used a plastic security card to gain entrance. Less than twenty seconds later he was easing his Mazda into the allotted parking space for unit 711.

Molly swallowed hard.

The curtain was about to go up on the biggest show of her life. For once, she was centre stage, the heroine of the play, with Liam her hero. Ten days ago this would have been unbelievable, unthinkable.

Yet here she was…

This is your one chance, Molly, a voice whispered in her head. Don't waste it.

I won't, she promised herself firmly.

Suddenly, the knots in her stomach began to unravel and a strange calm overtook her. Without waiting for Liam, she reached for the door handle and let herself out of the car. She felt oddly ethereal as she watched him climb out and walk round to join her. Almost as though she was having an out-of-body experience. She was here, yet she was also watching from afar.

'Are you all right, Moll?' Liam asked, frowning.

Her smile was dreamy. 'Yes. Fine.'

His frown deepened. 'You're not drunk, are you?'

'No. I don't think so.'

'You knocked back a lot of that wine over dinner. And you didn't eat much.'

'I didn't have much appetite,' she admitted. 'I was thinking of you, Liam. And of this.' Again without waiting for him she slid her arms around his neck, reached up on tiptoe and pressed herself against him.

He just stood there, deliciously acquiescent, while her lips found his in a series of light kisses which fluttered over his mouth like angels' wings. Molly was in seventh heaven, making soft, satisfied little noises in her throat. Her fingers stroked the back of his neck, her thumbs caressing the soft skin behind his ears.

Finally, Liam's lips parted and he sucked in a long, quivering breath. Molly's tongue immediately darted forward, connecting with his own tonguetip before it could retreat. She felt his hesitation, but ruthlessly ignored it, snaking her tongue deep into his mouth then winding it around the full length of his.

She was the original Eve, tempting Adam with the pleasures of the flesh, but combining her seduction with an even more subtle force. Her love for him. It gave her a power she could never have guessed at. And the will to exercise that power. She undulated her tongue—and her body—against his, and urged him on as females had been urging their menfolk since time immemorial.

His tortured groan startled her as his hands came up to grip her shoulders. His fingertips dug into her flesh and for a few moments his tongue took over and gave her a glimpse of how Liam might make love, once he really lost his head. Just as savagely he yanked her away from him, holding her at arm's length while he glared down at her with a blistering reproach in his blazing blue eyes.

'No, damn it,' he ground out. 'No!'

'But you said you wouldn't stop!' she cried in dismay.

'I'm not stopping, you little fool. I'm just changing the scene of the crime.' And, taking her hand, he began dragging her across the car park.

'The crime?' she echoed dazedly.

'Yeah. What you were doing to me just then was criminal. But don't you worry, Miss Moving On. I'll let you do whatever you fancy once we're in the privacy of my bedroom. In fact, I'll insist upon it!'

CHAPTER ELEVEN

LIAM'S apartment was on the seventh floor. It was expensive, spacious, modern. And practically empty.

'I have ordered furniture but it hasn't arrived yet,' he said as he ushered Molly across a huge expanse of pale blue carpet. 'But don't worry. I did manage to buy a bed before I moved in. I had them send one of the floor stock, complete with bedlinen.'

Molly's heart leapt. A brand-new bed, with virgin sheets, waiting for her and Liam. No bad vibes. No memories. No comparisons.

He led her into a huge master bedroom dominated by an equally huge bed with dark blue and maroon bedding. The large double-glazed window which stretched across behind it was covered with cream vertical blinds but no curtains. A door to the left led off to what she presumed was an *en-suite* bathroom.

'So what do you think?' he said as he shrugged out of his dinner jacket and reefed off his black bow-tie.

Molly tried not to stare when he began unbuttoning his shirt. She kept telling herself it wouldn't be the first time she'd seen Liam naked to the waist. He always mowed his mother's lawn like that in the summer. But this was different.

'I think we have all the essentials, under the circumstances,' she said, her crisp tone belying the thickening in her throat. 'A bed. A bathroom. And us.'

Liam laughed while he yanked the shirt-tails out from the waistband of his trousers. 'I don't know if I entirely approve of Moving-on Molly, but I won't deny you have me totally intrigued.'

'I would prefer turned on to intrigued,' she quipped, determined not to revert to the mouse she'd once been. Where had that got her? Certainly not into Liam's bedroom with Liam undressing in front of her!

'That goes without saying,' he said, and stripped off the shirt.

Molly swallowed. 'Does it? I've never turned you on before...' She locked eyes with his and by sheer force of will kept hers steady. She would not have been human if her earlier nerves hadn't returned—this was unknown territory, after all—but she was damned if she was going to show them.

'Shall I undress as well?' she asked, her hands going behind her back in search of the bow which anchored the laces. She could not find the ends and screwed her head round over her shoulder in a vain attempt to locate the wretched things.

Liam materialised behind her. 'Let me,' he said softly, and removed her shaking hands. 'I've been wanting to do this all night...'

Molly gasped when he bent to press tender lips to the nape of her neck, at the same time obviously pulling the right thread, for the restricting laces suddenly gave way. A tremor raced through her as he eased the narrow silk straps towards the edge of her shoulders, kissing her neck all the while. Another inch or two and the whole dress would fall from her body, slithering down to the floor to leave her near naked to his eyes, and to his touch.

Her heart turned over at the thought, then quickened. To have Liam touch her bare breasts...

His hands moved outwards and the dress slithered downwards. Molly gasped, then held her breath. It felt an eternity before his hands moved again. And when they did she moaned her frustration at his lack of speed.

They slid slowly up and down her goose-bumped arms before finally taking her arms and winding them around behind him.

'Yes,' he said thickly when she clasped them together at the back of his waist, effectively imprisoning herself against him. Her mouth dried at the feel of his bare chest pressing up against her own bare back. Her heart thudded heavily behind her ribs, her naked breasts jutting out impatiently for his touch. They seemed to swell with each passing moment, their eager tips stretching out and upwards in silent yearning.

Something else was swelling as well, making its presence felt against the cushioning curves of her bottom. Molly had never seen—let alone felt—an erect male before. She knew the theory, but somehow the reality felt different from her virginal imaginings.

Bigger. Harder. And with a mind of its own. Her own mind reeled at the inevitability of its final resting place tonight.

Dear God…

Liam's hands grazing down over her breasts brought her back to the present, thrusting any thought of pain to the back of her mind. Pleasure took its place—blissful, blinding pleasure. She gasped when his palms rolled over her nipples a second time, then groaned when he took each tender peak between his thumb and forefinger, playing with them till they burned and throbbed with the sweetest ache she had ever known.

But it wasn't only her breasts which burned and ached. Her whole body was swiftly becoming a furnace of frantic fire.

'Liam,' she whispered in pleading tones.

'Yes?'

'Please don't stop.'

'I won't,' he rasped, his mouth moving restlessly over her neck, kissing and sucking at her heated skin.

Molly shivered violently. 'I mean later. Don't stop. For anything.'

His hands froze on her breasts. His mouth lifted. 'Are you sure?'

'Yes.'

'What about pregnancy?'

Molly was taken aback. She'd actually been thinking of her pain stopping him. Now she realised what he was referring to, and shrank from the concept of him putting anything between them. She might only have this night with him and she wanted everything to be perfect.

'There's no danger of that tonight,' she reassured him hurriedly, desperate to have his hands and mouth back on her flesh once more. 'My period's due this week and I'm never late.'

'You haven't asked me if *I'm* any danger to *you*.'

Again that thought had not occurred to her. '*Are* you?' she asked, shaken.

'No.'

She shivered her relief. 'Then everything's all right, then.'

He spun her abruptly in his arms and cupped her face. 'Promise me you won't trust any other man like that,' he demanded. 'You've no idea the lies some creeps will tell not to use a condom.'

The realisation that he was already anticipating her sleeping with other men after him dismayed Molly. Silly, really. What had she expected? That he would discover how much he secretly loved her tonight and claim her as his and his alone for ever? What a romantic fool she was!

'Don't you worry about what I do with other men, Liam,' she said sharply.

'But I *do*. You're my friend and I care about you.'

'Really? You yourself said tonight this had nothing to do with friendship.' She stepped back and hastily stripped off her pantyhose and shoes, scooping the bundle of clothes to one side and straightening to stand naked in front of him. Her chin lifted defiantly, her green eyes glittering as she pulled the swinging earrings from her lobes one by one and tossed them on top of her green silk dress. 'You were quite right. This has *nothing* to do with friendship, Liam. Nothing at all!'

Too much passion in her voice, she realised.

But too late.

Liam frowned. Then frowned some more. 'And what has it to do with, Moll?' he asked slowly, his eyes searching hers all the while. 'I sure as hell hope Dennis wasn't right.'

'Dennis? What has Dennis got to do with this?'

'Nothing, obviously. But he seemed to think your feelings for me encompassed more than friendship. He said he was watching you while I made my speech tonight and he reckoned you were in love with me. He warned me not to tangle with your body since virgins in love were notoriously vulnerable. I didn't believe him at the time. I thought it was just Dennis making trouble. But now I'm beginning to wonder…'

Molly knew she had to act quickly or all would be lost. She hoped her laughter had just the right mixture of disbelief and dry amusement. 'In love with you? Oh, Liam, how very typically male! You and Dennis do have incredible egos, you know. In love with you, as well as my Mr X? I'm not that much of a masochist. But you *have* grown into a very attractive man, dear friend,' she said, undulating towards him with a sexy smile curving her mouth. 'And your experience with women is impressive. Why do you think I chose you for this exercise? No, Liam, I don't want your love tonight. I just want your body.' She pressed her palms against his naked chest and kissed the base of his throat, then slowly lifted her eyes back to his.

Was he angry with her? Or angry with himself?

Whatever, his blue eyes were blazing with something. He gripped her elbows and lifted her bodily off the carpet, carrying her over and tossing her back onto the bed. She lay sprawled there in a breathless silence, watching dry-mouthed as he proceeded to strip himself with rough, angry movements.

The sight of the unknown was as worrisome as she had feared. No doubt about it. This was going to hurt. She only hoped he remembered his promise not to stop. For anything!

CHAPTER TWELVE

LIAM joined her on the bed, scooping her up onto the pillows and taking her mouth in a savage kiss.

Molly didn't mind his anger. She welcomed it. Anger was much safer than far too accurate accusations. More kisses followed, not quite as savage, but definitely still on the merciless side, his tongue ravaging her mouth while his hands ravaged her body.

Molly was amazed at how arousing she found this less than gentle handling. She moaned when he kneaded her breasts, whimpered when he pinched her nipples. But they were moans and whimpers of pure pleasure. Yet nothing compared with the electric sensations his fingers evoked when they slid between her legs. Everything inside her leapt, then twisted tight. She gasped into his mouth, then held her breath.

But not for long. Soon she was whimpering beneath the twin onslaughts of his mouth and those knowing fingers. He seemed to know exactly where to touch her down there, teasing and arousing her till she was melting and burning for him. The blood pounded in her temples and her head swam. She felt as if she was going to burst.

Soon, Molly began to fear her body was heading for that explosive release which was much sought after, but which usually heralded a swift end to desire. She didn't want these delicious feelings to end. She wanted them to go on and on and on!

Liam seemed to know, however, just when to stop that particular activity, leaving her in a fever pitch of arousal. She was more than ready for him to stroke open the lips which guarded her virgin flesh, more than ready for him to slip his finger inside.

When that finger started sliding in and out, her flesh gripped him avidly, her low groans betraying her increasing frustration. She sucked frantically on his tongue. Her hips writhed on the bed. One finger eventually became two, then three, stroking her inner walls, making them swollen and slick with wanting.

Oh, God, the wanting. She had never felt anything like it; had never imagined, even in her wildest fantasy, that it could be like this. The twisting tension within her mounted, and gathered. If she didn't have him inside her soon, she would go mad.

One hand searched blindly for him; found him; caressed him. Her legs fell apart and her other hand came round to grip his bare buttocks and urge him to roll between her legs. His mouth burst from hers, his invading hand withdrawing to brush both of hers away. And then he was there, probing, taking her breath away.

It wasn't painful. But neither was it as pleasurable as she'd been anticipating. The feeling of pressure was intense, and almost uncomfortable. She could not help tensing and when he pushed a little harder she gave a muffled cry. Now there was real pain. Surely she must split open.

'Are you all right?' he asked, his hands cradling her face as he looked deep into her eyes.

'Yes,' she bit out. 'Don't stop.'

'But I'm hurting you.'

She clenched her teeth even harder. 'It doesn't matter.'

'Of course it matters!' And he withdrew.

She clutched at his shoulders in a panic. 'You promised you wouldn't stop,' she reminded him. 'You promised!'

'For God's sake, do you think *I want* to stop?'

The tears came then, and he cuddled her to him. 'Don't cry, Moll. Please don't cry.'

'But you mustn't stop,' she sobbed against his shoulder. 'You don't understand. You mustn't.'

'Hush, my sweet,' he crooned. 'Hush. I'm not really stopping. But you need to relax. We'll just talk for a while.'

'Talk?' she echoed, dashing the tears from her cheeks. 'What…what about?'

His smile was wry. 'How about my latest project? That's what I usually talk to you about.'

'There's nothing usual about this situation, Liam,' she said tautly.

'No,' he agreed slowly. 'No, there certainly isn't.'

Still, he did just that, nestling between Molly's legs while he explained his idea for his next computer game, to be accompanied by an original soundtrack.

As usual it was a brilliant idea which would amuse as well as entertain. Slowly, she did relax and was actually laughing at something he said when Liam made his move, penetrating her fully before she could do more than gasp in astonishment.

She stared up at him, eyes and mouth wide with wonderment. For there had been no pain. None at all!

'See?' he said. 'It was just a matter of relaxing.'

'Yes,' came her choked-out reply. The realisation that Liam was deep inside her, that they were one, that they were truly lovers now, was almost too much for her. She could feel her eyes pricking with tears. Her heart contracted, and so did her insides.

'Mmm,' Liam murmured appreciatively. 'That felt good. Do it again.'

'Do what?' she asked breathlessly.

'Squeeze me. With your insides.'

She did and Liam moaned softly.

'Don't stop,' he rasped.

She didn't, and soon he was surging into her body in time with her contractions, thrusting deep as she squeezed tight, then rocking backwards on her release. Any thought of tears was soon forgotten. Everything was forgotten except what she was doing, and what she was feeling.

Was it pleasurable?

Molly wasn't sure. But she could not have stopped for anything. Driven by a dizzying and compelling desire, she clung and clutched at Liam's bare back and buttocks, pulling him down onto and into her body, striving for an even deeper possession. He seemed of a similar state of mind, for he scooped his hands up under her buttocks and held her off the bed so that he could pump even more powerfully into her.

'God, Molly,' he muttered thickly. 'It's too much. I'm going to come. I can't stop it. I'm sorry…'

She wasn't. For so was she. She could feel it. And just as he exploded within her her own climax arrived, shocking her with its electric intensity, making her back arch and her lips fall apart as she gasped her ecstasy. Her spasming muscles gripped Liam's flesh with a fierceness which had him crying out loud. They shuddered together, moaned together, grew silent together as the spasming waves slowly subsided.

Liam eventually rolled over, but he did not withdraw. He took her with him, his hands stroking gently up and down her spine while she melted against his body.

Molly thought she had never felt anything as loving as those hands. She sighed a deep, shuddering sigh, then just lay there, savouring every precious moment, both of the present and the recent past.

Making love with Liam had been everything—and more than—she'd hoped for.

There again, she'd known she could not ever be really disappointed, no matter what. Even if she had not come, she would still have been satisfied, deep down in her heart. But she had to admit that finding such wondrous physical satisfaction had been an added bonus. If nothing else, she had experienced the ultimate with the man she loved. She only hoped Liam had enjoyed it as much as she had. He *seemed* to have done. But of course she had no way of knowing. Maybe he *always* came like that. Maybe what had been so special for her had been commonplace for him.

Suddenly, he sighed, his chest rising and falling beneath her. She turned her face and kissed him just above the heart, then laid her cheek against the spot. She could hear it beating strongly. Dear Liam. He had a good heart.

Molly yawned as the world started to slip away. Those hands kept stroking her and soon a blissful blackness claimed her mind—and her body.

She woke to find Liam shaking her shoulder and telling her it was time he took her home. He was dressed in his dinner suit once more, but without the tie. Her clothes, she saw, were laid out neatly for her on the foot of the bed.

'I'll be out in the kitchen,' he said brusquely. 'Don't be too long. It's after two already.'

Molly's heart sank as she watched him retreat from the room. She'd known Liam long enough to know when something was bothering him. He would go all quiet and brooding, a faint frown forming a permanent V between his brows as if he had a headache.

Did he now regret doing what he'd done? Was his conscience bothering him?

Perhaps he was worried about how this would affect their friendship. Or his relationship with Roxy.

Molly bit her bottom lip. Surely he wasn't going to *tell* her? There was really no need.

'Are you up yet?' Liam called out somewhat impatiently. 'I can't hear any movement in there.'

'Yes, I'm up.'

Molly scooped up her clothes and dashed into the bathroom, where, after a quick visit to the loo, she struggled into her pantyhose and dress. The big bathroom mirror showed a pretty ravaged sight. Her hair was all over the place and her lips looked bruised and swollen. With her purse left in the car she had no make-up or comb for repairs. She lifted her arms to finger-comb her hair back into place, the action making her aware of very tender nipples under her dress. Yet, surprisingly, she wasn't at all sore elsewhere. Maybe that would come later.

Finally, she replaced her earrings and slipped her feet back into her shoes. Pasting a smile on her face, she sallied forth from the room, determined to put Liam's conscience to rest.

He was standing at the counter of the sleek grey and white kitchen, sipping a mug of coffee, that troubled V firmly in place between his eyebrows.

'I'm ready,' she said breezily.

He lowered the mug and glared at her.

Molly was quickly unnerved. 'What's wrong?'

He shook his head, his face reproachful. 'You slay me, Moll. Anyone would think nothing had changed between us.'

'Nothing has. Or are you saying you don't want us to be friends any more?'

'I'm not sure what I'm saying!' he snapped irritably. 'All I know is I'm going to find it hard to forget what we shared just now. I hadn't realised how much I might enjoy making love with you. It has... complicated things.'

Molly could not believe it! He was upset because he had *enjoyed* her. He was thinking of breaking up their friendship because she now represented a temptation, a complication! She had never felt so hurt—or as angry—as she did at that moment.

'And you don't like complications in your life, do you?' she said caustically. What about *my* life? she was thinking. Why don't you give *that* a thought? I don't exactly do what I just did every night of the week, you know!

'No,' he replied slowly. 'I don't like complications.'

'Tough. Life is a bitch, Liam.'

'I don't know about life,' he growled, 'but I know a certain girl who's in danger of becoming one.'

'Then at least I won't be the odd one out with all the other bitches you've bonked!'

He slammed the mug down onto the benchtop, spilling coffee all over the grey granite surface. 'Don't you dare talk like that!'

'I'll dare whatever I like, thank you very much. You can't dictate to me! Who do you think you are, Liam Delaney? You're not my father, brother or boyfriend. You're not even my friend any more from what I can see!'

'And you're no longer the Molly I knew and loved. You've turned into a bloody monster. A sarcastic, stroppy, sex-mad monster!'

'Really! Sex-mad, am I? Well, I didn't see you knocking me back last night, Mr Perfect. Yet you're supposed to be getting back with sexy Roxy today, who I'm sure would have given you all the bonking you wanted. But you couldn't wait a few miserable hours to get a bit, could you? Not after doing without for four whole weeks! Yet *I* hadn't had the pleasure for twenty-five rotten years. But never you fear. I'm going to make up for lost time now. Just you watch me! Now I'd like to go home, please. Oh, and don't talk to me during the drive, thank you very much. I'm not in the mood for meaningless chit-chat with selfish, narrow-minded hypocrites!'

CHAPTER THIRTEEN

'SO HOW did last night go?' her mother asked when Molly struggled out of bed shortly before midday. 'You must have got home pretty late. I was still up reading at one-thirty.'

Molly knew she could not bear a full confession at that moment. She was still coming to terms with the end of her relationship with Liam. In the cold light of morning, it was a bitter pill to swallow that she'd exchanged a lifetime of friendship for one night of fantasy.

Liam had delivered her home around three-thirty, neither of them having said a word to each other on the trip. When he'd tried to say something in the driveway she'd stopped him with a look and quickly alighted. In her room, she'd felt too shattered to cry. She'd undressed and climbed into bed and just lain there, staring up at the ceiling, trying to make sense of the whole man/woman thing. No clear answers had come to comfort her.

She'd finally dropped off around dawn, and had one of those awful dreams where she was travelling on a train and had lost her luggage. It was a frustrating dream which she had from time to time. Inevitably, she woke feeling dreadful. Not that she needed an extra reason that morning.

Liam didn't like her any more. She'd become a sex-mad monster in his opinion; a…complication. Molly knew he would not come around any more. And pride would stop her seeking *him* out. Their friendship was over, ruined by her love for him.

'Molly?' her mother probed gently.

She shook her head, unable to say anything.

Ruth sighed. 'I presume it didn't work out like you hoped.'

'No,' Molly managed.

'I see. I'm so sorry, love. I know how much Liam means to you.'

'Meant,' Molly said with a sudden and unexpected determination. She stood up from where she'd been drooping over the kitchen table, her shoulders slumped in defeat. Now they straightened, her chin lifting in defiance of her depression. 'Liam is the past, Mum. Today is the first day of the rest of my life, and I don't aim to waste it moping around. I'm going out.'

'Out? Where, out?'

'I have no idea. Yet. I'll think about it while I have a bubble bath.'

'A bubble bath? In the middle of the day?'

'Why not? Do you realise I still haven't used the bottle of bubble bath Joan gave me for Christmas? I think it's way overdue.'

'What…what about the papers?'

'Papers?'

'The financial forms Liam was going to leave with me last night. He must have forgotten them. Did he mention anything to you about them?'

'No, he didn't. But I'm sure he hasn't forgotten, Mum. Liam's not like that.'

'Do you think I should go over and ask him about them? He must be there. His car's in the drive.'

Molly flinched. The thought that Liam was physically so close rattled her momentary resolve to get on with her life. How could she go on, having won him in a fashion for one short night, only to lose him for ever?

'Yes, I think that would be a good idea,' she said briskly. 'He's probably still asleep but I'm sure Mrs Delaney will be up.'

Molly turned and fled the room before she weakened in front of her mother. Stay strong, she kept telling herself on her way upstairs. You must stay strong!

One hour later she was bathed and dressed in blue jeans and her new lime T-shirt. Her hair was still a little damp but swinging nicely around her perfectly made-up face. She'd also hunted out some large round gold earrings she'd only worn once, but which now really suited her new look and new hair colour. She'd thought about putting on the new gold chain necklace Liam had given her, but didn't want the constant reminder of him, so it stayed at the back of her top drawer. She did, however, spray a whiff of Seductress behind her ears.

No one would have guessed just looking at her that inside she was having the mental and emotional battle of her life. It would be so easy to give in and give up, to sink back into the miserable mousy nothing she'd once been. But to do that would be to waste all the changes she'd made. If nothing else she would remain grateful to Liam for being the impetus behind her making those changes.

Neither would she ever regret losing her virginity to him. How could she? She loved him. It angered her, however, that Liam had never recognised her love for him, when everyone else had, even Dennis. It had been easier for him to believe she'd suddenly turned into a sex-mad monster than to face the fact that there could be something else behind her choosing him to become her first lover.

'Molly?' her mother called out from downstairs, and Molly immediately tensed. She recognised that slightly sheepish tone in her mother's voice.

'Yes?' she called back curtly.

'Um…Liam's here. He wants to talk to you.'

Molly squeezed her eyes shut. Oh, God, why couldn't Liam have left well enough alone? It was finished. *They* were finished. She'd risked the substance for the shadow and she'd lost. She understood that. Why didn't he?

It looked as if she would have to spell it out for him again, because no way was she going to let him play with her emotions any more, no matter how innocent his intentions. The way to hell was paved with good intentions. Maybe she should remind him of that.

'I'll be right down,' she said stiffly. Gathering herself, she slipped her bare feet into her brown sandals and forced herself to go down and face Liam. Her mother passed her on the stairs, obviously deciding to make herself scarce.

Liam was in the kitchen, standing with his back to the sink, his arms crossed.

'You look awful,' she said.

He didn't, actually. He looked fantastic, even with dark rings under his eyes and his clothing not up to his usual sartorial splendour. He too was wearing jeans. Grey. Stonewashed. But his white T-shirt was crumpled and there wasn't a jacket in sight.

'You don't,' he returned, blue eyes washing over her. 'You look great.'

Molly declined to make a comment on that comment. 'What is it you wanted, Liam?' she asked coolly.

'Your mother says you're going out.'

'That's right.'

'Where?'

'That's none of your business.'

'I'm making it my business. Where are you going?'

She shrugged. 'I'm not sure yet. Anywhere.'

'In that case you can come anywhere with me.'

'Can I, now?'

'Yes.'

'Why should I?'

'Because I'm asking you to.'

'Not good enough.'

'It was…once. You used to be happy to go along with anything I suggested.'

Her smile was not very nice. 'Times have changed, haven't they?'

'Yes. And so have you,' he bit out.

Molly raised her eyebrows. 'Do I detect a note of disapproval there? I must admit I'm at a loss. Because I actually *did* do everything you suggested. This is your creation, Liam,' she said, uncrossing her arms and sweeping them down over her body. 'You made me what I am today. You even gave me a splendid initiation into the pleasures of the flesh. I will be eternally grateful. They say a lot of girls' first experiences aren't anything to write home about. I don't know about you, but I found mine fantastic. If nothing else, I will be eternally grateful to you for that.'

'I don't want your bloody gratitude.'

'Oh? What is it you want, then?'

'You.'

There was no denying the dark intent in his smouldering blue eyes. They raked over her, showing her with more than words what he wanted. Not love. God, no. There was nothing of love in the way he was looking at her. Lust, hot and strong, burned across the distance between them, branding her with its stunning heat. Molly's surface coolness vanished momentarily, swamped by a white-hot deluge of answering desire.

'Don't tell me it's not mutual,' he ground out. 'I can see the truth in your face. You want me as much as I want you, Molly. As complicated as this might get, once was simply not enough.'

She wasn't going to deny it. Impossible. Her heart was off and running, and so was her conscience. If I can't have his love, she reasoned recklessly, then I'll settle for his lust. I'll settle for damned well anything at this moment.

This realisation made a mockery of her earlier vow to get on with her life without Liam. She was condemned to always being weak where he was concerned. Love made a woman weak, she accepted. It was a sobering thought.

'What about Roxy?' she asked, proud of herself that she didn't sound as shaken as she was.

'You let me worry about Roxy.' He held out his hand and waited. She knew that to place her hand in his was to surrender to his wishes without reserve. From what she could see, he wasn't offering her anything but sex. He hadn't even promised to get rid of his old girlfriend.

Molly knew she could not cope with that. 'I won't share you, Liam.'

'I won't share you, either.'

'You won't go back to her?'

'Not if you come with me right now.'

And give me what I want…

These unspoken words haunted Molly, for she found them both dismaying and wildly exciting. It wasn't exactly what *she* wanted. Still, becoming Liam's bedmate was a temptation beyond bearing. She hadn't yet had her fill of him in a sexual sense, either, had she? Difficult to knock back such a chance. Impossible, really.

His face held a blackly triumphant satisfaction when she placed her trembling hand in his. His fingers closed tightly around its slender width and he yanked her towards him. Her lips parted on a breathless gasp as their bodies collided.

'So you're my creation, are you?' he murmured in a low, dangerously menacing voice. 'In that case I've created a monster. A manipulative, demanding, conscienceless monster.' He began stroking her neck, making her quiver with arousal and expectation. His eyes dropped to her mouth and she could feel the heat of his desire in their blistering blue depths. Any moment he was going to kiss her. She wanted him to kiss her, ached for him to kiss her.

'No, I'm not going to kiss you,' he ground out, his fingers stilling on her throat. 'Even though you want me to. You're going to learn to wait. You're going to learn a lot of things before I'm finished with you. You think you can play with people? You think you can use me then just move on to other men, other lovers?'

His fingertips pressed into the soft skin of her throat. 'Think again, my darling,' he snapped, blue eyes gleaming. 'Last night was only the first of many nights. And all of them will be with me. No one else. Not Dennis or even your pathetic Mr X. Soon, your lovely little body will only respond to me because I aim to make enslaving it to my will my next project.'

He laughed. It was definitely a Mr Hyde laugh. It sent shivers down Molly's spine.

'You, better than anyone, know how obsessive I can get about my projects,' he went on in a fearsome fashion. 'Nothing sways me from my goal. I promise you I will devote every minute of every day to the task, all my intellect, and every ounce of my energy. I will become your tutor, your master, your own personal devil, taking you to levels of surrender undreamt of even in your darkest, most decadent fantasy! You want sexual experiences? My God, I'll give you all you damned well want. And more!'

Molly gaped up at him, her eyes round, her heart pounding. This was a Liam she'd never met before. A madly impassioned, out-of-control Liam whose dark side had him firmly in its grip. But oh, my, the insidious attraction of that dark side. What would it be like to be the object of such a wild, ruthless obsession, to become his next project? Molly knew you wouldn't need much incentive to surrender to his sexual will. His impassioned words were already sending her on the path to that particular hell.

And hell it would eventually be. For she knew Liam well enough to know that his obsessions always burnt out. Once a project was mastered, he quickly lost interest and abandoned it, moving on to the next project. And then the next.

'So what have you got to say to that?' he snarled.

Molly decided enough was enough. She might be dying to volunteer as his next project, but she would not be bullied, or abused.

'My goodness, you must be in even more desperate need of some sex today than you were last night,' she replied airily. 'Why didn't you just say so instead of going on with all that macho rubbish? So I say... Lead on, Macduff. I'm with you all the way.' And, without waiting for him to explode, she brushed past his temporarily stunned self and dashed upstairs. 'Mum!' she called out. 'Oh, Mum! Where are you? Liam and I are going out for the day and we might be late home, so don't cook dinner for me...'

CHAPTER FOURTEEN

ANOTHER talkless drive to Sydney. More nerve-racking tension.

And doubts. Terrible doubts.

What am I doing? Molly agonised. This isn't me. I'm *not* a sex-mad monster. I know I'm not. So what am I doing letting Liam reduce me to nothing but a sexual challenge?

Celine Dion was belting out a song, singing about love in her distinctive style.

Love! God, but she was beginning to hate that word. And the state. Being in love was totally self-destructive. Look what it had done to her mother. She'd loved her father who'd been a rotter and a wastrel. He'd brought her nothing but heartache and misery.

Now here *she* was, her mother's daughter, wasting her love on the wrong man. Maybe Liam wasn't a rotter or a wastrel but he had one major flaw. He didn't love her back. If he did, he wouldn't be doing this, would he? He'd be…

Molly sucked in a startled breath as a possible defect in her reasoning broke through her mental ramblings. The question she'd just asked herself could have been the wrong question. What if she'd asked how Liam would be acting if he definitely *didn't* love her? If he disliked and disapproved of her new self as much as he said he did.

For one thing he would not have come over today. He would have been only too happy to see the back of her. He certainly would not have raged at her then vowed to turn her into some kind of sex slave!

Molly took a deep breath and tried not to get too carried away with this new theory to explain Liam's somewhat alien actions. It was always possible that she'd somehow captured his sexual interest in a way previously unknown to him, and he just could not handle his new feelings towards her. Clearly he was jealous of the idea of her with any other man. Could that be the result of his having been her first lover? Maybe he'd never deflowered a virgin before. Maybe it had evoked a possessiveness over her body which his male ego interpreted as sole ownership. A bit like the little boy who could not bear to share his toys.

Their arrival at Liam's place brought a swift end to this new and rather exciting train of thought. Still, Molly vowed to stop being so obsessed with her own feelings and more observant about Liam's. She appreciated, however, that cool reasoning was difficult when your nerve-endings were dancing and all you could think about suddenly was what Liam would do when they were alone in his apartment.

He seemed a little tense himself, dropping his keys at the door then fumbling with the lock. He finally flung the door open and stalked inside. Molly let out her long-held breath then followed in his wake. She was about to say something when a voice interrupted her, a low, husky female voice.

'Glad to see you finally came home, darling. I don't know about you, but this last month has been the longest in my life. So I didn't want to waste any time…'

Molly could not see who it was who had spoken. Liam stood in her line of sight. But she recognised the voice. Roxy had a very distinctive delivery.

'For pity's sake, Roxy!' Liam exclaimed. 'I have someone with me.'

Molly stepped out from behind Liam's suddenly frozen stance to see what had shocked him. Roxy was draped in the bedroom doorway, stark naked.

If ever Molly had cause to feel inadequate, it was at that moment. She could not fault Roxy's tall, voluptuous body. Anywhere. The only remote flaw she could find was that Roxy's nakedness confirmed what a jealous Molly had always suspected—that Roxy was not a natural blonde.

Still, such a small imperfection was little comfort in the face of such an amazing figure.

Roxy was only slightly thrown by the unexpected presence of another woman. Her artfully raised arms dropped languidly to her sides and she rolled her eyes at Liam in mild exasperation. 'Really, darling. This *is* the day we agreed to get together again. Had you forgotten? Maybe I left you alone for too long…'

She actually sashayed into the room, utterly unabashed at her nudity. Her long blonde hair shifted in sensual disarray across her shoulders, her melon-like breasts undulating sensuously, bringing attention to their lush size, plus their very pink, very pointed nipples.

Molly would not have put it past her to have painted the damned things, then iced them to their present stunningly erect state.

'Why don't you tell this little sweetie to run along?' Roxy said, waving a dismissive hand in Molly's direction. 'You really don't want to stay, do you, sweetie? Liam has clearly been a naughty boy in not telling you he already has a girlfriend.'

Liam glared his fury at her while Molly gathered all her courage. 'Actually, my name is Molly, not sweetie,' she said coolly. 'And I'm afraid it's *you* who's going to be leaving, Roxy, dear. Liam has indeed been naughty, but only in not calling you today and telling you it's over between you two. He's decided to move on, haven't you, *darling*?' And she linked arms with Liam, fluttering her eyelashes up at him as she gazed adoringly into his stunned face.

Roxy at last looked annoyed. Her hands found her hips and she peered at Molly with narrowed eyes. 'Molly, did you say?'

She took an aggressive step forward and looked Molly up and down. 'My God, it *is*!' she sneered. 'It's the mouse from next door. I just didn't recognise her. I always knew you were a sly little piece. Did you think you had me fooled with your butter-wouldn'tmelt-in-your-mouth routine? I saw the way you drooled over Liam when he wasn't watching. I knew you were jealous as sin of me and you were just watching and waiting for your chance to get your hooks in. Just good friends, my foot. That's not what you wanted. Never was!

'So what did she do to get you, darling?' she directed up at Liam. 'Confessed her long-time love? Kissed your feet? Promised undying devotion? No, I don't think that would have worked if I know you. You would have run a mile. You like your women assertive and independent, not simpering and clinging.'

She gave Molly another savage glance, then laughed. 'I get it. She played the make-over game. Changed her hair and clothes. Worked on her previously pathetic body, then threw you the oldest line in the book. Said she was off to spread her wings.'

'That's enough!' Liam ground out.

'Oh, no, it's not,' Roxy returned, scornful and defiant. 'It's not nearly enough. I'm going to have my say. I'm not going to crawl out of here with my tail between my legs. If nothing else I'm going to make you see that that bitch there is even more of a schemer than I am. And that's saying something, lover.

'So what carrot did you dangle for him, princess? Your priceless virginity?' When Molly's face flamed, Roxy sniggered. 'Oh, that *is* priceless. And you fell for it, Liam? I'm surprised. I thought you had more sophistication than that. But I guess deep down all men are suckers for supposedly untouched flesh, the poor misera—'

Roxy never got to finish her tirade of insults. She was too busy squawking when Liam threw her over his shoulder and marched her to the door. But she soon found her voice again, screaming a string of obscenities at Liam when he dumped her, in a none too flattering heap, in the hallway. Her clothes followed, then her purse—minus a key, an open-mouthed Molly noticed.

'Goodbye, Roxy,' he said coldly. 'I would have liked to have done this decently. But decency would be wasted on you. I'm sure you won't have any trouble finding some sucker who has the same low standards as yourself. And as filthy a tongue. *Hasta la vista*, baby.' And he slammed the door shut on her, shooting the lock across with a savage flick of his wrist.

When he turned, he actually shuddered. 'I can't believe I ever considered going back to that…that *creature*!'

Molly's estimation of Liam went up a thousandfold. Which meant it was now off the planet. 'She is…was…very beautiful,' she said. 'And I dare say she was good in bed.'

Liam grimaced. 'I doubt anything about her is good except her acting. I would rather have five minutes in bed with you, Moll, than a lifetime with her. You leave her for dead in every department. And you're just as beautiful.'

Molly's heart caught. 'Not really, Liam,' she murmured. 'But it's nice of you to say so.'

'No, I mean it. You have a beauty which will last, because it comes from within. Not that I don't think you're very attractive,' he said as he drew her into his arms. 'You are. And very sexy too. In fact you're more sexy with your clothes on than Roxy is stark naked. I see now that true sexiness comes from what a woman subtly offers a man. A willingness to give as well as receive. And trust. It wasn't so much your virginity I found enchanting last night, but your trust. You trusted me with your body, and even your life. That blew me away. *You* blew me away. I couldn't sleep all night for thinking of you, and wanting you again. What I said to you earlier, Moll… I didn't really mean that. I would never do anything to hurt you. I was simply off my head with wanting you. And I was in a flat panic that you were going to go off and find someone else.'

She cupped his handsome face and tried to still her racing heart. 'You mean you're not going to bow me to your will through fair means or foul? You're not going to try to turn me into some kind of sex slave?'

'God, no. I don't know what got into me.'

'Well, that's a real shame,' she said, smiling saucily into his very serious face. 'I was rather looking forward to it.'

His blue eyes jerked wide, then narrowed.

'I have an awful feeling you mean that.'

'I do…in a fashion.'

'What kind of fashion?'

'I certainly wouldn't want you to ever hurt me. But I *was* looking forward to all those experiences you promised. And I rather fancied the idea of your becoming my sexual tutor...'

She reached up to kiss him lightly on the lips.

'And my master...'

She kissed him again, not quite so lightly.

'And my own personal devil...'

Her third kiss left him breathing heavily.

'But most of all,' she whispered huskily, 'I was counting on you taking me to that mysterious level of surrender not even dreamt of in my darkest, most decadent fantasy.'

His expression had darkened during her provocative confession. She wasn't sure if she'd shocked him to the core this time or not. He was certainly pretty still. But then a slow smile pulled at his nicely shaped mouth, and a wicked gleam brightened his beautiful blue eyes.

'You do know what happens to little girls who play with fire, Moll, don't you?'

She gulped. Had she gone too far?

'Er...'

'Too late,' he snapped, and scooped her up into his arms. 'You can't throw down a challenge like that to a man like me, then try to back out.' He began to stride towards the bedroom.

'But I... I...'

He halted in the doorway. 'You what? Speak now, woman, or for ever hold your peace.'

Molly bit her bottom lip and Liam swept into the room. At least he'd called her a woman!

CHAPTER FIFTEEN

'MOLL?'

Molly was lying crossways on the bed with her head cradled in the small of Liam's back. Liam was stretched out on his stomach, face buried in the pillows. Till a moment ago, she'd thought he was asleep.

And well he might have been. He had to be utterly exhausted. She herself was bone-weary.

But what an afternoon it had been! She would never have believed she could come so many times in a few short hours. Or that a man and woman could make love in so many different ways and positions.

Liam had seemed to delight in witnessing her shock at each successive and seemingly outrageous suggestion, before seducing her to his will with an ease that made a mockery of her initial inhibited reaction. How quickly he'd routed those inhibitions, showing her pleasures undreamt of, once she'd put aside—or at least learnt to ignore—that squirming embarrassment which came whenever he looked upon her body in some new and increasingly intimate fashion.

He'd become her own personal devil all right, tempting her in ways she might have read and dreamt about, but which she would never have believed she would dare to do.

Her stomach fluttered at what he might be going to suggest now, just when she'd thought everything had come to a satisfying conclusion. Was there anything else? She doubted it.

'Yes?' she murmured warily, her own eyes staying shut.

'Lift your head for a second, will you?'

She did, and he rolled over onto his back. 'Right. You can put your head back down again.'

Her head now nestled into his stomach, Molly's own stomach contracted. The nearness of his slumbering penis brought back hot memories of the last time she'd encountered his flagging desire, less than thirty minutes before. Liam had carried her into the shower after one of their torrid matings and, after washing her all over, had given her the shower gel and the sponge and set her to returning the favour.

She'd been shy at first, as she always was when confronted by one of Liam's new suggestions. Her hands had initially been hesitant on him, but not for long.

How exciting it had been to bring him to life again in such a stunningly intimate way. There'd been a dizzying sense of power at the sight of him growing harder and larger by the second, his moans letting her know how much he was enjoying her ministrations. The decision to sink to her knees and do to him what he'd already done to her more than once had come without conscious thought. It had seemed perfectly natural, yet at the same time the most wildly exciting thing she'd ever done.

Liam, however, had not been as comfortable with her bold lovemaking. His thighs had alternately trembled and tensed as he'd struggled to control himself.

'Stop,' he'd rasped at last, stiffening and bracing himself back against the cool, wet tiles. 'You must stop.'

But she had not stopped. If he'd been her own personal devil before, she was his at that moment, her lips tempting him with the dark excitement of total surrender to *her* will this time.

And while the hot water beat down on them both and the bathroom filled with steam Liam had finally lost his battle of the flesh, and she'd had her wicked way with him.

'Moll?' he said again, snapping her out of her erotic reverie.

She shivered then glanced up at him. 'What?'

He was staring down at her with heavy-lidded eyes.

'Why is it, do you think, that everyone seems to believe you're in love with me?'

Molly froze, then forced a light laugh. 'I didn't know everyone did. Surely you're not talking about Roxy? She was so green-eyed she couldn't see straight!'

'I realise that. But Dennis seemed to think so too. Then this morning even Mum hinted the same.'

Molly gulped. 'Really?'

'Yes, she said how much you cared for me and if

I hurt one hair on your head I'd have her to answer to.'

Molly was touched, but also flustered. Was this the moment to confess, to tell Liam the truth? How would he react, she wondered, to finding out *he* was the enigmatic and mysterious Mr X? Even if he was initially flattered, he might also be annoyed. He might think she'd made some kind of fool of him by playing with his own identity like that.

Liam would not like thinking that she'd been mocking him, or amusing herself at his expense. Which she *had* been, in a way. Though never maliciously.

Then there was his possible reaction to finding out she'd been pining for him all these years like a lovesick cow. Even Roxy had realised that if she declared a lifelong love and undying devotion Liam would have run a mile. His mother's advice had been similar. Liam was captivated by spirited women who went after what they wanted, not little mice who languished for years from an unrequited passion.

No, she could not tell him the truth. She could not risk losing Liam's respect, and possibly losing Liam. She might only have won his lust so far, but it was a start.

'Well, of course I *do* care for you, Liam,' she confessed rather nonchalantly. 'I always have.'

'Yes, but it's this Mr X you're in love with,' he muttered, none too happily. His disgruntlement gave Molly hope. He lifted his head to glare down at her. 'You *are* still in love with him, aren't you?'

She didn't know what to say. She really had to get rid of that infernal Mr X once and for all. He'd become a nuisance and an embarrassment.

But how?

'*Well?*' Liam glowered at her.

Incredibly, she blushed.

Liam took that for an admission, and scowled. 'What in God's name has *he* got that *I* haven't got?'

Now Molly was rattled. 'Er…nothing, I guess.'

'Then there's no reason why you can't fall out of love with him and in love with *me*, is there?'

Molly's mouth dropped open. 'What…what are you saying?'

'What am I saying?' He bent down and scooped her up on top of him. 'I'm saying I'm mad about you, Moll. And I won't rest till you're just as mad about me.' He rolled her under him and kissed her with a breathtaking hunger, his hands cupping her face and keeping it solidly captive beneath his. 'I know I can make you want me sexually,' he muttered after he'd reduced her to a panting mess. 'But that's not enough. I want to drive all thoughts of Mr X from your mind. I want you to love me as you've loved no other man.'

'But I already have, Liam. Loved you as I've loved no other man.'

His head jerked back. 'What?'

'Do you think I've done any of the things I've done with you today with any other man?'

He frowned. 'But I thought…I mean… Look, lots of girls out there are technically virgins these days, but that doesn't mean they haven't done plenty. I thought…in the shower…I mean… My God, Moll,' he said, awe in his voice, 'you're damned good at that for a beginner.'

'Perhaps I just have a damned good tutor,' she murmured, smiling. 'And perhaps you were right about Mr X. What I felt for him was probably only infatuation, a fantasy. To be honest, I haven't given him a thought all the time I've been with you.'

'So, you're not in love with him any more?'

'I can't see how I can be.'

His triumphant smile sent shivers down her spine. 'In that case *that's* going to be my next project— making you fall in love with me.'

Molly tried not to stare too hard. Or to cry.

But it was just too good to be true.

She swallowed and tried not to let her feelings overwhelm her. Common sense dictated she be careful and not get her hopes up too high. Liam might be mad about her at the moment but that didn't mean he genuinely loved her. It might all be one of his passing passions, a temporary obsession. He'd probably been mad about Roxy at one point, plus all those other girls.

'And how do you aim to do that?' she asked him with a saucy smile.

He pursed his lips and made a thoughtful sound. 'I'm not quite sure yet. You're much more of a mystery than I ever imagined. A highly complex girl, not the simple creature I thought I knew so well. And you're far naughtier than I'd imagined, too,' he added, his eyes gleaming.

'Really?' She laughed. 'Well, you're *exactly* as I always imagined.'

'Is that good or bad?'

'Oh, definitely good. *And* bad. You are as selfish as you said you were, but not in bed, thankfully.'

'I'm not going to be selfish any more,' he vowed. 'I'm going to change.'

She smiled. 'And the sun's going to rise in the west.'

'You just wait and see. Besides, who are you to talk? Moved-on-Made-over Molly isn't exactly all Miss Sweetness and Light. You could have knocked me over with a feather the way you stood up to Roxy out there.'

'Whereas the Molly I used to be would have stood there and not made a sound, not even a little squeak.'

'Hey. Don't run her down. I really liked that girl. She was sweet.'

Molly's eyebrows lifted. Yes, but you didn't fall in love with her, came the rueful thought.

'She was a bore!'

'She was *very* nice,' he defended hotly.

'She's dead and gone. Banished!'

'No, she's not,' he said, his voice dropping to a soft and sentimental timbre. 'She's still there, hiding underneath your new red hair and your newly found assertiveness. I think that's why my feelings for you are different to what they were with any of those other girls. Different, and deeper. Because *you're* different. I've always liked you, Moll. You're not a vain little puss. And you're honest as the day is long. You'd never lie to me, or try to manipulate me. You're the sort of girl a man is proud to take home to his mother. The sort of girl a man wants to m—'

She pushed her fingers against his mouth, panic flowering all through her. 'Hush! Don't say that, Liam. Don't!'

He groaned, then picked up her fingers and kissed the trembling fingertips. 'I'm rushing you, I know. I can be like that once I set my sights on something. I can see it's the wrong thing for me to do. Only yesterday you were a virgin, and in love with another man. I can understand you might be a little confused. But I can also be patient too,' he vowed passionately. 'And very single-minded. You're going to be mine, Moll. Fight me if you will. I enjoy a good fight. But come the new year you will be my fiancée, with my ring on your finger and true love for me in your heart.'

She stared at him with wide, blinking eyes. She almost told him then, but didn't. For she knew she had to make sure of him, had to let him fight his good fight for her, and for her love. It was fitting, after all the years of heartache and longing she'd been through, that he should not win her too easily.

Men did not value what they gained easily. And Liam was going to value her. She deserved it.

'The new year?' she said, her mind racing. That was ten months away, ten months of him chasing her, courting her, pursuing and seducing her. It was an irresistibly exciting thought. 'Well, I suppose by then I should know if it's a true love I feel for you and not just infatuation. After my fiasco with Mr X, I would want to be sure…'

'You'll be sure, my darling. Don't worry. I'll make sure of that!'

CHAPTER SIXTEEN

THE party was in full swing, a large and motley collection of people having gathered in the Delaney house to celebrate New Year's Eve, plus the engagement of Liam to his long-time girlfriend and next-door neighbour, Molly McCrae.

As the glamorous guests of honour, the happy couple were dressed for the part. The proud groom-to-be was resplendent in stylish navy trousers, an open-necked blue shirt and a suave cream silk sports jacket. His bride-to-be was stunning in a strapless party dress of emerald satin, with an even more stunning emerald and gold choker gracing her long, elegant neck. It had been a Christmas present from her adoring fiancé, one of many he'd lavished on her during the past year.

Liam had, in fact, spoiled Molly rotten with gifts of expensive clothes and jewellery, not to mention his myriad smaller purchases of chocolates, flowers and perfume. He'd taught her to drive in his precious new Mazda, and would have bought her a car, if she'd let him. Then there were the fantasy getaways he'd taken her on, weekends here and there at romantic places designed to seduce and soften even the hardest of hearts.

Not that Molly was a hard girl. Liam knew she wasn't.

But she'd been surprisingly difficult to win, he'd found to his consternation. He'd never been quite sure of her feelings. She'd kept him dangling, had often been late for dates, and had sometimes even dared to cancel them. He'd never quite known where he stood with her, which had been both irritating and intriguing.

Only in the lovemaking department had he been sure of his domination over her. There, she was putty in his hands, melting at his touch, quick to be aroused and always willing, no matter how often he wanted her, or where.

She'd never said no, even when there'd been some danger of being discovered. His choosing precarious places—such as behind rocks at the beach or in a sparsely filled movie theatre—had sometimes soothed the sense of emotional insecurity she instilled in him. At those moments when she'd been prepared to take any risk to have him, he'd almost felt loved. There'd been no doubt she craved him sexually; could not deny him. But was that love?

She'd never said she loved him. Not in so many words.

Till Christmas Day, when he'd produced an engagement ring for her which would have done Elizabeth Taylor proud. It was a huge brilliant-cut yellow Argyle diamond, set in gold. But it had been his words as he'd given it to her that had seemed to do the trick.

'This cost me a fortune, Moll,' he'd said. 'But a fortune means nothing to me without you. Marry me, my darling. I love you so much, and I think you love me. You don't have to say you do if you don't want to but it would be nice, just once, to hear it from your lips.'

Molly had stared at him and then burst into tears. He'd gathered her to him and heard the words he'd been dying to hear all year. 'Of course I love you. Don't you know that yet? I love you, Liam. Love you... Love you...'

He looked over at her now across the crowded living room and caught her eye. She smiled at him, green eyes sparkling. It wasn't so much different from smiles she'd given him before, but tonight he saw the love in them. Why hadn't he seen it before?

Liam was about to walk across the room to join her when someone tapped him on the elbow. 'Hello, you gorgeous hunk, you. If I wasn't married, you know, I'd have given Molly a run for her money.'

It was Joan, from the library, Molly's friend.

Liam smiled. 'You would have had to be good.'

Joan nodded up and down. 'You're right. Molly's a grand girl and I'm very happy for her. You don't know how lucky you are.'

'Oh, I think I do...'

'She's loved you for so long, you know.'

Liam was about to say he didn't know at all when

he stopped himself. It was then he realised Joan was off in another world, smiling at something in her head.

'I can still remember the day she came into the library and told me about Mr X. You must remember Mr X, Liam,' she added, glancing up at him.

'Only too well,' Liam said drily, and lifted the glass he was holding to his lips.

Joan chuckled. 'I nearly cracked up when she told me about him, especially when she said you hadn't twigged. I mean…you have to admit it's very funny, but rather typical of men, not seeing beyond their nose. But I dare say you've laughed together about it since.'

'Laughed about what?'

'About your being Mr X, of course.'

Liam's drink froze midway to his mouth. He stared at Joan over the glass. She grimaced, then groaned. 'Oh, dear heaven, you didn't know. I always assumed she'd told you. Oh, Lord!'

Liam could hardly think. *He* was Mr X. His head spun with the news, and all it implied. Molly had loved him all along. But she'd also lied to him, laughed at him, manipulated him. She'd been a schemer, as Roxy had warned she was.

He recoiled at this thought, and his feelings showed on his face.

'Don't you *dare* take that attitude,' Joan warned. 'Don't you *dare!* That girl loves you. No, she adores you. Always has done. But did you ever see it? Not on your nelly! You sailed on through your glamorous, privileged life, tossing her a few crumbs from your table when it suited you. You didn't give a fig for her feelings. You took her for granted and you broke her heart.'

'But that's not—'

'Oh, do shut up and listen!' Joan snapped. 'So what if she protected her self-esteem by inventing a Mr X? So what if she had some fun with it? She'd had little enough fun in her life at that point in time. Give credit where credit is due, Liam. When she saw her chance, she went after what she wanted. She changed for you, lied for you, fought for you. And she won you, by God—won your love and your respect. Look at her, Liam. She's a beautiful and very brave woman; a woman in a million. Don't you dare tell her I told you about Mr X. Don't take away her pride. Go on letting her think you believe she once had a Mr X in her life, because maybe she needs that. Maybe she… Oh, my God, she's coming over. Promise me, Liam. Promise me you won't tell her I told you.'

'I promise, Joan,' he said faithfully. 'And thank you…for making me finally see the light.'

Liam watched the girl he loved walk towards them, a lovely smile on her lovely face. He felt humbled and incredibly moved as the full import of Joan's words sank in. Molly had always loved him. Oh, how cruel life could be sometimes. And how wonderful.

He saw now why he loved her so much. Because she loved *him* so much. He must have sensed it at some subconscious level, had known that to let her go would be the worst, most stupid thing he could ever do. He vowed now he would never let her go. Never!

'What are you two sneaky devils talking about over here?' she asked, glancing from one to the other. 'You were looking very serious, Joan. You too, darling.'

Liam's heart kicked over. Never had the word 'darling' on her lips sounded so sweet, or so touching. He wound his arm around her slender waist and pulled her against him.

'We were having a very serious discussion on having children in this day and age, weren't we, Joan? We agreed it's a difficult task being a parent, but I'm willing to risk it anyway.'

He could see the flicker of surprised pleasure in her eyes. 'I've been wanting to discuss children with you. I…I would like to have a baby quite soon, but I wasn't sure about you…'

No, he thought, understanding dawning. She still wasn't sure of him. It was a cruel legacy of all those years when he hadn't noticed her, hadn't wanted her. That was why she'd kept *him* unsure. She'd been protecting herself, had made him keep proving his love over and over. There was still a lot of work to be done, he realised, before she would feel totally secure in his love. But having children together would be a good start.

He gave her a reassuring smile, and a loving little squeeze. 'How soon is soon?'

She gave a self-conscious laugh. 'How about nine months after the wedding day?'

'How about six?' he returned, squeezing her again. The wedding date had been set in March.

'I think this conversation is getting too private for me,' Joan quipped, and was off.

Liam laughed. 'I like your Joan. I think we'll ask her to be godmother to our first child.'

'Our…*first* child?'

'You don't honestly think we're going to have only one child, do you? Only children are notoriously spoiled.'

'Yes, well…'

He kissed her. Then kissed her again. 'Do you think we might slip away somewhere?' he murmured against her trembling mouth.

'Where? We can't possibly be gone long and people have infiltrated your whole house, even your bedroom.'

'What about yours?'

Molly sucked in a startled breath. 'Mine? But it…it only has a single bed in it.'

Liam took her hand and began drawing her from the room. 'Single beds were just made for lovers.'

Midnight came with cheers and shouts, whistles and car horns. People spilled out of houses into the street below. Everyone was kissing.

No one missed the guests of honour.

Nine months later, a baby was born to Mr and Mrs

Liam Delaney. A boy. The grandmothers were delighted, and even approved of his name. Saxon. But their joy was nothing compared to the mother's. Having Liam's child in her arms finally put to rest that little niggle of doubt which till then had plagued Molly: that it wasn't *her* he really loved, but the myth she'd created, that made-over moved-on version who was partly a pretend person.

But she'd known, during the long, painful hours of labour, when she'd hardly been looking her best, when she'd been crying and swearing and sweating, that the man holding her hand and mopping her brow really loved *her*, Molly, the person. She'd seen it in his concern, his patience, his tenderness. But mostly she'd seen it in his eyes, his beautiful blue eyes, the windows to his soul.

And that soul was full of true love for her.

Liam loved her, Molly, the simple, solid girl who'd always loved him.

She would never doubt it again, and he would never give her cause to.

Initially a French/English teacher, **Emma Darcy** changed careers to computer programming before marriage, motherhood, and the happy demands of keeping up with three lively sons and the very social life of her businessman husband, Frank. Very much a people person, and always interested in relationships, she finds the world of romance fiction a thrilling one and the challenge of creating her own cast of characters very addictive.

**Don't miss Emma Darcy's spectacular story
coming in March 2003,
Modern Romance™:**

THE BLIND-DATE BRIDE

THE MARRIAGE DECIDER

by

Emma Darcy

CHAPTER ONE

IS YOUR MAN ABOUT TO DUMP YOU?
SPOTTING THE EXIT SIGNS

THE headline teaser on the glossy cover of her favourite magazine caused a roll of nausea through Amy Taylor's stomach. It was the new December issue, out today, and the advice it contained was too late to be of any help. A pity the article hadn't been written months ago. She might have recognised what had been going on with Steve, at least been somewhat prepared for the bombshell that had hit her over the weekend.

Though that was doubtful. She wouldn't have applied the exit signs to her relationship with Steve. Although neither of them had pushed for marriage—free spirits should never shackle themselves, he had insisted—after *five* years together—a mini-marriage in anyone's book—continuity had become a state of mind. She'd been hopelessly blind to what was really happening.

Free spirits! Amy gnashed her teeth over that remembered phrase. There was nothing free-spirited about rushing headlong into marriage with someone else! The blonde he'd bedded behind Amy's back, was shackling Steve with an ease that was painfully insulting. With the result that Amy was certainly being left *free!* Though hardly free-spirited.

Here she was, comprehensively dumped, twenty-eight years old, single again, and suffering the worst case of

5

Monday blues she could ever remember having. It was sheer masochism to pick up the new issue of the magazine with *that* article in it—a clear case of punishing herself—but maybe she needed to have all the signs spelled out so she'd know better next time. *If* there ever was a next time.

At her age, the market for unattached men was slim, especially men worth having. Amy brooded over that depressing fact as she paid the news vendor for the magazine and walked down Alfred Street to her workplace, the last office building facing the harbour on Milsons Point, a highly privileged piece of real estate which she was in no mood to appreciate this morning.

Ahead of her, summer sunshine had turned Sydney Harbour into a glittering expanse of blue, patterned harmoniously by boats and ferries carving white wakes across it. To her left, Bradfield Park offered the peaceful green of newly mown lawns, invitingly shadowed by the great Coat-hanger bridge that dominated the skyline, feeding the city with an endless stream of commuter traffic. Amy was totally oblivious to all of it. For her, there was only the dark gloom of her thoughts.

Dumped for a blonde, a smart, pregnant blonde. Nobody got pregnant by accident these days. Not at thirty-two. Amy was sure it had been a calculated gamble, the hook to pull Steve in and tie him up for better or for worse. And it had worked. The wedding date was already set. One month from today. New Year's Eve. Happy New Year, Amy thought bitterly, seeing a long stretch of loneliness for herself.

Maybe at thirty-two, she'd feel desperate enough to snitch someone else's man. After all, if he was willing, as Steve must have been…but how could you ever really trust a man who cheated on the woman he was living with? Amy wrinkled her nose. She'd be better off on her own.

But she didn't feel better off. She felt sick, empty, lost in a world that had suddenly turned unfamiliar, hostile, her bearings torn away. Tears filled her eyes as she pushed open the door to her workplace and barged into the foyer, needing the safe mooring of her job to fight the flood of misery she could barely contain.

"Hi! Boss in?" she aimed at Kate Bradley, her vision too embarrassingly blurred to meet the receptionist's eyes directly. Besides, Kate was a gorgeous blonde, a typical choice for Jake Carter's front desk woman, and another reminder of pain for her right now.

"Not yet," came the cheerful reply. "Something must have held him up."

Jake was an early bird, invariably in his office ahead of Amy. She was intensely relieved to hear he was late this morning, giving her time to get herself together before those yellow wolf eyes of his noted anything amiss.

She certainly didn't need the humiliation of having to explain why her mascara was running, which it probably was from her furious blinking. Moisture had to be clinging to her lashes. She pressed the elevator button, willing the doors to open instantly.

"Have a good weekend?" Kate asked, addressing Amy's back, blithely unaware of any problem.

Amy half turned, not wishing to appear totally rude. "No. It was the pits," she blurted out, giving vent to some of her pent-up emotion.

"Oh! Guess things can only get better," Kate offered sympathetically.

"I wish," Amy muttered.

The elevator doors obligingly opened. The ride up to the floor she shared with Jake was mercifully brief and she headed straight for the washroom to effect repairs. Once safely enclosed in privacy she tore tissues from the box on the vanity bench and began wiping away the smeared make-up around her eyes.

She couldn't afford to look as though she was falling apart. As Jake Carter's personal assistant, she had to stay on top of everything, as well as maintain the class image of the company. *Wide Blue Yonder Pty Ltd.* sold its services to the mega-rich who had no tolerance for bungling. Perfection was expected and perfection had to be delivered. Jake had drummed that into her from day one.

Two years she'd been working with him and she knew him through and through. Nothing escaped his notice and she needed cast-iron armour to stop him from getting under her skin. He was a brilliant salesman, a masterly entrepreneur, a stickler for detail, and a dyed-in-the-wool womaniser.

He was certainly single, and frequently unattached, but the chance of forging anything but a brief physical affair with him was nil. She couldn't help fancying him now and then—no woman alive wouldn't—but Amy had too much self-esteem to ever allow herself to be used for fun. Casual intimacy did not appeal to her.

Jake was into *experiences* with women, not relationships, the more exciting and varied the better. To Amy's accumulated knowledge, he had a low threshold of interest in any woman. They came and went with such regularity, she lost track of their names.

Though they did have one thing in common. They were all stunning to look at and made no secret of their availability to answer any need Jake Carter might have for them. He didn't have to chase. He simply had to choose.

Jake the rake, Amy had privately christened him. As far as she could see, he never scratched more than the surface of those who rolled through his life. Amy had figured very early on that keeping an impervious surface to Jake Carter was a prime requirement for keeping her job. Let other women fall victim to his animal magnetism. She had Steve.

Except she didn't anymore.

Tears welled again.

She stared at the soggy mess of herself in the mirror, battling the sense of defeat that was swamping her. Maybe she should dye her hair blonde. The ridiculous thought almost made her laugh. Her emphatically arched eyebrows and the double rows of lashes were uncompromisingly black, her eyes such a dark blue they were almost violet. She'd look stupid as anything other than a brunette.

Besides, she liked her hair. It was thick and glossy and the feathery razor cut around her face gave the shoulder-length bob a soft frame for her rather angular features. She didn't mind them, either. The high slant of her cheekbones balanced her squarish jawline and although her mouth was on the wide side, it did not look disproportionate. It more or less complemented the slight flare of her nostrils and the full curve of her lips was decidedly feminine. Her nose was straight, her neck was long enough to wear any jewellery well and her figure was fine, curvy enough in the right places and slim enough to carry off the clothes she liked.

There was nothing wrong with her looks, Amy fiercely asserted to herself. Jake Carter wouldn't have hired her if he'd found her wanting in that department. His clients expected glamour. After all, they bought or chartered luxury yachts and jet planes. *Wide Blue Yonder* catered to their every whim, and charged them the earth for it. Jake insisted that his staff be as pleasing to the eye as everything else connected to his business. Image, he preached, was every bit as important as supplying what was demanded.

Though Amy had little doubt he was pleasing himself as much as anyone else. He made no secret of enjoying the visual pleasure of his female work force. He might call it *class,* but he was such a sexy beast, Amy was certain he revelled in exercising his right to choose a stimulating environment for himself.

She took several deep, calming breaths, opened her handbag, fished out her emergency make-up kit, and set to work, creating an unblemished facade to present to her boss. His lateness this morning was a stroke of luck. She couldn't bank on any more luck running her way. Somehow she had to shut Steve and his pregnant wife-to-be out of her mind and concentrate on performing every task Jake handed her with her usual efficiency. It was the only way to avoid drawing unwelcome attention.

Satisfied she looked as good as she could in the circumstances, Amy returned her make-up kit to her handbag. Having washed and dried her hands, she smoothed the skirt of her scarlet linen shift over her hips, wishing linen didn't crease quite so much. But it was *in* this season, despite its crushability, and the bright colour was a much-needed spirit-booster. At least, that was what she'd argued as she'd donned it this morning.

Pride had insisted the expensive dress should not be wasted. She'd bought it last week, planning to wear it to Steve's office Christmas party. Now she saw it as a too belligerent statement that she would not mourn for him, a pathetic statement, given the heartsickness she was trying to hide. Still, it was too late to change her mind about it now and it might distract Jake Carter from picking up on her inner distress.

The tension of having to face him eased when she discovered his office empty and there was no sign of his having arrived for work. Puzzled as she was by his un-characteristic lateness, Amy was nevertheless relieved to have the extra time to establish an air of busy occupa-tion.

She settled at her desk and slipped the magazine she'd bought into the bottom drawer, out of sight and hope-fully out of mind until she could read it in private. Concentration on her job was top priority now. She turned on her computer, connected to the Internet and brought up the E-mail that had come in over the week-end.

She was printing it out for Jake's perusal when she heard the telltale whoosh of the elevator doors opening to the corridor which ran adjacent to their offices. Her nerves tightened. Her mind raced through defensive tac-tics.

Jake would probably drop into her office to explain

his lateness, then use the connecting door to enter his own. After a perfunctory greeting she could plunge straight into discussing the mail with him. It contained a number of queries to be answered. The sooner they got down to business, the better.

Jake had a habit of throwing personal inquiries at her on Monday mornings and she desperately wanted to avoid them today. This past weekend didn't bear thinking about let alone commenting upon. Not to Jake Carter.

If there was one thing more difficult to deflect than his sizzling sex appeal, it was his curiosity. Give him even a hint of an opening and he'd capitilise on it, probing for more information every which way. The man had a mind as sharp as a razor.

The door to her office rattled as it was thrust open. Amy's heart kicked in trepidation. She kept her gaze fastened on the printer as she steeled herself not to reveal even the tiniest crack of vulnerability to the dangerous impact of her boss's strong charisma.

In her mind's eye she ticked off what she had to meet with perfect equanimity; the tall, muscle-packed physique exuding male power, skin so uniformly tanned it seemed to gleam with the warm kiss of sunshine, a face full of charm, a slight smile accentuating the sensuality of a mouth that somehow combined strength and teasing whimsy, an inviting twinkle in eyes all the more fascinating for their drooping lids, causing them to look triangular in shape, accentuating the intensity of the intelligence burning through the intriguing amber irises. Last, but not least, was an enticing wealth of dark, wavy hair, threaded with silver, giving him an air of maturity that encouraged trust in his judgement, though Amy knew him to be only thirty-four.

She suspected he'd look no different in ten or even twenty years' time. He'd still be making every woman's heart flutter. It was a power she resented, given his fickleness, and she clung to that resentment as she looked up from the print-out to give the necessary acknowledgement of his presence.

Her gaze caught on the capsule he was carrying.

Shock wiped out her own concerns.

Jake the rake with a baby?

A baby?

Steve's pleas for understanding pounded through her mind...responsibility, commitment, the rights of the child, being a full-time father...

Jake the rake in that role?

Amy lost all her moorings. She was hopelessly adrift.

"You don't think fatherhood becomes me?"

The amused lilt of his sexy, purring voice jerked her gaze up. He chuckled at her confounded expression as he strolled forward and plonked the capsule on her desk.

"Cute little tyke, isn't he?"

Amy rolled back her chair and stood up, staring down at what looked like a very small baby who was blessedly fast asleep. Only its head and a tiny clenched hand were visible above the bunny rug tucked snugly around the mound of its body. How old it was Amy couldn't guess, but she didn't think it was newborn.

"This...is yours?" Her voice came out like a strangled squawk, disbelief choking more than her mind.

He grinned, enjoying having provoked her obvious

loss of composure. "More or less," he answered, his eyes agleam with wicked mischief.

She belatedly registered the teasing. Resentment flared out of her control, fuelled by the pain of having to accept Steve's full-on commitment to fatherhood with a woman other than herself.

"Congratulations!" She arched her eyebrows higher. "I take it the mother is happy with this more or less arrangement?"

"Uh-oh!" He wagged a finger at her, his sparkling amusement scraping her nerves raw. "Your bad opinion of me is showing, Amy. And it's absolutely undeserved."

Like hell it was! She hastily constructed a deadpan look to frustrate him. "I do apologise. Your personal affairs are, of course, none of my business."

"Joshua's mother trusts me implicitly," he declared loftily.

"How nice!"

"She knows I can be counted upon in an emergency."

"Yes. You always do rise to an occasion."

He laughed at the dry irony in her voice. "I see you've recovered. But I did have you lost for a word earlier on," he said triumphantly.

"Would you like me to be speechless more often?"

"What fun would the game be then?" Sheer devilment in his eyes.

Amy deliberately remained silent.

He heaved a sigh. "Determined to frustrate me." He shook his head at her. "Challenge is the spice of life to me, Amy."

She ignored the comment, giving him nothing to feed off.

"Okay," he conceded. "Joshua's mum is my sister, Ruth. Everything fell in on her this morning. My brother-in-law dislocated his shoulder, playing squash. She had to take him to hospital. I was elected as emergency baby-sitter so I got landed with my nephew for the duration. Ruth will come by here to pick him up when she can."

Light dawned. "You're the baby's uncle."

"And his godfather." The teasing grin came back. "You see before you a staunch family man."

From the safe distance of being once removed, Amy thought cynically.

"I'll just pop him down here." He lifted the capsule off her desk and placed it on the floor beside the filing cabinets. "Great little sleeper. Went off in the car and hasn't budged since."

He was leaving the baby with her!

Amy stared at the tiny bundle of humanity—the result of intimacy between a man and a woman—a bond of life that went on and on, no matter what the parents chose to do—a link that couldn't be broken—a baby.

Her whole body clenched against the anguish flooding through her. For this Steve had left her. For this Steve was marrying another woman. Their years together meant nothing…compared to this. He'd covered up his infidelity. Amy hadn't even suspected it. It was the baby who had ended their five-year-long relationship…the baby the man-trap blonde was having…part of Steve he couldn't let go.

And Amy couldn't blame him for that, however deeply it pained her.

A baby deserved to have its father.

But the betrayal of all they'd shared together hurt so much, so terribly much…

"This today's mail?"

She hadn't been aware of Jake backtracking to her desk. The question swung her head towards him. He'd picked up the sheets from the printer. "Yes," she answered numbly.

"I'll take it into my office." He made a beeline for the connecting door, waving at the capsule as he went. "There's a bottle of formula and a couple of disposable nappies in that bag at Joshua's feet. Shouldn't be a problem."

So arrogantly casual, dumping his responsibility for the baby onto her!

Resentment started to burn again.

He opened the door and paused, looking back, oh so sleekly elegant in his grey silk suit, unruffled, uncreased, supremely self-assured, the tantalising little smile quirking his mouth.

"By the way, you look utterly stunning in red, Amy. You should wear it more often."

He winked flirtatiously at her and was gone, the door closing smoothly behind him.

Amy saw red.

Her mind was a haze of red.

Her heart pumped red-hot blood through her veins.

Her brain sizzled. All of her sizzled.

Since Jake Carter enjoyed cracking her composure, he could damned well enjoy a monumental crack! She was *not* going to look after someone else's baby…a baby who had no connection to her whatsoever. It wasn't her job. And today of all days, she didn't need a vivid reminder of what she had lost and why. Let Jake Carter look after his own…the staunch family man! The Godfather!

She looked down at the baby, still peacefully asleep, oblivious to the turbulent emotions it stirred in Amy. She looked at the plastic bag at the foot of the capsule. It was printed with fun Disney characters. Today, Jake Carter could have *fun* with his nephew. The game with her was over and she didn't care if he fired her for it. In fact, if he dared to try any pressure on her over minding his nephew she'd get in first and dump him.

It would probably be a new experience for him, getting dumped by a woman. And he wouldn't be expecting it, either. There hadn't been any exit signs for him to spot.

A savage little smile curled her lips.

She was about to give Jake Carter a red letter day.

And serve him right, too!

CHAPTER TWO

AMY barged into her boss's office, wishing the capsule swinging in her hand was a cudgel to beat him with. It infuriated her further to find him leaning back in his executive chair, feet up on his executive desk, hands cupping the back of his head, gazing smugly at the panoramic harbour view through his executive windows.

No work was being done. The mail she had printed out for him had been tossed on the in-tray. He looked as if he was revelling in recalling the pleasures he had undoubtedly indulged in over the weekend. While she had been dealt one killing blow after another.

It wasn't fair!

Nothing was fair!

But by God! She'd make *this man* honour his commitment!

Her unheralded entrance drew a bland look of inquiry. ''Some problem?''

Welcome to hell on wheels! she thought, marching straight up to his desk and heaving the capsule onto it. She did refrain from knocking his feet off. She didn't want to wake the baby. It wasn't the infant's fault that his uncle was a male chauvinist pig.

With her hands free, she planted them on her hips and took her stance. Apparently fascinated by the vision of his normally cool personal assistant on the warpath, Jake stayed locked where he was, which suited Amy just fine. She opened fire at point-blank range.

"This baby…is your responsibility."

Her voice shook, giving it a huskiness that robbed it of the authority needed. She hastily worked some moisture into her mouth and resumed speaking with more strength.

"Your sister elected *you* to be her son's baby-sitter."

She stretched her mouth into a smile designed to turn Medusa to stone. It must have worked because he still didn't move. Or speak.

"She trusts you implicitly," Amy said sweetly. "As she should since you're his godfather. And a staunch family man."

It gave her a fierce pleasure to throw that claim back in his face, an even fiercer pleasure to see him look so stunned and at a loss for a ready reply. Join the club, brother, she thought, and fired the last volley.

"Looking after your nephew is not my job. Hire someone who specialises in baby-sitting if you can't do it yourself. In the meantime, he belongs with you."

She swivelled on her heel and headed for the door, her spine stiff, her shoulders squared, her head tilted high. If Jake Carter so much as breathed at her she would wheel and attack him again.

There wasn't a sound.

Silence followed her to the door.

She didn't look back.

She made her exit on a wave of righteous fervour.

It wasn't until the door was shut and she was alone in her own office, that the silence she'd left behind her took on an ominous quality in her mind.

Silence…

Like the silence after Steve had walked out.

She'd lost her man.

Amy closed her eyes as the realisation of what she'd done rushed in on her.

She was about to lose her job.

Lose everything.

This black day had just turned blacker.

CHAPTER THREE

AMY lost track of time. She found herself sitting at her desk and didn't remember sinking into her chair. It was as though she'd pressed a self-destruct button and her whole world had slipped out of control, shattering around her.

Vengeance…that's what she'd wreaked on Jake Carter…paying him out for what Steve had done to her. And she'd had no right to do it. No right at all.

A personal assistant was supposed to personally assist. That was what she was paid for. Any other day she wouldn't have blinked an eyelid at being left with a baby to mind. She would have taken it in her stride without so much as a murmur of protest, cynically accepting that Jake, the rake, wouldn't want to be bothered by a baby. Besides which, in business hours, his time was more important than hers. He was the one who pulled in the profits.

She slumped forward, propped her elbows on the desk and dropped her head into her hands. Dear merciful God! Was there some way out of the hole she'd dug for herself?

She couldn't afford to walk away from this job, not now she was alone. Steve's departure meant the rent on the apartment would double for her unless she got someone else in to share the cost. These few weeks before Christmas was not a good time for changes.

Besides, who would pay her as much as Jake did? Her salary was more than generous for her qualifications. And she would miss the perks that came with meeting and doing business for rich and famous people.

Her gaze lifted and ruefully skirted the photographs hanging on the walls; celebrities on their luxury yachts, on board their private jets, travelling in style to exciting places, wining and dining in classy surroundings, perfect service on tap.

Of course Jake was in all the photographs, showing off his clientele and what he had provided for them. The man was a brilliant salesman. The photographs were public proof that he was the one to deliver what was desired.

And the plain truth was, however much he provoked her with his teasing and wicked ways, Amy did, for the most part, enjoy the challenge of matching wits with him. He kept her on her toes, goaded her into performing at her best, and the work was never boring. Neither was he.

She'd miss him.

Badly.

Especially with Steve gone.

She'd miss this plush office, too.

Where else would she get a workplace that could even come near to matching what she had here at *Wide Blue Yonder?*

Her gaze drifted around, picking up on all she could be about to lose. The carpet was the jewel-like turquoise colour of coral reef lagoons, the paintwork the mellow yellow shade of sandy beaches, outlined in glossy white. Fresh arrangements of tropical flowers were brought in every week, exotic blooms in orange and scarlet mixed with glowing greenery. Every modern technological aid for business was at her fingertips—no expense spared in providing her with the best of everything.

Then there was the million dollar view—an extension of the vista that could be seen from Jake's office—Darling Harbour and Balmain directly across the water, Goat Island, and stretching along this shoreline, Luna Park with its cluster of carnival rides and entertainment booths.

Mortified at her own lunacy for giving none of this a thought before barging in to confront Jake, Amy pushed out of her chair and moved over to the picture window overlooking the grinning clown face that marked the entrance to the old amusement park. Fun, it promised. Just like Jake. Except she'd hot-headedly wiped fun off today's agenda.

She should go back into his office and apologise.

But how to explain her behaviour?

Never had she struck such a blistering attitude with him. He was probably sitting in there, mulling over what it meant, and he wouldn't gloss over it. Not Jake Carter. No way would he leave it alone. If he wasn't thinking of firing her for insubordination, he was plotting how to use her outburst to his advantage.

She shivered.

Give Jake even a molehill of an advantage and he could build it into a mountain that put him on top of any game he wanted to play. She'd seen him do it over and over again. If he let her stay on...

The sound of the door between their offices being opened froze her train of thought. It raised prickles around the nape of her neck. Panic screamed along her nerves and cramped her heart. She'd left it too late to take some saving initiative. In helpless anguish she turned to face the man who held her immediate future in his hands.

He stood in the doorway, commanding her attention by the sheer force of his presence. The absence of any hint of a smile was stomach-wrenching. He observed her in silence for several tension-riven seconds, his eyes focused intensely on hers. Amy's mind screamed at her to say something, offer an olive branch, anything to smooth over what she'd done, but she couldn't tear her tongue off the roof of her mouth.

"I'm sorry."

Soft words…words she should have said. She stared at his mouth. Had they really come from him or had she imagined it? Yet how could she imagine an apology when she hadn't expected it?

His lips twisted into a rueful grimace. "I was out of line, dumping Joshua on you and taking it for granted you'd mind him for me."

Incredulity held her tongue-tied.

The grimace tilted up into an appealing smile. "Guess I thought all women melted over babies. I didn't see it as an imposition. More like a novelty."

She felt hopelessly screwed up. Her hand shot out in an agitated gesture. "I…over-reacted," she managed, her voice a bare croak.

He shrugged. "Hell, what do I know? You're so buttoned up about your private life. There must be some reason you're not married to the guy you've been living with all these years." His eyebrows slanted in an expression of caring concern. "Is there a problem about having a baby?"

The sympathetic tone did it.

Like the trumpets that brought down the walls of Jericho, it struck chords in Amy that triggered a collapse of her defences. Tears welled into her eyes and she couldn't find the will to stop them. She wanted to say it wasn't her fault but the lump in her throat was impassable.

She had a blurry glimpse of shock on Jake Carter's face, then he was moving, looming towards her, and the next thing she knew his arms had enveloped her and she was weeping on his shoulder and he was muttering a string of appalled comments.

"I didn't mean it... Honest, Amy!... I was just testing...never thought it was true..."

"'Snot," she sobbed, her hands clenched against his chest.

"Not true?" His bewilderment echoed in her ears.

She couldn't bear him thinking she was barren, making her even less of a woman than Steve had left her feeling. She scooped in a deep breath and the necessary words shuddered out. "He didn't want a baby with me."

"Didn't?" He picked up sharply on the past tense.

The betrayal was so fresh and painful, it spilled out. "Having one with her."

"He knocked up some other woman?"

Jake's shock on her behalf soothed her wounded pride. "A bwonde," she explained, her quivering mouth not quite getting around the word.

"Well, I hope you've sent him packing." A fierce admonition, giving Amy the crazy sense he would have done it for her, given the opportunity, probably cracking a bullwhip to effect a very prompt exit.

"Yes," she lied. It was too humiliating to confess she'd sat like a disembowelled dummy while Steve had gone about dismantling and removing his half of their life together.

"Good riddance," Jake heartily approved. "You wouldn't want to have a baby with him, Amy. Couldn't trust a man like that to stick around."

"'Sright." She nodded mournfully, too water-logged to make any cynical parallel to Jake's attitude to women.

"Still feeling raw about it," he murmured sympathetically.

"Yes."

"Guess you only found out this weekend."

"Tol' me Sat'day."

"And I had to slap you in the face with Joshua."

The self-recrimination stirred her to meet him halfway. "Not your fault." There, she'd finally got it out. "Sorry," she added for good measure.

"Don't worry about it, Amy. Bad timing, that's all."

He was being so kind and understanding, patting her on the back, making her feel secure with him, cared for and valued. His warmth seeped into her bones. Her hands relaxed, fingers spreading out across the comforting heat of his chest. She nestled closer to him and he stroked her hair.

Like a wilted sponge, she soaked in his tender compassion, needing it, wanting it. She'd felt so terribly alone these past two days, so bereft of anyone to care about her…

A baby cry pierced the pleasant fuzziness swimming

around in her mind. Joshua! Left alone in the other office! Amy lifted her heavy head, reluctant to push out of Jake's embrace but she couldn't really stay there. Kind understanding only went so far. This was a place of business. A line had to be drawn.

Jake might start thinking she liked being this close to him. In fact, weren't his arms tightening around her, subtly shifting their body contact, stirring a consciousness of how very male he was? To Amy's increasing confusion, she found she wasn't immune to the virility she'd always privately scorned. For several electrifying moments she was mesmerised by its effect on her.

Another baby cry escalated into a wail, demanding attention.

"Responsibility calls, I'm afraid," Jake said wryly, confusing Amy further as he gently loosened his hold on her.

Had she imagined the slight sexual pressure?

He retained one supporting hand at her waist as he lifted his other to tilt her face up. His eyes were a warm, caressing gold. "Got your feet back?" he softly teased.

It drew a wobbly smile. "Firm on the floor again."

"Good!" He nodded approval. The warm molten gold hardened to a glitter. "Better go and wash that guy off your face, as well as out of your mind."

In short, she was a mess and he wanted his personal assistant back in good form. Of course that was all he wanted. Jake Carter was too smart to muddy up his business with pleasures he could get so easily elsewhere.

Then his fingertips brushed her cheek. "Okay?"

Her skin tingled, most probably from the flush of embarrassment rising to her cheeks. ''Yes,'' she asserted as strongly as she could.

He gave her a lopsided grin as he dropped his hand and stepped away. ''The godfather is on duty. Got to see to Joshua.''

He was already at the door before she summoned breath enough to say, ''Thanks, Jake.''

''Any time. My shoulders are broad,'' he tossed at her good-humouredly, heading into his office to tend to his nephew.

Amy took several deep breaths to re-stabilise herself, then forced her legs into action. She picked up her handbag and strode off to the washroom, determined on being what she was supposed to be for Jake. She wouldn't forget his forebearance and kindness, either. Nor the moral support he'd given her. He almost counted as a friend, a solidly loyal friend.

On second thought, she shouldn't go overboard with that sentiment. Jake Carter was her boss. It was more efficient to get his personal assistant back in good working order than to train someone else to meet his needs. She was well aware of Jake's strong dash of pragmatism. Whatever it took to get the end he wanted was meticulously mapped and carried through.

All the same, she deeply appreciated his…well, his sensitivity…to her distress just now. He was also right. She *was* well rid of a man who cheated on her. She should stop grieving and start getting on with the rest of her life.

Though that was easier said than done.

At least she still had her job.

The black hole had closed up before she'd fallen right to the bottom of it, thank God!

Proving she was back in control again, her hand remained absolutely steady as she once more cleaned off her face and re-applied some masterly make-up. Then feeling more in command of herself, she hurried to Jake's office, determined to offer any assistance he required. After all, Joshua was not Steve's baby. She could handle looking after him.

As for Jake…well, she'd been handling him for the past two years. Nothing was going to change there. She just had to keep her head and not let him close to her body again. Business as usual.

CHAPTER FOUR

JAKE had left the door to his office ajar and Amy paused there before entering, amused by the crooning voice he was using for the baby.

"We're on a winning streak now, Josh. Oh, yes, we are, my boyo! We've got Amy Taylor right where we want her."

The smile was jolted off her face by those last words. Though hadn't she known not to trust his benevolence? Jake Carter always took advantage of what was handed to him. Always. If it suited him. One way or another he was going to capitilise on her lapse in professionalism.

"Well, not *precisely* where we want her," he went on.

Good! She'd show him she wasn't putty in his hands. One breakdown didn't mean she was a pushover. She knew where the line was drawn when it came to working with Jake Carter.

"Bit of patience needed, Josh. Bit of manoeuvring. That's a good chap. Hold it right there."

Unsure of how much of this speech applied to her, Amy stepped into the office to take in the scene. The capsule was on the floor and the baby laid out on the bunny rug which had been spread across the desk. Little legs and arms waved haphazardly as Jake triumphantly shoved a used disposable nappy into a plastic bag.

"Clean one coming up," he assured his nephew.

Deciding it was safe to interrupt without giving away the fact she'd been eavesdropping, Amy moved forward to offer the assistance she'd resolved to offer. "Would you like me to take over?"

Jake glanced up and shot her a grin. "Nope. I've got this all figured out." He grabbed Joshua's ankles, raised his bottom off the bunny rug and whipped a clean nappy into place. "Just a matter of getting the plastic tabs the right way around," he informed her.

Since Amy had never changed a nappy in her life, she was grateful Jake had acquired some expertise. It was quite fascinating, seeing the deft way he handled fastening the absorbent pad on the squirming little body.

"You could heat up his bottle for me." Jake waved towards the capsule. "Ruth said to stick it in the microwave for thirty seconds."

"Okay."

Glad to be given something positive to do, Amy quickly found the bottle in the Disney bag and raced off to the kitchenette where she usually made morning or afternoon teas for clients. She wasn't sure what temperature to set on the microwave, decided on medium, then watched the bottle revolve for the required time. A squirt of milk on her wrist assured her it wasn't too hot, and she carried it back to Jake with a buoyant sense of achievement.

Joshua was reclothed and clinging like a limpet to his uncle's shoulder as Jake patted his back. That makes two of us this morning, Amy thought ruefully. Guilt over her earlier refusal to have anything to do with the baby prompted her to offer full services now. Besides which, she didn't want Jake holding anything against her. Power came in many guises, and Jake Carter was a master of all of them.

"I can take him into my office and feed him," she said as *un*grudgingly as she could.

"It's my job," Jake insisted, holding his hand out for the bottle.

She passed it over, frustrated by his righteous stance. Paying *her* back, she thought. Rubbing it in.

"You can read me the mail while I take care of Josh," he added, granting her professional purpose. "I'll dictate whatever needs to be answered or followed through and leave that to you."

"Fine!" she agreed and darted into her office for her notebook, determined not to be faulted again. He already had too much ammunition against her...when he decided to use it.

The man was devilishly clever. She had never trusted him with personal information, suspecting he would somehow wield it to gain more power over her. All along, she had instinctively resisted his strong magnetism, perceiving it as a dangerous whirlpool that sucked people in. Especially women. Amy was in no doubt it paid to be wary around Jake Carter.

She deliberately adopted a business-like air as she seated herself in front of his desk, preparing to sort through the mail with him. However, despite her sensible resolution to take guard, she found the next half hour highly distracting to her concentration on the job.

Jake had settled back in his chair, feet up, totally relaxed as he cradled the baby in the crook of his arm and tilted the bottle as needed for the tiny sucking mouth. He looked so natural about it, as though well practised in the task. He even burped the baby halfway through its feed, propping it on his knee and firmly rubbing its back. Amy herself wouldn't have had a clue how to do that, let alone knowing it should be done.

"Good boy!" Jake crooned as two loud burps emerged, then nestled the baby back in his arm to continue the feeding.

Amy was amazed. Maybe, however improbable it seemed, Jake Carter *was* a staunch family man when it came to his immediate family. Or maybe his self-assurance simply extended to anything he took on. It was all very confusing. She could have sworn she had her buccaneer boss taped to the last millimetre, but he was certainly adding several other shades to his character this morning. Unexpectedly nice shades.

When they'd dealt with the last letter, Amy felt reluctant to leave the oddly intimate little family scene. It was Jake who prompted her, raising a quizzical eyebrow at her silence.

"All finished?"

"Yes."

"Anything I haven't covered?"

"No." She stood up, clutching the letters with her attached notes.

Jake smiled at her, a genuinely open smile, nothing tagged onto it. "Let me know if you run into any problems."

"Okay." She smiled back. Unreservedly.

It wasn't until she was back in her own office with the door closed between them, that it occurred to Amy how much better she was feeling. The day was no longer so gloomy. Steve's betrayal had gathered some distance, making it less overwhelming. She could function with some degree of confidence.

Had she nursed unfair prejudices against her boss?

Had loyalty to Steve pushed her into casting Jake Carter as some kind of devil's advocate who could shake the foundations of a life she valued?

Only one certainty slid out of this musing.

She didn't owe Steve loyalty anymore.

Nevertheless, she'd be courting real trouble if she ever forgot the reasons she'd named her boss Jake the rake!

Amy spent the next half hour diligently working through his instructions, her concentration so intensely focused, she didn't hear the elevator open onto their floor. The knock on her office door startled her. She looked up to see a woman already entering, a tall, curvaceous redhead, exuding an air of confidence in her welcome.

Amy felt an instant stab of antagonism. Some of Jake's women had a hide like a rhinoceros, swanning in as though they owned the place. This one was new. Same kind of sexy glamour puss he usually picked, though—long legs, big breasts, a face that belonged on the cover of *Vogue,* hair obviously styled by a master cutter, very short and chic, designer jeans that clung seductively, a clingy top that showed cleavage.

"Hi! I'm Ruth Powell, Jake's sister."

Amy was dumbfounded. There was no likeness at all. If she hadn't been presented with Jake's nephew this morning, she would have suspected a deception. Some women would use any ploy to get to the man they wanted. Though on closer scrutiny, and with the help of the identification, Amy did see one similarity in the triangular shape of the eyes. The colour, however, was deeper, Ruth's more a sherry brown than yellow-gold.

She had paused beside the door, returning Amy's scrutiny with avid interest. "You're Amy Taylor?" she asked before Amy thought to give her own name.

"Yes," she affirmed, wondering about the testing note in the other woman's voice.

A grin of pure amusement flashed across Ruth's face. "I see," she said with satisfaction.

Perplexed, Amy asked, "See what?"

"Why you dominate so much of Jake's conversation."

"I do?" Amy was astonished.

"So much so that amongst the family we've christened you Wonderwoman," Ruth answered dryly.

Amy flushed, suddenly self-conscious of how less flatteringly she had privately christened Jake.

"Actually, we weren't sure if you were a firebreathing dragon who kept his machismo scorched, or a stern headmistress who made him toe your line. Now I'll be able to tell everyone you're Irish."

"I'm not Irish," Amy tripped out, feeling more flummoxed by the second.

"Definitely Black Irish." Ruth started forward, gesturing her points as she made them. "You've got the hair, the eyes, and the spirit. You had me pinned like a butterfly for a minute there. Lots of power in those blue eyes."

"I'm sorry if you thought me rude," Amy rushed out, trying to get a handle on this strange encounter.

"Not at all. Call it a revelation. You must have Jake on toast." She laughed, bubbling over with some wicked kind of sibling pleasure as she strolled over to Amy's desk. "I love it. Serve him right."

Amy mentally shook her head. It was an absurd comment—her having Jake on toast. He had enough women to sink a ship. He was hardly dying of frustration because she refused to rise to his bait.

We've got Amy Taylor right where we want her…

The insidious words suddenly took on extra meaning. With Steve written out of the picture…

Held in Jake Carter's seductive embrace…

But not *precisely* in his bed!

Amy almost rolled her eyes at the totally over-the-top train of thought. Imagination gone wild. Jake's sister obviously enjoyed teasing as much as he did. None of it was to be taken seriously and it was best to put a stop to it.

"I beg your pardon, but…"

"Oh, don't mind me." Ruth twirled one perfectly manicured hand dismissively. "Relief loosening my tongue. I thought Martin's injury was worse that it is. It was hell waiting around in Casualty, fretting over what was happening or not happening."

Martin… that had to be her husband. "His shoulder is all right then?" Amy asked, belatedly recalling it had been dislocated.

"They put it back in. He's sleeping off the anaesthetic now so I thought I'd pick up Josh." Her gaze swept the area behind Amy, frowning at not spotting the capsule. "Where is he?"

"With Jake." Amy nodded towards the connecting door.

Ruth looked her surprise. "You mean he didn't ask you to look after him?"

Amy grimaced. "Well, we had a little contretemps about that. As I understood it, you entrusted him with your baby, so…"

"You insisted he do it?" Ruth's eyes shone with admiration.

"I hope that was right," Amy appealed. "He does seem very good at it."

Ruth broke into laughter again, her eyes twinkling merry approval. "You are priceless, Amy. I'm so glad I got to meet you. As for Jake being good with Josh, he is. Dogs and children gravitate naturally to my brother. So do women. As I'm sure you've noticed," she added with arch understanding.

"Hard not to," Amy returned dryly.

"Too used to getting his own way, my brother."

She was right about that but Amy decided some loyal support was called for. "He does work at it. Not much is left to chance, you know. His background research on every project is very thorough."

"Oh, I wasn't besmirching his professionalism. Jake was always an obsessive perfectionist. A born achiever." Her mouth twitched sardonically. "But some things do tend to fall in his lap."

Like a pile of willing women, Amy silently agreed, but it wasn't her place to say so. She smiled. "Well, Joshua was in his lap, last time I saw him."

"Right! It's been fun talking to you, Amy. Hope to see you again someday," Ruth said warmly, taking her exit into Jake's office.

Fun… Jake's family seemed addicted to fun. Amy

wondered what it might have been like, growing up in that kind of atmosphere. She remembered her own childhood as being dominated by fear of her father. Not that he had ever stooped to physical abuse. He didn't have to. He could cut anyone down with a word or a look. In hindsight, she could identify him as a control freak, but at the time, he was the authority to be escaped from whenever it was possible.

Her mother had been completely cowed. The only escape for her had been in death, and it was her death that had released Amy from staying any longer in her father's household. Her two older brothers had already gone by then, driven away by their father's unreasonable demands. She hadn't seen them in years. She no longer had any sense of family.

What she did have was a strong belief in living life on her own terms. Which was probably why she hadn't pushed for marriage with Steve. The thought of a husband was too closely connected to her father. She didn't want to be owned like that. Ever. In fact, she'd found Steve's much quoted term of being ''free spirits'' very attractive. Until she found out what ''free'' meant to Steve.

What a stupid, blind fool she'd been!

Amy shook her head at herself and turned back to work. There was nothing to be gained by maundering over her mistakes. Her best course was to learn from them and move on. She was briefly tempted to pull out the magazine she'd bought this morning and read the article on exit signs. The thought of Jake catching her at it put her off. No more gaffes today, she sternly told herself.

We've got Amy Taylor right where we want her…

Amy didn't like that smug little boast. She didn't like it at all. She liked *not precisely* much better. She hadn't spent two years honing her defensive skills with Jake Carter for nothing. Whatever he had in mind, she was not going to be a patsy, falling into his lap.

It was Jake who'd made a gaffe, blabbing to the baby. She'd be on her toes from now on, ready to block whatever little one-upmanship game he was planning to play. This time she'd be one step ahead of him.

Yes…she was definitely feeling better.

Jake certainly had a knack of putting zest into her life.

Which was a big improvement on the black hole.

CHAPTER FIVE

IT WASN'T long before Jake came in to check how Amy was doing. Ruth had apparently left through his door to the corridor since there was no sight or sound of her and the baby. "On top of it?" he asked casually.

"No problem," she answered, nodding to the printout of the work she'd done.

He picked up the sheets, then propped himself on the front edge of her desk to read them. As always, his proximity put her nerves on edge and she had to concentrate harder on keeping her fingers moving accurately on the keyboard. She was even more aware of him than usual, remembering how he'd held her earlier...his body, his touch. She wondered if he was a sensitive lover.

Her gaze flicked to his hands, the long tapered fingers wrapped around the sheaf of paper. They'd stroked her hair so gently. She reminded herself Jake was very smooth at everything he did. Sexual sensitivity didn't necessarily mean he actually cared for the person. Stoking his own pleasure more likely. Though he had seemed to care about her this morning. Had it been entirely a pose for an ulterior purpose?

"Couldn't have worded this better myself," Jake said appreciatively. His smile had a caressing quality that almost made Amy squirm. "You have a great knack of filling out my instructions, Amy, applying the right touch to get through to people without pushing too hard.''

She quelled the whoosh of pleasure at his praise. ''I have been learning off a master the past two years,'' she pointed out, her eyes lightly mocking.

''And an apt pupil you've proved,'' he was quick to add, his admiration undimmed. ''Don't know what I'd do without you. You're my right hand.''

He was laying it on with a trowel. Amy instinctively backed off. ''So what's next on the agenda?'' He was probably buttering her up to land some task he didn't want to do himself in her lap.

''Two years, mmh?'' he mused, ignoring her question. ''You deserve a raise in salary. Ruth is right.''

''About what?'' This was very doubtful ground.

He grinned. ''You're priceless.''

Amy frowned. ''Do you make a habit of discussing me with your family?''

He shrugged. ''Perfectly natural. You are my closest associate. Don't you mention me to yours?''

''I don't have a family.'' It slipped out before she could catch it back.

His eyebrows shot up. ''An orphan?''

The interest beaming at her was not about to be side-tracked. Amy sighed. All this time she'd worked with Jake Carter and managed to keep him at arm's length where any personal issues were concerned. Today she'd blown it in more ways than one.

''Not exactly,'' she muttered, telling herself her family was so far removed from her it didn't matter. ''My mother died when I was sixteen. My father's remarried and we don't get on. I have one brother living in the

U.K., and another settled in Alaska. Hardly what you'd call close.''

Having rattled out the bare facts, Amy constructed a dismissive smile which she found difficult to hold when faced with Jake's appalled reaction.

''You mean you're alone? Absolutely alone with no one to turn to? No backup support?''

''I'm used to it,'' she insisted. ''I've been on my own a long time.''

''No, you haven't,'' he fired back at her. ''Which was why you were weeping on my shoulder this morning.''

Amy gritted her teeth and glowered at him. ''Must you remind me of that?''

''At least *I* was here for you. Just remember that, Amy. When your scumbag of a lover let you down, I was here for you.''

''You're my boss! You weren't here for *me*,'' she argued hotly. ''It was purely a matter of propinquity.''

''Nonsense! I took your side immediately. I know what you're worth. Which is a damned sight more than that fool did.''

She knew it! He just had to take advantage of any slip she made. He *revelled in it.* ''I do not wish to discuss Steve any further,'' she grated out.

''Of course not. The sooner he's wiped out of your life, the better. Eminently sensible. Though there are practical matters to take into consideration.''

''Yes. Like getting on with work,'' Amy tersely reminded him.

''You might need help in shifting to a new apartment.''

''I like the apartment I've got, thank you.''

"Not a good idea, keeping it, Amy. Memories can be depressing. I realise shifting would be another upheaval you might not want to face right now, but a clean break is the best medicine. Gets rid of the hangover."

"Well, I'm sure you'd know that, Jake," she said with blistering sarcasm.

The acid didn't make a dint. "I'll help you," he said, as though she'd conceded to his argument instead of commenting on his quick turnover in women.

"I don't need your help."

He smiled and blithely waved her protest aside. "Consider me family. It's times like these that family bucks in and picks up the slack. Since I'm the closest thing you've got to family..."

"I do not...remotely...associate you...with family," Amy stated emphatically.

"Well, yes..." One shoulder lifted and fell. Devilment danced into his eyes. "...That probably would be a bit incestuous, wouldn't it?"

"What?" she squawked.

"I can't lie to you, Amy," he declared loftily. "What zips between you and me could not be called sisterly...or brotherly...or motherly...or fatherly."

She flushed, biting her tongue so as not to invite more along this line.

"However, I am genuinely concerned about you," he said, projecting such deep sincerity it swallowed up the devilment and threatened to suck Amy in right after it.

She fought fiercely for a bank of common sense, needing some safe ground between her and Jake Carter. The danger of him infiltrating her private life felt very acute and every instinct told her it wasn't wise. He could bad-mouth Steve as much as he liked but was he any better? His record with women was hardly in his favour!

"I'll ask around," he burbled on. "Find you a nice apartment. Closer to work so you won't have far to travel. Bondi Beach isn't really suitable for you."

"I like Bondi," she protested.

He frowned at her. "Not good for a woman on her own. A lot of undesirables gather out there at weekends. You wouldn't be safe going out at night without an escort."

He had a point, but where was safe at night without an escort? Life without Steve was going to take some adjustment.

"Why not have a look around Balmoral if you want to live by a beach?" Jake suggested. "It's a respectable area. Doesn't draw any trouble."

She rolled her eyes at him and his big ideas. "It's also a very expensive area."

"No more than Bondi. And being on the north side of the harbour, it's much handier to Milsons Point. You won't have to drive across the bridge to work."

"I can't afford it. I can't afford where I am without a partner."

"I said I was upping your salary. Let's say another twenty percent. That should let you live decently."

Amy's mouth dropped open. Her mind flew wildly into calculation mode. "That's more than Steve earns!"

He grinned. "You're worth it. I'll just go and ring a few estate agents I know. See what they can come up with. In the meantime, send these off." He handed her the replies she'd printed out. "They're all fine."

He hitched himself off her desk and left her gaping

after him like a goldfish caught in a bowl, looking out at a foreign world. Jake Carter had always been a shaker and a mover, but never before on her behalf. Was it out of concern for her or did he have other motives up his sleeve?

Amy ran her fingers through her hair, trying to steady the mad whirl in her mind. What could she believe as irrefutable fact? Both Jake and his sister were into game-playing, scoring points. Nothing they said could be taken too seriously.

On the other hand, Jake always delivered what he promised. He wouldn't backtrack on the money. Her salary would now be more than she'd ever dreamed of earning, putting her on a financial level where she was truly independent. Which meant she had options she didn't have before.

A grin broke across her face.

Such a large salary would certainly make her life considerably brighter and it was wonderful to be valued so highly. This morning she'd felt her future had fallen into a black hole, but it wasn't true. There was life after Steve. And she was going to make the most of it, thanks to Jake.

Though if her devious boss was thinking he could attach personal strings to that big hunk of money he'd just handed her, he could think again!

CHAPTER SIX

AMY had just finished filing copies of the letters she'd sent when Jake erupted into her office.

"Grab your handbag," he commanded. "We're off."

"Where to?"

"I'll explain on the way." He checked his watch as he crossed her office to the door. "We've got precisely twenty-five minutes to make the rendezvous."

Amy grabbed her handbag and scooted after him. Jake had the door open for her. She strode into the corridor and summoned the elevator, glad they were going to be involved in some outside activity. Jake would be busy with other people who would take his focus off her and she could get back to feeling relatively normal in his company again.

She always enjoyed these meetings with clients, watching Jake work his brand of magic on them. "Who's the target?" she asked as they stepped into the elevator together.

"Not who. What," he said enigmatically, pressing the ground floor button.

"A new boat?"

He shot her a look of exasperation as the elevator descended. "We do not deal in boats, Amy. Only in yachts," he reminded her.

"Sorry. Slip of the tongue."

"Watch it," he advised darkly. "I want my P.A. to impress the man we're going to meet."

"What's his name?"

"Ted Durkin of Durkin and Harris. Big property dealers."

The name meant nothing to her but clearly it was well known to Jake. The elevator opened onto the reception area before she had time to question him. Jake steered her out and pointed her to the stairwell that led down to the back of the building where he parked his car in a private yard reserved for himself and clients.

"Kate," he called to his front woman, "we're out of the office. Take messages."

"When will you be back?"

"Don't know. If it's anything urgent I can be reached on my mobile."

He hurried Amy down the stairs and outside, using the remote button on his key to unlock the BMW M3 supercar which he currently fancied. Amy headed for the passenger side of the two-door coupe. Haste precluded courtesy. They both took their seats and Jake handed her a folded piece of notepaper as he switched on the ignition.

"What's this?"

"Where we're going. Better get out the Gregory's Street Directory and navigate for me. Haven't got time for wrong turns. I'm right to Military Road. After that, you direct me."

She extracted the guide book from the glove box and settled back for the ride. The scribbled list on the notepaper did not enlighten her as to their destination. In fact, it looked as though Jake had picked up the wrong sheet. What was written appeared to be information about a woman.

Her mouth curled. It seemed he did research on them, as well. "This says, 'Estelle, 26, 8, no smoking, no pets, no WP…'"

"Wild parties," Jake elaborated. "The address is 26 Estelle Road, Balmoral. Apartment 8. The rest are the conditions for rental."

Amy's sardonic humour dried up. Her heart performed a double loop. She waited until it settled back into seminormal rhythm, counting to ten in the meantime. "I take it this is for me," she said as calmly as she could.

"If you like it and if we can swing it."

"Jake, this is not your business." He'd been encroaching on her private life all morning. She had to put a stop to it before it got completely out of hand.

"I said I'd look into it for you," he replied, unshaken from his purpose.

"You said you'd make some calls, not escort me to view places during business hours. I cannot accept…"

"It's almost the lunch hour," he reasoned. "You're always obliging about working overtime in emergencies. The least I can do is this small favour in return."

"This is not an emergency, Jake," she argued, barely holding on to her temper. "I can look for an apartment—if I want to move from the one at Bondi—in my own time."

He frowned at her. "Why are you nit-picking? There's no harm in looking at a place you might like. It could be the ideal change for you."

Amy stubbornly stuck to her guns. "You could have given me the address and…"

"No good! You need me with you for this one. I'm your reference. I pressured Ted into showing it to you ahead of his listing it and he's on his way there now to meet us. He's a handy business contact, Amy. I wouldn't like to waste his time."

She heaved an exasperated sigh, accepting she'd been outmanoeuvred. He was her boss. It would be wrong for her to mess with his contacts. But a stand had to be taken. She didn't want him pulling strings on her behalf, entangling her in them without her knowledge or permission.

"You should have discussed it with me first. I haven't made up my mind on this." And she hated the feeling of being steam-rollered by Jake.

"There's no obligation to take it. Sounded like a great deal for you, though. Worth seeing if it's as good as Ted says. And I might add, he's proved spot-on in his advice to me in the past."

"What's so great about it?" she demanded tersely.

"Location for a start. Ted reckoned it was a pearl for the rent being asked."

"How much?"

He rolled out a sum that was only marginally lower than the rent for the Bondi apartment. Even with her new salary, it would take a bigger chunk of her income than she felt was reasonable for her.

"Ted told me it could command a much higher rent," Jake burbled on. "But the owner's fussy about getting the right tenant in and has scaled the rent to suit. The apartment was recently purchased and is in the process of being refurbished. The owner doesn't want any damage to it, so…''

''No smoking, no pets, no wild parties.'' Amy looked at the list again. ''What does 'SCW' stand for?''

''Single career woman. Someone who respects property and has a tidy mind.'' Jake flashed her a teasing smile. ''I said you fitted the bill. Never met a woman more intent on keeping things in order.''

Including you, Amy thought darkly. He was such a tempting devil, too attractive for his own good, and he thought he could charm his way into anything. Not my life, she fiercely resolved. It was bad enough being dumped by Steve. If she let Jake get too close to her, she had a terrible suspicion he had the power to steal her soul. Then where would she be?

Every self-protective instinct screamed alarm in his presence and today the scream was louder than ever. Raw and vulnerable from the weekend's revelations, Amy admitted to herself she was frightened of Jake slipping past her guard, frightened of the consequences. She fretted over the knowledge he now shared that Steve couldn't be used as a barrier between them anymore.

Though that wasn't entirely right.

Steve had been much more to her than a barrier against Jake.

Much more, she insisted to herself.

She opened the Gregory's Street Directory and started plotting their course to Estelle Street, trying her utmost to ignore the man beside her. His power was threatening to swamp her; powerful masculinity, powerful car, powerful friends, and they were all being used on her. Or so it felt.

We've got Amy Taylor right where we want her.

Not precisely.

A bit of manoeuvring.

The provocative words clicked through her mind again, conjuring up another scenario. An apartment in Balmoral was Jake's idea. He'd given her a raise in salary so she could afford it. He'd found one for her, supposedly to order. He'd tricked her into his car so he could take her there, pressured her with the importance of a business contact.

Was it some kind of put-up job between him and his friendly property dealer, Ted Durkin?

But why?

What good would it do Jake to have her in Balmoral?

He was screwing her up again.

The only way to be sure of anything was to thwart him by making her own decisions her own way. In the meantime she'd play along like a good little girl. Which meant giving directions from the directory.

Amy had never lived on the north side of Sydney and didn't know the Middle Harbour area at all. Her only previous reference to Balmoral was an interview she'd read about a TV celebrity who lived there and loved it. Which undoubtedly meant it was very classy. And expensive. Any place on the harbour was expensive.

Having found Estelle Street on the map, Amy stared at its location with a sense of disbelief. It was only one block back from The Esplanade which ran around the beach. It faced onto a park that extended to The

Esplanade, giving residents a view of greenery, as well an uninterrupted vista of the water beyond it. This had to be a prime location.

She frowned over the rental Jake had mentioned. It was steep for her to pay alone, but it had to be amazingly cheap for an apartment on this street. Even the most run-down place would surely command double that amount, and Jake had said it was being refurbished.

"This doesn't make sense," she muttered.

"What?" Jake inquired.

"I've found Estelle Street. It's almost on the beach. The property there has got to be million dollar stuff. Even with the strict rules, the owner could ask a really high rent."

Jake must have made some under-the-table arrangement with Ted Durkin. She just didn't trust this sequence of events. Or coincidences.

"I did tell you Ted said it was a bargain. For the right person," Jake reminded her. "There is the catch of the six months' lease," he added in the throwaway tone of an afterthought. "But even if this is only a stopgap place for you…"

"What catch?"

She'd been waiting for a "catch." Jake was being altogether too persuasive about this wonderful chance for her. There had to be a "catch."

"Seems the owner plans to take up residence there. Only waiting on selling the current home. Doesn't want to hurry that." He sent her a wise look. "Always best to hang out for the asking price. It's a losing game, selling in haste."

"So it's only for six months."

''Mmh… more like a house-sitter than a tenant, according to Ted. Someone who'll value the place and look after it. Never a good idea to leave a property empty for an extended period of time.''

It was beginning to make more sense. Maybe her suspicions were unwarranted. It wasn't beyond the realm of possibility that Jake might want to do her a good turn. If she hadn't overheard those words…was she reading too much into them?

Whatever the truth of the matter, it didn't make a great deal of sense for her to shift house if she had to shift again in six months' time. Changing apartments was a high-cost exercise what with putting up bond money and the expense of moving her furniture, not to mention the hassle of packing and unpacking. Nevertheless, she was curious to see the apartment now. Especially since Jake was investing so much time and talk on it. She still wanted to know why.

They were well along Military Road so she started giving him directions. Within a few minutes he'd made the turns she gave and they were heading down a hill to Balmoral Beach. Amy was entranced by the view. The water was a dazzling blue this morning. A fleet of small yachts were riding at anchor, adding their interest to the picturesque bay. The curved shoreline had a welcoming stretch of clean sand, edged by manicured lawns, beautiful trees and walkways.

This beach had a quiet, exclusive air about it, unlike the broad sweep of Bondi which invited vast public crowds. Even the populated side of The Esplanade looked tidy and respectable, no litter, no grubbiness, not a tatty appearance anywhere. Amy was highly impressed by its surface charm, wishing she had time to explore properly. She made a mental note to come here another day. After all, with Steve gone, she would have plenty of *free* days to do whatever she pleased.

They turned off into the street beside the park and found the address with no trouble at all. The block of apartments was on the next corner, a fairly old block in red brick and only four storeys high with garages underneath. Amy guessed Apartment 8 would be on the top floor, and found herself hoping it was on the corner with the balcony running around two sides, both east and north.

''There's Ted waiting for us,'' Jake pointed out, waving to the man standing by the entrance to the block.

As they cruised past in search of a parking place, Amy caught only a glimpse of the agent, a broad, bulky figure, smartly attired in a blue business shirt, striped tie, and dark trousers. Jake slotted the car into the kerb only twenty metres away. Amy checked her watch as they alighted. Twelve-thirty. They were on time. Ted Durkin had arrived early. No fault of theirs, but both she and Jake automatically covered the distance at a fast pace.

Amy was conscious of being scrutinised as they approached. It wasn't a sexual once-over, more a matching up to specifications. The agent looked to be in his late forties, his iron-grey hair thinning on top, making his slight frown very visible. It only cleared when Jake thrust out his hand to him, drawing attention away from her.

"Good of you to give us this opportunity, Ted," he enthused genially.

"Not at all. You've put business my way in the past, Jake. Appreciate it."

"This is my P.A., Amy Taylor."

"Pleased to meet you, Mr. Durkin," Amy chimed in, offering her hand.

He took it and gave her a rueful little smile. "To tell you the truth, Miss Taylor, I wasn't expecting someone quite so young."

Single career woman—had he been envisaging a spinsterish woman in her late thirties or forties, someone entrenched in her career with little else in her life?

One thing was suddenly clear. This had to be a *bona fide* deal or Ted Durkin wouldn't be raising questions.

Without pausing to examine her eagerness to dismiss objections to her possible tenancy, Amy rushed to reassure him.

"I'm twenty-eight, Mr. Durkin, and I've held a job since I was sixteen. That's twelve years of solid employment, working my way up to my current position."

"Very responsible," Jake slipped in emphatically.

Ted Durkin shot him a chiding look. "You didn't mention how very attractive your P.A. is, Jake." Another apologetic look at her. "No offence to you, Miss Taylor, but the owner of the apartment was very specific about..."

"No wild parties," she finished for him. "That's not my style, Mr. Durkin."

"Amy's been with me for two years, Ted," Jake said. "I really can vouch for her character. An ultra-clean living person."

"Uh-huh." He raised his eyebrows at her. "No boy-friend? I don't mean to get personal. It's a matter of satisfying the owner. Did Jake explain…?"

"Yes, he did."

Regardless if she was prepared to take the apartment or not, Amy bridled against the sense of being rejected, especially after the painful blow from Steve. She found herself pouring out a persuasive argument, uncaring that it was personal business. Jake knew it anyway and she felt compelled to convince Ted Durkin she was an appropriate tenant.

"Actually I'm looking for time to myself, Mr. Durkin. I've been in a rather long-term relationship which has just broken up." She grimaced, appealing to his sympathy. "No chance of a reconciliation, so I really am on my own and I don't intend rushing into socialising. Six months here would do me very nicely, right away from where I've been."

"Ah!" It was the sound of satisfaction. "Well, I'll take you up and show you around. It's not quite ready for occupation. Painters are in at the moment."

Won a stay of judgement, Amy thought, ridiculously pleased. She glanced at Jake as they entered the build-ing, wanting to share the achievement with him since he'd helped. He wasn't looking at her but she caught a smug little smile on his face and then wanted to kick herself.

She'd ended up playing *his* game, showing positive enthusiasm for *his* plan to move her out of Bondi and to Balmoral.

I was only saving *his* face in front of Ted Durkin, Amy quickly excused herself. She could still say no to the apartment. There was no commitment until she signed the lease for it. In fact, if she decided to move—in her own good time—it was much more practical to find a place that didn't have a time limit on it.

Jake Carter hadn't won this round yet!

CHAPTER SEVEN

THEY rode a small elevator up to the top floor. It opened onto a broad hallway, lit by the multicoloured panes of glass which ran down the opposite wall, making an attractive feature for the stairwell next to it. Ted Durkin ushered them to an opened door on the left hand side. Amy's heart gave an excited skip.

It *was* the apartment with the east-north balconies.

They walked into a wonderfully light, airy, open-plan living area and for Amy it was love at first sight. To live here—if only for six months—it was irresistible—an incredible bargain!

The floor was covered with marvellous tiles, the pearlescent colour of sea-shells crushed into a wavy pattern that instantly suggested a seabed of gently undulating sand. The wall facing the bay was almost all glass, offering a panoramic view and a wealth of sunshine. Other walls were painted a pale cream. The kitchen was shiny new, all blonde wood and stainless steel, fitted with a dishwasher and a microwave oven, as well as a traditional one.

In the living room, two men in paint-spotted overalls sat on foldaway chairs, eating their lunch. A spread-sheet was laid out on the floor underneath them. Tins of paint stood on it in a tidy group.

"How's it going?" Ted asked them.

"One more coat on the skirting boards and architraves and we're finished," the older one answered.

These were being painted a pearly grey, picking up on some of the grains in the tiles and making a stylish contrast to the cream.

"Still wet?"

"Should be touch-dry by now. It's safe to move around."

"Fine." Ted turned to Amy. "The old carpet's been ripped out of the bedrooms for the carpenter to fit the cupboards properly. The new one won't be laid until later this week," he warned.

"There's more than one bedroom?" Amy asked, stunned by the spaciousness of the apartment.

"Two."

Jake wandered over to chat to the painters as the agent steered Amy towards an archway in the back wall of the living room. Apparently he didn't intend to participate in her decision, which made a mess of her line of logic.

She made a determined effort to shake off her pre-occupation with his influence, realising she must have misread the situation, possibly blowing it completely out of proportion. When all was said and done, he had only followed through on what he had advised her. Having her right where he wanted her could simply mean keeping her happy as his assistant.

Through the archway was a short hall with doors at both ends of it and two more doors facing the wall with the arch. The latter pair were opened first. "Laundry and bathroom," Ted pointed out.

The laundry held a linen and broom cupboard, washer, dryer and tub. All new. Amy was delighted to see the washer and dryer since Steve had taken those in the division of their property, leaving her with the refrigerator and the TV. She'd envisaged visits to a laundrette, an inconvenience she wouldn't have to put up with here.

The bathroom was positively luxurious. It had obviously been renovated, the same tiles in the living area being carried through to it and the same blonde wood in the kitchen being used on the vanity bench. Incredibly, it featured a Jacuzzi bath as well as a shower and everything else one could need.

"These old places were built to be roomy. Couldn't put a bath like that in most modern apartments," Ted remarked, probably noting her stunned expression. "You don't often see such high ceilings, either. All the rooms here have bigger dimensions than usual."

And there'd been an enormous amount of money poured into making the most of them, Amy thought. No expense spared. Little wonder that the owner didn't want it damaged by careless tenants.

The second bedroom was larger than average. The main bedroom was larger still, with glass doors that led out onto the north-facing balcony. "What colour is the new carpet?" Amy asked.

Ted shrugged. "Don't know. The owner picked it. I could tell you on Friday."

Amy shook her head. "It doesn't matter. I've never been in such a lovely apartment. Believe me, Mr. Durkin, it would be an absolute pleasure to keep this in mint condition. Do you think the owner will accept me as a tenant?" she pressed eagerly.

His face relaxed into an indulgent smile. His eyes twinkled at her in approval. "Why not? I can sell anything if I believe in it and I'm inclined to believe you, Miss Taylor.''

"I promise your faith won't be mislaid.''

"Well, I do have Jake's word for that, as well, so we'll call it a done deal.''

"Thanks a million, Mr. Durkin.'' She grabbed his hand and shook it vigorously, feeling as though she'd won a lottery.

His smile turned slightly ironic. "Guess you should thank Jake, Miss Taylor. He did the running.''

"Yes, of course. I will.''

Jake! He would probably be insufferably smug about it, but right at this moment Amy didn't care. He'd done her a great favour. A fabulous favour! She floated back out to the living room on a cloud of happy pleasure. The apartment was hers. Six months of blissful living in this beautiful place! It was better than a vacation! New surroundings, new people, new everything!

Jake turned from chatting to the painters and raised his eyebrows at her.

She couldn't help it. She grinned at him like a cheshire cat.

He grinned back.

Understanding zinged between them.

It was like a touch of magic, a fountain of stars showering her, lifting her into a new life. She barely stopped herself from pirouetting across the tiled floor and hugging Jake Carter.

"A done deal?'' he asked.

"A done deal,'' she affirmed exultantly.

"Then let's go to lunch and celebrate,'' he said.

"Yes," she agreed, too happy to worry about caution. Besides, he was part of this. Without Jake she wouldn't have got this apartment. It was only right to share her pleasure with him.

CHAPTER EIGHT

THE restaurant Jake drove her to was on the beach side of The Esplanade, just along from the old Bathers' Pavilion, which he pointed out in passing, informing her it was a historic landmark at Balmoral. Amy smiled over the name. It conjured up men in long shorts and singlets, and women in bathing costumes with skirts and bloomers.

The past, however, was wiped out of her mind as Jake led her into an ultra-modern dining room that shouted class with a capital C. "Table for Carter," he murmured to the woman who greeted them, while Amy was still taking in the huge floral arrangement in the foyer—a splendid array of Australian flora in an urn. The waratahs alone would have cost a small fortune.

Her heels clacked on polished floorboards as Jake steered her into following the woman. Well-dressed patrons sat in comfortable chairs at tables dressed in starched white linen and gleaming tableware. They bypassed a bar that curved around from the foyer and headed towards a wall of glass which seemed to rise from the water beyond it.

This was an illusion, as Amy realised when she was seated right next to the window. There was a strip of beach below them, but they were so close to the waterline, the sense of being right on top of it stayed. Outside, a long wharf was lapped by waves and pelicans were using it as a resting place. Inside, she was handed a menu and asked what she'd like to drink.

"Two glasses of champagne," Jake answered, and gave Amy a smile that fizzed into her blood.

"And a jug of iced water, please," she quickly added, telling herself she needed to keep a cool head here.

She'd been in classy restaurants many times with Jake and a party of his clients, but never before alone with him. The setting engendered a sense of intimacy, as well as a sense of special occasion. A glance at the prices on the menu left Amy in no doubt she was being treated to top class, and the dishes described promised gourmet standard from the chef. She wasn't sure it felt right to be sharing this much with her boss.

"Did you book a table before we left the office?" she asked.

He looked up from his menu, his golden eyes glowing warm contentment. "Yes, I did. Great forethought, wasn't it?" he said with sublime confidence in her agreement.

"There might not have been anything to celebrate," she pointed out.

"Then it would have been a fine consolation for disappointment. Besides, it's lunchtime. On the principle we have to eat, why not eat well? Superb food here. Have you chosen yet?"

"No. It all looks marvellous."

"Good! I figured you needed your appetite tempted. Can't have you pining away on me."

Relieved of any cause for battle, Amy returned her attention to the menu, satisfied she understood Jake's motives. This lunch was part of his program to push her into forgetting her grief and promote the attitude that life was still worth living. Put her in a new environment, lift her spirits with champagne, stuff her up with delicious comfort food, and Amy Taylor would be as good as gold again.

She smiled to herself as she made her choice, deciding on her favourite seafoods. Making the most of Jake's fix-it ideas was definitely the order of the day. He probably didn't have a clue about broken hearts. He never stayed in a relationship long enough to find out. Nevertheless, Amy had to admit he was positively helping her over a big emotional hump.

After this sinfully decadent lunch, they'd be dropping in at Ted Durkin's office to sign the lease on the apartment. She could take up occupation next Saturday. What had loomed as a long, miserable, empty week ahead of her would now be filled with the business of organising the move and coloured with the anticipation of all it would mean to her. To some extent, Jake was right with his practical solutions. Life didn't stay black when good things happened.

Their champagne arrived and their orders were taken. Jake lifted his glass, his eyes twinkling at her over it. "To the future," he toasted.

Amy happily echoed it. "The future. And thanks for everything, Jake. I really appreciate your kind consideration."

"What would I do without your smile? It makes my day."

She laughed at his teasing, then sat back in her chair, relaxing, allowing herself the luxury of viewing him with warmth. "I like working with you," she admitted. "It's never boring."

"Amy, you're the best assistant I've ever had. In fact, you're the perfect complement to me."

He was talking about work, nothing but work, she insisted to herself, yet there was something in his voice that furred the edges of sharp thinking and her heart denied any breakage by hop, skip, and jumping all over the place.

"Jake, darling!"

The jarring intrusion snapped Amy's attention to the woman who had suddenly materialised beside Jake. A blonde! A very voluptuous blonde! Who proceeded to stroke her absurdly long and highly varnished fingernails down Jake's sleeve in a very provocative, possessive manner.

It was like a knife twisting in a fresh wound. Amy could see Steve's blonde getting her claws into him, never mind that he belonged to another woman. A marauding blonde, uncaring of anything but her own desires. This one was insinuating herself between Amy and Jake, splitting up their private celebration party, stealing the lovely comfortable mood, demanding to be the focus of attention.

"What a surprise, seeing you here today!" she cooed to Jake, not asking any pardon for intruding.

Amy hated her. She wanted to tear that hand off Jake's sleeve and shove it into the woman's mouth, shutting off the slavering drool of words.

"An unexpected pleasure, Isabella," Jake returned smoothly, starting to rise from his chair, dislodging her hand.

Isabella! Of course, she'd have a name like that, Amy seethed. Something sexy and exotic.

"No, please stay seated." It was another excuse to touch him, to curl her talons around his shoulder. The blonde bared perfect teeth at Amy. Piranha teeth. "I don't think I've met your companion."

"Amy Taylor...Isabella Maddison," Jake obliged.

"Hi!" the blonde said, the briefest possible acknowledgement.

Amy met her feline green eyes with a chilly blue blast and nodded her acknowledgement, not prepared to play the all jolly friends game. She didn't want to know Isabella Maddison, didn't care to greet an uninvited intruder, and would not pretend to welcome a predatory blonde into her company.

Her and her "Jake, darling!" How rude could you get? It was perfectly obvious the blonde was putting in her claim in front of a possible rival and didn't care what it took to win. Never mind dimming Amy's pleasure, taking the shine off the day, pushing herself forward to block Amy out.

"Great party on Saturday night, Jake," Isabella enthused, giving it a sexy innuendo.

"Yes. A lot of fun," he replied.

Fun! The urge to have a bit of fun herself blew through Amy's mind. "What a pity I couldn't be there!" she said ruefully. "Jake and I have the best fun together, don't we, darling?"

His head jerked to her, eyes startled. He recovered fast, his mouth curving into his whimsical smile. "Ain't that the truth?" he drawled.

'Jake always says we complement each other perfectly,'' Amy crowed, buoyed so much by his support, she batted her eyelashes at the blonde bombshell.

''Then you should have been there, shouldn't you?'' came the snaky return comment, accompanied by a suggestively raised eyebrow.

''Oh, I don't know.'' Amy shrugged and swirled the champagne around in her glass as she gave Jake a smouldering look. ''Some men like a bit of rope. I don't mind as long as I can reel him in whenever I want to.''

''Amy is very understanding,'' Jake said, nodding his appreciation.

''Well, perhaps another time, Jake,'' Isabella purred, undeterred from a future romp.

''Oh, I doubt it.'' Amy poured syrup into her voice. ''He rarely dips into the same well twice.'' She bared her teeth. ''Take a friendly word of advice. Best to move on to greener pastures. He is sort of stuck with me for the long haul.''

Isabella started to retreat. ''If you'll excuse me…''

''With pleasure,'' Amy said to speed her on her way, then downed half the champagne to celebrate her going.

Jake's eyes were dancing with unholy amusement. ''My wildest fantasy come true…you fighting another woman for me.''

''Huh!'' Amy scoffed. ''That'll be the day.''

''Am I not to believe my ears?''

''She had the wrong coloured hair.''

''Ah!'' His wicked delight took on a wry twist. ''The other woman.''

''Sorry if I've queered your pitch with her.'' She wasn't sorry at all, but it seemed an appropriate thing to say. After all, when all was said and done, he was still her boss. Though he could have stopped her roll if anything important was at stake. She would have taken her cue from him.

"No problem," he said carelessly.

"No, I don't suppose it is." Cynicism streaked through her. "If you snapped your fingers she'd come again."

"Isabella has no claim on me." It was a surprisingly serious statement, and his eyes held hers intently, as though he was assuring her he spoke the truth.

It was meaningless to Amy. No woman ever seemed to have a *claim* on him. "Is she your latest interest?" For some reason, she really wanted to know.

"No," he answered without hesitation.

"Just one of the hopeful crowd that trails after you," Amy said dryly.

He shrugged. "It hardly matters if I'm not interested, does it? To be blunt, Isabella doesn't appeal to me. She never will appeal to me. Any hope she might be nursing is therefore futile."

Goodbye, Isabella.

Amy was pleased that Jake had more taste than Steve. For both the men in her life to fall into the clutches of predatory blondes would have been altogether too wretched to bear. Not that Jake was an *intimate* part of her life, but he was a big chunk and she wanted to respect his judgement of character.

His quirky little smile came back. "You are quite a formidable fighter, Amy."

She shrugged. "You did encourage me, taking my side. If you'd clamped down on me..."

"And miss that performance?" His eyes sparkled admiration.

"The fact remains..." It felt really good that he'd supported her. "...You let me win, Jake."

He lifted his glass of champagne in another toast. "We're a team, Amy. A great team."

"A team," she echoed happily, and drank to the splendid sense of well-being flowing from being a solid team with Jake.

Their first course arrived.

Amy ate with gusto. Not only was the food fantastic, her tastebuds were fully revived from the weekend when everything she'd tried to eat seemed to have the texture of cardboard, indigestible. Maybe having a healthy appetite was a side effect from feeling victorious. Defeat was certainly the pits.

"More champagne?" Jake asked, seeing her down the last drops in her glass.

"No, thanks. I'd better move on to iced water. I think I've been hot-headed enough today."

He grinned. "Some things need letting out of your system. Especially the deep down and poisonous stuff."

"Well, I'm almost squeaky clean again."

"What a shame! So much volatile passion flying around. It's been quite an exciting experience watching it in action. Intriguing, too. Shows me a side of you you've kept under wraps. Not that I didn't suspect it was there."

Amy sat very still because her heart was fluttering extremely fast. Jake was regarding her with simmering speculation. The cat was out of the bag, well and truly, and she'd let it out with her wild flights off the rails. If she wasn't careful, the cat would feel free to pounce!

Twice she'd zoomed out of control, losing any semblance of the cool she'd kept with Jake. She could make excuses for herself. Jake was obligingly accepting them. But that didn't put things back the way they were between them.

"Anything else you'd like to spit out? Get off your chest?" he invited, clearly relishing exploring this newly revealed side of her.

Amy needed a safe topic fast, preferably focused on him instead of her.

"Yes. Since I've now been introduced to your sister, would you mind telling me about your family?" Her curiosity had been piqued by Ruth's revelations this morning.

"Not at all. What do you want to know?"

"Is there only you and Ruth?"

"Ruth is the youngest. I'm the next youngest. Above us are two older brothers, both very respectably settled down with families. Mum does her best to rule over us all and Dad lets us be."

"Do they all live in Sydney?"

"Yes."

"And you're the wild one."

He laughed. "They called me the adventurer when I was a kid."

He still was, Amy thought. "Tell me why," she prompted, eager to know more about him, to understand where he came from.

Again he obliged her, putting her at ease by regaling her with amusing stories from his childhood. Freed from the disturbing sexual pull he could exert on her, Amy enjoyed listening.

It was easy to imagine a little Jake trotting off on his own to explore the exciting things the world had to offer, worrying his mother, trying the patience of his older brothers who were sent to find him after they'd neglected to mind him properly. Ruth had become his partner in voyages of wonder when she was old enough, happy to be led anywhere by Jake.

The first course was cleared from their table. The main course was served and consumed. They were both persuaded to order the divine-sounding apple and brandy soufflé served with a lemon and kiwi fruit compote to finish off the meal.

The stories went on, eagerly encouraged by Amy. Hearing about a happy childhood, and a family that wasn't in any way dysfunctional, was something new to her, almost magical. She tended not to think about her own—no happy memories there—and Steve had been an only child whose parents had divorced when he was eight. He'd virtually lived in a world of computer games through his teens and they were still an escape for him whenever an argument loomed.

She wondered if his blonde knew that about the man she'd snaffled. Avoidance was Steve's answer to confrontation. Which was probably why Amy had been presented with his fatherhood and the date of his marriage, showing in one inarguable stroke there was no point in fighting.

Anything for a peaceful life. Steve's philosophy. She'd thought it was good but it wasn't really. Problems never got properly aired.

"I've lost you."

Jake's dry comment drew her attention back to him. She smiled. "No. I was just thinking how lucky you are not to have any fears. Or inhibitions. You were very blessed being born into your family, Jake."

He cocked his head slightly. The speculation in his eyes gradually took on the wolfish gleam that usually played havoc with her nerves. Maybe she'd been lulled by her good fortune, the champagne and fine food. Instead of alarm, she felt a tingling thrill of challenge.

"Everyone has fears, Amy," he drawled. "And inhibitions are placed upon them, whether they want them or not."

"Like what?" she said recklessly.

"Well, take you and me. I'd like nothing better than to race you off to bed and make mad passionate love for the rest of the afternoon."

For one quaking moment, Amy was tempted.

Then Jake gave his quirky smile and added, "But if I had my wicked way, I'm afraid you might bolt out of my life, and I wouldn't like losing you. So here I am…hopelessly inhibited."

The soufflés arrived.

"Consolation," Amy said, doing her utmost to hide both the shock and the relief she felt.

Jake laughed and picked up his spoon. *"Bon appétit!"*

Off the hook, Amy thought gratefully. The temptation had come so swiftly and sharply, she was still quivering inside. She sternly bent her mind to reasoning it away.

It was because the physical attraction had always been there, and with Steve's defection, pursuing it was no longer forbidden. And it felt great having Jake at her side, fighting on her behalf against Steve, against the blonde, treating her as though she was precious to him.

But it would be crazy—absolutely crazy—to get sexually involved with Jake. She'd only be one of an endless queue—another little adventure—and how on earth would she be able to work with him afterwards? She'd hate it when he dumped her and took up with someone else. As he surely would.

Besides, she didn't really want to make love with him. It was just that he'd made her feel desirable, like a winner instead of a loser and a reject. It was simply a seductive situation. And he'd thought better of it, too, applying solid common sense.

Here she was on a winning streak and it would be really silly to spoil it. Today had brought her a wonderfully ego-boosting salary, and an apartment that was close to paradise. However tempting it might be to add a new lover to the list, it was best to get any thought of tangling with her boss in bed right out of her mind.

She put down her spoon and then realised she'd shovelled the soufflé down her throat without really tasting it. Wasted, she thought. Which was a pity. A delight missed.

A glance across the table showed Jake had finished his, too. She didn't know for how long but she suddenly felt him keenly observing her and had the awful sense he'd been reading her thoughts. She glanced at her watch, anxious to divert any further disturbing exchanges between them.

''Good heavens! The afternoon's almost gone!'' Her gaze flew to his in sharp appeal. ''We'd better leave, Jake.''

He checked his watch, raising his eyebrows in surprise. "You're right. Got to get that lease signed on our way back to the office." He signalled for the bill and smiled at Amy. "A good day's work."

She laughed, trying to loosen up. "We've played hookey for hours."

"There's a time and place for everything," he answered blithely.

And this wasn't quite the time and place...yet...for what he had in mind.

Amy tried to scotch the thought but it clung. "I'll just make a quick visit to the powder room," she said, rising from the table, hoping she wasn't appearing too skittish.

"Fine. I'll meet you in the foyer."

She had her armour in place when she emerged from the powder room. Jake was waiting, looking well satisfied with his world. He wasn't about to race her off, not without appropriate encouragement from her, anyway. She was safe with him as long as she kept herself under control.

"What's the name of this restaurant?" she whispered as they headed outside.

"The Watermark."

"Ah! Very appropriate. It was a wonderful lunch, Jake. Thank you."

"I enjoyed it, too."

No doubt about that, Amy thought. The teasing twinkle in his eyes was not the least bit dimmed. Jake Carter always lived to fight another day. He settled her in his car with an air of the man in possession.

But he wasn't.

Thanks to Steve, Amy *was* a free spirit.

The name of the restaurant lingered in her mind as they drove towards completing the business of the day. *The Watermark…* It made her think of tides. When one rolled out, another rolled in. High points, low points. She wondered if making love with Jake Carter would be like eating a soufflé—a delight and then nothing.

Sex without love.

Forget it, she told herself.

Missing it didn't hurt her one bit.

CHAPTER NINE

AMY did her best to carry a positive attitude home with her that evening. She didn't allow the emptiness of the apartment she'd shared with Steve swamp her with depression. Soon it would be empty of both of them, she told herself. This phase of her life was over. Another was starting and she was going to make the most of it.

She made lists of what had to be done; contact the agency that handled the Bondi apartment and give notice of moving, telephone and electricity bills to be finalised, look up removalists and get estimates, collect boxes for packing. She was mentally arranging her furniture in the new Balmoral apartment when the telephone rang, jolting her back to the present.

Amy felt reluctant to answer the call. It might be for Steve, someone who didn't know he was gone, and she would have to explain. Shock and sympathy would follow and she'd be forcefully reminded of her grief and humiliation. She glared at the telephone, hating its insistent burring, wanting to be left alone to pick up her new life.

The summons finally stopped. Amy sighed in relief. Maybe it was cowardly not to face up to the truth, but it was such a hurtful truth she just wanted to push it aside. To her increasing chagrin, however, she was not left in peace. The telephone rang on and off for the next hour, demanding an answer. She balefully considered taking the receiver off the hook, then realised that could instigate an inquiry from the telephone company since the caller was being so persistent.

In the end, the need to cut off the torment drove her to snatch up the receiver. "Amy Taylor," she snapped into it.

"Thank heaven! I was getting really worried about you, Amy. It's Brooke Mitchell here."

Brooke! Amy instantly grimaced. Her least favourite person amongst her acquaintances.

"When Ryan came home from work and told me what Steve had done, I just couldn't believe it at first," she blathered on. "Then I thought of you and how you must be feeling, you poor dear…"

"I'm fine," Amy interrupted, recoiling from the spurious gush of sympathy.

Gush of curiosity more like! Brooke Mitchell lived for gossip, revelled in it, and Amy had never really enjoyed her company. Brooke just happened to be married to Ryan who worked with Steve and the two men were both computer heads, moving their common interest into socialising occasionally.

"Are you sure? When you weren't answering the phone…"

"I've only just come in," Amy lied.

"Oh! I had visions of you…well, I'm relieved you haven't…uh…"

"Slit my wrists? I assure you I'm not the least bit suicidal, Brooke. No drama at all." *For you to feed off,* Amy silently added.

"I didn't mean…it's just such devastating news. And I can't say how sorry I am. I don't know how Steve could have done it to you. Infidelity is bad enough but getting the woman pregnant and deciding to marry her…after all the years you've been together…''

Amy gritted her teeth. Brooke was rubbing salt into the wound.

''…It's just terrible,'' she went on. ''Though I've never thought living together was a good idea. You should have nailed him down, Amy. It's the only way to be sure of them.''

It was the smug voice of a married woman. Amy refrained from saying divorce statistics didn't exactly prove Brooke right. It would have sounded like sour grapes.

''If you need a shoulder to cry on…''

The memory of Jake holding her brought a sudden rush of warmth, taking the nasty chill off this conversation. ''I'm really fine, Brooke. In fact, I've had a lovely day. Jake Carter, my boss, took me out to lunch to celebrate my new freedom.''

Which was almost true.

''You told him about Steve?'' Real shock in her tone this time.

Caught up on a wave of bravado, Amy ploughed on in the same vein. ''Yes, I did. And Jake convinced me I was well rid of him, so don't be concerned about me, Brooke.''

''I see.'' Doubt mixed with vexation at this turn of events. ''Didn't you tell me your boss was a rake?''

''Mmh. Though I'm thinking it might well be a worthwhile experience being raked over by Jake Carter.''

''Amy! Really!''

''Yes. Really,'' she echoed, determined on wiping out

any image of her being thrown on the scrap heap, too crushed to raise any interest in another man.

"Well…" Brooke was clearly nonplussed. "I was feeling so awkward about bringing up next Saturday's party. I mean, when I invited you and Steve, I expected you to be together. Now…well, it is awkward, Amy. Ryan says Steve will want to bring…"

"Yes, of course," Amy rushed in, her heart contracting at the thought of the pregnant blonde on Steve's arm, queening it in Amy's place. And the plain truth was, Steve was far more Ryan's friend than she was Brooke's.

"But if you want to bring Jake Carter…" Her voice brimmed over with salacious interest.

"I was about to say I have other plans, Brooke. It was kind of you to be concerned about me and I'm glad you called. I'd forgotten about the party. Please accept my apologies. And I do wish you and Ryan a very merry Christmas."

She put the receiver down before Brooke could ask about her plans, which were none of the other woman's business. It gave Amy some satisfaction to think of Brooke speculating wildly about Jake, instead of pitying her, but it had probably been a rash impulse to use him to save her pride. The word would be quickly spread…

So what? Amy thought miserably. It would probably salve everybody's unease about excluding her from future activities. Brooke had been angling to cancel the party invitation and she wouldn't be the only one to dump Steve's ex-partner in favour of his wife-to-be.

When couples broke up, it forced others to make choices and the pragmatic choice was to accept a couple rather than a suddenly single woman who could either be a wet blanket at a social gathering or a threat to other women's peace of mind.

Depression came rolling in as she realised she was now a social pariah and she didn't really have friends of her own. The five years of sharing her life with Steve had whittled them away, and the past two years as Jake's personal assistant had kept her so busy, she literally hadn't had the time to develop and nurture real friendships. In fact, she felt closer to her boss than she did to anyone else at the present moment, and that brought home what a sorry state she was in.

Jake had filled the emptiness today but she knew how foolish it would be to let herself become dependent on him to fill her future. She had to take control of her own life, find new avenues of meeting people. The need-to-do list she'd made seemed to mock her. It would get her through the next week, but what then?

Amy couldn't find the energy to think further. She went to bed and courted oblivion. Being without Steve had to get easier, she reasoned. Everyone said time was a great healer. Soon she'd be able to go to bed and not think of him cuddled up to his blonde. In sheer defence against that emotional torment, she started visualising what it might be like to be cuddled up with Jake Carter. It was a dangerous fantasy but she didn't care. It helped.

Though it didn't help her concentration on work the next day. It made her acutely aware of every physical aspect of the man, especially his mouth and his hands. Even the cologne he wore—a subtle, sexy scent—was an insidious distraction, despite its being the same cologne he always wore. It didn't matter how sternly she berated herself for imagining him in Steve's place, the fantasy kept popping into her head, gathering more and more attractive detail.

It was terribly disconcerting. Thankfully, Jake didn't notice how super-conscious she was of him. He seemed totally tied up with business, not even tossing her teasing remarks. Certainly there was no allusion to any wish to race her off and make mad passionate love, nor any suggestion it was on his mind.

Amy hoped her stupid boast to Brooke Mitchell would never reach his ears. Not that she'd meant it. It was purely a reaction to circumstances, not a real desire. She knew better than to actually *want* Jake Carter in her bed. In the flesh.

The only personal conversation came at the end of the day as she was preparing to leave. Jake stood in the doorway between their offices, watching her clear her desk. "Are you holding up okay, Amy?" he asked quietly.

She flushed at the question. "I am *not* suicidal!" she snapped, the conversation with Brooke all too fresh in her mind, plus everything else that had flowed from it.

Jake's eyebrows shot up. "The thought never entered my mind."

"Then why ask?" she demanded, dying at the thought he'd noticed how jumpy she was around him.

His mouth quirked. "Guess you've already had well-meaning friends nattering in your ear."

"You could say that."

"Do you still plan to move house on Saturday?"

"Absolutely. Saturday can't come fast enough."

The quirk grew into a grin that seemed to say *That's*

my girl! and Amy's heart pumped a wild stream of pleasure through her body, spreading a warm, tingly feeling.

"You seemed rather unsettled today," he remarked with a shrug. "It made me wonder if there was too much on your plate. Moving can be a hassle if you intend to do it without the help of well-meaning friends."

"I've got it all lined up," she informed him, although it wasn't quite true. She had spent the lunch hour on the telephone, organising what she could.

"Fine! If you need some time off, just ask. If there's anything I can do to facilitate the resettling process…"

"Thanks, Jake." She smiled, relieved he'd put her edginess down to her emotional state over Steve. "I think I can manage but I'll let you know if I need some time off."

He nodded, apparently satisfied. "One other thing, Amy. You know we've sent out brochures and invitations to the New Year's Eve cruise on *Free Spirit.*"

"Yes." The magnificent yacht came instantly to mind, pure luxury on water. The cruise, which would feature the fireworks display over the harbour on New Year's Eve, had a guest list of potential clients, all of whom could be interested in chartering the yacht for either business or pleasure. As Jake had it planned, New Year's Eve was the perfect showcase for *Free Spirit.*

"Well, if you're not tied up that evening, I'd really appreciate your hostessing for me on the yacht. I know it's work on a holiday night, but you would get a front-line view of the fireworks and they're supposed to be the best ever."

Amy barely heard his last words. Her mind was stuck

on *not tied up*. Steve would certainly be tied up. It was his wedding night. He and his blonde bride would be…

"I'll be happy to hostess for you," she rushed out, welcoming any distraction from those thoughts and the curdling that had started in her stomach.

"Thanks, Amy. It should be a most productive evening."

No, it won't, she thought. The production was already in place. The only difference would be the wedding rings, holding it together.

"And a fun time, as well," Jake went on.

Fun! Well, she could always fall overboard and drown herself. Except she wasn't suicidal.

"You can count on me," she said dully.

"Good!" He gave her a casual salute. "Happy packing."

It was more a case of ruthless packing, than happy. In sorting through the contents of drawers, Amy discovered Steve had left behind all the photographs of their life together, as well as mementos from their skiing trips and seaside vacations. She threw them out. Threw out the clothes that reminded her of special occasions, too. If he could walk away from it all, so could she.

When tears occasionally fell over silly, sentimental things, she dashed them away, determined on not faltering in her resolution. It occurred to her that death would be easier to accept than betrayal. At least you were allowed to keep good memories when someone died, but all her memories of Steve were tainted now. She could never again feel *good* about him. Best to let him go. Let the hurt go, too.

Unfortunately, however hard she worked at achieving

that end, she couldn't make the awful sense of aloneness go. Even the strong connection she felt with Jake Carter was not enough to dispel it. That couldn't be allowed to progress to real intimacy, so the pleasure of it was always mixed with a sense of frustration. Which added to her feeling of defeat, as though she was fated to be drawn to men who would never ultimately satisfy her.

She welcomed the weekend, eager for the move to Balmoral and the change it would bring to her life. No one except Jake knew about it. Easier to cut her losses, she'd argued to herself. Those who might try to contact her were all connected to Steve and she guessed that any caring interest would quickly fade once she was completely out of the picture. In any event, it was better for her to move on.

She did not regret walking out of the Bondi apartment for the last time on Saturday morning. It was a glorious summer day, an appropriate omen to leave gloom behind and fly off to the *wide blue yonder*. She smiled over her use of Jake's company name. It did have a great ring to it, promising an adventure that obliterated the greyness of ordinary day-to-day life.

As she followed the removalist's van across the Sydney Harbour Bridge, her spirits were buoyed by the sense of going somewhere new and exciting, and when she arrived at Balmoral, it was every bit as lovely as she remembered it. So was the apartment.

She did, however, have an odd sense of *déjà vu* on looking into the master bedroom. The new carpet was turquoise, almost the exact shade as used in the offices at Milsons Point. Then she realised the paintwork was similar, too. It felt uncanny for a moment, almost as if

Jake had left the imprint of his personality here. But the colours were easy to live with and an attractive combination. Anyone could have chosen them.

Having already planned where to place her furniture, Amy was able to direct the removalist men efficiently. They came and went in very short time. She spent the rest of the day, unpacking suitcases and boxes, exulting over how much space she had in cupboards and arranging everything to please herself.

When she was finally done, fatigue set in, draining her of the excitement that had kept her fired with energy. She was here, old shackles cut, bridge crossed, ready to write a new page in her life, yet suddenly it didn't mean as much as she wanted it to. There was no one to show it to, no one to share it with, and the black beast of loneliness grabbed her again.

She wandered around, still too wired up to relax. Watching television didn't appeal. She plumped up the cushions on her cane lounge suite, eyed its grouping with the small matching dining setting, and knew she'd only be fiddling if she changed it. The view should have soothed her but it didn't. Somehow it imbued her with the sense of being in an ivory tower, separated from the rest of the human race.

The ringing of her doorbell made Amy almost jump out of her skin. A neighbour? she wondered. Even a stranger was a welcome face right now. In her eagerness to make an acquaintance, she forgot to take precautions, opening the door wide and planting a smile on her face.

Jake Carter smiled back at her.

Jake, exuding his charismatic sexiness, looking fresh and yummy and sun-kissed in an orange T-shirt and white shorts, lots of tanned flesh and muscle gleaming at her, taunting her with its offering of powerful masculinity, accessible masculinity, his wicked, yellow wolf's eyes eating up her dishevelled state and his smile saying he liked it and wouldn't mind more.

Amy's impulses shot from wanting to hug him for coming, to a far wilder cocktail of desires running rampant. Or was it need clawing through her? It was madness, anyway. She felt virtually naked in front of him, clothed only in skimpy blue shorts and a midriff top that she usually wore to her aerobics class. Quivers were attacking her stomach and her breasts were tightening up. Indeed, she felt her whole body responding to the magnetic attraction of his.

It was scary.

Alarming.

And the awful part was she sensed he knew it and wasn't the least bit alarmed by it. He was positively revelling in it. And he'd come here at this hour, when she was so rawly vulnerable, having burnt all her bridges, making himself available to her, seeking entry…Jake, the rake.

The moment those words slid into her mind, sanity bolted back into it, repressing the urges that had been scrambling common sense. In sheer, stark defence, words popped out of her mouth, words she would have given anything to take back once they were said, but they hung there between them, echoing and echoing in her ears.

"I'm not going to bed with you."

CHAPTER TEN

"ACTUALLY, I was thinking about feeding other appetites," Jake drawled, holding up a plastic carrier bag that held takeaway containers and a paper bag bulging with bottles of wine.

Amy flushed scarlet. She knew it had to be scarlet because her whole body felt as though it was going up in flames. Even her midriff.

"First things first," Jake burbled on. "Moving is a hot, thirsty business and you've probably been run ragged today, too tired by now to think of bothering with a proper dinner, even if you did get provisions in."

Which she hadn't, except for absolute basics.

"And since you insisted on doing all this on your own, I thought you might welcome company at this point. Winding down at the end of the day, putting your feet up, enjoying some tasty food and a glass of wine…"

He was doing it to her again, pouring out a reasonable line of logic she couldn't argue with. Except he was here at the door of her home. And it wasn't business hours. And he certainly wasn't dressed for business. This was personal.

With Jake Carter, personal with a woman meant…

His eyes twinkled their devilish mischief. "But if you want to change your mind about going to bed with me later on in the evening…"

"There! I knew it!" she shot at him triumphantly, having worked her way out of the hot fluster.

"Whatever you decide is okay by me, Amy," he blithely assured her. "I wouldn't dream of going where I wasn't wanted."

"I didn't invite you here, Jake," she swiftly pointed out.

"Telepathy," he declared. "It's been coming at me in waves all day. Couldn't ignore it."

"I haven't thought of you once!"

"Subconscious at work. No one here to share things with. Low point coming up."

Suspicion glared back at him. "Sounds more like psychology to me." *Get the girl when she's down!*

"Well, you could be right about that," he grandly conceded. "I guess I was compelled by this sense of responsibility towards you."

"What responsibility?"

"Well, I said…Jake, my boy, you more or less pushed Amy into that apartment. There she is, without her familiars, and the least you can do is turn up and make sure she's okay."

"I'm okay," she insisted.

His mouth moved into its familiar quirk. His woman-trap eyes glowed golden with charming appeal. "I brought dinner with me."

No one, Amy reflected, knew the art of temptation better than Jake Carter. She could smell the distinct aroma of hot Chinese mixtures. Her stomach had un-knotted enough to recognise it was empty. More to the point, sparring with Jake had banished the black beast of loneliness. If she sent him away…

"Dinner does sound good," she admitted.

"I hate eating alone," Jake chimed in, pressing precisely the button that had Amy wavering.

"I wouldn't mind sharing *dinner* with you," she said with arch emphasis.

"Sharing is always better." He cocked an eyebrow in hopeful appeal. "Can I come in now? I promise I won't even ask you to show me the bedroom."

No, he'd just sweep her off there, Amy thought, and the awful part was, the idea had a strong attraction. But he didn't know that…couldn't know it…and she was making the rules here.

"Be my guest," she said, standing back to wave him in. "You know where the kitchen is," she urged, not wanting him to linger beside her.

He breezed past, never one to push his luck when the writing was on the wall. As Amy shut the door after him, it occurred to her she might be driving the loneliness beast out, but she'd let the wolf in, a wolf who'd huffed and puffed very effectively, blowing her door down, so to speak.

On the other hand, he wasn't about to eat her for dinner. He'd brought Chinese takeaway. She could manage this situation. But she wouldn't feel comfortable staying in these clothes. She was too…bare.

Jake was happily unpacking his carrier bag, setting out his offerings along the kitchen counter. His white shorts snugly outlined the taut curve of particularly well-shaped buttocks. When it came to cute butts, Jake Carter could line up against any gym buff. As for power-packed thighs… Amy took a grip on herself, wrenching her mind off the seductive promise of so much impressive male muscle.

Looks weren't everything.

So what if Steve had been on the lean side in comparison?

"Lemon chicken, sweet and sour pork, Mongolian lamb, braised king prawns, chilli beef, fried rice." Jake shot her a dazzling grin as he finished listing his menu. "All ready for a banquet."

"Good choice," she commented as blandly as she could.

He laughed. "I have acquired some knowledge of your preferred tastes, Amy."

It surprised her. "You noticed?"

"There isn't much I haven't noticed about you in the two years you've been at my side." His gaze skated over her skimpy clothes. "Though I haven't seen you look quite so fetching as you do this evening. Very *au naturel*."

Amy instantly folded her arms across her midriff but she was acutely aware the action didn't hide the tightening of her nipples.

His eyes teased the flare of hard defence in hers. "Just as well I'm a man of iron control."

The need for evasive action was acute. "I was about to take a shower and clean up."

"Go right ahead." He waved expansively. "Make yourself comfortable. I'll get things ready for us here."

If he thought she was going to reappear in a sexy negligee, he was in for severe disappointment.

All the same, as Amy stood under the shower, soaping off the stickiness of the long, humid day, she couldn't help wondering how well she stacked up against Jake's other women. Thanks to her aerobics classes and a healthy diet, she was in pretty good shape, no flab or cellulite anywhere. No sag in her breasts.

She'd always been reasonably content with her body and normally she wasn't self-conscious about being nude. Not that she intended stripping off for Jake Carter. Besides which, he probably only fancied her because she remained a challenge to him. What physical attributes she had were really irrelevant.

With Jake it was always the challenge. Had to be. Which was why he lost interest once he'd won. At least, that was how it looked to Amy. Though she couldn't see there was much winning in it when women fell all over him anyway.

She decided to wash her hair, as well. It would do him good to wait. Show him she was not an eager beaver for his scintillating company. Besides, she felt more in control if she was confident of her appearance; fresh, clean, tidy, and properly clothed.

By the time she finished blow-drying her hair it was full of bounce and so was she, looking forward to keeping Jake in his place. She left her face bare of make-up since she wasn't out to impress. Jake could have that part of her *au naturel*.

Deciding jeans and a loose T-shirt would make a clear statement—demure and dampening—she tied the belt firmly on her little silk wraparound for the dash from bathroom to bedroom, opened the door to the hallway, and was instantly jolted from her set plan by a flow of words from Jake.

"She's in the shower, making herself comfortable."

He had to be talking to someone.

"Would you like a glass of champagne?" he burbled on, apparently having invited the someone into her apartment! "I've just poured one for Amy and myself."

"What the hell is going on here?"

The incredulous growl thumped into Amy's heart. It was unmistakably Steve's voice!

"Pardon?"

"Amy can't afford a place like this." Angry, belligerent suspicion.

The shock of hearing her ex-partner gave way to a fierce wave of resentment. How dare he judge or criticise!

"I gave her a raise in salary," Jake blithely replied. "She deserved it. Best P.A. in the world. Is it yes to the champers?"

"No. I only came to see that she was all right."

Guilt trip, Amy thought, writhing over how she'd been so hopelessly devastated last week.

"From the look of it I could have saved myself the trouble," he went on, the sneer in his voice needling Amy beyond bearing.

She whirled through the archway in a rage of pride, coming to a stage-stop as she took in the scene, Jake by the table he'd set for their dinner, brandishing a bottle of champagne, Steve standing by the kitchen counter, keeping his distance, obviously put out by her luxurious living area and Jake's presence.

His carefully cultivated yuppie image—the long floppy bang of hair dipping almost over one eye, the white collarless linen shirt and black designer jeans—somehow looked immature, stacked up against the raw male power so casually exhibited by Jake, and for once Amy was pleased Steve came off second-best in comparison. She fully intended to rub it into her ex-lover's ego. Let *him* be flattened this time!

"Good heavens! How on earth did you get here, Steve?" she trilled in amazement.

He gawped at her, making her extremely conscious of her nakedness under the silk and lace bit of froth, which, of course, he recognised as part of the seductive and sinfully expensive lingerie she'd bought herself for her last birthday, intending to pepper up their sex life. The outcome had been disappointingly limp, undoubtedly because he'd been bedding the blonde.

"Mmmh..." The sexy purr from Jake was meant to inflame. "I love your idea of comfortable."

"I'm so glad," she drawled, seized by the reckless need to prove she wasn't a downtrodden cast-off. Abandoning all caution, she ruffled her squeaky-clean hair provocatively as she sauntered towards Jake, knowing full well the action would cause a sensual slide of silk over her curves. "Champagne poured?"

"Ready to fizz into your bloodstream, darling."

The wicked wolf eyes were working overtime as he handed her a brimming glass. One thing she could say for Jake, he was never slow on the uptake. Right at this moment, his response was positively exhilarating. In the hunk stakes, Jake Carter was a star.

"Darling!" Steve squawked.

Hopefully he was feeling mortifyingly outshone! And very much the odd one out in *this threesome!*

"I've always thought she was," Jake tossed at him. "I should thank you for bowing out, Steve. It freed Amy up for me, got rid of her misplaced loyalty, opened her eyes…''

''I didn't do it for you,'' Steve chopped in, furious at finding himself upstaged by her boss.

''Which reminds me, where is your bride-to-be?'' Amy asked silkily, having fortified herself with a fine slug of alcohol. ''Lurking outside to see that you don't stay too long?''

''No, she's not!''

''Well, if I were her, I wouldn't trust you out of my sight. Not after working so hard to get a ball and chain on you.''

Let his *free spirit* wriggle on that barb, Amy thought bitterly. She sipped some more champagne to dilute the upsurge of bile from her stomach.

Steve's face bloomed bright red. To Amy, it was a very satisfying colour. Much better than the pallid white he'd left on her face a week ago.

''She knows I'm here. I told her…''

''And just how did you know where to come, Steve?'' she inquired with sweet reason. ''I haven't given this address to anyone.''

''Except me,'' Jake popped in, shifting to slide his arm around her shoulder in a man-in-possession hug. ''We've moved so much closer in the past few days.''

Amy snuggled coquettishly, getting quite a charge out of the hip and thigh contact.

Steve looked as if he was about to burst a blood vessel. Which served him right, having thrown a blonde and a baby in her face. He clenched his jaw and bit out his explanation.

"I went to the Bondi apartment this morning and saw our stuff being carried out to the removalist van…"

"*Our* stuff?" She couldn't believe he was backtracking on the division of their property. How crass could he get in the circumstances? "It was agreed this was *my* stuff."

"Mostly, yes. But there were little things I left behind. Overlooked in…well, not wanting to make things worse for you."

"Worse for whom?" she demanded with arch scepticism. "The great evader couldn't get out fast enough. That's the truth of it, Steve."

He flushed. "Have it your way. But I still want my things. And since you'd obviously packed up the lot, I followed the van here, then gave you time to unpack…"

"How considerate of you! What things?"

"Well, there were photographs and mementos…"

"I threw them all out."

"You…what?"

Amy shrugged. "Unwanted baggage. What's gone is gone," she declared and proceeded to drain her glass as though to celebrate the fact.

"One never enjoys being reminded of mistakes, Steve," Jake remarked wisely.

"You could have called me first," Steve spluttered accusingly.

"Sorry." She slid a sultry look up at Jake. "I've been somewhat distracted this week."

He instantly brushed his mouth over the top of her hair, murmuring, "Amy, I've got to tell you that scent you wear is extremely stimulating."

She wasn't wearing any scent. Unless he meant her

shampoo and conditioner. It occurred to her she was playing with fire but the warmth coursing through her felt so good she didn't care.

"Goddammit! I did my best to be decent to you," Steve bellowed.

"Oh? You call getting another woman pregnant being decent?" Amy flared.

"I bet you were already sneaking behind my back…"

"Amy sneak?" Jake laughed at him. "She is the most confrontationist woman I know. Sparks and spice and all things nice."

Steve glared furiously at her. "And I was fool enough not to believe Brooke when she told me you just couldn't wait to have it off with him."

"Well, sometimes Brooke does get things right," Amy fired back heedlessly.

"I feel exactly the same way," Jake declared with fervour. "In fact, I can hardly wait for you to leave."

"And you do have Brooke's party to go to," Amy pressed. "Apart from which, I'm sure your wedding will supply more suitable photos and mementos for your future." She lifted her glass in a mock toast. "Happy days!"

Unfortunately there was no champagne left in it to drink.

"Darling…" Jake purred "…let me take that empty glass." He plucked it out of her hand and set it on the table. "Bad luck you didn't get what you came for, Steve," he burbled on as he swept Amy into his embrace. "But as my girl here says, what's gone is gone. And it's well past time you were gone, too. Would you mind letting yourself out?"

''You know what she called you, Carter?'' Steve yelled at him, his face twisting in triumphant scorn. ''Jake the rake!''

''Well, fair's fair,'' Jake said, totally unperturbed. He whipped off his T-shirt and spread her hands against his bare chest. ''You can do some raking, too, Amy. I'd like that. I'd like that very much.'' And his voice wasn't a purr anymore. More like the growl of a wolf with his dinner in view.

It should have frightened her. This whole scene was flying out of her control. Yet the fierce yellow blaze in his eyes was mesmerising and his skin had a magnetic pulse that compelled contact.

''You'll regret it,'' Steve jeered, but the words seemed to come to her through a fog, setting them at an irrelevant distance, and the door slam that followed them was no more than an echo of the throb in her temples.

''Let me rake you as you've never been raked before,'' Jake murmured, the low throaty sound hitting on some wild primitive chord that leapt in eager response, and his fingers were running through her hair, tilting her head back.

Then it was too late to pull away, even if she'd found the will to do it, because his mouth took possession of hers and she was sucked into a vortex of irresistible sensation from which there was no escape, nor any wish to. The desire to drown in what Jake Carter could do to her was utterly, savagely overwhelming.

CHAPTER ELEVEN

THE sheer passion of that first kiss blew Amy's mind. Conscious thought was bombarded out of existence. An insatiable hunger swept in and took over, demanding to be fed, to be appeased, to be satisfied.

He tasted so good, his tongue tangling with hers in an erotic dance, arousing explosive tingles of excitement across her palate, stirring sensations that streamed through her body which instantly clamoured for a bigger share of what was going on, a more intense share.

Her hands flew up to get out of the way and her breasts fell against the hot heaving wall of his chest, squashing into it, revelling in the rub of silk and firm male flesh and muscle. Her fingers raked his shoulders, his hair, his back, finding purchase to press him closer. She squirmed with pleasure as his hands clawed down her back to close over her buttocks and haul her into a sweet mashing contact with even more prominent and stimulating masculinity.

Clothes formed a frustrating separation.

They got rid of them.

Then everything felt so much more delicious, incredibly sensual, body hair tickling, hard flesh sliding against soft, mouths meshing, moving to taste everything, greedy, greedy, greedy, loving it, relishing it, feeding on each other in a frenzy of wanting, licking, sucking, hands shaping pathways, beating rhythms, wildly pushing for

99

the ultimate feast of co-mingling, yet not wanting to forgo any appetiser along the way.

Exquisite anticipation, pulse racing, an urgent scream shrieking along nerve-endings, craving…and he lifted her up to make the most intimate connection possible and she wound her legs around his hips and welcomed him in, her muscles rippling convulsively, ecstatically as he filled the need.

And they were one—this wonderful man-wolf and the animal-woman he'd taken as his—as he went down on all fours, lowering her with him to some flat furry surface on the floor, and she tightened the grip of her legs around his hips, fearing the emptiness of losing him. But there was no loss. No loss at all.

With the purchase of ground beneath them he drove in deeper… oh, so soul-shakingly deep, the power of him radiating through her, waves and waves of it, building an intensity that rippled through every cell so it felt as though they were coalescing, melting, fusing with the thunder of his need to possess all of her, and she gave herself up to him, surfing the peaks he pushed her to, wallowing voluptuously in the swell of them, urging him on with wild little cries, exulting in the hot panting of his breath on her, the nails digging into her flesh, the pound of his heart, and the sheer incredible glory of this mating.

Even the ending of it felt utterly fulfilling, climactic in every sense, the shudder of his release spilling her into an amazing, floating, supernatural experience where all existence was focused internally and he was there— the warm, vital essence of him—and that part of him would always be part of her from this moment on.

Then his body sank onto hers, covering it in a final claim, imprinting the power, intoxicating her with it, lulling her into a peaceful acceptance of an intimacy which blotted out everything else because this had a life of its own and it was complete unto itself…like a primitive ritual enacted in a different world.

How long she lay in a euphoric daze, Amy had no idea. Somewhere along the line her mate had shifted both of them to lie on their sides, her body scooped against his spoon-fashion, one of his arms around her waist, the other cushioning her head. Gradually her eyes focused on the balcony she was facing and she became conscious of a strange reality.

Her two cane armchairs were sitting out there, along with the coffee table that served her lounge setting. She hadn't put them on the balcony. The glass doors were open and somehow those pieces of furniture had got out there without her knowledge. The table should be right in the centre of the mat in front of the lounge…except she was lying on the mat instead…and Jake Carter was lying right behind her…both of them very, very naked!

The slowly groping activity in Amy's mind stopped right there. A shock screen went up, forbidding any closer examination of how and when and why. A soft breeze was wafting in. It was pleasantly cool, certainly not cold enough to raise goose bumps, yet Amy's skin prickled with a host of them. Jake moved a big muscly leg over her thigh, nuzzled the curve of her shoulder and neck with a soft, seductive mouth, and slid his hand up from her waist to warm her breasts, his palm gently rotating over her highly sensitised skin.

"Getting cold?" he murmured.

''Yes.'' It was a bare whisper. Her throat had seized up, along with her shocked heart and frozen mind. She felt as paralysed as a rabbit caught in headlights.

''A hot spa bath should do the trick,'' he said, and before Amy could even begin to get herself into a semblance of proper working order, he'd somehow heaved them both off the floor and was carrying her to the bathroom, and she was staring over his shoulder at the mat where it had all happened.

Well, not quite all.

It had begun near the table. His orange T-shirt was hanging off one of the dining chairs. Her silk wraparound lay in a crumpled heap on the floor between the table and the lounge. A pair of white shorts had been pitched right across the room to droop drunkenly over the television set. She couldn't see what had happened to the sandals he'd been wearing.

Her view was blocked off as Jake moved through the archway and into the bathroom. He sat on the tiled ledge around the Jacuzzi, settled her on his lap and turned on the taps full blast. Amy didn't know where to look. Luckily he started kissing her again so she just closed her eyes and let him do whatever he liked.

Which he was extremely good at.

She certainly had to grant him that.

Though she was equally certain he had taken advantage of her…her susceptibility…to his…his manpower…which was stirring again and her body was riven by an uncontrollable urge to shift to a more amenable position, like sitting astride those two great thighs instead of across them.

As though Jake instinctively knew this was more appropriate, he rearranged her with such slick speed, it seemed like one lovely fluid movement with him sliding right back into the space that wanted him, filling it with a really delicious fullness.

It felt great. Even better when he started drawing her nipples into his mouth, tugging on the distended nubs, setting up a fantastic arc of sensation that zipped from her breasts to the deep inner sharing, driving her awareness of it to a kind of sensual madness that refused to be set aside.

The taps were turned off, the jets of water switched on and they slipped into the bath, still revelling in the erotic intimacy of being locked together. One part of her mind warned Amy she would have to face what she was doing with Jake Carter, but most of it just didn't want to think at all. Feeling was much more seductive and satisfying.

"Warm now?" he asked.

"Mmmh…"

He laughed, a low throaty gurgle coated with deep satisfaction. "Can't hold it in water, sweetheart, but let me tell you I've never had it so good."

She sighed over the inevitability of their connection ending, though she even found pleasure in his shrinking, feeling the relaxation of her inner muscles as the pressure decreased and tantalisingly slipped away. She peered through her lashes at the happy grin on his face and privately admitted she'd never had it so good, either, but she wasn't sure she should echo his words.

He was still Jake the rake.

Still her boss.

Letting him know he'd won first prize on the sexual

front might mess up things even worse than they'd already been messed up. Amy didn't know how to deal with this situation. Another bridge had been burnt and the future was now a lot murkier than it had been before. She pushed herself down to the other end of the bath and tried to get her mind into gear. Some straight thinking might help.

Jake raised his eyebrows at her in teasing inquiry while his eyes danced with the wicked knowledge that she couldn't ignore what they'd just shared.

Then she remembered the heart-sickening frequency of his sharing with other women. What if he told all of them he'd never had it so good? A charming ego-stroke to top everything off? And just in case he forgot their names in the heat of the moment...

"Don't call me sweetheart!"

The words shot out of her mouth with such vehemence, both of them were startled by their passionate protest. Amy was shaken by how violently she recoiled from having joined an easily forgotten queue, and Jake's good humour instantly lost its sparkle, his eyes narrowing, focusing intensely on her. His sudden stillness suggested he was harnessing all his energy to the task of perceiving the problem.

"I don't use that endearment loosely, Amy," he said quietly. "You *are* sweet to my heart. But if you don't like it..."

"I have a name. I'm not one of your passing parade, Jake. I'm your P.A.," she cried. "Just because I've committed the ultimate folly of going to bed with my boss, doesn't turn me into a no-name woman."

"You? Amy Taylor a no-name woman?" He threw

back his head and laughed. "Never in a million years!" A golden star-burst of twinkles lit his eyes. "And you know we didn't go to bed, Amy. You specifically said you weren't going to bed with me and I respected that decision."

Her insides were mush, churning with a million uncertainties, yet being hopelessly tugged by the sheer attraction of the man. Was she sweet to his heart? All she really knew was they'd done it, bed or no bed, and she was in a state of helpless confusion over what it meant or might mean to either of them.

Before she could think of any reply to him, he shook his head at her and offered a wry little smile as he made the pertinent comment, "Neither of us can blame ourselves for spontaneous combustion."

This implied he hadn't planned what happened, any more than she had. An accident of Fate? Or a convenient excuse?

"Was it?" she asked suspiciously.

"What?"

"Spontaneous combustion."

"It felt like that to me." His brow puckered for a thoughtful moment. "I remember I was swinging in with all the support I could think of for your out-of-my-life act, socking it home to your ex, then…yes, I'd definitely have to call it spontaneous combustion. Mind you, the chemistry was always there. No denying it."

Amy had to accept the undeniable truth that she'd played with fire, tempted the devil, and the ensuing conflagration could not be entirely laid at Jake's door. She sighed, letting go the craven wish to dissolve in the bath. There was no escaping what had to be faced.

"So what do we do now?" she asked, looking for some signal from him.

He grinned at her. "I suggest we have dinner. Both of us need re-fuelling."

Pragmatic Jake. One appetite burnt out...might as well get on with feeding another.

Which could then re-ignite the first and... Amy clamped down on that thought. She had to get sex with Jake off her brain. More practical matters needed to be settled.

"Okay," she agreed. "You dry yourself off first and I'll follow."

He eyed her quizzically. "You're not going shy on me, are you, Amy?"

It triggered a nervous laugh. "A bit late for that. I just want the bathroom to myself while I tidy up."

In truth, Amy didn't want to risk tangling physically with Jake, with or without towels. She needed some clear space here to tidy up her responses to him.

"Fair enough," he said and whooshed out of the bath, the massive displacement of water almost causing a tidal wave.

He was a big man. Stark naked, there was a lot of him, all of it impressive. Amy couldn't help staring. In every male sense he was well proportioned, well muscled and most decisively well endowed. Very well indeed. Her vaginal muscles went into spasms of excitement just looking at him, remembering how he'd felt and what he'd done.

It was just as well she was still lying in the bath. Jake didn't even have to apply the art of temptation in the nude. He was *it*. He turned to reach for a towel and his backside scored a perfect ten beyond a shadow of a doubt.

Amy was struck by a powerful insight. Lust was not a male prerogative. Lust could hit a woman like a runaway train. She was left wondering how on earth it could be stopped.

A more urgent question was…did she *want* it to be stopped?

CHAPTER TWELVE

DINNER was good. Jake didn't press anything but food on her. He played the charming host, ready to serve her every whim, encouraging her to try everything he'd brought, pleased when she did, obviously resolved on giving her a breathing space and setting a relaxed mood.

Amy appreciated it. She appreciated the food, too. It seemed to stabilise her stomach and clear her head. Her confusion over the sexual element that had scrambled their relationship, gradually sorted itself out into various straight avenues of thought.

Of course, it helped that Jake was fully clothed again. And she felt...safer, protected...in the jeans and T-shirt she'd planned to wear before Steve's fateful intrusion. Probably her choice of clothes had alerted Jake to her nervous tension and reservations about any further intimate involvement. He was never slow on picking up signals.

Nevertheless, there could be no avoiding a discussion on where they went from here. As they cleared the dishes from the table, transferring them to the kitchen counter, Amy decided it couldn't be postponed any longer. She could only hope Jake would understand her position.

"Coffee on the balcony?" he suggested.

Her gaze zapped to the armchairs and coffee table he must have put outside while she'd been in the shower prior to Steve's arrival. "You thought of that before," she blurted out, flushing with embarrassment as she recollected precisely when she'd noticed their removal to the balcony.

He shrugged. "It seemed a pleasant way to finish off the evening."

She looked him straight in the eye, something she'd had difficulty in doing throughout dinner. "You didn't come here to jump me, did you, Jake?"

"No," he answered unequivocally. His face softened into a warm, whimsical smile. "I do genuinely care about you. I didn't want you to feel alone."

Her heart turned over.

Maybe caring made the difference.

"Besides, jumping isn't my style," he went on. "I'm only interested in mutual desire."

Desire...lust...he'd probably *cared* about all the others, too.

His eyes gleamed their dangerous wolf-yellow. "And it is very mutual, Amy. Don't put other labels on it."

Don't put *love* on it...that was certain.

Mutual desire was not going to lead anywhere good and it was no use wishing it might. Heat raced into her cheeks again as she tried to explain her spontaneous combustion away.

"Jake...it was just a moment in time...because of Steve...and..."

"No." He shook his head at her. "At least be honest, Amy. We're not ships passing in the night. What happened has been building between us for a long time. A progression..."

"But we don't have to choose it," she cried, agitated

by the way he was validating what had been madness on both their parts. ''We work together, Jake. Please don't make it impossible for us to keep on working together.''

He frowned as though he hadn't taken that factor into consideration.

''I'll make the coffee,'' she said, scooting off to the kitchen, hoping to keep the counter between them for a while.

Clothes didn't really help, not when he started radiating physical charm and reminding her of the desires they had indulged so…so wildly. If he reached out and touched her, she wasn't sure she could resist touching back. She had the feeling an electric current would sizzle her brain and her body would proceed on its own merry way to meltdown.

To her intense relief, Jake wandered out to the balcony. She stacked the plates and cutlery into the dishwasher as the coffeemaker did its job. The activity covered her inner turmoil as she clung desperately to what was the only sensible resolution to this volatile situation.

It couldn't go on. Couldn't! Jake's idea of a *progression* threw her into a panic. The sex had been good. Amazing. Incredibly marvellous. But it wouldn't stay that way. Moods and feelings were rarely recaptured. Lust did peter out. She had the evidence of Jake's many affairs to demonstrate how quickly it passed.

The article in the women's magazine which still lay in the bottom drawer of her desk came sharply to mind. If she indulged herself in more physical pleasures with Jake Carter, she'd be looking for the exit signs, every minute of every day, not trusting their togetherness to last long. Then how awkward would it be when he started looking for a fresh experience? How destroying it would be!

No, it was wrong for her. It would mess her up even more than she was already messed up. No matter what he said or did, she couldn't allow herself to be tempted. Now was the time to start building a hopeful future for herself, not plunge down a sidetrack to more misery.

The coffeemaker beeped. She filled two mugs, steeled herself for the stand she had to make, then set out to fight the man who was undoubtedly plotting a different scenario. Her hands shook so much the coffee slurped over. She put the mugs on the counter and walked slowly around it, clenching and unclenching her hands. Her chest was so tight, her heart felt as though it was banging against it, stifled for proper room. Nevertheless, she did manage to carry the mugs out and set them on the coffee table without further spillage.

Jake was leaning on the balcony railing, apparently taking in the night view. He didn't turn even though he must have heard her. Having got rid of the mugs from her nervous hands, Amy fidgeted. Sitting down didn't feel right. It was impossible to relax enough to make it look natural. Yet to join Jake at the railing in the semi-darkness…

''Tell me what you want, Amy.''

The soft words caught at her heart, turning her doubts and fears into silly trivialities. Jake had moved on to the big picture. He was simply waiting for her to paint in how she saw it.

Without any further hesitation, she stepped over to the railing and took a deep breath of fresh sea air. The winking myriad of lights around the bay assured her of life going on in a normal fashion, despite the ups and downs everyone was subjected to from time to time. It was normality she needed now.

"I want to keep my job," she said simply.

He didn't move, not even to glance at her. She had the sense of him being darkly self-contained, waiting and listening, biding his time until he had what he needed to work with.

"There's no question of your losing it," he assured her.

"I want to feel comfortable in it. I need to feel secure in it," she explained further. "It's my anchor right now. If you take that away from me…"

"Why on earth would I?"

He sounded genuinely puzzled.

"You could make it too difficult for me to stay."

"You think I'm going to chase you around the office?" he asked, the dry irony in his voice mocking such a notion. "It's a fool's game, mixing business with pleasure, Amy. Have I ever seemed that much of a fool to you?"

"No."

"I respect you far too much to press unwanted attention on you anyway."

"I'm sorry. I…maybe I've got this wrong," she rushed out in an agony of embarrassment. "I shouldn't have assumed you'd want to…"

"Oh, yes, I want to, Amy. I really would be a fool not to want to make love with you whenever I can. Outside of office hours."

He spoke matter-of-factly yet Amy was left in no

doubt he meant every word of it. One taste was not enough for him. He wanted more, and just the thought of him wanting more aroused all the sensitised places in her body that craved the same.

"But I'd hate you to feel…under duress," he added, his voice dropping to a low rasp of distaste.

The choice was hers, he was saying, and she should have felt relieved, except she was so twisted up inside, her mind couldn't dictate anything sensible.

"It has to be freely given," he went on. "As it was tonight." He half turned to her, a lopsided smile curving his mouth. "You did want me, you know. Not because of Steve. You wanted *me*."

Amy was further shaken by the passion creeping through the quiet control he'd maintained. "Any woman would want you, Jake," she blurted out.

"You're not…any…woman." He flashed her a scathing look. "For God's sake, Amy! Do you think it's like that every time I turn around?"

"How would I know?" she flared back at him, losing the sane control she'd tried so hard to hold on to. "You turn around so often…"

"Because once I know it's not going to work I don't string a woman along as a convenient backup while I cheat on the side, as your precious Steve did," he shot at her.

Pain exploded through her. "Fine!" she fired back at him. "Just don't expect me to give repeat performances until you decide it's not working for you anymore. I'd rather choose my own exit, thank you very much."

He straightened up, aggression emanating from him in such strong waves, Amy almost cringed against the railing. Pride stiffened her spine. She was not going to be intimidated. The memory of her mother being cowed by her father flashed into her mind. Jake had that kind of power but she would not give in to it. Never! She would stand up for what was right for her, no matter what the consequences.

Maybe he sensed her fierce challenge. Something wrought a change. The aggression faded. She felt him— the strength of his will—reaching out to her even before he raised a hand in a gesture of appeal.

"It could be something special for both of us, Amy," he said in soft persuasion.

The fire in her died, leaving only the pain. "It *was* special. Please…leave it there," she begged. "I don't want to fight with you, Jake."

He sighed and offered a wry smile. "I don't want to fight with you, either. Nor do I want you to regret tonight."

She had a hazy memory of Steve yelling, *you'll regret it,* and everything within her rebelled against his mean-minded prediction. Besides, *he* had never once given her so much intense pleasure, never once swept her into such an all-encompassing sensual world. That belonged to Jake and she would never forget it…surely a once-in-a-lifetime experience which had exploded from a unique set of circumstances.

"I'll never regret it, Jake. It was something very special," she reiterated, because it was the truth and it was only fair to admit it to him.

His smiled widened, caressing her with his remembered pleasure. "Then you'll keep it as a good memory?"

He was giving in…letting go…

"Yes," she cried in dizzy relief.

"Of course, if you ever want to build on the good memory, you will keep me in mind," he pressed teasingly.

She laughed, the release of tension erupting through her so suddenly she couldn't help but laugh. It was the old Jake back again, the one she was used to handling, and she loved him for giving him back to her.

"I couldn't possibly consider anyone else," she promised him.

"I can rest content with that," he said, sealing the sense of security she'd asked him for. "And just remember, Amy, you're not alone. You do have me to count on."

Unaccountably after the laughter, tears swam into her eyes. "Thank you, Jake," she managed huskily, overcome with a mixture of sweet feelings that were impossible to define.

"It's okay," he assured her, then stepped over, squeezed her shoulder in a comradely fashion, gently pushed her hair aside and dropped a kiss on her forehead. "Goodnight, Amy. Don't you fret now. It's back to work on Monday."

She was swallowing too hard to say anything. He touched her cheek tenderly in a last salute, and she could only watch dumbly as he walked away from her. All the way to the door she felt the tug of him. Her body churned with need, screaming at her to call him back, take him into her bed, have him as long as she could.

But she stayed still, breathlessly still, and listened to the door closing behind him.

"Goodnight," she whispered.

It had been good.

Best that it stayed good.

CHAPTER THIRTEEN

DESPITE Jake's assurances, Amy's nerves were strung tight as she walked down Alfred Street on Monday morning. Resolutions kept pumping through her mind. She was not going to look at Jake and see him naked. She had to focus every bit of her concentration on the job. And act naturally.

Acting naturally was very important. No overt tension, no signs of agitation, no silly slips of the tongue. Think before you speak, Amy recited over and over again. Pretend it's last week. Pretend it's next week. No matter what she felt in the hours ahead of her, it would pass.

Determined not to falter, Amy pushed past the entrance doors to their office building and strode down the foyer to the elevators. "Hi, Kate!" she called to the receptionist, and practised a bright smile.

"Well, that's a happier start to the week," Kate remarked, smiling back. "No Monday blues. Things must have picked up for you."

Had it only been a week since Steve dumped her? Amy felt as though she'd shifted a long way since then. And she had. All the way to Balmoral. Which was absolutely lovely.

"Feeling good," she declared, pressing the Up button with blithe panache. Positive thinking had to help. "Boss in?"

"Up and running."

"How did your weekend go?" Amy asked, wondering if she could make a friend of Kate.

"I Christmas shopped till I dropped," she replied with a mock groan.

Christmas! Barely three weeks away. And she had no one to share it with this year. No one to buy presents for. But that didn't mean she couldn't celebrate it herself, buy a Christmas tree for the apartment and think of different things to do. She was not going to feel depressed. She had her composure in place and she simply couldn't afford to let anything crack it.

The elevators doors opened and Amy stepped in, throwing Kate a cheery wave. "See you later."

The ride in the elevator was mercifully short. Amy carried the power of positive thinking right to Jake's office. Their connecting door was open. She gave a courtesy knock and stepped inside, exuding all the confidence she could muster.

"Good morning," she trilled, smiling so hard her face ached.

Jake was reading a brochure on planes, chair leaning back, feet up on the desk. He looked over it, cocked an eyebrow at her and said, "The top of the morning to you, too."

"Start with the mail?" she asked.

"I've already looked at the E-mail messages. Go and read the inbox and get up to date. We'll deal with the Erikson inquiry first. And check the diary, Amy. We'll have to set up a meeting with him."

"Right!"

She was almost out of his office when he raised his voice in command.

"Hold it!"

Amy's heart jumped and pitter-pattered all around her chest. She held on to the door and popped her head around it. "Something else?" she inquired.

Jake had swung his feet off the desk and was leaning forward, beetling a frown at her. "You're wearing black. Didn't I specifically tell you my P.A. was not to wear black?"

It was true. He had. "I forgot," she said. Which was also true.

"Black does not fit our image, Amy," he said sternly. "Black is safe. Black is neutral..."

Which was precisely why she had chosen it this morning, having dithered through her entire wardrobe.

He wagged a finger at her. "Black is not to be worn again."

"Right!" she agreed.

"Just as well we don't have any important client meetings today," he muttered, then shot her a sharp look. "You're not in a black mood, are you?"

"No!" she denied swiftly.

"Good!" His expression brightened. The familiar teasing twinkled into his eyes as he lifted his feet back on the desk. "You can wear red anytime you like. You look stunning in red."

He picked up the brochure again and Amy skipped out to start work, her heart dancing instead of pitter-pattering. Everything was normal. Everything was fine. Jake was as good as his word. Life could go on as it had before.

Almost.

Amy found the to-and-fro between them wasn't quite

as easy as the day wore on. Not that she could lay any fault at Jake's door. Not once did he do or say anything to discomfort her along intimate lines. The problem was all hers.

When Jake bent over to pick up some papers he'd dropped, and the taut contours of his backside were clearly outlined, his trousers just disappeared and she could see him stepping out of the bath in all his natural glory. When he sat down and crossed his legs, the bulge of his powerful thighs vividly reminded her of their strong, bouncy support when she'd sat astride them. His mouth generated quite a few unsettling moments, too. She hoped Jake didn't notice these little distractions.

Lust, she decided, was not a runaway train. It was more like a guerilla soldier who could creep up and capture you before you even knew he was coming. But the memories of that *special* time with Jake were still very fresh, she told herself. Given a few days, they wouldn't leap to the forefront of her mind quite so much.

As it turned out, by the end of the week, Amy was really enjoying her job again, feeling a sense of achievement in meeting the challenges Jake regularly tossed at her, countering his bouts of teasing with the occasional smart quip, helping with the deals he set up and made for their clients. Best of all, without her old hackles rising all the time, she was open-minded enough to realise Jake truly did value and appreciate her contribution to his business.

He showed it in many ways, generous with compliments if what she'd done warranted them, giving consideration to her opinions and impressions of clients, readily taking suggestions if he thought them effective.

She was also more acutely aware of the close rapport they shared, where just a look conveyed a message which was instantly understood. Two years of familiarity did build that kind of knowledge of each other, she reasoned, yet she was beginning to feel she was more attuned to Jake's way of thinking than she'd ever been to Steve's, so the longevity of a relationship did not necessarily count.

As she left the office on Friday, she was wishing there was no weekend and it would be work as usual tomorrow. Which showed her she was becoming too dependent on Jake's company. Get a life, she sternly told herself.

On Saturday she canvassed several gyms between Balmoral and Milsons Point to see what equipment and classes they offered, comparing their fees, chatting to instructors, appraising their clienteles. She did some research on dance schools, as well, having always fancied learning tap-dancing. Wait for classes to be resumed in the new year, she was advised.

Saturday night proved difficult. It didn't matter what she tried to do, her mind kept wandering to Jake. She couldn't imagine him sitting at home by himself. He'd be involved in some social activity—a party, a date— and one or more women would be enjoying his charm and attention, beautiful sexy women who wouldn't say no to an experience with Jake Carter.

Envy frayed any peace of mind over her decision to cut any further intimate involvement with him. But it was the right decision, she insisted to herself. At least she was saved from the bitterness of becoming his ex-lover when he started favouring someone else. And her job was safe. No risk of a nasty blow-up there. But "the good memory" lingered with her a long time when she finally took herself off to bed.

She spent Sunday on the beach, determined to relax and enjoy what she had within easy reach. It passed the time pleasantly. She succeeded in pushing Jake to the edge of her mind for most of the day. On Monday morning, however, her hand automatically reached for the scarlet linen shift. She told herself it was stupid to want to look "stunning" for him, but she wore it anyway.

"Ah!" he said when she walked into his office to greet him. It was a very appreciative "Ah!" and the wolfish gleam in his eyes as he looked her up and down put a zing in her soul.

"Image," she said pertly. "We're meeting with Erikson today."

"Of course," he said and grinned at her.

She felt ridiculously happy all day.

The buoyant mood continued for most of the week.

The first niggle of worry came on Friday.

She'd finished the monthly course of contraceptive pills she'd been taking for years and her cycle always worked with clocklike regularity. Her period should have started today. So why hadn't it?

Her mind kept zinging to the night she'd forgotten to take a pill, but she'd taken two the next day to make up for it. Though it was actually the next night—not the morning or the day—when she'd discovered the error and taken double the dose. One missed night. It wouldn't matter normally. She had doubled up before, when she'd accidentally missed one over the years, and nothing had gone wrong.

But this time…this time…

Impossible to forget which night it was…she and Jake losing themselves in spontaneous combustion…and the deep, inner sense of mingling…melding inextricably.

Had their mating…such a terribly evocative word—borne fruit?

It was a nerve-shattering thought. Amy kept pushing it away. It would be the worst irony in the world if she'd fallen pregnant, just when she was trying to get her life in reasonable order after her long-term partner had taken off because he'd got another woman pregnant. Not that she wanted Steve back. That was finished. But Jake…as the father…it didn't bear thinking about.

Her cycle was messed up a day. That was all it was. Any minute it could correct itself. Tomorrow she'd be laughing about this silly worrying. One missed pill…it was nothing in the big picture. Her body wouldn't play such a dirty trick on her when she'd been protecting it against such a consequence for years.

Saturday brought her no relief. By Sunday afternoon Amy was in full panic. She bought a pregnancy test kit from a twenty-four-hour pharmacy. She couldn't bear the uncertainty.

The uncertainty ended on Monday morning.

It didn't matter how much she wanted to disbelieve the results of the test, two deadly pink lines were looking her in the face, not changing to anything else, and according to the instructions with the test kit, this meant she was pregnant. She checked the instructions again and again. No mistake. Pink was positive.

Just maybe, she thought frantically, the kit was faulty. Best see a doctor. Get a blood test. She looked through the telephone directory, found a medical centre at Mosman along the route she drove to work, then considered what lie she could tell to cover her late arrival at the office.

Impossible to say she needed to see a doctor. Jake would ask why. Jake wouldn't leave it alone until he found out. A flat tyre on her car, she decided. It could happen to anyone.

The visit to the doctor was a nightmare. Yes, missing a pill at a critical time could result in pregnancy. Test kits were usually reliable but a blood test would give absolute confirmation. Amy watched the needle going in and almost fainted as the blood started filling up the tube, blood that was going to tell her the awful truth. A baby! She closed her eyes. No, no, no, she begged. Having a baby—Jake's baby—made life too impossible.

She'd have the results in twenty-four hours, the doctor said. All she had to do was telephone the surgery and ask for them. She checked her watch. Nine-thirty. Twenty-four more hours of hell to get through, a third of those hours with the man who'd done this to her.

Not intentionally.

Though he should have used protection...should at least have asked her if she was protected. In which case she would have said yes, so there was no point in blaming him. Nevertheless, she might have remembered to take the wretched pill if he'd asked. Spontaneous combustion might be a very special experience but the ''good memory'' was swiftly gathering a mountain of savage regrets.

Jake, the rake... How would he react to being told he'd sown one too many oats? With his P.A., no less.

But she didn't have to face that yet.

Not yet.

Twenty-four hours.

Amy didn't know how she got through the day with Jake. He asked about the flat tyre and she blathered on about it, excusing the time away from the office. She was aware of him frowning at her several times. It was almost time for her to leave when he asked, "Is something wrong, Amy?" and her glazed eyes cleared enough to see he was observing her very keenly.

Would their child have those wolf eyes?

Her stomach cramped.

"No," she forced out. "Everything's fine." *Except I'm probably pregnant.*

"You haven't been with me, today," he remarked testingly.

"Sorry. I have been a bit scatter-brained. Christmas coming on…"

"Planning anything special?"

The excuse had popped into her mind but she was totally blank about it and had to grope for a reply. "No. Not really. Just…well, I guess I was thinking about the family I don't have. Kate Bradley was saying she'd shopped till she dropped and…" Amy shrugged, having run out of ideas to explain herself. "At least I'm saved that hassle."

Christmas…celebrating the birth of a child…

Dear God! Please don't do this to me.

"Uh-huh," Jake murmured noncommittally. "Not a good thing, spending Christmas alone. No fun in all. I'll speak to my sister about it."

"What?" Amy didn't understand what his sister had to do with it.

"Leave it to me," he said and went back into his office.

Amy shook her head in bewilderment. She simply wasn't in tune with Jake's thought processes today. But at least he'd stopped questioning her and she wasn't about to chase after him and invite more probing into her own thought processes, which were hopelessly scrambled by the waiting to know.

The next morning, she wasn't free of Jake's presence until ten-thirty. Almost sick with apprehension, she pounced on the telephone and called the surgery, all the while watching the door she'd closed between Jake's office and hers, desperately willing it to stay closed. Which it did, thankfully, because the news she received, although expected, still came as a shock.

No doubt about it anymore.

She *was* pregnant.

To Jake Carter.

And she had no idea in the wide world what to do about it.

An abortion?

Instant recoil.

Tell Jake.

No, she wasn't ready for that. She needed time to armour herself against…whatever she had to armour herself against.

An unworthy thought flashed through her mind. Steve's blonde had used her pregnancy to pull him into marriage. Would Jake…

No, Amy fiercely decided. She couldn't—wouldn't—

go down that road. Marriage could be a trap, as she well knew, and using a baby to seal the trap would be a terrible thing to do to all three of them. Jake wasn't the marrying kind. He was the perennial bumblebee flitting from flower to flower.

He'd probably be appalled at the prospect of fatherhood being thrust upon him…a long-term relationship he couldn't get out of. Unless she had an abortion. Would he ask it of her?

She'd hate him if he did.

She remembered the lovely, natural way he'd handled his baby nephew, Joshua. Surely, with his own child…

The telephone rang.

Amy picked up the receiver, struggling to get her wits together to handle a work-related call.

"Good morning…"

"Amy, is that you? Amy Taylor?" an eager female voice she didn't recognise broke in.

"Yes…"

"Good! It's Ruth Powell here, Jake's sister."

"Oh?" The coincidence of having just been thinking of Ruth's son dazed Amy for a moment. "How can I help you?"

"We'd all love you to come for Christmas Day, Amy. It's at my house this year. Well, mine and Martin's, naturally. The rest of the family will be here and they're dying to meet you. Jake said you didn't have family of your own to go to, so how about joining us? It'll be such fun!"

This was rattled out at such high speed, Amy was slow to take it in. "It's…very nice of you, Ruth…"

"Please say you can. It's no trouble, I promise you.

We'll have food enough for an army. Mum's bringing the turkey and my sisters-in-law are providing the ham and the pudding, and Jake, of course, is in charge of the drinks. We've told him, nothing but the best French champagne…''

Which had probably contributed to the mess she was in, Amy thought miserably.

"So you see,'' Ruth went on, "we'll have the best time. All the festive stuff has been thought of and you must see my tree. It's Joshua's first Christmas and Martin and I bought the most splendid tree you can imagine. Fabulous decorations. Please say you'll come, Amy.''

She never had got around to buying a tree. Too much else on her mind. Jake's baby. And this was his family—her baby's family—inviting her to meet them. Suddenly it felt important to do so, to see Jake in action with his family, to see him with children…

"Thank you, Ruth. It's such a kind thought…''

"You'll come?'' she cried excitedly.

"Yes. I'd like to.''

"Great! Jake will pick you up at…''

"No, please, I don't want that. He should be with you.''

"He won't mind.''

"Ruth, *I'd* mind.'' She could cope with him in office hours. Outside of them…her stomach quivered. "I'd rather come and go by myself,'' she stated firmly.

Ruth laughed. "Still keeping him in line. Good for you, Amy! Does eleven o'clock Christmas morning suit you?''

"Yes. Where do you live?''

The address was given and the call ended, Ruth sounding triumphantly satisfied with the arrangements.

It was really Jake's doing, Amy realised, remembering how he'd questioned her about Christmas yesterday.

He didn't like the idea of her being alone.

The irony was the last time he'd acted to save her from being alone, he'd left her pregnant, ensuring she wouldn't be alone in the future.

But where was he going to stand in her future?

He did care about her.

But how much? ...How much?

Christmas...

Maybe that would be the day she'd find out.

CHAPTER FOURTEEN

CHRISTMAS day with the Carter family was happy chaos. From the moment Amy arrived at the Powell home, Ruth linked her arm with hers in warm welcome and whizzed her into a wonderfully large family room which opened out onto a lovely patio and pool garden area. People were scattered everywhere and introductions were very informal.

"Amy, this is my dad, trying to clear the room of wrapping paper."

"Hi, Amy!" An elderly version of Jake grinned at her over the mountain of brilliantly printed Christmas gift wreckage he held in his arms. "I'm sick of wading through this stuff. Might stub my toe on something."

She grinned back. "I can see it might be a problem. Nice to meet you, Mr. Carter."

"And this is our tree," Ruth went on proudly, not giving Amy time to get into conversation. It didn't really seem expected. Which was totally unlike any visitor's encounter with *her* father, who would have demanded full and absolute attention.

The tree was, indeed, fabulous—three metres tall, at least, towering up towards the cathedral ceiling, a green fir draped in red and purple and silver ornaments and hundreds of fairy lights.

Amy was swept into the adjoining kitchen where two women were gathered around an island bench loaded

130

with festive food. "Grace, Tess, here she is. These two busy bodies are my sisters-in-law, Amy."

She managed a "Hi!" before being interrupted.

"At last!" Grace, a plump and very pretty brunette exclaimed, brown eyes twinkling triumphant delight. "You're making our day, Amy. We can really henpeck Jake about you now."

"Pardon?" The word tripped out as alarm shot through Amy. She didn't want to be a target of teasing, no matter how good-natured it was. The situation was too serious for her to respond light-heartedly.

Tess laughed. She was a honey-blonde and obviously pregnant, making Amy even more conscious of her own condition. "Don't worry, Amy," she was quick to assure. "We won't embarrass you. It's just that our brother-in-law is such a slippery customer when it comes to women, it's nice to hang one on him."

"I am only his P.A.," she reminded them.

"Don't say *only*," Ruth instantly expostulated. "We think you're marvellous. The only constant female in Jake's life, apart from his family."

"And he cared enough to want you here," Grace put in.

"Which proves he *can* care," Tess declared. "We were beginning to doubt he was capable of it. You're the only one he's ever wanted to share his Christmas with, Amy."

"Well, we do share a lot of days," Amy explained, trying to hide the flutter of hope in her heart. "I guess he thought this was just another."

"Nope. It's definitely caring," Grace insisted.

"Trust, too," Tess said decisively. "You've given us

hope for him, Amy. He actually trusts you to survive meeting his family. Obviously a woman of strength.''

Amy smiled at their free flow of zany humour. ''Are you so formidable?''

''Dreadful en masse,'' Ruth said, rolling her eyes to express the burden of belonging to them. ''Loud and competitive and opinionated and everyone tells horrible stories. You'd better come and meet the rest so you can sort them out.''

Ruth's husband, Martin, Jake and his two older brothers, Adam and Nathan, were all in the pool, playing water games with five children. ''Hannah's the eldest at ten. Olivia's eight. Tom's seven. Mitch is four and Ashleigh's three,'' Ruth rattled out. ''It's a rule in this family that everyone has to learn to swim before they walk.''

They all yelled out, ''Happy Christmas!'' and Amy was struck by their happiness and harmony as they continued their fun. Jake was holding a big plastic ball, ready to throw, and the cries of ''Me, Uncle Jake, me!'' rang with excitement and pleasure.

She would have liked to stop and watch him frolicking with his nieces and nephews but Ruth steered her to where an elderly woman sat in the shade of a vine-covered pergola, nursing a wide awake Joshua on her lap. ''Mum, this is Jake's Amy,'' she announced.

''Ruth, do try to introduce people properly,'' her mother chided, and Amy instantly had a flash of Jake saying, ''Mum does her best to rule over us all.''

''Amy Taylor, please meet Elizabeth Rose Carter,'' Ruth trotted out in mock obedience.

Her mother sighed. She was still a striking woman,

however old she was. A lovely mass of white wavy hair framed a face very like Ruth's, but her brown eyes were more reserved than openly welcoming.

"It's very kind of you all to include me in your family Christmas, Mrs. Carter," Amy said, aware she was being given a keen scrutiny by Jake's mother during this mother-daughter exchange. "It's a great pleasure to meet you."

"And you, my dear," came the dignified reply. "Jake has spoken so much about you."

"I enjoy working with him," was the only comment Amy could think of.

It was rather disconcerting being measured against whatever Jake had said about her, and being visually measured from head to toe, as well. It was silly to feel self-conscious in her white pantsuit since the other women wore similar casual clothes, but she suddenly wished she'd worn a loose shirt instead of the figure-moulding halter top. *I might be pregnant to him but I'm not a brazen hussy out to trap your son,* she found herself thinking.

"I understand you have no close relatives," Elizabeth Carter remarked questioningly, making Amy feel like a reject of the human race.

"My parents emigrated from England and my brothers now live overseas," she answered. "This kind of gathering is quite remarkable to me. You're very lucky, Mrs. Carter."

"Yes, I suppose I am. Though I tend to think one makes one's own luck. I did bring my children up to value the close bonds of family."

"Then they were very fortunate in having you as their mother."

"What of your own mother, Amy?"

"She died when I was sixteen."

"How sad. A girl needs her mother. So easy to go off the rails without good advice and support."

"I suppose so," Amy said noncommittally, feeling she was being dissected and found wanting. No solid family background. No wise maternal guidance in her life.

"Mum, do you think it's kind to ram that stuff down Amy's throat on today of all days?" Ruth demanded in exasperation.

"Amy!"

Jake's shout saved the awkward moment. They all looked to see what he wanted. He'd hauled himself out of the pool and was striding towards them, rubbing himself vigorously with a towel. Amy's heart caught in her throat. He was so…vital…and stunningly male.

She forced her gaze to stay fixed on his face as he neared them. The rest of his anatomy held too many pitfalls to her peace of mind. Not that she had any peace of mind, but her knees suddenly felt very shaky and if there was ever a time to appear strong it was now, especially in front of his mother's critical eye.

"Sorry I wasn't out of the pool to greet you when you arrived," he said, his smile aimed exclusively at her, a smile that tingled through her bloodstream and made her feel light-headed.

"No need to apologise. Ruth is looking after me," she said, struggling to be sensible. "Go back if you like. I don't want to interrupt the game."

He shook his head. "You look great in that white outfit. Why haven't I seen you in white before?"

"You would have said it's a neutral, not fitting our image," she said dryly.

He grinned, the yellow wolfish gleam lighting his eyes. "Definitely a positive. Give me five minutes to get dressed and I'll be at your side to protect you from the hordes."

"Well, if you're going to poke your nose in, I'm taking Amy back to the kitchen so we women can get some chat in first," Ruth informed him archly.

He laughed. "I can feel the knives in my back. Take no notice of them, Amy. The women in this family have mean, vicious hearts."

"Oh, you…" Ruth tried to cuff him, but he ducked out of reach and was off, still laughing.

"Are you still okay with Joshua, Mum?" Ruth asked.

"Yes, dear." The dark eyes pinned Amy purposefully. "Perhaps we'll have time to converse later."

"I'm sure we will," she answered, forcing a smile she didn't feel. The impression was too strong that Elizabeth Rose Carter did not consider her a suitable person to be the one woman her youngest son chose to share Christmas with his family, let alone be the mother of his child.

It hurt.

And the natural acceptance given her by all the others as the day wore on, didn't quite overlay that initial hurt. It preyed on her mind more and more as she watched the Carter family in action over the long and highly festive Christmas luncheon.

They connected so easily and they had no fear of saying anything they liked to each other. There was no tension. Laughter rippled around the table. Children were lovingly indulged. Good-natured arguments broke out and became quite boisterous but there wasn't a trace of acrimony, merely a lively exchange of opinions accompanied by witty teasing. It was interesting, amusing, and most of all, happy.

Jake didn't allow her to be simply an observer. Neither did his siblings nor their partners. It seemed everyone was keen to draw her into being one of them, inviting her participation, wanting it, enjoying it. Occasionally Jake's father would stir the pot with provocative remarks, then sit back, his amber eyes twinkling like Jake's as comments bounced around the table.

They knew how to have fun, this family. To Amy it was a revelation of how a family could be, given a kindly and encouraging hand at the helm. She wished her baby could know this, know it from the very beginning…to grow up without fear, with an unshakable sense of belonging to a loving circle. Maybe she was idealising it, but the contrast from what she'd come from was so great, it all seemed perfect to her.

The rapport she shared with Jake was heightened in this company. There were times when their eyes met, the understanding felt so intimate she was sure she could tell him she was pregnant and it wouldn't cause any problem between them. He would want his child. He would love it. Family was natural to him.

Then she would catch his mother watching them and knew there was no easy solution to her situation. Elizabeth Carter did not approve of her. Besides, the sense of intimacy was an illusion, generated by the special harmony of a happy Christmas day. Jake might care for her and trust her. It didn't mean he would want to be bound to her through their child.

She was his P.A.

He wasn't in love with her.

He probably wasn't the type to fall in love since he'd never brought any other woman to a family Christmas. Brief affairs was his style when it came to women. She probably wouldn't be here if she was still one of his "brief" affairs. He undoubtedly thought she was *safe,* not expecting anything of him.

After the feast had been devoured to everyone's satisfaction, they drifted out to the patio. Nathan had set up a badminton net beside the pool, and the two older brothers challenged Jake and Ruth to a game. The rest of the family took up spectator positions, ready to barrack for their team. The children sat around the pool, making up their own competition about diving in to retrieve the shuttlecock should it be hit into the water. Elizabeth Carter invited Amy to sit with her under the pergola.

Here comes *the conversation,* Amy thought, and wondered why Jake's mother was bothering. Didn't she know her own son?

"I hope you've been enjoying yourself," she started.

"Immensely," Amy returned with a smile.

"This badminton match is something of a tradition. Jake started it years ago. They'll play on for a while. It's the best of five games."

"Closely fought, I'd imagine."

She actually unbent enough to laugh. "Very. And

they use outrageous tactics. Which is why their father has to umpire.''

''But all done in the spirit of fun, I'm sure,'' Amy commented.

''Oh, yes.'' The amusement faded into a shrewd look. ''Though life isn't all fun. I've found it's a lot less complicated if one follows a straight path.''

''How do you mean?'' Amy prompted, thinking they might as well get to the meat of this talk.

''Well, as I understand it from Jake,'' she started tentatively, ''You've been…attached…to a relationship for many years.''

''Most people do get attached,'' Amy said dryly. Not counting Jake, she could have added even more dryly.

Elizabeth Carter gathered herself to spit out what was on her mind. ''I must say I don't hold with this modern custom of moving in together,'' she plunged in, her expression implying she was giving Amy the benefit of her wisdom. ''I don't think it does anyone any good in the long run. No clear-cut commitment to a shared future. No emotional security. It's not the right way to go, Amy. Your mother would have told you that,'' she declared with confidence.

''You didn't know my mother, Mrs. Carter,'' Amy said quietly. ''Nor what she suffered in her marriage. What we all suffered. You may see marriage as a safe haven where people can grow happily. It's not always so.''

Silence.

Amy watched the badminton game, her stomach churning over the judgement Jake's mother had made on her—a loose-living woman without commitment. It wasn't fair. It wasn't right. And her defences were very brittle today. She didn't need this. She needed...support.

"I'm sorry. I can only assume your mother made a bad character judgement in her husband," came the gentle rejoinder.

The criticism hit Amy on the raw. One didn't have a clear-minded choice over everything. She hadn't chosen to get pregnant. Especially to a man who didn't love her!

"Perhaps you'd like to give me a reading of Jake's character, Mrs. Carter." Amy swung a hard gaze on her, giving no quarter. "From where I've sat over the past two years, he's a rake with women. A very good boss, a very charming man, but not someone I'd trust to make me happy in the long run, as you so succinctly put it. His turnover rate hardly makes him a good choice, does it? Or do you see it differently?"

The recoil of shock was written all over Elizabeth Carter's face. Being hit by a such a direct and pertinent challenge had certainly not been anticipated. Do her good, Amy thought grimly. Stop her from thinking her youngest son was a glittering prize any woman would love to snatch.

Shock was followed by bewilderment. "Why did you come here today, Amy?"

"I wanted to see what Jake's family is like," she answered bluntly. "It can tell you a lot about a person."

"Then you must understand Jake is looking for the complement to what we have here. He'll keep on looking for it because he won't settle for anything less."

Amy gave her an ironic look. "He's been looking a long time, Mrs. Carter, without success. I may have *moved in* with a man but at least I was constant for five years, which I'm sure Jake told you, and it was my partner's infidelity that broke up the relationship. Infidelity does not appeal to me.''

She frowned. ''I did not mean to offend you, Amy.''

In that case, tact certainly wasn't her strong point, Amy thought.

The frown deepened. ''I know Jake wouldn't cheat on anyone. It isn't in his nature.''

He'd said as much himself, on the balcony after…but that didn't mean he'd stay with one woman for the rest of his life. And Amy suddenly realised it was what she'd want of him…a commitment to her and their child…and it wouldn't happen…so to tell him she was pregnant would almost certainly result in an intolerable situation for both of them. It wouldn't be happy families. It would be emotional hell.

''Don't worry, Mrs. Carter,'' she said ruefully. ''I will not embroil your son in a relationship you wouldn't like.''

''Amy…'' She shook her head in distress. ''Oh, dear… I just wanted to help. I know you've been hurt. Sometimes people just don't see straight and they keep repeating their mistakes instead of learning from them. Moving in together is so…so messy.''

So is divorce, Amy thought, but she held her tongue. The couples in the Carter family looked far too solid for her to make that sour comment.

''I have no intention of moving in with your son,'' she stated flatly. ''I work for Jake. We get on well. This invitation to join you for Christmas was a kindness on his part. It's unnecessary to make more of it than that, believe me.''

And I won't intrude again.

''Jake is kind,'' his mother said, as though preparing to build a case for her son's *good* character.

''Yes, he is,'' Amy agreed.

''Underneath all his wild ways, he has a heart of gold. He wouldn't hurt anyone. He goes out of his way not to hurt anyone.''

Amy sighed. ''You don't have to defend him to me, Mrs. Carter. I guess I don't like being put in a position where I'm pushed to defend myself. Shall we leave it at that?''

She knew she sounded hard, but she was in a hard place and Jake's mother hadn't made it any easier. Not that anything would, she thought despairingly.

Elizabeth Carter was clearly upset by this outcome. ''I'm sorry…'' she began again.

''It's okay,'' Amy rushed out dismissively, wanting the conversation dropped. She couldn't bear it on top of everything else. ''Let's just watch the match through and then I'll go.''

''Jake won't want you to go.''

''I make my own decisions, Mrs. Carter.''

She had for a long time. A very long time. Starting when she'd decided independence was the only way to survive intact in her father's household, not to care, not to want, not to need what she didn't have. And now she looked out over Jake's family, feeling like a disembodied outsider, watching a magic circle she could never hope to join. Not freely.

Her baby might be a passport to it in a limited sense—

Jake was kind—but that kindness could be a terrible cruelty, too—to be given a taste while not truly belonging. The only way she and their child could properly belong would be if Jake were her husband, and she couldn't trap him into marriage like that. Marriage should not be a trap. For anyone.

It hurt to watch him. She tried to move her attention to the others but her gaze kept being drawn back to him…the father of her child…the accidental father…unaware that part of him was growing inside her. Was it right not to tell him? Was it best, in the long run, to just disappear from his life?

She didn't know.

She felt as though she didn't know anything anymore.

She was in chaos. It wasn't the happy chaos of a Carter family Christmas. It was the dark chaos that came with the constant beating of uncertainties.

Finally the game was over, Adam and Nathan conceding victory to Jake and Ruth, and Jake was coming for her, wanting her to play.

And she had to find an answer.

CHAPTER FIFTEEN

"WINNER'S choice now," Jake crowed. "Amy and I challenge Ruth and Martin."

"You can have it, boyo," the oldest brother, Nathan, groaned. "I'm for a long cool drink."

"Me, too," Adam agreed. "Preferably in the pool."

"Ah, the frailties of age," Jake teased.

"You'll get yours," Nathan retorted. "Martin will wipe you off the court."

"Huh! You don't know my Amy."

My Amy...and the glorious grin he aimed at her...she couldn't take any more turmoil.

"Not me, Jake," she quickly protested. "Take Grace as your partner. I really must be going now." She stood up, preparing to make her farewells.

"Going?" He looked incredulous.

"It's been a wonderful day..."

"It's not over yet," he argued. "We light up the barbecue at about seven and..."

"I'm sorry. I can't stay."

"Why not?" Ruth demanded, getting in on the act. "We need you to balance up the party, Amy."

She forced a smile. "The truth is I have a raging headache. Too much champagne over lunch, I guess. Please don't mind."

Elizabeth Carter leapt up from her chair. "You should have said, Amy. I'll get you some pills to take."

143

"You could lie down for a while," Ruth suggested.

"No, please…" Amy reached out to stay Jake's mother, unaware her eyes filled with anguished appeal. "Just let me go. All right?"

The older woman hesitated, then blurted out, "I'm so sorry…"

"For what, Mum?" Jake asked sharply.

"That I'm not up to more fun and games," Amy hastily explained. She forced another smile. "I'd like to say my goodbyes, Jake."

He searched her eyes, obviously sensing something wrong beyond the headache. However, much to Amy's intense relief, he decided not to press the point. "You're the boss today," he said with his quirky smile. "Mum, would you mind getting the headache tablets for Amy to take before she goes?"

"Of course, dear."

"Can't have you driving in pain," he said, then raised his voice. "Hey, everyone! Amy has to leave now so come and wish her well."

They all bunched around, shaking hands, kissing her cheek, saying what a pleasure it was to have met her. It passed in a blur to Amy. She hoped she made suitable responses. Jake's mother handed her a glass of water and two pills. She took them. The raging headache was very real. The crowd around her receded. So did the noise. Finally, there was only Jake who took the glass from her, set it down on a table, then wrapped her arm around his.

"Are you sure you're fit to drive, Amy?" he asked in concern as he walked her into the house.

It was all she could do not to tremble at his touch, his

nearness. He didn't realise the effect he was having on her, the sheer torture of being so closely linked, yet impossibly far from what she wanted of him. "I'll be fine," she insisted huskily.

He paused her in the family room. "I'll sit with you for a while if you like. Some quiet time won't go amiss."

"No. I don't want to be a trouble." It was hard to keep a frantic note out of her voice. She broke away from him to pick up her handbag which she'd left on a chair by the Christmas tree.

Christmas…peace, hope and goodwill…it was a joke… a wickedly painful black joke!

"It's no trouble," Jake assured her.

"I'll be fine," she insisted more firmly, and having collected her bag, she headed for the foyer, every step driven by the need to get away from the torment he stirred.

He followed. "Amy, did Mum say anything to upset you?" Urgent concern in his voice now.

"Why should she?" she flipped back.

"Because my mother has a habit of thinking she knows best," he grated out.

"Most parents do." *Except me,* Amy thought, in helpless panic. Here she was, a parent in the making, with no idea what was best.

"You're not answering my question," Jake persisted.

"It doesn't matter."

He halted her by stepping in front of her, right in the centre of the foyer which served the front door. "*You* matter," he said with quiet force. "You matter to *me*."

Do I?…Do I?

The words pounded through her mind as she lifted her head to search his eyes for how much she mattered to him. Golden eyes, burning fiercely. But what did it mean?

She didn't see him lift his hand. Her cheek quivered under its tender touch, a touch that was only there fleetingly, because fingers were suddenly raking through her hair and his head bent closer and his mouth claimed hers.

Amy completely lost track of what happened after that. The pain in her head was pushed to some far perimeter, her mind filling up with a host of clamouring needs, every one of them chorusing yes to the connection being forged…yes, to the sweet caress of his lips, yes to the seductive slide of his tongue, yes, yes, yes, to the passionate plunder that followed, a wildly exhilarating, intensely evocative reminder of sensations she'd known before with this man…only this man.

She wasn't aware of moving her body to meet his, of clinging to him, of basking in the heat he generated, the strength emanating from him, surrounding her, cocooning her in a place that felt safe and right. Her whole being was swimming in a sea of bliss, feeling—knowing on some deep subconscious level—this was the answer, the answer to everything.

"Uh-oh…"

Ruth's voice…intruding, jarring.

"…Slice of Christmas cake for Amy… I'll just leave it here."

The pain in Amy's head crashed through the wall of sensation that had held it at bay. The realisation of what she was doing—what Jake was doing—exploded through her mind. This physical compulsion…sexual attraction…*didn't answer anything!*

She tore her mouth from his. Her hands were buried in his hair. Her body was plastered against his, his arms, hands, ensuring she was pressed into maximum, intimate contact, and she'd not only allowed it, she was actively *clinging,* as though he was the only rock that could save her from going under.

Clinging…like's Steve's blonde…for whom she'd felt contempt.

Such a wretched lack of understanding on her part.

Yet she was appalled at her own weakness.

"It's the same," Jake murmured near her ear, his voice furred with satisfaction.

She jerked her head back. Her hands scrambled out of his hair to push at his shoulders, frantic to make some space between them. "You shouldn't have done this. You agreed!" she cried, her eyes meeting his in agitated, anguished accusation.

"It *is* out of office hours," he reminded her in mitigation of the offence. His mouth—his damnably mesmerising mouth—curved into a soft, sensual smile. "And I'd have to confess the temptation to refresh the memory got the better of me."

The memory…still physically surging between them. Flustered by her own complicity in reviving it, Amy broke his embrace, her hands fluttering wildly over his chest as she forced a step back from him, her eyes begging for release.

"You took advantage." Blaming him didn't excuse herself, but she had not invited this. He couldn't say she had.

"Mmh…" He was not the least bit abashed. The smile still lingered on his lips and the molten gold in his eyes remained warm, twinkling with the pleasure of a desire fulfilled. "Look up, Amy."

"What?" She *was* looking up, her gaze trained directly on his, desperately seeking the heart of this man.

"Right above your head is a bunch of mistletoe hanging from the light fitting."

She looked up. There it was, just as he said.

"A man's entitled to kiss a woman standing underneath the mistletoe on Christmas day."

Fun, she thought despairingly. He was having his wicked way with her, out of office hours, just because he wanted to. Never mind how she felt or what it would do to her. Jake, the rake, couldn't resist an opportunity to satisfy himself. Fury swept through her, a fury fed by fear and frustration.

"You deliberately stopped me here," she hurled at him, her hands dropping from all contact from him, curling into fists, her whole body bristling with fierce aggression. How dare he touch her *in fun!* It was monstrous, without care or conscience.

He frowned, perceiving her sense of violation and not liking it. "I'm simply letting you know there's no reason to be fussed by it, Amy."

Fussed! It was the most contemptible word he could have used, making light of what he'd done when it wasn't light at all. Nothing about her situation was *light*. She hated him in that moment, hated him with a passion.

"That was not a Christmas kiss," she bit out, her eyes furiously stripping him of any further attempt at levity.

Any trace of a smile was wiped from his face. His

eyes suddenly gathered an intense focus, gleaming more yellow than gold. A wolf on the hunt, Amy thought wildly, determined on tracking through anything to get to her.

"No. It was much more," he quietly agreed.

Her heart squeezed into a tight ball. He was going to close in on her no matter what she said or did. She could feel the power of his purpose, and couldn't move away from it.

"Don't you find that curious, Amy?" he asked.

She had no answer. Her mind had seized up on the idea of his being an irresistible force.

"How well we get on now that Steve's out of the way?" he went on, the words seeming to beat at her in relentless pursuit. "How perfectly we click when we come together?"

Perfectly!

That triggered a rush of hysteria which was impossible to contain. The words bubbled out of her mind and spilled into irretrievable sound.

"Oh, so *perfectly* I'm pregnant, Jake!"

Her hands flew up in dramatic emphasis.

"How do you like that for perfect?"

CHAPTER SIXTEEN

SHOCK!

Amy saw it, felt it reverberating through Jake just as it quaked through her. It was like a live thing, with writhing tentacles, reaching and changing everything. She couldn't believe she'd done it…set this irrevocable happening in motion without any rational planning for consequences…just blurted it out…here it is…

"Pregnant."

The word fell from Jake's lips as though there was too much to take in and he couldn't quite cope with it.

Amy flapped her hands helplessly. "I'm sorry… I'm sorry… It was that night you came to my apartment and…and I forgot to take the pill after…after you'd gone. I took two the next day but…"

Her voice faltered as she saw the shock clear from Jake's face, to be replaced by a strange, wondrous look.

"You're pregnant to me," he said.

Amy didn't understand. He sounded as if he liked the idea. Maybe his thinking had been knocked haywire. "Jake…" It was of paramount importance to get through to him. "…It wasn't meant to happen…"

"But it did." He grinned from ear to ear.

Amy started to panic. His reaction wasn't right. He certainly wasn't thinking straight. "Are you listening to me?" she cried.

"You're carrying my child…mine!" He spoke as

though he'd won the best lottery in the world. "For a moment there, I thought it was Steve's, and that would have been hard, Amy. A hell of a reminder…"

"Jake, this is not okay!" she hurled at him, desperate to get the conversation on some kind of clear track. "It was an accident. I didn't want to hang it on you."

"Hang it on me! Hang it on me!" He repeated in a kind of dazed incredulity. "I'm the father. You're not hanging anything on me. The biological fact is…" He paused, apparently having been struck by a different thought. "How long have you known?"

"What?" Amy just couldn't get a handle on how Jake's mind was working. It was totally incomprehensible to her.

"About the baby."

"Oh!" She flushed. "I got the results of the blood test two days ago."

He grinned again. "So it *is* absolutely certain."

"Will you stop that?" she cried in exasperation.

"Stop what?"

"Looking so damned pleased about it!"

"I can't help it. It's not every day a man gets told he's going to be a father. We're talking about our first child…"

"Jake! We're…not…married," she almost shouted at him.

"Well, we can soon fix that," he said, his delighted expression moving swiftly to purpose.

Amy glared at him in helpless frustration. The man did not have his feet on the ground at all. Maybe he was besotted with the idea of being presented with a child of his own, having been surrounded by his siblings' children all day. Whatever the reason, there was no sense coming from him. He probably needed a few days to think about it, do some sober reflection on their situation.

"I'm going home," she stated firmly. "I've got a headache."

As she started to step past him his arm shot out to prevent it.

"Wait! Please..."

It was too much. Tears welled into her eyes. She was too choked up to speak, too distressed to look at him.

"I'm sorry. I'm not getting this right, am I?" he said softly, apologetically.

She shook her head.

"Don't cry, Amy. I'll do better, I promise."

The tears flowed faster.

Then his arm was around her shoulders, hugging her close for comfort. "I'll take you home."

She swallowed hard, struggling to get control of her voice. "Your family..."

"You're my family now, Amy. Let me at least take care of you."

That did it, speaking to her so gently, saying what she'd been secretly craving to hear. The tears were unstoppable now and he was already urging her to the front door, opening it for her. She didn't have the strength to fight him, didn't have voice enough to argue. They were out of the house and walking down the path to the street before he spoke again, his sympathetic tone soothing some of the turmoil inside her.

"It must have been rough on you the past two days, worrying about what to do."

"Yes," she managed to whisper.

"You're not…umh…thinking of a termination, are you, Amy?"

"No."

"Good!" His sigh expressed deep relief. "I'm not sure I could have borne that, either."

This was muttered more to himself than to her and Amy briefly puzzled over it. She was the one who had to do the bearing. Jake seemed to be off on another plane again. Though it was clear he wanted her to have the baby. He hadn't left her in any doubt about that. Though she had a mountain of doubts surrounding what would eventuate from it.

"The car key?" he prompted.

They'd reached the sidewalk where her car was parked at the kerb. She fumbled in her handbag and found the key, found a tissue, too, and wiped her weepy eyes. She was feeling slightly more in control, though still very shaky on how to proceed from here with Jake.

He held out his hand. "Better let me drive, Amy. I don't think you're in a fit enough state to concentrate on it."

Taking care of her…being kind. Jake *was* kind. For a moment Amy wallowed in the warm reassurance. He wasn't going to make this hard for her. He was prepared—more than prepared—to take responsibility. Which reminded her of other more immediate responsibilities.

"What about you? The champagne?" she asked, unsure how many glasses he'd consumed over lunch. The last thing she needed was to end up today in a police station with Jake charged for drunk driving.

"No problem." He gave her his quirky smile. "Sober as a judge."

Somehow that typical little smile put things on a more normal footing. She sighed, trying to loosen the tightness in her chest, and handed over the key, relieved he could take care of the driving, relieved also that he appeared to be more himself now.

Despite her headache, Amy decided it would be good to get a few things settled so she had some idea where she stood with him. And with her job. There was no longer any escape from the truth, so the sooner they talked it over, the better.

Jake unlocked the car, saw her settled in the passenger seat, then moved quickly to the driver's side, sliding in behind the wheel and closing them in together. *Together* was the operative word, she thought ruefully. They'd made this baby together and now they were stuck together until something was sorted out.

"One thing I want to say, Amy, before you do any more thinking."

She could feel him looking at her with urgent intensity but she couldn't bring herself to let him see just how vulnerable she was to whatever he had to say. It was easier to stare straight ahead, easier for steeling herself to face the difficulties he would certainly bring up.

"Go on," she invited, hoping she could cope with the outcome.

"Don't rule marriage out," he said quietly. "I want to marry you, Amy. I think we could have a good life together. So please give it your serious consideration while I drive you home."

He didn't wait for a reply, which was just as well,

because Amy was too poleaxed to speak. He switched on the engine and got on with driving.

She didn't really notice the journey home, wasn't aware of time passing. Her mind was in a ferment. How could she give marriage to Jake Carter serious consideration? What was he thinking of? It was time to take a wife and have a family and she'd do as well as anyone else, especially since she was already pregnant to him? The good old chemistry spark was there so why not?

Never mind that the spark might go out before she even had the baby! There was always a host of other available women to have on the side when that happened. Did he think he could fool her when she knew so much about him? It was true they got on well together, but how long would that last under pressures they'd never had before? She could not live with infidelity for a start!

It was all very well for his mother to say it wasn't in Jake's nature to cheat. Without love, they'd be cheating each other anyway if they got married. Besides, Elizabeth Rose Carter certainly wouldn't welcome her as a daughter-in-law. Though Jake could probably charm his mother into accepting anything if he worked at it.

Amy was only too aware of how charming he could be. She couldn't let it work on her. There was too much at stake here. Her happiness. Their child's happiness.

Their child…

Misery swamped her. It wasn't right to bring a child into the world when neither parent had planned for it. What was she to do? What did she want Jake to do?

Dazedly, she looked around for landmarks and realised they were heading down the hill to Balmoral Beach.

It reminded her of the day Jake first drove her here, the day she'd told him Steve was going to marry his pregnant blonde.

Pregnancy…marriage.

Did all men think like that?

No, of course they didn't. If men were so committed to their children there wouldn't be so many single mothers. Not that she wanted to be a single mother. That would be a very hard road. But getting married because of a baby…the thought of an oppressive prison loomed darkly on the edges of what looked like an easier road. Becoming dependent on a man who didn't really want to spend his life with her…

We could have a good life together.

Amy rubbed at her temples.

Did Jake really believe that?

''Headache worse?'' he asked in concern.

''No. Just trying to think.''

''Leave it until we get home,'' he advised. ''Almost there.''

It wasn't his home, Amy thought crossly. He was going to invade it again, as he had before…invading her life…but they did have to talk. He was the father of her child and there was no locking him out of their future. One way or another, he would always be in it. Especially if he kept up his current attitude.

He parked the car in her garage slot underneath the apartment block. She vaguely wondered how he knew which slot was hers. Probably a lucky guess.

As they rode up to the top floor in the elevator, Amy became acutely aware of Jake's physical nearness. She started remembering the kiss underneath the mistletoe and how she'd clung to him…how he'd felt, how much he could make her feel, the sheer power of his sexuality drawing on hers. If he started that again…tried to use it…she must not let him.

He held out her car key. She snatched it off his palm, frightened of any skin-to-skin contact with him. For a moment Jake's palm hung there empty and her graceless behaviour shot a wave of heat up Amy's throat.

Thankfully Jake made no comment. He lowered his hand to his side and Amy busied herself with her hand-bag, putting away the car key and finding the one for her front door.

Her inner tension increased, screaming along every nerve in her body as Jake accompanied her out of the elevator. Fortunately he had the good sense not to touch her. She would have snapped.

Once the door was unlocked, Jake gestured for her to precede him into the apartment, so she went ahead and left him to follow, grateful he was tactful enough not to crowd her and she had the chance to establish a com-fortable distance. Having dropped her handbag on the kitchen counter, she walked straight across the living room to open the doors to the balcony.

The instant waft of fresh sea air on her hot face felt good. Unbelievably, despite her fevered thoughts, her headache had eased. If she could just keep enough cool to handle Jake in a calm and reasonable manner, maybe they could come to some workable agreements.

"Can I get you something, Amy? A cup of tea or…"
"No."

His voice came from the kitchen area. He'd probably paused there, watching her. She took a deep breath and turned to face him, forcing an ironic smile to ease the concern he was expressing. He was behind the counter, hands resting on it, poised to minister to her needs, but he was no more relaxed than she was.

His shoulders looked bunched, his facial muscles were taut, a worry line creased the space between his brows, his triangular eyes were narrowed, sharply scanning, weighing up her body language.

"Thank you," she added belatedly, "but I doubt anything would sit well in my stomach right now. I wasn't ready for this, Jake. Telling you, I mean."

He nodded. "Better done than churning about it, Amy."

"Yes. Though I didn't mean to mess up your Christmas day with your family. I only went to see…" She trailed off, finding it too difficult to describe all the nuances of her observations.

"What it might be like if you joined it?"

His quick perception jolted her. "I can't marry you," she blurted out more baldly than she had meant to.

He frowned. "Because of my family?"

"No…no…" She shook her head, berating herself for being as tactless as his mother. "You have a great family. It must be wonderful to belong to them. For you, I mean. For them. All of you…"

Now she was blathering. She stopped and took another deep breath. Her heart was fluttering. She couldn't seem to keep two coherent thoughts in her head.

"There's no reason why you couldn't belong, Amy," Jake said with serious intent. "And our child certainly would, as naturally as all the other children. You met

Tess and Grace and Martin today. You must have seen how they…''

''Please…'' She waved an emphatic dismissal. ''That's not the point, Jake.''

''What is the point?''

''I wouldn't be living with them day in and day out. I'd be living with *you*.''

''So?''

Living with anyone wasn't simple. Amy knew from living with Steve…the adjustments, the compromises. It was hard enough *with love*. Without it…and always worrying about Jake connecting with other women, beautiful women running after him all the time…

She shook her head. ''I can't do it.''

''Why not?''

The need for this torment to be ended formed her answer. She looked at him squarely, defying any further persistance on this question, sure there was no way of refuting what was necessary to her.

''I don't love you, Jake.''

He stiffened. A muscle in his cheek contracted. It was as though she'd hit him physically and Amy had the strangest feeling—a strong, unshakable feeling—that she'd hurt him. Hurt him badly. Which rattled her. She hadn't considered Jake would be hurt by her rejection. Frustrated at not getting his own way, but not hurt.

She stared at him in wretched confusion and was caught by the changing expression in his eyes, the sharpening of his focus on her, the gathering of an intensity that felt like a powerful concentration of his will and energy, burning a challenge straight into her brain…a challenge that denied the knowledge she thought she had of him, denied even her knowledge of herself.

For a few riveting moments he seemed like a total stranger to her…or he took on dimensions she had not been aware of before. It gave her the scary feeling she was dealing with much more than she had anticipated, and she was suddenly riven with uncertainties. She almost jumped when he spoke.

"There is such a thing as a marriage of convenience, Amy. I believe it could work very well," he said quietly.

One certainty instantly exploded from all the thinking she'd done and because he'd unsettled her so deeply, she answered with fierce emphasis. "I will not be a *convenient* wife to you. That might suit you, Jake, out and about your life, but I don't see myself as the little woman at home, subservient to your needs."

"Subservient! Since when haven't I considered your needs?" His tone was harsher, edged with angry disbelief. "I've spent most of my time with you, putting your needs above my own. Can we have a bit of fair-mindedness here, Amy?"

She flushed, unable to pluck out one pertinent example of inconsideration on his part, and he'd been especially sensitive to her needs since Steve had dumped her. The long shadow of her parents' marriage crossed her mind…her mother serving her tyrannical father like a slave…but there was nothing tyrannical about Jake. He was more like a free-wheeling buccaneer, happy to lead anyone into adventurous fun.

"I want a marriage of sharing, Amy," he pressed. "We happen to do that well."

"Am I supposed to share you with all the women you

fancy?'' she flared, fighting her way out of being in the wrong.

''That's enough!''

He slammed his hand down on the counter, the angry frustration he'd repressed erupting with such force, Amy shrank back against the door. Then was angry at herself for being intimidated.

''Don't like the truth, Jake?'' she challenged, her chin lifting into fighting mode.

''You want the truth?'' he flung back at her, too incensed to back down this time. ''I'll give it to you. The high turnover of women in my life can be placed entirely at your door.''

''Mine?'' she retorted incredulously.

''Yours!'' He stabbed a finger at her. ''So try swallowing that for a change instead of spitting out slurs on my lack of staying power.''

''And just *how* can it be my fault?''

''Because what we sparked off each other—and don't you deny it, Amy—was stronger than anything I felt with the women I tried to relate to. Tried, because you made yourself inaccessible to me and it seemed pointless to wait for something that might never happen.''

The sheer passion in his voice rocked her into silence.

His eyes flashed with savage mockery. ''Oh, you did your best to block it out…the natural connection that was always there between us. With two long years of blocking it out, it's become a habit, hasn't it? Keep Jake at a distance. Don't let him close because something big might slip out of your control.''

A fierce pride hardened his features. ''Which it did.

The night we made a baby was bigger than anything I've felt in my life. And I'll bet my life it was for you, too.''

His mouth twisted into a bitter grimace. "Two years wasted while I was fool enough to respect your commitment to a guy who ended up cheating on you. Two years...and now you want to waste the lot, clinging to some prejudicial rubbish.''

His eyes glittered derision at her. "Give her more time, I told myself. She's still getting over that bastard. You'll win her in the end, Jake.''

He shook his head. "You're not even prepared to give me a chance for the sake of our child.''

The indictment he was delivering was so devastating, Amy could do nothing but listen, absorbing shock after shock as he forced her to recognise and acknowledge a different perception from what she had allowed herself. And the worst of it was, there was ample evidence to back up all he was saying.

She *had* used Steve as a barrier between them, no denying it if she was truly honest.

Once the barrier was gone...

She remembered Jake rattling on to baby Joshua after he'd learnt Steve was out of her life... *We've got Amy Taylor right where we want her...well, not precisely.*

Then later when she'd said she was on her own, Jake reminding her...*I was here for you. When your scumbag of a lover let you down, I was here for you.*

You do have me to count on.

Ruth's attitude to her...the Wonderwoman in Jake's life ever since she'd begun working for him. Even his mother saying Jake had talked so much about her... And they'd all told her she was the only woman he'd ever wanted to share his family Christmas.

The night of their *mating* flooded back into her mind... Jake asking her not to forget it, a special memory...uniquely special...and it truly had been...but she'd twisted it all to fit a different picture to the real truth...the truth he'd just forced her to see...the truth that damned everything she'd said and thought.

She saw the anger drain out of him, saw the passion give way to sadness, and had the sinking feeling she had dug her own grave and there was no way out of it.

"One day you'll have to explain to our child why you wouldn't marry me," he put to her, his eyes dull and opaque, blocking her out of his heart. "If you have to keep lying to yourself...well, I guess that's your choice. But don't lie to my child about me, Amy. I don't deserve that."

Her heart felt like stone. She had done him so many terrible injustices. And for what? To ensure she was protected against her own natural impulses, her own instincts? Jake was twice the man Steve was. More. She'd always known it. Of course she had. And told herself he was too much to handle, too risky to take on. He was too handsome, too attractive, and there was too much competition for him. She wasn't good enough to hold him.

Not good enough...

It was what her father had always said to her.

So she'd stayed with less, chosen safety, and told herself it was sensible, right, for the best.

Jake stepped back from the counter, stood very straight and tall, a man who'd fought and lost but not without dignity, not without courage and fire and belief in himself.

"Ask whatever you want of me and I'll give it to you," he said flatly. "But let's leave it for a few days. When you come back to work will be soon enough. I'll listen to your plans then. I've lost any taste for them right now."

He nodded to her. "If you'll excuse me…"

Without waiting for a reply, not expecting one, he moved out of the kitchen and headed for the front door. For several seconds, Amy was completely paralysed. The click of the knob being turned snapped her out of it.

"Wait!" Her voice was little more than a hoarse croak. She rushed to the far edge of the kitchen counter, desperately calling, "Jake, please wait!"

He stood at the end of the short hall, his back turned to her, his hand still on the doorknob, his shoulders squared, but his head was thrown high as though in acute listening mode.

He *was* waiting. Not inviting any more from her, but prepared to hear why she wanted to stop him from going. If she didn't get it right, he would go. She knew he would.

"What is it?" he rasped, impatient with her silence.

What could she say? Amy only knew she had to stop him from walking out of her life. Then the words came, sure and true.

"I'll marry you. I will. If you'll still have me."

CHAPTER SEVENTEEN

TENSION racked Amy as she watched Jake's shoulders rise and fall. It had to be a deep, deep breath he was taking and she had no idea what emotion he might be fighting to control.

Then he turned.

Slowly.

Amy *held* her breath.

He looked at her as though he didn't know her, scanning for a recognition which should have been there, but had somehow slipped past him. "Why, Amy?"

"Because…" The grave she'd dug for herself was so huge, so deep, she quailed at the task of climbing out of it. Her stomach contracted in sheer panic. Her mind skittered all over the place, finally grasping a hook Jake had given her. "What you said is true. I've lied and lied and lied, to stop myself…to stop *you* from getting too close to me."

His face tightened. His eyes gleamed yellow, hard and merciless. "That hardly makes marriage desirable for either of us," he bit out derisively.

Her hands fluttered out in desperate appeal. "I don't know how to explain it to you."

"Try!" It was a harsh, gutteral sound, scraped from wounds too freshly delivered for him to accept any evasion from her.

Amy knew it was a demand she had to meet, yet

165

where to start, how to make him understand? She hadn't understood it herself until he'd started putting it together for her.

"No backward steps now, Amy," he warned.

"You once asked me about my family," she plunged in, her eyes begging his forebearance. "I glossed over it, Jake."

Impatience exploded from him, his hands cutting the air in a sharp-scissor motion. "What can your family possibly have to do with us? You told me they've been out of your life for years."

"Control," she answered quickly, frantic to capture his attention and keep it. "With your upbringing, you couldn't imagine what my childhood was like…the constant emotional abuse from my father…having to wear it…trying not to be crushed. When I left home at sixteen, I swore never to let anyone have control over me again…not…not in an emotional sense."

"You expect me to accept that? After all the emotion you spent on your ex-lover?" he hurled at her in disgust. "Was it five years of nothing? Is that what you're telling me?"

"It wasn't like that!" she cried.

"You're not making sense to me, Amy."

"With Steve…there was never any talk of marriage between us. He called us *free spirits*. I felt…*safe*…with him."

"Safe!" Jake jeered.

"Yes, *safe!*" she snapped. "If you don't want to hear this, just go," she hurled back at him, driven to the end of her tether.

"Oh, I wouldn't miss this story for anything," he retorted scathingly. "Do go on."

Amy paused, taking a deep breath to calm herself. Her heart was thundering. The pulse in her temples was throbbing. There was no escape from this pain. It had to be faced, dealt with. Then the choice of what to do would be Jake's.

"If you want to understand anything about me instead of leaping to your own coloured judgements, then you'll listen," she told him as forcefully as she could. "If only for the sake of your child, you should listen."

The mention of the baby visibly pulled him back from the more personal issues between them. He took on an icy demeanour. "I'm listening."

They were so cold those words, Amy shivered. Nevertheless, she stuck grimly to her course, determined now to lay out the truth, whatever the consequences.

"To get back to Steve. He came from a damaged family, too. It effects people, Jake. You want someone—no one likes being alone—but you don't want to be owned. Because that's threatening."

He frowned, assessing what she was saying.

Encouraged, Amy rushed on to the vital point. "You threatened my sense of safety, Jake."

It startled him. He cocked his head on one side, considering this new perspective, his eyes still reserved but intensely watchful.

"You had the power to get at me, no matter how guarded I was against it. I guess you could say Steve was my bolthole from you."

Another jerk of his head, seemingly negative to Amy's view.

"Call me a coward if you like," she offered, feeling a heavy load of self-contempt for all the running away she'd done. "I *was* a coward with you."

"No." His eyes flashed hard certainty. "You always stood up to me."

"That wasn't brave. It was the only way to retain control," she pressed, trying to reach him on what she saw as the crux of everything. "I lost it the night you came here. I didn't listen to what you were saying afterwards. I was fighting to regain *control,* fighting your power to…" She paused, trying to get it right for him. "…To take over my life and do whatever you wanted with me."

He shook his head, patently appalled at how she had thought. "Amy, you'd always have a say in it. I've respected your wishes. I'd never not respect them," he argued, fiercely dismissing what probably seemed to him a gross allegation.

"I realise that now," she acknowledged. "But I was too frightened to see it then. I kept pushing you away from me, trying to protect myself. I tried to cling to the idea of *spontaneous combustion.* It was like an excuse. But you said it more truly a few minutes ago… *something big slipping out of control.*"

"But our child…" he burst out in angry confusion. "Didn't the baby we made…and its future…deserve some re-thinking?"

"I've been frightened of that, too, pushing it away from me," she confessed.

"But you want the baby. You said…you assured me…"

"That I wasn't thinking of a termination," she finished for him, leaping ahead, anxious to get it all out now. "I couldn't, Jake. Not because it was my baby. This will probably sound unreal to you, but from the moment the pregnancy was confirmed, I thought of the baby as *yours*."

"Blaming me?"

"No…no…" She shook her head vehemently, anguished by his misunderstanding. "I meant…you have this power, Jake. It…it clouds everything. I didn't think of it as *my* baby. Not even an entity by itself. It was like a bond you'd made with me. A tie. And I see-sawed between wanting the link with you and being frightened of what it might mean to me."

"Frightened… you're *frightened* of marrying me?" He looked repelled by the idea.

"I was. I'm not anymore," she cried in a fluster. "Don't you see?" she pleaded. "There was no way out because of the baby. And if you hurt me…it's like a trap. I can't bring myself to let you go…yet you have the power to damage me far more than my father ever did. For far longer."

"You have the same power over me," he said tersely. "Don't you realise that?"

It jolted her. She hadn't realised it. Hadn't even thought of it. Yet she'd seen the hurt she'd given him, was watching the pain of her rejection working through him now as she pleaded her case.

"The power goes both ways," he said less harshly. "It's up to both of us not to abuse it."

She rubbed at her forehead. "I don't know what to do. The baby…" She looked down at her stomach, touched it tentatively. "It's still unreal to me as mine.

Maybe I'm not maternal. I wanted it to belong to your family. I don't think I know how to be a mother. My own mother…'' She raised anguished eyes. ''…She was too frightened of my father to stand up for us.''

''It only takes love, Amy. Freely given.'' He grimaced. ''Maybe your mother didn't feel free to give it. But there's no reason you can't. At least to our child.''

Freely given…he'd said that to her before…the night they'd made the baby…their baby. She wished she could feel good about it, that it wasn't some kind of a trap for either of them. Maybe that would come. She hoped so. She needed to feel good. Good enough, anyway.

Jake still didn't know all he had to know, and she had to tell him. No more lies. No evasions. Her eyes ached with the need to reach him as she said, ''I do want you, Jake. I've wanted you for so long… I said I didn't want to go to bed with you but that was another lie. I lied because I didn't want you to know how much I had thought about it, how much I wanted it. Wanted you…''

She could read no reaction from him. He was completely still. Whether he was absorbing what she said or shutting it out she couldn't tell. She felt drained from the effort of unburdening herself to him, yet the compulsion to draw him back to her would not let her rest.

''Today, when you kissed me under the mistletoe… I wanted to believe what you made me feel was forever. It meant…too much. It scared me again. And then you said…it was only a Christmas kiss…''

''No,'' he denied vehemently. ''I said a man was entitled to kiss a woman standing under a mistletoe on Christmas day.''

"So I screwed that up, too," she said helplessly. "I guess I've made it too hard for you to believe me now."

"What's too hard for me to believe, Amy?"

Not too hard. Impossible. But she said it anyway.

"I love you, Jake."

It was true. She loved everything about him, loved him so much it hurt. Her heart was bleeding with all she felt for him. And it hurt all the more because he hadn't said he loved her. He wasn't saying it now, either. He just stood there, staring at her with seemingly unseeing eyes.

Maybe he didn't love her and was shocked by her confession. She'd assumed…but it could have been his ego hurt by her blanket rejection, not his heart. Why hadn't she thought of that? Because she needed… Dear God! She *needed* his love. *She couldn't marry him without it.*

"Jake…" His name scraped out of her convulsing throat. She swallowed hard. Her hands lifted in agitated appeal. "…If you don't love me…"

He moved then. Before Amy could take a breath she was wrapped in his arms and held so close she could feel his heart beating and his warmth flooding through her. She wrapped her own arms around his neck, buried her face against his broad shoulder, and hung on for dear life as tremors racked her body and her mind slipped into meltdown, knowing only that Jake had taken her back, he was holding her safe, and they were together again.

He rubbed his cheek against her hair, tenderly soothing. "Don't be frightened of me. Not ever, Amy," he said, his voice furred with passionate feeling. "If you'll just open your heart to me, I'll listen. We'll work things out together. That's how it should be.''

He'd forgiven her. The relief of it went through her like a tidal wave.

"Maybe I should have spoken…instead of holding back," he went on, his own torment pouring out. "I guess we all try to protect ourselves from hurt. You'd been with Steve for so long… I was wary of a rebound effect. I wanted you free and clear of him, Amy, before I told you how I felt."

How could she blame him? She'd given him so little to work on.

He sighed, his warm breath caressing her ear. "I've loved you for a very long time. I can't imagine not loving you."

He loved her.

It wasn't just for the baby.

It wasn't only the pull of physical chemistry.

He loved her.

The wonderful surge of energy that shot through Amy pushed her head up. She wanted—needed—to see. There was no mistake this time. No misreading. The molten gold in his eyes glowed with such rich depth of feeling, she knew instinctively this was only the tip of a river that flowed through every part of him.

"But I do need some love back from you without having to fight for it," he pleaded, searching her eyes for it. "Do you understand?"

"Freely given," she whispered, awed by the strength of his giving.

"Yes."

She didn't hesitate. She went up on tiptoe, pulled his

head down to hers and kissed him with all the passion his giving had released. A storm of passion. Years of pent-up feeling, freed at last, to be expressed, revelled in with joy and love and the deepest, most intense pleasure. No fear. Not the tiniest hint of fear or worry or doubt about anything. He loved her. She loved him. And the baby made a beautiful bond between them.

She took him to bed with her, showing him it was her choice, her desire, her wish to share everything with him, openly and honestly, and they made love for a very long time. There was no need to stop and every need to experience and learn all they wanted to learn of each other. The wonder of touching—touching without any inhibitions—was incredibly marvellous.

Jake was the most magnificent man. In every way. She adored him. And he adored her right back...sensually, sexually, emotionally. And when he kissed and caressed her stomach so lovingly, and she saw the happiness and pleasure in his eyes at the thought of her carrying his baby inside—their baby—she suddenly felt an intense wave of love for the life they had created, Jake and her together...their child...who would be brought up with love...freely given.

Instead of being dark and fearful and threatening, the future now shone with so much glorious promise.

Except...

"Jake!" In a rush of agitation, she lifted his head up.

"Mmh..." He smiled at her, his eyes dancing with teasing wickedness. "Can't I do what I want with you now?"

"Yes, but..." She sighed. "Your mother doesn't like me, Jake. She won't approve of us marrying."

"Ah!" He sobered into serious speculation. "I suspected something had gone on between you today. So what did?"

Amy grimaced at the unpleasant memory. "Your mother thinks I'm loose…living with Steve…not marrying him. She said my mother would have advised me it wasn't good. Wasn't right."

"She spoke out of ignorance, Amy," he said soothingly. "That can easily be fixed."

"It was like she was warning me off you, Jake."

"No." He gave his quirky smile. "Just warning you off living with me. She got upset about me giving you the apartment."

"What?"

"Okay…" He rolled his eyes. "I've been a bit devious, but it was for your own good, Amy."

"This is your apartment?" she squeaked. The colours used in the decor…his knowledge of her garage…

"I just wanted you away from any memory of Steve, so I fixed it with Ted Durkin and…"

"You made up all those conditions?"

"Well, the rent was too steep so I had to bring it down in a way you'd accept."

"And Ted Durkin was in on it?" She remembered her suspicion at the time, the suspicion she'd dismissed because of Ted Durkin's manner.

"He helped me make up a credible cover story."

"Oh!" She didn't know whether to feel outraged or…beautifully taken care of.

"Anyhow, Mum thought I was plotting to set you up as my mistress. But I wasn't, Amy. I truly wasn't. Marriage was always on my mind."

She laughed, suddenly remembering something else. "You just wanted to get me where you wanted me." Her eyes danced back at his.

"Precisely," he agreed, completely unabashed.

And she laughed some more, all the doubts of the past behind her.

"Mum probably thought, because you'd lived with Steve, you might choose to do that with me, too, so she was trying to steer you straight." He heaved an exasperated sigh. "She just can't keep out of things."

Amy sobered up. "I'm afraid I said some harsh things to her, Jake. About you and your women. Sorry, but…" She shook her head regretfully. "I was really quite rude, cutting her off when she tried to defend you."

He shrugged. "All's well that ends well, Amy. I'll call her now, fix it up."

His confidence amazed her. He leaned over, picked up the bedside telephone, dialed, listened, then said, "It's Jake, Ruth. Is Mum still there?"

He sighed as his sister apparently rattled on.

"Never mind that, get Mum for me." He smiled at Amy. "Ruth's all excited about seeing us kissing. She knows how I feel about you."

"Do they all?" Amy asked curiously.

"More or less. I'm no good at hiding things from my family," he confessed.

Then he'd be no good at hiding things from her anymore, either, Amy happily decided. Not that he was trying to. She thought fleetingly of Steve who'd clam up like an oyster whenever she'd tried to dig anything out of him. It was so different with Jake, ecstatically different.

"Mum?"

Apparently his mother rattled on to him, too. His family were certainly great talkers. Which was good. Great! Nothing repressed or suppressed.

"No, you haven't ruined everything." His eyes twinkled at Amy. "In fact, things couldn't be better. Amy loves me and she wants to marry me. Except she thinks you don't approve of her."

Another long speech which Jake interpreted for Amy as it went on.

"Mum is very sorry…she didn't mean to give that impression…she thinks you're beautiful…she thinks we're well suited…and you obviously have good sense and taste to choose me as your husband…she's relieved she didn't upset the applecart, so to speak…we're invited to lunch tomorrow…so she can show you how happy she is about us…is that okay, Amy?"

She nodded.

"We'll be there, Mum." He grinned as he put the receiver down. "She says this is the best Christmas ever. The last one of her brood finally settling down." He laughed, all his shadows gone, too. "It certainly is the best Christmas for me, Amy."

"Me, too," she agreed, her heart brimming over with happiness.

Jake gathered her close and kissed her, and she stretched against him languorously, provocatively, wanting all of him again. He was not slow to oblige, and Amy exulted in the sense of belonging to him, not Jake the rake, *her* Jake, always and forever.

And she'd belong to his wonderful family, too.

No more being alone.

Not for her nor her baby.

Their baby.

The miracle of love, she thought, and gave herself up to it.

Freely.

CHAPTER EIGHTEEN

NEW Year's Eve...

Amy watched *Free Spirit* gliding through the water to the wharf. It was a beautiful yacht, long sleek lines, exuding luxury, glamour, no expense spared in design or amenities. Murmurs of excitement and pleasurable anticipation ran around the select group of Jake's clients as they waited to board.

Free Spirit...

The name reminded her of Steve. And his blonde. Tonight was their wedding night. But she was not going to drown herself. No way. She was going to have a wonderful night with Jake, a wonderful life with him, too. In fact, she was more free with Jake than she'd ever felt before.

The men in the group wore formal dinner suits, adding style and class to the festive evening. Amy couldn't help feeling pride in the fact that not one of them looked as handsome as Jake. He outshone them all. The strange part was, she didn't feel the least bit insecure about it. Jake had only to glance at her and she knew no other woman here—regardless of beauty or finery—held a candle to her, not in Jake's mind.

She smiled to herself, remembering the women's magazine with the article on exit signs. It was still in the bottom drawer of her desk at the office, still unread. No need to read it now. Or ever. Jake believed implicitly in the marriage vows. Absolute commitment. For better, for worse...until death do us part.

Since Christmas, she had seen so much more of his family, and they all shared the same attitude. They'd been brought up to view a good marriage as the most desirable state in life, with children as the blessed bonus. Not one of them had anything negative to say when Jake had made the announcement about the baby. Expressions of delight, congratulations, offers of help from all the women were instantly forthcoming. And Jake's mother could not have been nicer, only too happy to push wedding plans.

Amy shook her head over her initial impression of Elizabeth Rose Carter. Jake's mother was really a very generous person, wanting everything to be lovely and possibly a little too concerned that it be so. His father had more of an optimistic, let-it-be outlook, confident his children would work out what was best for themselves. Amy considered him a real darling.

As the yacht docked and two of the deckhands started sliding out the boarding ramp, Jake hooked Amy's arm around his and smiled at her. "Ready to start hostessing?"

"Lead on." she replied happily.

His smile turned quirky. "Actually you don't have to hostess. I've hired people to do the necessary."

"But you said..."

"I needed some excuse to get you on this cruise with me." His eyes sparkled wickedly. "It was my seduction plan. And I see no reason to change it."

She laughed, hugging him closer to her as they walked to the ramp.

"You know, Amy, you look stunning in red but I've got to say, that blue you're wearing completely knocks me out." he declared decisively.

"You really like this outfit?" It was a long skirt and tunic in a soft, slinky, royal blue fabric, to which she'd added an ornate silver belt, silver shoes and silver jewellery.

His eyes gleamed gold. "You give it the magic of the night, my love."

"Mmh…keep up that seductive talk and who knows where it may get you?"

He laughed.

They were both of them bubbling with good humour as they preceded their party onto the yacht. A flight of steps led up to the main sundeck, an outdoor entertainment centre with a long bench lounge, table, chairs. Two hostesses hovered by a bar table which had been set up with wines, beer, fruit juice, iced water.

"Champagne, sir?" one of them instantly asked Jake, her eyes feasting on his every feature.

"Two, thank you." he replied, indicating Amy be served first.

Jake in control, and not the least bit interested in other women's interest, Amy observed. As he'd once said to her, any amount of interest was futile when it wasn't returned.

They moved to a position by the door leading in to the formal saloon, ready to greet everyone as they passed through to check out the luxurious appointments of the yacht.

In the saloon, three long deeply cushioned sofas, their cream upholstery trimmed with terracotta piping, were positioned around a polished granite coffee table, graced by an artistic floral arrangement. Beyond it was the formal dining room, its black lacquered table surrounded by black leather chairs.

Below, there were two queen-size staterooms with full ensuites and two twin bedrooms with ensuites, as well, all of the rooms designer decorated. The rear deck featured a spa-pool, and the bridge deck above them provided more lounging space for a topside view of their cruising around the harbour.

Amy was ready with all the facts and figures about the yacht should anyone ask. Mostly, the clients and their guests wanted to see for themselves, passing by her and Jake after a few words, happy to explore and assess everything on their own.

"Jake, darling!"

Amy glanced back from chatting to one couple to find the voluptuous blonde who'd fallen on Jake at *The Watermark,* coming on strongly again... Isabella Maddison...red talons raised ready to grab and dig in.

The sight of Amy stepping back to Jake's side stopped her in mid-pounce. The feline green eyes flashed venom.

"Oh! I see you have your companion with you."

"More than that, Isabella." Jake informed her, sliding his arm around Amy's shoulders and bestowing a smile lit with very possessive love on her. "My wife-to-be. Amy has finally agreed to marry me."

"Finally?" Isabella echoed in shock.

"Yes." Amy confirmed, ostentatiously holding up her left hand where Jake had placed a magnificent solitaire diamond ring on her third finger. She wriggled her fingers to make it flash under Isabella's catty eyes. "I decided to haul him in for good. It's time we had a family.''

''Well…congratulations.'' came the weak rejoinder.

''Do help yourself to champagne.'' Amy invited sweetly. ''This is a cruise to really enjoy.''

''Yes…thank you.''

Off she moved in a daze and Amy couldn't help grinning at Jake.

His wolf eyes gleamed. ''You *were* jealous of her that day at *The Watermark*.''

''I could have scratched her eyes out.'' Amy admitted.

''I should have raced you off to bed that afternoon.''

''You can do it tonight instead.''

''Oh, I will. I will.'' he promised her. ''Though I doubt we'll make it as far as the bed.''

Which put Amy in such a high state of sexual arousal, she barely tasted the gourmet food circulated by the hostesses; smoked salmon with a sprinkling of caviar, swordfish wrapped in Chinese spinach, little cups of sweet lamb curry and rice, deep-fried corn fritters, tandoori chicken kebabs. She tried them all, wanting to experience everything about tonight, but her awareness of Jake was uppermost.

It was a beautiful evening, a clear sky filling with stars as it darkened, only a light breeze ruffling the water, the warmth of the long summer day still lingering in the air.

The harbour was almost a maze of yachts, all sorts of small crafts, pleasure boats, the tall ships that had sailed in from around the world, ferries trying to weave through them all.

Crowds had gathered at vantage points around the foreshores, some of them virtually hanging on cliffs, clinging to rocks, waiting to see the fireworks display. It seemed as though all of Sydney had come out to watch the spectacle and celebrate New Year's Eve together.

The captain positioned *Free Spirit* mid-harbour, quite close to Fort Denison, giving a centre-stage view of the Opera House and the great Coat-hanger bridge which would be highly featured by the fireworks. As twilight sunk into the darkness of night, most of the guests moved up to the top deck, Jake and Amy with them. The display was scheduled to begin at nine o'clock, so families could enjoy it before children became too tired.

Amy leant against the waist-high railing. Jake stood behind her, his arms encircling her, holding her close, letting her feel his arousal, exciting her with it. There might have been only the two of them, alone together. Everyone was looking skywards, waiting for the darkness to light up with colour.

Then the fireworks began, shooting up from the great stone pylons that supported the bridge—huge explosive bursts of stars, balls of brilliant colour growing bigger and bigger before showering the sky with a brilliant rain of sparks, the whole skyline erupting in a wildly splendid mingling of reds and blues and greens and gold and silver. It was magical, glorious, totally captivating. It went on and on, becoming more and more surprising, stunning, fantastic. The whole span of the bridge came alight, streams of gold pouring down to the water far below it.

"What are you thinking?" Jake murmured in her ear.

"I was thinking of our wedding night and how it will feel." Amy whispered.

"How do you imagine it will feel?"

"Like this, Jake. Like this."

Suddenly, flashing across the huge coat hanger arch were the two curved lines of a smiling mouth, outlined in brilliant gold.

"Yes." Jake breathed in awe. "Just like that."

Amy's heart swelled with love and happiness and wonder.

A smile…

The smile of fulfilment…

On their wedding night.

Lindsay Armstrong was born in South Africa but now lives in Australia with her New Zealand-born husband and their five children. They have lived in nearly every state of Australia and have tried their hand at some unusual – for them – occupations, such as farming and horse-training – all grist to the mill for a writer! Lindsay started writing romances when their youngest child began school and she was left feeling at a loose end. She is still doing it and loving it.

Lindsay's latest book is on sale in February. So look out in Modern Romance™ for:
HIS CONVENIENT PROPOSAL

MARRIED FOR REAL

by

Lindsay Armstrong

CHAPTER ONE

ARIZONA Adams flung her large black hat on a settee, crossed the lounge to the mirror over the fireplace and withdrew the pins securing her thick hair. She ran her fingers through it as it fell to her shoulders in a rich river of chestnut. It was strong, abundant hair with a bit of a wave in it, and she could do pretty much as she liked with it. Her late husband, who had died a year ago and whose memorial service she'd just attended, had often commented that it had a life of its own.

She sighed and looked at her elegant outfit, an almost ankle-length slim black dress worn with a long cream jacket, and thought he would probably have approved of it. He'd also often said that she had an innate but different sense of style, although he'd been fond of adding that she could wear anything and look good. But the truth was, she did her own thing when it came to clothes, and for some reason it generally came out right—then again, according to her mother, she always did her own thing pretty much, which was fairly ironic coming from her mother, who had named her only daughter after a song first and a state in the USA quite incidentally. Yet here she was, Arizona reflected also with irony, feeling tense and uneasy as well as sad and not at all sure whether she would be allowed to continue to do her own thing.

She turned away from the fireplace and glanced at

5

her watch. Nearly six o'clock, which left six more
hours of this day—would he come?

He came five minutes later.

Arizona heard the doorbell chime just after she'd shed
her jacket and was picking up her hat. She stilled, and
right on cue the double lounge doors opened and
Cloris stood there.

'Sorry, Arizona,' she said diffidently, 'I know you
didn't want to be disturbed but it's Mr. Holmes. I—
well, I didn't like to say no.'

'That's all right, Cloris,' Arizona said resignedly,
laying her hat and jacket down with exaggerated care.
'I'm sure Mr. Holmes is a hard man to say no to.'

Cloris, who liked to think she enjoyed a more ex-
alted station than housekeeper but who nevertheless
was a marvellous housekeeper, smiled gratefully. 'He
was at the service,' she confided. 'At the back—I
don't think many people saw him. I only saw him
because I was at the back myself and, well—' she
gestured '—that's Mr. Holmes.'

'That's Mr. Holmes,' Arizona echoed. 'Show him
in, please, Cloris.'

Cloris beamed then hesitated. 'Would you like me
to bring in some, er, drinks and snacks?'

'No,' Arizona said definitely.

Cloris opened her mouth but detected the gleam in
Arizona's grey eyes, and she withdrew with a suddenly shuttered expression. Arizona grimaced. Ten
seconds later Declan Holmes walked into the room.
He was, as Arizona had often heard commented, a
fine figure of a man. Tall and well built, he had thick
dark hair and Irish blue eyes. That he often had a

saturnine, cynical look in those blue eyes didn't seem to lower him in the estimation of many women by an iota. If anything, it was the opposite. Which was a fact that she'd thought about once or twice with some cynicism herself—her own sex's preference for dark, damning men. And, as she'd often seen him, he was faultlessly outfitted in a dark grey suit that hid neither his powerful shoulders nor lean hips and justly became his position of wealth and power.

'Hello, Declan,' she said coolly and with some idea of taking the initiative as he stopped a few feet from her. 'So you did come.'

He raised a wry eyebrow at her. 'I don't break my word lightly, Arizona. How are you? I believe I'm to be denied the pleasure of having a drink with you.'

She narrowed her eyes and said a bare, 'Yes.'

'That's a bit harsh, isn't it?' he murmured amusedly. 'You look as if you could do with one yourself. It can't have been an easy afternoon.'

'And about to become even harder, I imagine.'

'We'll see,' he said placidly. 'Did you really think I wouldn't come? I thought you knew me better than that, Arizona.'

'It's strange you should say that, Declan, because I hardly know you at all,' she retorted.

'Now that, my dear, is not quite true,' he replied. 'I think it's fair to say we've been—eyeing each other over the fence for a couple of years now.'

A flash of anger lit her eyes. 'I have not been eyeing you or anyone else over any fence,' she said precisely.

He moved his shoulders slightly. 'Well, put it this way— I've certainly been eyeing you, Arizona. And

I'm equally certain that you have not been unaware of it.'

She tensed inwardly and would have loved to be able to deny this with composure and surety. Unfortunately, although he'd made no overt moves at all, she had been aware, by some inner sense, of Declan Holmes's interest. There had been times right from the day they'd first met when she'd looked across a room and encountered his blue gaze, times, she couldn't deny to herself, when something within had responded, some curl of interest had awoken— which she'd thoroughly despised herself for. And correspondingly there had been times when she'd gone out of her way to avoid him, only to be visited by the uncomfortable feeling that he'd known exactly what she was doing and why… *But I'm damned if I'm actually going to admit anything to him.*

She said matter of factly, 'A lot of men look.'

He smiled a little dryly. 'One of the hazards of being such a good sort, I guess.'

Arizona shrugged. 'I don't really care whether you think I'm vain, Declan.'

'As a matter of fact I don't—just honest, in this case. Do they all ask you to marry them?' he enquired guilelessly.

Arizona was saved having to reply as there was a knock at the door. It was Cloris, looking pink and determined, which didn't happen often, but when it did she was as tenacious as a miniature bulldog with faded blonde curls. She had with her a trolley with an array of drinks and a plate of snacks, and she stood in the doorway staring beseechingly at her boss.

Arizona closed her eyes then said in a goaded sort of voice, 'Bring it in, Cloris, bring it in.'

And so Cloris spent a few fluttering minutes deploying her trolley and departed finally in an even worse flutter after a few kind words from Declan Holmes.

Who said to Arizona once the door was closed again, 'Routed, I'm afraid, Arizona—are you going to take it in good grace? In other words, may I pour you a drink and myself one and may we then sit down and discuss—things more comfortably?' But there was a gleam of mockery in his blue eyes.

Arizona breathed deeply, shrugged and sat down. 'Thanks, a brandy and dry,' she said briefly.

He poured two of the same, handed her hers then sat down opposite her. 'Cheers. Well, here's to the fact that I'm here to ask you to marry me as I promised I would twelve months ago—to the day,' he said gently, sipped his drink then placed it beside him.

'And you haven't, in the intervening twelve months, reflected that if nothing else it was pure bad taste to ask me that on the day of my husband's funeral?' she retorted.

'On the contrary, I think advising you of my intentions but allowing a whole year to pass before I acted on them was observing all the proprieties. Particularly in view of the fact that your last marriage was a marriage of convenience, Arizona.'

'How dare you?' She stared at him coldly.

'Let's examine the facts then,' he replied smoothly, 'and don't forget I knew Pete well. But you came here to Scawfell as a penniless governess, didn't you, Arizona? To look after the four motherless children

of a man twice your age. Less than a year later you
married him, and all this—' he gestured, taking in the
elegant room and somehow more, the whole beautiful
estate of Scawfell '—became yours.'

'No, it didn't,' Arizona contradicted through lips
pale with anger. 'It's held in trust for his children, as
you very well know, Declan. After all, you're the
trustee.'

'All the same, you have the use of it guaranteed
until you remarry, Arizona,' he said coolly, 'and the
means so that you can continue to use it in the manner
to which you've become accustomed.' His eyes lingered on the smooth skin of her bare arms then drifted
down the exquisitely tailored black dress.

'I didn't want that, I didn't know it was in his will,'
she said steadily. 'Nor have I done anything in the
manner to which I had become accustomed, quote
unquote, since Pete died, other than look after his
children and—'

'How are they?' he broke in.

'Fine,' Arizona said briskly. 'Why don't you ask
them how I rate as a stepmother, incidentally?'

'I've never accused you of not being a good stepmother, Arizona,' he returned mildly.

'Only a fortune huntress,' she said with soft mockery.

'Well, why did you do it?' he countered.

'Marry Pete?' she said with hauteur. 'That's my
business, Declan, and I'm afraid you're destined to
remain in ignorance.'

'Even when you're married to me?'

She took this without a blink and said thoughtfully,
'Tell me something—considering what good friends

you were, didn't you think it was in incredibly bad taste to be eyeing your friend's wife across the fence, as you put it yourself, Declan, if *nothing* else?'

'Unfortunately one can't help one's—instinctive reactions. And as I did nothing but look on the odd occasion, no, I don't.'

'And what would have happened if Pete hadn't died?' she asked caustically.

He shrugged wryly. 'Who knows? I might have got tired of looking, although I'm not sure about that. Or you might have got tired of Pete.' He grimaced.

Arizona ignored this and said, 'But, and this does puzzle me, you now want to marry me, despite the fact that you think I only married Pete with an eye to the main chance. That doesn't altogether make sense, if you'll forgive me.'

'I think it makes perfect sense,' he responded. 'I have a much larger fortune than Peter ever had, which makes me an excellent candidate for your hand—provided, of course, you reserve that lovely, sexy—' he looked her up and down '—body for my exclusive use,' he finished, looking into her eyes with a gleam of pure insolence in his.

'That's incredbly—that's diabolical,' Arizona said with an effort, an effort to stay calm. 'You're talking about trade, nothing else—'

'I rather thought you understood about trade all too well, Arizona,' he broke in.

'Contrary to what you think, Declan, I was extremely fond of Pete,' she said, and stood up restlessly.

'But you weren't in love with him?' he said after

a moment as he sat with his arm along the back of the settee and watched her thoughtfully.

'I…' She stopped then looked directly into his blue eyes. 'It wasn't a grand passion, *if* they exist.' She shrugged. 'But yes, I loved him in a way. A warm, committed way that I can't imagine ever loving you.' And her grey eyes were suddenly challenging.

'Would it surprise you to find yourself loving me in a different way?'

'Are you talking about love or lust?' she asked with an insolent glint of her own.

'They're not always easy to separate, Arizona,' he drawled.

'Oh, I think they would be in this case.'

A faint smile twisted his lips, then he sat forward, picked up his drink and regarded its depths for a moment before he said, 'Well, my dear, this may be the moment to talk turkey then. Pete's rather complicated estate has finally cleared probate, and unfortunately, the outlook is not good at all.'

Arizona frowned at him. 'What do you mean?'

'You may not have realized this, but Scawfell is heavily mortgaged and was, to an extent, mortgaged against Peter's future income, which should have payed it off—he was one of the most famous, sought-after architects in the country. What he neglected to do, however, was take out any insurance against, well, the unknown happening such as did happen.'

Arizona sat down rather suddenly. 'What are you saying?'

'I'm saying,' he said levelly, 'that although he was the finest architect, he wasn't much of a businessman. He was also very secretive so that not even I knew how complicated his affairs were or how unwise some of his investments. What it boils down to is that Scawfell will have to be sold to save anything of his estate for his children, let alone the provisions he made for you, but in the real estate climate of the moment, it's debatable if there will be anything left for any of you.'

'But I don't understand,' Arizona whispered, paling as his words sank in. 'He never said a word to me about all this, not—' she stopped then continued '—not that I ever asked him. But he didn't seem to have any worries about finances.'

'He wouldn't have had if he hadn't died so unexpectedly.'

'But...' She stood up again, uncaring that he was watching her like a hawk now. 'This is terrible! It was bad enough for them to lose their father like that, in a car accident, after losing their mother to an incurable disease and with no living relatives—'

'Which was why as their trustee I agreed to them staying with you, Arizona,' he said with a significant little look. 'They don't have anyone else, no grandparents left alive, aunts or uncles et cetera because both their parents were single children.'

'I *know* that. And to lose Scawfell as well,' she said hollowly. 'Are you sure?'

'I'm sorry to have to say I'm all too sure.'

'So...what will we do?' She stared at him dazedly. 'Ben is enough of a handful at the moment as it is.' She stopped abruptly and bit her lip.

'So they're not all fine—what about the others?'

Arizona closed her eyes briefly then said a little

bitterly, 'I'm sure fifteen-year-old boys can be a handful without the trauma he's gone through—'

'Oh, I'm sure they can,' Declan Holmes replied dryly. 'Especially without a father. What about ten-year-old twins—and Daisy?'

'How did you find them on the last of your monthly visits?' Arizona countered.

He looked amused. 'My monthly visits that you so pointedly went out of your way to avoid whenever you could? Daisy was—Daisy,' he said. 'The twins were extremely taken up with the model I brought down, and Ben was out, too.'

Arizona sighed. 'Sarah and Richard do seem to have bounced back, but then they have each other,' she said of Peter Adams's ten-year-old twins. 'As for Daisy, it took her months to understand he was never coming back, then she got weepy for a while, but I think she's forgetting now, although she tends to cling, but I'm always here so—Ben is the only real problem.'

'How so?'

'He's moody, he seems to have given up on school—he seems to hate the whole world, other than his horse and riding, at times.'

'I see.'

'That's a great help,' Arizona remarked after a pause.

'I didn't think you wanted my help.'

'I don't, but you insisted on knowing. Look,' she said impatiently, 'this is getting us nowhere. How come no-one has seen fit to let me know about all this before today?'

'A lot of it wasn't known for a time. There were

offshore ventures that took quite some time and patience to unravel.'

'But I don't understand,' she said, perplexed. 'How have we been going along in the meantime?'

Declan Holmes paused, narrowed his eyes and said, 'I hope you don't hate this too much, Arizona, but with my help.'

She gasped. 'Do you mean you've been supporting us?'

'Precisely.'

'But why didn't you tell me?'

He said reflectively, 'I had several motives, Arizona. I didn't want to add any more burdens for the kids to have to cope with so soon after losing their second parent, and I thought it would be difficult for you to carry on unconcernedly once you knew.'

'Well, you're right,' she said through her teeth, 'but it would have been on their behalf not mine that I would have been unable to remain unconcerned despite what I have no doubt you're implying!'

'Perhaps,' he said mildly.

'So what were your other motives?' she demanded.

He raised an eyebrow. 'I guess I wanted to see how you did—conduct yourself over the last twelve months.'

'Before you came back and asked me to marry you again? How do you know I haven't taken a legion of lovers in the interim?'

'Have you?'

Arizona made a sound of pure, despairing exasperation.

'Look, don't answer—I know you haven't,' he said with a lightening grin.

Arizona opened her mouth, closed it then all but spat, 'Have you been having me followed or something like that?'

'No, nothing like that, but I do have my sources,' he replied imperturbably. 'In fact,' he continued softly, 'it's almost as if you've been waiting for me, my dear.'

'So…it's never entered your calculations,' she said with difficulty, 'that I might just have been grieving and not interested in forming any liaisons?'

'Well, one day I'll probably know a lot more about you, but in the meantime, will you marry me, Arizona?'

'No. Definitely not,' she added to give it more force and then tried a little more force. 'It would be the very last thing I'd do. Do I make myself clear?'

His blue gaze didn't alter much—perhaps a tinge of amusement crept into it. 'Not even if I told you that it was one way, probably the only way, to save Scawfell for Pete's kids?'

Arizona realized suddenly that she could hear her heart beating heavily, that her lips were dry and her breathing ragged. And nearly a minute passed before she said in a voice quite unlike her own, 'What do you mean?'

'I mean that if you married me I would pay off the mortgage on the estate so that the children had something to inherit as well as a familiar beloved spot to live out their childhood, and I would support them as my own—as our own.'

'Do you mean you would bring them up as your children?' she said uncertainly.

'We could bring them up as ours.'

Arizona stared at him dazedly then licked her lips. 'What's the alternative—for them, I mean?'

'Well, I would certainly never let Pete's children starve, but taking them on single-handedly wouldn't be the same for them— I'd probably have to relocate them. I wouldn't have a great deal of time for them although I suppose I could always get another governess for them.'

'Stop,' she whispered then cleared her throat. 'This is the most arrant blackmail I've ever heard—*why?*' she asked intensely.

'Why?' he mused. 'I should have thought that was obvious—I want you, Arizona!'

'There's a saying about hell and fury and women scorned—are you sure you're not suffering from being scorned, Declan?' she asked scathingly.

He laughed. 'It could be a bit of that, too, I guess.'

'On the other hand what would you have thought of me if I had responded to your eyes across the fence?'

'Well, I probably wouldn't have had to marry you, would I?' he said placidly.

'That doesn't make sense—it's worse,' she declared bitterly. 'It puts me in a no-win situation, which is simply crazy!'

'Well, now, that remains to be seen. Being married to me won't be nearly so bad as you're cracking it up, Arizona. At one stroke you'll retain Scawfell, you'll retain four children you're very fond of and who need you—think of that if nothing else.'

Arizona closed her eyes and for the life of her couldn't help thinking of it. Thinking of Daisy, whose natural mother had died when she was two, Daisy who didn't remember her and didn't understand about stepmothers and thought Arizona *was* her mother, Daisy who worried... Thought about Sarah and Richard, charming twins so long as you understood the full extent of their dependence on each other, and Ben. Poor, tortured Ben who was still bereft without his father, who now viewed the world with cynicism and disenchantment and was increasingly disruptive... She opened her eyes and stared blankly at Declan Holmes.

'Also,' he said quietly, 'you'll have your sex life taken care of—and an awful lot of pin money to spend, Arizona.'

'If I didn't hate you before, I do now,' she responded equally quietly.

He smiled briefly. 'But you'll do it?'

'Only because I have no choice.'

'Not entirely true,' he drawled, 'but nevertheless, when?'

'Oh, I think I'll leave it to you to name the day, Declan.'

'Is that some kind of a cop-out, Arizona?' he murmured.

'No,' she said baldly. 'Merely an indication of my lack of interest.'

His lips twisted but he said only, 'How about a month from today then? It will give the kids a bit of time to get used to the idea.'

'If you say so—me, as well, I suppose.' She grimaced.

'You've had a lot longer than that,' he remarked softly. 'If it's so repugnant I'm surprised you haven't left the country or something equally dramatic.'

'But you knew damn well you had me here as some kind of a hostage, didn't you, Declan?'

'Did I?' he reflected. '*Exactly* what *kind* of a hostage, is what one wonders, to be honest. While I don't doubt your devotion to the kids—oh, well—' he gestured with one long, strong hand '—time will no doubt tell. Why don't you invite me for the weekend, Arizona? We could start the process of apprising the world of our intentions.'

'Come, by all means,' Arizona replied with utterly false cordiality. In fact her stance and the look in her eyes said something quite different—come and do your damnedest, in other words.

To which, after a long, challenging moment, he merely smiled gently as if to say, *We'll see, we'll see...*

'Dearest Mother,' Arizona wrote that night. 'I suppose it's still all right to call you that and not Sister Margaret Mary, but I digress. The news is that I'm getting married again—now I know how you opposed, from the seclusion of your convent, my first marriage but from a purely materialistic sense, this one is even better. You've probably heard of Declan Holmes—who hasn't? Yes, the same one who took over his father's media empire (small media empire) at the age of twenty-six and now, at about thirty-three, could probably be justifiably termed a media magnate. Well, he was a good friend of Peter's, he's the children's trustee and guardian and as I'm the children's stepmother, it seems like a good idea. So far as your objections to my previous marriage go, he's only ten years older than me, he's not a father figure or anything like that, he's a mighty marriageable man, but no, I'm not in love with him and I don't think he's in love with me. What else can I tell you? It's to be a month from today…'

Arizona lifted her head and stared into the middle distance. *Can I tell you that I'm incredibly confused, desperate and afraid? That I'm wondering whether I should leave the country or something like that—but how to leave the kids?*

She closed her eyes then impatiently tore the sheet off her notepad and threw it into the wastepaper basket. A moment later she reached down and tore it up into little pieces, which she let fall like confetti into the basket, thinking at the same time that it was a cheap shot writing to her mother like that, that it was continuing a feud that should be over, that if the one thing her mother had done right in her life, it seemed she was making a good nun.

The next morning as she dressed, she observed the slight shadows under her eyes, grimaced then tossed her head. She pulled on jeans and a blue sweater, tied her hair back and went on her rounds of waking the children. And when they were dressed and assembled at the big table in the kitchen, she went out of her way to be as normal as possible over breakfast, served by Cloris.

'Let's see, Sarah and Richard, you have drama this afternoon after school. Daisy, you're going to play with Chloe straight from school and I'll pick you up at five o'clock and Ben—'

'I know exactly what I've got on, thanks, Arizona,

you don't have to treat me as a child,' Ben interrupted intensely.

'Okay!' Arizona smiled at him and got up to give Cloris a hand with the school lunches. 'Oh, by the way,' she said casually over her shoulder, 'Declan is coming to spend this weekend with us.'

'Yippee!' the twins chorused, and Daisy followed with a similar exclamation.

It was Ben who said moodily, 'What's he coming for? I thought he was here yesterday.'

Arizona narrowed her eyes. 'And I thought you liked Declan, Ben.'

'He's all right,' he said ungraciously. 'But what is he coming for?'

'It doesn't matter what he's coming for, Ben,' Daisy said earnestly. 'What matters is that he's nice and we should be nice back, shouldn't we?'

'For God's sake,' Ben entreated, 'can't you make her stop lecturing us, Arizona? She's only six—'

'Ben—'

'And you shouldn't say that,' Daisy continued solemnly. 'Should he, Arizona? I mean talk about God like that?'

'Eat your breakfast, Daisy,' Arizona said smoothly.

'But I'm right, aren't I?'

'Yes, you're right,' Arizona replied with the patience of long practice.

'Well, for crying out loud then,' Ben muttered moodily, 'what happened to the old saying about children—' he glared at his baby sister '—being seen and not heard?'

'Daisy not heard!' Sarah said with a giggle.

Richard piped up, 'That'll be the day!'

Whereupon Ben got up and flung out of the kitchen with his breakfast half eaten.

Cloris wrung her hands and murmured something about growing boys, Daisy embarked upon the hazards of not eating one's meals and wasting away, Sarah and Richard became convulsed with giggles, and Arizona raised her eyes heavenwards as she wondered where this golden, solemn little girl had inherited her lecturing and worrying tendencies from—because Daisy worried dreadfully about everything and never hesitated to expound upon it.

'It's all right, pet,' she said to Daisy. And later when she dropped Daisy off, last, at school, reassured her once again.

'Ben's not really cross with me is he, Arizona?' Daisy hung back in the car.

'No, but it might be an idea not to, well, lecture Ben at the moment.'

'What's lecture mean?'

'Uh—tell him what he's doing wrong all the time—'

'Because he might go away and never come back? You wouldn't ever go away and never come back like Daddy did, would you, Arizona?' Two large tears began to glisten on Daisy's lashes.

'No, no,' Arizona said hastily and gave her a quick hug and a kiss. 'Look, sweetheart, there's Chloe waiting for you. Now, don't forget you're going home with Chloe and her mum after school!'

When she got back to Scawfell it was to find Cloris in a suppressed state of excitement. 'Staying for the whole weekend, Arizona?' She beamed widely. 'I've already started on the blue bedroom and I've made a little list of menus—what do you think?' She fluttered a piece of paper at Arizona.

'I have absolute faith in you, Cloris, just don't make it too grand.'

Cloris managed at the same time to look pleased yet slightly crestfallen. 'Well, all right,' she said slowly then smote her cheek. 'The garden,' she said anxiously. 'It's in a bit of a mess and we've only got two days, it's Thursday today—'

'I'm about to attack it, Cloris,' Arizona reassured her.

'Well, you are so good at it, but I did wonder if we shouldn't get a gardening firm in, and then there's Ben!' she added dramatically. 'What do you think is wrong with the poor boy?'

Arizona looked at her ruefully. 'Still missing his father I would say—Cloris, don't get into too much of a flutter about Declan Holmes, he's only a man.'

'I know.' Cloris blushed nevertheless. 'But it is a bit of an honour to know him, don't you think, Arizona?'

'As a matter of fact I don't.' *Oh, hell,* Arizona thought immediately, *I'm going to have to do a bit of an about-face soon, aren't I?* And with an impatient grimace, took herself off to attack the garden.

She backed the ride-on mower out of the shed and started on the wide expanse of lawn in front of the house. Scawfell, which Peter Adams had inherited from his parents, was situated on the south coast of New South Wales and comprised about fifty acres. The house was old, two-storied, large and rambling on the outside, but over the years Peter had redesigned the inside so that it was light, modern and very comfortable. It stood with its back to a tree-lined ridge and faced, over its several acres of lawn, the sea. There was a fairly steep cliff face beyond the lawn down to a perfect little bay with a crescent of sandy beach. It was a wonderful place to live if you liked the outdoors, sweeping vistas and the sea. Arizona, born in a city and carted from city to city, excepting while she'd been training to be a teacher, had taken to Scawfell and country life as if she'd been born to it. Always an energetic person, she'd found she loved gardening, grew her own herbs and vegetables and had reclaimed the orchard from a charming wilderness to a garden of bounty. She'd also had the stables renovated, and at present they housed three hacks and three ponies. All of which Declan Holmes had been paying for, she thought with a sudden pang.

Which led her to think further, as she drove the mower expertly and the scent of freshly cut grass filled the air, that she'd been proud of her achievements in her three years at Scawfell, proud in her first year as governess of what she'd achieved with Pete's children, then in her second year all she'd achieved with his estate. *And I even thought I was holding it all together over this last year,* she reflected a little bitterly. *Little to know…at least I was a model of thrift and resourcefulness. Little to know that the money Declan was feeding into the bank as per the arrangement after the will was read and until probate was his own. Not that it's helped me much, being so thrifty and resourceful, he still views me with the utmost cynicism and he's still determined to marry me…*

She sighed again and thought of Peter Adams, who had been a vague, warm, friendly man, a genius at designing buildings but not a good businessman, apparently, yet a man who had understood her and had known something of the forces that had moulded her. *Why did he have to die?* she thought sadly. *For the first time in my life I felt...safe.*

She spent that day and the next working extremely hard, often alongside Cloris although certainly not in the same mood. But she couldn't deny that she was also motivated to have Scawfell looking its best. It was unfortunate that Declan Holmes, who'd said he would arrive on Saturday morning, arrived late on Friday afternoon, catching her unkempt after a bout in the orchard. But the news he brought with him upset her all the more...

CHAPTER TWO

SHE was crossing the driveway, hauling the dead bough of a peach tree, when he drove up in his dark red convertible Saab.

She dropped the bough and stood with her hands on her hips as he stopped the car only feet from her. It was a windy, cool dusk with the promise of rain in the air, and she wore a pair of denim dungarees over an ancient checked shirt, wellingtons, gardening gloves and had her hair bundled into a red scarf.

On the other hand, as he opened the door and stepped out of the Saab, she saw that he was wearing well-pressed khaki trousers, highly polished brown moccasins and a white knit sports shirt beneath a beautiful dark brown leather jacket.

'What are you doing here *today*?' she said crisply as his blue eyes drifted amusedly over her.

'Came a bit early, that's all,' he drawled. 'Is there a problem?'

'You could have warned us!'

'Sorry,' he said entirely unrepentantly. 'But if you're embarrassed about how you look, may I say that it makes no difference what you wear, you still look like a goddess, Arizona. Although in this case an avenging goddess,' he added with soft mockery.

Arizona's expression defied description for a moment, then she said tautly, 'Cloris will be thrown into despair. She'd planned to roll out the red carpet for you and make every meal a masterpiece, whereas it could well be mince on toast tonight.'

He laughed. 'I quite like mince on toast, and I loathe red carpets, but I will make my formal apologies to Cloris.'

'Not to me, though.' She gazed at him coolly.

'I really don't think there's anything I need to apologize to you for, Arizona, is there?' He raised an eyebrow at her.

'No, nothing!' she marvelled. 'Well, if you'll excuse me, I'll get rid of this and—'

'Incidentally,' he broke in as she turned away, 'I'll be staying for the week.'

She turned back immediately. 'A *week*! Why?'

'I felt like a break, that's all.' He shrugged. 'And seeing as we're betrothed, who better to spend it with than you? Of course I didn't expect the prospect to fill you with *undiluted* joy, but—'

Arizona muttered something under her breath and went to turn away again, whereupon he stopped her with a hand on her wrist. 'But we do have a bargain, don't we, Arizona?'

'Let me go,' she said proudly.

'In a moment. Don't we, Arizona?' he repeated evenly.

'Yes,' she said through her teeth. 'However, in *private*, Declan, *don't* expect much joy at all!'

His blue eyes narrowed but he said merely, 'And in public, Arizona?'

'I have no idea how—things will come out,' she said through her teeth.

'Then you better start thinking about it,' he replied dryly. 'Or thinking about the kids,' he added with all the pointedness of an unerringly aimed arrow. 'Are they all home?'

'No. Ben is out camping with his scout group.' She paused then decided not to tell him that Ben had not intended to go on this camp—until he'd heard about Declan Holmes spending the weekend with them. So she added instead with a scornful toss of her head, 'I'm not in the habit of placing children in the line of fire, Declan.'

'Good,' he murmured. 'Then allow me.' And he picked up the bough. 'Where do you want it?'

Arizona gazed at him for a long moment but his eyes were a placid, mild blue. 'Over there, thanks,' she said briskly, pointing towards a pile of timber. 'I thought we might have a bonfire tomorrow night, if it doesn't rain.'

'Sounds like fun,' he said casually. 'Stay there, I'll drive you up to the house.'

'Won't you be bored stiff—here for a whole week?' she said abruptly as he drove the short distance to the front door.

'No. Why should I?'

'It's not exactly a dashing lifestyle we pursue,' she said with irony.

'It's not exactly a dashing lifestyle I'm after. And I thought it would be nice to—ride with you, swim with you, that sort of thing. We could also,' he went on as she cast him a weary look, 'go over the estate together and decide what needs to be done.'

'There's quite a lot—' She broke off and castigated herself mentally.

'Quite a lot to be done? Good—we're here,

Arizona,' he murmured gravely, but his eyes were full of amusement.

'Well, would you mind if I left you to Cloris's tender mercies for a while, Declan?' she returned swiftly and sweetly. 'I rather desperately need a bath.'

'Not at all, Arizona, not at all.'

She took with her, upstairs to the privacy of her own suite, a raging tendency to want to swish her tail like an angry lioness.

Her suite, which Pete had designed specially for her, comprised a bedroom, bathroom and study. The bedroom faced the sea and was large and airy with a pale green carpet, an exquisite, riotous bedspread with the same green background and dusky pink and soft lemon tulips all over it, and draped green curtains. The study overlooked the rose garden she'd started at the side of the house, and each piece of furniture, the desk, the lovely winged armchair with matching foot-stool, the bookcase, were lovingly chosen antiques.

None of it, although it was usually a haven of peace and privacy for her, brought her any peace, however, as she strode into the peach marble bathroom, ran the taps and stalked to her walk-in wardrobe. And she rifled through her clothes impatiently before choosing a pair of slim cream pants and a taupe knit top.

In fact it wasn't until she was lying in the bath, surrounded by a sea of bubbles with her hair tied on top of her head, that she started to relax at all, and even then it was only in a limited sort of way. *How am I going to cope with him in front of the children?* she wondered despairingly. *If they haven't sensed my antipathy by now they must at least know we're not the best of friends.*

But although she soaked thoughtfully, then scrubbed and finally got out to dry herself on one of the outsize peach towels, no inspiration came to her. *Perhaps I can only follow his lead,* she mused dismally as she drew on her underwear and then her clothes and sat at the vanity table.

An *avenging goddess*, she thought bitterly as she studied her reflection. Damn the man! *But I can't go on thinking like that, can I? So what do I think about instead?* she asked herself dryly as she brushed her hair until it shone and left it loose to float in a chestnut cloud to her shoulders. *What it will be like to be married to him?*

She closed her eyes briefly then smoothed moisturizer onto her skin and made up her face lightly, just a touch of foundation, a light lipstick and shaped her eyebrows with a little brush, and answered herself, *No, I just can't picture it but then again, I can't picture how to extricate myself, either!*

She stood up suddenly and caught sight of herself in the full-length mirror on the opposite wall. She was five foot nine and knew that she had a willowy figure with some luscious curves that attracted men like bees to a honeypot. Her mother had had the same kind of figure.... To go with it, she had smooth skin like pale honey, luminous grey eyes with dark-tipped lashes, a well-defined mouth, and she could look thoughtful and serious, sometimes serene and happy, often impatient and autocratic but always, according to Peter Adams, amazingly good to look at.

She sighed and turned away abruptly.

*   *   *

What she found when she went downstairs was not exactly what she'd expected. The table was laid for dinner in the large, bright kitchen, which was normal. But it could have only taken Declan's charm to persuade Cloris to feed *him* in the kitchen. And he, the twins and Daisy were working on a model galleon in the rumpus room adjacent to the kitchen, separated by a half wall. Cloris was happily attending to a leg of lamb. It was a contented, domesticated scene. She paused just inside the doorway and thought of Ben, out camping in the windy darkness rather than being here, with a little sigh. But the only living thing that seemed to afford Ben any consolation these days was his horse, Daintry.

Declan Holmes looked up and saw her. 'Arizona—' he straightened '—you look…refreshed.'

'Thanks,' she said briefly, bit her lip then walked into the rumpus room. 'How's it going?'

'I think we're making progress.' He looked at the three absorbed, bent heads around him, and Arizona suddenly remembered that he'd brought the galleon for the children on his last visit.

'That was a good idea,' she murmured, gesturing. 'We keep it for that rather difficult hour to fill between bath time and dinner time.'

'Yes,' Daisy said earnestly. 'We're not allowed to touch it until we've had our baths.'

'That's why we've been so slow,' Richard said ruefully. 'We could have finished it weeks ago, couldn't we, Sarah?'

'Sure could.' Sarah didn't raise her head, so engrossed was she.

'But that wouldn't have been right,' Daisy began.

Whereupon both the twins raised their heads and said exasperatedly, 'Daisy, don't *start*.'

'I only mean—'

'Come and have a drink,' Arizona said wryly to Declan Holmes.

'With pleasure.' And when they were sitting in the lounge with their drinks, he said, 'How do you cope with her?'

'With patience and humour and just sometimes a desire to tear my hair out. Ben—' She stopped.

'Go on.'

'Ben,' she said after a moment, 'is finding it particularly hard to take at the moment, but then he's finding it all hard to take. I suppose—' she bent her head and paused in thought then shrugged. 'I don't know. But I'm worried about Ben. I can't get through to him.'

'I'll have a chat to him when he gets home.' He stretched his legs out and looked at her reflectively. 'In some respects you're amazingly mature, Arizona.'

'And in other respects?' she countered coolly.

'That wasn't meant as an insult.'

'Perhaps I'm so used to them from you I just expect them.'

'Or perhaps you're determined to turn everything I say into one. But before—' his lips twisted '—this degenerates into a slanging match, I meant that for someone of only twenty-three you're—capable. You run this place well, you look after the children well.'

'That still doesn't explain what you meant by in some respects.'

'At times,' he said slowly, 'your attitude to me is, well—' he shrugged '—quite naive. And sometimes, very rarely, you look young and untouched—but that's only when I catch you off guard.'

Arizona stared at him and felt an odd prickle beneath her skin. She was saved having to make a reply by Cloris announcing dinner.

'For a mince-on-toast type of dinner, that was excellent,' Declan murmured to her after they'd partaken of roast lamb with mint sauce, roast potatoes, pumpkin and sweet potato, baby green peas and rich gravy followed by an apple crumble and cream.

Her mouth curved into a fleeting smile. 'I would dearly have loved to serve you mince on toast tonight but of course I didn't reckon on Cloris.'

'Mince on toast!' Cloris said right on cue and in a scandalized manner. 'I only ever give you that for breakfast. What could you have been thinking of, Arizona?'

'Don't worry about it, Cloris,' Arizona murmured with a wry look. 'Just me being foolish, or is it naive? Okay, kids.' She stood up. 'One hour of television since it's Friday night and your favourite program is due to start in ten minutes, which will give you time to give Cloris a hand! And we could take our coffee into the office, Declan. There are a few things you might be interested to see.'

Declan Holmes stood up. 'Unfortunately I have a few calls to make, Arizona. May I use the office for those first? And your fax? We can have our little get-together when I'm finished.'

'By all means,' Arizona replied airily, although she was actually seething inside. 'I have a million things to do myself—in fact I have a better idea. Let's leave it until tomorrow!'

'Oh, no,' he said smoothly. 'Later this evening will do fine.' And he further infuriated her by helping Cloris and the children clear the table.

It was nine o'clock—she'd spun out the bedtime stories and rituals as long as she could, consoling herself that it was Friday night—before they came together again. And this time he was waiting for her in the lounge when she came downstairs, slightly dishevelled, after an energetic romp with the children before putting their lights out firmly.

'How about that coffee now, Arizona?' he drawled and indicated the trolley with a bubbling percolator that Cloris had left.

'Thank you, yes.' She walked over to the mirror above the fireplace and ran her fingers through her hair.

'All bedded down and correct?' he queried as he poured. She turned away from the mirror.

'Hopefully.'

'Lucky kids,' he commented and handed her a cup.

She sat down in her usual chair, wondered what to say but before she had a chance to wonder much, he said, 'There are a couple of things we ought to discuss, Arizona.' And sat down opposite her.

'I'm sure there are.' She shrugged. 'I don't feel much like it at the moment, though.'

'Well—' he paused and looked at her wryly '—perhaps that's what we should discuss first.'

'I don't know what you mean,' she murmured and smothered a yawn.

'I mean, taking the first step towards—putting you in the mood for everything we need to sort out.'

'I still don't know what you mean,' she said and stopped abruptly.

'My dear Arizona,' he said a little dryly, 'we're going to have to start somewhere and some time.'

'If you're talking about going to bed—'

'By no means,' he interrupted with an amused, mocking little look. 'Just getting to know each other a little better. I certainly wouldn't expect you to sleep with me without some sort of a—courtship before-hand.'

'Declan, if you expect me to indulge in some *petting* with you,' she said witheringly, 'you're wasting your time!'

'Don't you go in for that sort of thing? I don't blame you,' he said ruefully. 'It sounds awful.'

'Then what?' she demanded.

'We could try something a bit more sophisticated,' he suggested.

'Along the same lines but by a different name?' she said bitterly. 'No, thanks.'

'So you object to it by any name,' he murmured. 'Only with me?'

She stared at him and frowned. 'I don't think I get your drift.'

'I was just wondering whether you're at all awak-ened, Arizona. I've wondered it before, and then you did tell me that Pete wasn't a grand passion, if they exist, quote unquote,' he said gently, but it was a fairly lethal sort of gentleness.

Arizona reacted in several ways. She mentally bit her lip at the same time as she mentally took umbrage and finally came out fighting. 'Wouldn't that be a disaster,' she murmured with a faint smile. 'To think that you, Declan Holmes, who could probably have any woman he chose, took a frigid bride—dear me!'

'I didn't say frigid,' he replied after subjecting her to an insolently considering little scrutiny—from her head to her toes but particularly the curves in between. 'I said unawakened, which is an entirely different thing, Arizona.'

'Oh, I know!' she conceded with some mockery and added an insolence of her own. 'I also know how particularly prone men are to imagining they and they alone will be the one to do this...awakening.'

He narrowed his blue eyes thoughtfully. 'And that sounds as if you have cause to be particularly cynical on the subject, Arizona. Like to tell me why?'

'No—that is,' she amended after the first bleak negative sprang to her lips, 'you don't have to be a genius or particularly cynical to work it out. Men—' she waved a hand '—are men.'

'How entirely magnificently damning,' he said, but this time with genuine amusement.

'Not especially,' she said with a shrug. 'Just realistic.'

'Do you really believe that?'

'Why shouldn't I?'

'Was Pete like that?'

She looked at him straightly. 'I've told you before, Declan, that's none of your business.'

'And I disagreed with you, Arizona, but we won't pursue it at the moment—'

'You're going to find it hard to pursue at any moment,' she said impatiently and stood up. 'I think I'll go to bed, if you don't mind.'

'Yes, I do mind,' he said simply.

She looked at him incredulously. 'You don't imagine you can dictate what time I go to bed, surely?'

'Do you usually go to bed at this time?' he countered.

'No,' she said unwisely, 'but—'

'Then you're only being childish,' he said mildly. 'Sit down and finish your coffee.'

Sheer frustration caused her to sit down. 'I'm *not* a child—how dare you treat me like one?'

'All right.' He laid his head back and regarded her with a wicked glint in his eyes. 'Would you rather I said you were being tiresomely female?'

'No, I would not,' she replied shortly. 'Because, if anything, you're being tiresomely male. If you want me to stay we'll need to talk about something else.'

'Such as?'

'Scawfell, the kids, the weather—we have a huge range at our disposal.' She regarded him with a tinge of malice.

He laughed. 'Why don't we try something a bit more interesting. How you grew up and where, for example.'

'Wherever it was the whim of my mother to be at the time,' Arizona said briefly.

'What about your father?'

'I never knew him. He…deserted my mother upon discovering she was pregnant.'

'Ah,' Declan Holmes said.

'What does that mean?' she enquired tartly.

'Why you're anti-men—'

'I'm not. I would never have marrried one if that was the case.'

'Perhaps you married Pete for other reasons. Such as security, all this.' He overrode her as she opened her mouth. 'And perhaps,' he continued, 'it wasn't only the security of his supposed wealth you sought, Arizona, but protection from other men.'

Arizona set her teeth and gazed at him angrily. 'Such as you, Declan? You could be right.'

'Am I?' he murmured, unperturbed.

'That's something you'll have to work out for yourself,' she returned. 'I'm amazed the thought occurred to you,' she added candidly. 'I assumed you thought I was all bad.'

'Not at all. I've told you you're a good stepmother, a good manager et cetera.'

'You've also offered me, by way of marriage, the inducement of your wealth, Declan. If that's not the ultimate insult, I don't know what is.'

'You forget that I also offered you the means to keep together a family that means a lot to you. But principally, you're forgetting the kind of...pleasure we could bring to each other.' He looked at her blandly.

'Yes, well, I only have your word for that—it didn't take long to get back to that subject, did it? I am really going to bed now, Declan.' She stood up with an air of finality written all over her.

He laughed at her softly and wickedly but stood up. 'Very well, my dear. Good night.'

'Is that all?' Arizona said unguardedly and feeling as if she'd had the wind taken out of her sails.

'What more would you like?' he asked with a hatefully raised eyebrow. 'I thought you were dead set against any demonstrations of…affection.'

She turned away abruptly and with a slight flush staining her cheeks. 'I am.'

'Although we could always shake hands,' he murmured from right behind her. 'Would that be in keeping with your view of our relationship, Arizona? A purely business affair.'

'*Yes*,' she said through her teeth, swinging back. 'You've got *one* thing right at last, Declan.'

But he still looked only wickedly amused, and she was suddenly acutely conscious of his height and physique, the way his clothes sat on his well-built frame and how wide his shoulders looked beneath the white-knit sports shirt, how lean his torso and long his legs in his khaki trousers…

She realized suddenly and too late that she'd unwittingly fallen prey to that curl of interest Declan Holmes had been able, always able, she thought with a pang, to arouse in her, but not only that, make her hate herself for. *All right,* she thought then and tossed her head, *you've always dealt with it before, do so again, Arizona!*

She held out her hand. 'A businesslike handshake, Declan? Why not.'

He took her hand but didn't shake it. Instead, he examined it thoughtfully and said finally, 'An elegant hand, Arizona. But I'm glad you don't go in for long, talon-like nails.'

She looked at her short, oval, unvarnished nails and grimaced, taken a bit by surprise. 'They're not exactly practical, long nails, are they?'

'Many women have them, however.'

'I would have thought…' She stopped.

'Go on,' he prompted.

'I would have thought you liked your women ultra-sophisticated, Declan,' she said deliberately.

He smiled enigmatically. 'Which just goes to show you shouldn't have too many preconceived ideas about me, Arizona. Mind you, I've seen you looking pretty sophisticated at times.'

She grimaced. 'Sophisticated clothes, perhaps. But since I'm happiest when I'm gardening or making plans for this place or with the kids, I don't think I'm particularly sophisticated at all.' She stopped rather suddenly and looked defiant first then weary.

'What?' he said softly.

'Didn't I give myself away—*making plans for this place*,' she repeated ironically.

'A little,' he said reflectively, 'but I'd always rather you were honest with me, Arizona, so don't worry about it too much.' And so saying, he raised her hand to his lips and kissed it.

Arizona was frozen for a long, strange moment during which she was assaulted by the oddest sensations. She seemed to tingle all the way up her arm. If she'd thought she was conscious of Declan Holmes before, she was doubly so now, and she got the unnerving impression that if he chose to draw her into his arms, she'd be unable to resist.

What did happen was that the door opened and Ben stood there, damp, windblown and breathless, and he took one look at the frozen little scene before his eyes and said in a voice quite unlike his own, 'Let her go, damn you, Declan! I *knew* that's what you were here for, but she was my father's *wife*.'

'Ben!' Arizona protested, as Declan released her hand unhurriedly. 'Ben, what are you doing here anyway? You—'

'You thought I'd be well out of the way, didn't you, Arizona? Well, I couldn't stand those stupid boys so I came back.' And with a furious gesture he turned and flung out of the room, slamming the door.

'Ben!' Arizona whispered and turned to Declan Holmes. 'Now look what you've done!'

'Something that doesn't quite meet the eye?' he suggested with his own eyes narrowed and thoughtful. 'If he's run away from his troop, is there any way you can get in touch with them to let them know he's safe?'

'I…yes,' Arizona said agitatedly. 'They have a mobile phone with them that they operate from the battery of their vehicle, only I can't remember where I put the slip of paper…' She looked around feverishly then took hold. 'I know where it is—I'll ring them. But what are we going to do with him? He—'

'Leave him to me,' Declan said evenly. He added, 'Don't go to bed until I see you again, Arizona.'

She opened her mouth to say something angry but changed her mind at his look and turned away as he strode out.

It was an hour before he came back to her, during which she'd been able to settle to nothing, and she was sitting disconsolately drinking another cup of coffee.

'How is he? Is he all right? You weren't too hard on him, were you?'

He answered none of her questions as he closed the door and poured himself a cup of coffee.

'Well?' Arizona said impatiently.

'Calm yourself, my dear,' he murmured. 'He's fine—or rather, he will be fine soon. I made a suggestion to him that will, I think, solve a lot of his problems.'

'What?'

'Boarding school.'

'No! Don't you think he's feeling lonely enough as it is without being sent away from us? And then there's Daintry—'

'He can take Daintry. The school I have in mind, as well as being a particularly good school, has a riding school attached.'

'But—'

'Just listen to me, Arizona,' Declan Holmes commanded and waited pointedly.

'Go on,' she said with a shrug after their gazes locked and she detected a will in this matter stronger than her own.

'Thank you,' he said with irony. 'He can come home for the weekend once a month and we can visit him one Sunday a month.'

'It sounds as if we're putting him in jail,' she commented curtly.

'What we'll be doing, in fact, is putting him in the company of other boys his age, providing him with a first-class education, plenty of sport and little time to—mope.'

Arizona stood up. 'I still don't like the thought of it one little bit.'

'Then let me tell you what else we'll be doing for

him,' he said dryly. 'I hadn't wanted to go into this and I promised him I wouldn't so *you'll* have to act as if you don't know, but we'll be removing him from the sheer torment of your presence.'

Arizona turned and stared incredulously at Declan Holmes. 'What do you mean?' she whispered.

'I mean that Ben is wildly, miserably and hopelessly in love with you, my dear Arizona, or thinks he is.'

She gasped and paled. 'I…he *told* you this?'

'Yes, but only because I suspected it and—' he gestured '—brought the subject up.'

Arizona sat down abruptly. 'But he's only a boy!'

'He's fifteen, Arizona, and I can assure you it's neither impossible nor anything particularly unusual.'

She blinked rapidly. 'But—I feel terrible!'

Declan Holmes smiled slightly. 'It's not your fault. But do you see now why he'll be much better off at boarding school?'

'I suppose so,' she said miserably then looked at Declan suddenly. 'What does *he* think, though?'

He shrugged. 'He's not exactly jumping for joy at the moment, but I think it's helped to have a man-to-man chat, and I promise you, he'll be fine.'

'A man-to-man chat,' she echoed.

'Yes.' He grimaced. 'I told him I was in a similar position.'

She stared at him and felt herself colour. 'Not wildly, miserably, hopelessly in love with me, surely!' she said to cover it.

He returned her look with a little glint in his eyes of wicked amusement. 'I told him I was greatly attracted and planned to marry you—after the first shock of it and after relieving himself of some bitter sentiments on the subject, we discussed it more rationally. I don't suppose he'll get over you immediately, Arizona, but he's at least admitted to himself now that it's out of the question.'

'And he doesn't—hate you?'

'No—would you like him to?'

'Of course not! I just…' She looked confused and exasperated.

'Don't understand men?' he said with a genuine grin. 'He is only fifteen, not too young to think he's in love but young enough for someone like me to be firm but understanding with him. I'm quite sure that before long a girl of his own age will come along and…'

'Oh, I do hope so,' Arizona said fervently. 'Poor Ben.'

Declan Holmes raised a wry eyebrow at her. 'No spare sympathy for me? Considering that we were more or less in the same boat.'

She tightened her lips and started to say something scathing but stopped as she was attacked by another thought. 'So he knows—that means they'll all know by tomorrow!'

He regarded her narrowly. 'Yes. But they had to know sooner or later. Why does it suddenly upset you, Arizona?'

'Because I feel more trapped than ever.' The words were out before she could stop them, and she saw his eyes change and harden. 'I mean—' But she couldn't go on, and she was suddenly claimed by exhausted frustration so that the only thing to do was turn and walk out. He didn't attempt to detain her.

CHAPTER THREE

THEY had a custom, she and Cloris, that on Saturday mornings, Cloris brought her tea and toast in bed, and on Sunday mornings she did the same for Cloris. Not that Arizona took the opportunity to rise late often on Saturdays, but Cloris very much enjoyed being cosseted on a Sunday morning and having the opportunity to read the Sunday papers that were delivered early in peace.

But on this Saturday when Cloris came with her tea, Arizona woke from a deep sleep after spending most of the night tossing and turning, felt dreadful and unwisely mentioned this to Cloris while she was still half asleep then said that she wouldn't be down early if Cloris could hold the fort.

The result of this was that ten minutes later there was a knock on her door. She called out wearily to come in, expecting one of the children, but it was Declan Holmes who did.

She was lying back against the pillows with her knees drawn up and her cup of tea in her hands resting on them, and for a moment she stared at him, stunned. He wore jeans, a khaki shirt with patch pockets and short brown riding boots, he was shaved, his thick dark hair was still damp from the shower and he looked alert but inscrutable.

'What are you doing here?' she got out at last as their gazes clashed.

'Morning, Arizona,' he replied, his blue gaze drifting from her unbrushed hair looped behind her ears to her pink cotton nightshirt with a teddy bear's picnic on the front, then moving briefly around the lovely room. 'What's wrong with you?' he added.

Her lips parted and she frowned. 'Nothing's wrong with me and I don't know why you feel you have the right to—'

'Then why is Cloris convinced you're sickening for something?' he broke in.

Arizona closed her eyes. 'I didn't tell her I was feeling *sick*!'

'She said you said you were feeling dreadful and that it was quite unlike you to want to stay in bed and she's wondering whether she should ring the doctor.'

Arizona muttered something inaudible then took a deep breath and gazed bitterly at Declan Holmes. 'I don't know how I put up with her sometimes.'

His lips twisted in a faint smile. 'She has your best interests at heart.'

'I *know* that. I…' She tailed off frustratedly.

'So you didn't tell her you were feeling dreadful and wanted to stay in bed?'

'Yes…no…I mean, yes, I did, but not because— look, I'm fine,' she said coldly, 'and I don't appreciate your being here like this, so—'

'Then if it's not your health—' he overrode her coolly '—you've been working yourself into a state about this self-imposed trap you're walking into. Is that it, Arizona?' he drawled, his eyes curiously mocking. 'May I give you some advice?'

She opened her mouth, closed it then said wearily,

'I don't suppose I can stop you. Just don't expect me to act on it, Declan.'

He paused, glanced out of the window and said as if changing topics, 'It's a beautiful morning, Arizona. The rain has gone, the ground is steaming gently in clear bright sunshine and smelling delicious. Two horses are saddled, moreover, as eager to have a good gallop before breakfast as I am, and you would be, too—if you weren't lying in bed feeling sorry for yourself and building *traps*,' he said softly and significantly.

Arizona put her cup down, tossed aside the bedclothes and sprang up. 'Go away!' she commanded. 'I will not be treated like this.'

He looked her up and down, and his gaze lingered on the long expanse of slim legs her nightshirt exposed. 'Like a child?' he suggested gently, his eyes coming back to hers. 'Then why don't you stop behaving like one? Do you always wear teddy bears to bed?' he added quizzically and went on thoughtfully. 'I would have imagined you in something sexier, to go with your lovely bedroom.'

'I've told you once, go away,' Arizona said through her teeth.

He shrugged and looked amused. 'Only if you'll come riding with me.'

'Now it wasn't such a bad idea after all.'

They had dismounted at the cliff top above the beach, and their horses were cropping the grass. It had been a good gallop, and he'd been right about the sheer magic of the morning.

Arizona was sitting on the turf, staring out to sea, a glittering, dancing sea. 'No,' she said briefly.

'Not still sulking?' he murmured and sat down beside her.

She shrugged and thought a little dismally that she probably was but then again, didn't she have cause? She decided to opt for honesty. 'Most victims of blackmail probably don't like it.'

'Even when the results are this pleasant?' He raised a wry eyebrow at her.

'That sounds as if you're a great believer in the end justifying the means,' she countered.

He grinned. 'In this case, yes.'

'Is that how you've got where you are?'

'Are you asking me whether I'm unscrupulous and immoral, Arizona?' he queried gravely.

'Yes,' she said baldly.

'No, I'm not.'

She glanced at him through her lashes, but that was a mistake, she discovered, as she encountered a grave blue gaze that didn't for one moment hide from her the fact that he was laughing at her inwardly.

She looked away. 'That's easy enough to say.'

'True,' he agreed blandly.

'And not so easy to believe, particularly in light of your dealings with me,' she murmured.

'On the contrary, I feel I'm being highly honourable in my dealings with you. And before you say that I'm forcing you to marry me, Arizona—'

'You are.'

'With your connivance, my dear,' he drawled. 'Also your hidden interest, to yourself, that is. Do you know what Cloris said to me when she heard the news?'

Arizona turned to him quite openly this time but once again looked stunned. 'She knows!'

'She knows,' he agreed.

'How? Has Ben—but he wasn't up! None of the kids were.'

'I told her. And what she said was this—that she'd thought it might be on the cards, that she was very happy for us both, that she thought I was the ideal person for you and she had the feeling you thought so too but you were a very stubborn person so not to feel too downhearted if you proved a little difficult.'

'Of all the…I don't believe it!'

'Her exact words,' Declan assured her. 'Well, interspersed with typical Cloris kind of stops and starts. She must have sensed,' he added, 'your interest.'

'I don't at all see how she could have,' Arizona said moodily. 'It was all I could do not to let on how much I disliked you.'

'Maybe it was just that, an irrational sort of dislike that made no sense. Perhaps that's what alerted her.'

Arizona lay back on the thick turf disgustedly. 'The whole business annoys me intensely,' she said tautly.

He smiled unexpectedly. 'That's what I like about you, Arizona. One of the things.'

'What?' she asked irritably as he said no more. 'That I get annoyed? I wouldn't have thought it was an asset in a wife at all.'

'Oh, it has its moments. You're not dull to be with.'

'I—' But she stopped abruptly as he propped himself on his elbow beside her and stared into her eyes.

'You?' he murmured with a wryly raised eyebrow.

'Nothing,' she said shortly and would have moved away if a curious sense of, as it turned out, misplaced bravado hadn't claimed her.

'May I make another suggestion?' he said after a minute or two.

'Seeing as you're so full of them this morning, why not?'

'Here goes then,' he said with a humorous quirk to his lips. 'Now we've had a little spat, well, two, and it is only eight o'clock in the morning, now you've done that and done yourself proud, so to speak, don't you think it would be all right to let yourself relax a little and—go with the flow? For a while at least?'

'That's the most illogical thing I've heard! It's worse, it's insulting!'

'Depends how you take it.'

'No! I mean there is no other way to take it. You're saying in effect that…' Words failed her.

'All I'm saying is, until you relax and try it, you really don't know what you're fighting about.'

'Try being kissed by you?' she suggested ominously.

'Uh-huh.'

'You never let up, do you?'

'I thought we'd established that.'

'All right,' she said abruptly, 'then let's establish something else—go ahead.' She closed her eyes and lay still.

'I hesitate to disturb you, Arizona,' he said quite gently after a pause, 'but you look a bit ridiculous.'

Her lashes flew up and her grey eyes flashed. 'How dare you? You—'

'You keeping saying that to me,' he murmured.

She sat up, her cheeks flooded with colour but her eyes just as angry, then she sprang up and caught her poor horse, taking it quite unawares, and swung herself into the saddle. She also yelled something pithy and highly uncomplimentary to Declan Holmes as she galloped off, and heard him laughing at her clearly.

Breakfast was awaiting her in the kitchen. The children had theirs, Cloris informed her, and Ben had got away safely.

'Got away? Where?' Arizona said bewilderedly.

'Didn't Mr. Holmes tell you?'

'No, Cloris, he did not!'

Cloris shrugged. 'He arranged for him to spend the weekend in Sydney with some friends of his. They have a yacht and a boy Ben's age—he knows him, so that's what they'll be doing this weekend, sailing. I do think it was a lovely thing to do for Ben, don't you, Arizona? He does need something to take him out of himself at the moment.'

'But how did he get—'

'I arranged for a car to come down and pick him up,' Declan Holmes said smoothly, coming in through the back door.

'You might have told me,' Arizona protested, still feeling enraged and embarrassed.

'Slipped my mind.' He sat down at the kitchen table. 'I'm starving.'

Cloris glowed. 'Well, I've got a lovely breakfast for you, Mr. Holmes. Do sit down, Arizona, it's your favourite, too. You're looking much better!'

Arizona took a deep breath—and sat down. Cloris

bustled about for a few minutes then produced perfectly cooked bacon and eggs with fried tomatoes and banana. It was as she poured their coffee that she produced her second bombshell. 'Goodness me!' she exclaimed. 'I don't know where my wits are this morning. Rosemary Hickson called, Arizona, to remind you of her dinner party tonight. I told her it was just as well she had called because I'd forgotten and I thought you might have, too. But I explained why,' she added anxiously.

Arizona took another deep breath. 'Why?'

'Why what?' Cloris looked at her, perplexed, and Declan ate the last of his breakfast serenely.

'Why would we have forgotten, Cloris?' Arizona said deliberately.

'Oh, hadn't you, Arizona? I thought you must have because you were talking about a bonfire tonight—'

'Cloris, I *had* forgotten,' Arizona said, goaded, 'as you very well know, but the why is what I'm trying to establish!'

'Oh, that!' Cloris brightened. 'Because of Mr. Holmes coming to stay unexpectedly, of course—not to mention, well, other things, but,' she said hastily, 'when I told Mrs. Hickson, she said it wasn't a problem. In fact she said she'd be thrilled to have you to dinner tonight, Mr. Holmes. She said it would even up her table delightfully.' Cloris paused, eyed Arizona nervously then suddenly came round the table and put her arms around her. 'I'm so happy for you, pet, I know I sometimes can be trying and—well, all the same, I often think of you as a daughter, you've been so very, very good to the children and I hope you'll be very, very happy.' She withdrew her arms and wiped a tear from her cheek.

Arizona stared at her, thought, *Oh, hell, I feel like a real heel!* And put her arms around Cloris, saying huskily, 'Thank you, I love you, too, you know, and I'm sure that of the two of us, I'm the trying one.'

'Your Saturdays are pretty busy,' Declan Holmes said as he steered the Saab towards the Hickson property, which adjoined Scawfell.

Arizona shrugged.

'What with pony club, Brownies et al., I'm surprised you're not exhausted,' he added and glanced sideways at her.

Arizona smoothed the short skirt of her yellow silk cocktail dress. The Hicksons always dressed formally for their dinner parties, and she'd put up her hair. She wore sheer pale nylons and grey kid high-heeled shoes. She also said witheringly, 'Well, I'm not. Physically, that is.'

'But you're all tense and wrought up mentally,' he commented dryly. 'It shows.'

Arizona laid her head back with a sudden little sigh. 'Yes. Mightn't you be if you were in my shoes?'

'If I knew a bit more about you and why you're so determined to hate me but still marry me, perhaps I could answer that.'

Arizona closed her eyes briefly. 'Never mind, just take it as read,' she said wearily. 'Are you going to break the news to the Hicksons, as well?'

'Would you like me to?'

'No.'

'Then I won't,' he said mildly. 'We're nearly there.

From what I remember, Rosemary Hickson is an overwhelming, high-powered blonde.'

'You're not wrong—but she's been a good friend,' Arizona added thoughtfully. Then she said on a downbeat, 'We are here.'

He stopped the car, but before he switched the engine off, he put a hand over hers and said surprisingly, 'Look at it this way for a change, Arizona. You're quite stunning, you have an unusual and beautiful name, you're young, spirited and intelligent, you smell delicious—why not drop the weight of the world off your shoulders for an evening?'

Her eyes flew to his full of puzzled surprise. 'I—'

'Just give it a try.' And he turned the key off, got out and came round to open the door for her. Arizona hesitated then swung her legs out, saw the way his blue gaze lingered on them then met her eyes expressionlessly—and she found herself looking away with a curious tingling of her nerves.

'Darling, so lovely to see you!' Rosemary Hickson gushed, as usual sporting her impressive bust in a very low-cut black dress. 'And how are you, Declan—we have met before, so delightful to have you both, especially—' she lowered her voice fractionally '—in view of the good tidings Cloris passed on this morning, although she did make me promise not to mention it—she wasn't sure she should have said anything, you see, so I haven't said a word to anyone else!'

Grey eyes met blue ones, and for a second outrage glinted in Arizona's gaze but then—perhaps it all just become too much? she wondered—she found herself laughing just a touch hysterically. And felt Declan's hand enclose her own as he said gravely, 'How are you, Rosemary? Thank you for inviting me, and if you wouldn't mind, we'd like to keep our engagement a secret for a bit longer.'

'Of course! Of course! But I'm thrilled to be one of the first in the know. Now come and meet everyone—we're twelve tonight so we should have great fun.'

But as she turned to lead the way, Declan held Arizona back for a moment and said very quietly, 'All right?'

'I...I'm working on it. Perhaps I will do as you suggested in the car.'

'Good girl.'

'Not so bad, was it?'

Arizona laid her head back against the leather car seat. 'That's the second time you've said that to me today.'

'Was it?'

'No.' She closed her eyes and thought over the evening. Peter had designed the Hicksons' home, so it was elegant and beautifully appointed. The food had been superb, the company entertaining and by some mysterious means, she'd transformed herself into the person Declan had advised her to be—untouched by the weight of the world, good company although with just a hint of reserve at times when she became conscious of the admiration she saw in the men's eyes and the speculation she saw amongst the women of the party concerning her relationship with Declan. But for the most part it had been a relaxed evening for her, and she might have been not a widow with four stepchildren but the youngest member of the company who had charmed and held her own. 'I feel like Cinderella now, however,' she murmured involuntarily.

'Thanks,' he said dryly.

She glanced at him briefly. 'Sorry, I should be thanking you for—well, I don't quite know what, but I guess for bringing out the best in me for a while.'

'Do you really mean that, Arizona?'

'Yes, surprisingly I do,' she murmured. 'It's a pity it can't last.'

He pulled the car up in front of the house and turned to her. 'It could, you know,' he said quietly. 'Take your shoes off and come for a walk with me. Just down the lawn to the cliff. If nothing else it will help dispose of a very rich meal.'

'To around about the same spot where I made myself ridiculous this morning?' she queried wearily.

'Perhaps the moonlight on the sea and a clear, scented, beautiful night will help you to be less so.'

'I wonder,' she said barely audibly, dropped her face into her hands for a second then kicked off her shoes. 'Okay, you're on,' she added with something more like defiance, and she got out of the car and started to stride across the lawn in her stockinged feet.

He caught up with her halfway to the cliff top and took her hand, resisting her attempt to pull away saying abruptly, 'Stop it, Arizona.'

So she slowed with a show of obedience that was a mockery but said nothing. And he was right, when they got there, the moon was shining on a pewter sea and picking the crescent of beach up below, turning it to a dazzling white. There were night scents on the air, honeysuckle and jasmine mingled with the sea air, dew-damp grass.

'It is…it is lovely,' she said shakenly after they'd said nothing for long minutes, just drunk it all in. 'Now do you understand why I'm marrying you, Declan?'

He hadn't let go of her hand and his grasp tightened fractionally. 'Is that why you married Pete? For Scawfell?'

'Of course, I thought you knew. And his money.' Her voice still shook slightly. 'Although I may have miscalculated there.'

'What about this?' He released her but put his hands on her shoulders and stared at her narrowly. 'This,' he repeated very quietly and steadily. 'Having a man run his hands over your skin.' He did so, down her arms and back again, then slid his long fingers beneath the straps of her dress. 'Being held and having your breasts touched, your nipples stroked, your beautiful mouth claimed.' And he did just that, drew his hands down the front of her dress to cup her breasts and run his thumbs over her nipples beneath the yellow silk and the lace of her bra—and as they hardened and she breathed erratically, he tantalisingly slid his hands away, around her waist, and pulled her closer so he could kiss her lips.

She kept them stubbornly closed then parted them involuntarily as his hands moved again, to her hips, to trace the outline of her bikini briefs beneath the thin silk, exploring, stroking, moulding her to him at the same time. He bent his head then and started to kiss her deeply.

It was, as she'd always feared and suspected it would be, impossible to remain unaffected. There was between them a surge of sheer magnetism, a physical match between the tall hard planes of his body and the soft curves of her own despite or perhaps even heightened by their mutual animosity. And it had been there ever since the first time she'd found him watching her out of those clever, sometimes so cynical blue eyes.

How can I handle this, she found herself thinking chaotically, *when I don't even know what it is, love or hate, a new war or—but I must.* And she managed at last to draw away, although not completely. He allowed her to rest against the circle of his arms and take several unsteady breaths before she murmured ingenuously, 'Oh, yes, but I must say I hadn't expected you to be so expert, Declan. I'm quite impressed—yes, *quite* impressed.'

Oddly enough, it gave her no satisfaction that he called her a bitch then in cold clinical tones and released her. In fact, instead, she felt something shrivel inside her, although she said, albeit a bit raggedly, 'But you knew that, too, didn't you—do you still want to marry me? I'll understand if you've changed your mind. You know, I've been thinking, if you kept Scawfell for the children, you could always keep me on instead of getting them a new governess. After all, that seems to be the one thing you admire me for—'

She stopped because he'd turned away from her for most of her speech but he turned back and for a moment she was frightened by what she saw in his eyes. But he said almost leisurely, 'Oh, no, Arizona. If you want Scawfell and the children, it has to be on my terms or not at all.'

'But I don't understand.' She stopped again as she heard the note of fear in her voice. 'I mean…why?' And heard something else in her voice that made her cringe inwardly, a sort of desperate uncertainty.

He laughed softly. 'For the pleasure of bringing you to your knees, for one thing, Arizona. You see,' he drawled, 'you've resisted all my efforts to make some sense of this, so I'm afraid that now, my dear, you're going to have to put up with the consequences—me and Scawfell. Or nothing.'

And he walked towards the house without a backward glance.

She was awoken the next morning by Sarah and Richard leaping onto her bed. 'What the…what are you doing?' she said groggily.

'Waking you up, sleepyhead!' Sarah replied obligingly.

Her twin brother added, 'It's six o'clock!'

Arizona groaned as they slipped in on either side of her. 'It's also Sunday! What have I done to deserve this on a Sunday morning?'

They giggled and enveloped her in a bear hug, and Declan walked in on them.

Arizona froze but the twins released her and sat up interestedly. 'Hi, Declan,' they chorused, and Richard said, 'We were wondering, since you're going to marry Arizona, what we should call you. I mean is it okay to go on calling you Declan?'

'Because we don't think we should call you Dad really,' Sarah said.

'Declan will do fine,' he murmured. 'Do you always wake Arizona up at this ungodly hour of the day?'

'Well, you're here, too,' Richard pointed out, and Arizona couldn't help the slightly ironic glint that came to her eye as his gaze caught hers.

'I'm here to tell her that Daisy's crying,' he said to the twins, but returned the irony directly to Arizona.

She sat up. 'What—'

'That's what we came to tell her!' Sarah said triumphantly. 'We think she's sick or something.'

'Well, why didn't you say so!' Arizona scrambled out of bed, once again caught in her teddy bear's picnic nightshirt, and was in no way mollified as Declan reached for the dressing gown lying across the bottom of the bed and handed it to her gravely.

'Daisy—Daisy, darling, what's wrong?' Arizona knelt beside the bed and smoothed Daisy's forehead. Declan and Richard and Sarah stood behind her.

'You're not going to go away, are you, Arizona?' Daisy wound her arms around Arizona's neck and pressed her hot, wet cheek to Arizona's.

'No, Daisy, I told you—'

'Ben's gone,' Daisy wept.

'Only for the weekend, sweetheart, and not because he was cross with you, I promise you.'

'But you're getting married, you told me so yesterday—I don't know what that means—and I feel horrible.'

'Daisy, Daisy,' Arizona said gently and unwound her arms, 'let me have a look at your chest, honey bunch, because I think I may know why you're feeling horrible.' She opened Daisy's pink pyjama jacket, and the rash on her little chest was quite visible. 'Is your throat sore, pet?'

Daisy nodded, still weeping copiously. 'And my head.'

'Measles?' Declan said quietly, behind her.

'Looks like it. She's very hot. Daisy, guess what, I'm going to call Dr. Lakewood, now you like her, don't you? And she'll help us make you feel better.'

'Am I sick?' Daisy said, suddenly looking more alert. 'Sam Johnson had to go home early from school the other day because he was sick.' She sat up with her blonde hair sticking to her forehead, her cheeks flushed but her eyes brighter. 'Will this make me more important? It did for Sam, Teacher made him lie down next to her on a cushion until his mother came!'

'Oh, tremendously important, darling!' Arizona said with a loving smile, while Sarah and Richard cast their eyes heavenwards but came to perch on the end of their little sister's bed.

'You'll have to stay in bed for days, Daisy. We know because we had it when we were six—' Arizona breathed relievedly when Sarah said this '—but we'll read you stories and play games with you.'

'But you'll look after me, won't you, Arizona?' Daisy said anxiously.

'Of course. Don't I always?' Arizona said lightly as she dropped a kiss on her head and stood up. 'Now I'm just going to ring the doctor, then I'll come straight back and make you more comfortable.' But as she turned around, it was to see a curiously intent look in Declan Holmes's eyes as they rested on her. She thought, as she moved past him, *I don't know why you're looking at me like that, but at least I've got something else to think about!*

It was four o'clock in the afternoon before she stopped and sat down to have a cup of tea on the front veranda, where Cloris had set it out on a white-clothed table. Tea and crumpets. Sarah and Richard had homemade lemonade before racing off, leaving her alone with Declan. It was a hot, bright afternoon.

'Phew!' She sat down and lifted her hair off her neck.

'Hot?' he queried and poured her a cup of tea.

'Hot and bothered, but she's asleep now, and a lot less emotional,' she added wryly.

He said nothing.

'Thanks for taking the twins off my hands,' she said a few minutes later.

'Not a problem,' he murmured and smiled suddenly. 'I've had quite an—instructive day. They're inexhaustible, aren't they?'

Arizona laughed. 'You're not wrong. It's strange—' She stopped.

'What is?'

She looked at her cup and cursed herself inwardly for letting her tongue run away with her unwittingly.

'Arizona?' he prompted quietly.

She looked up at last and shrugged. 'I had no idea how I was going to face you today, that's all.'

'Saved by a case of measles, of all things.'

She searched his expression for mockery or irony,

but his eyes were enigmatic. 'I guess so,' she said expressionlessly.

'Were you really worried, Arizona?'

She hesitated. 'I couldn't help wondering where we would go from—there.'

'And I couldn't help wondering how much of what you said last night was...believable.'

'Not at the time, you didn't,' she countered dryly then bit her lip.

'True,' he agreed reflectively. 'But when I saw you with Daisy this morning, it struck me that there are two sides of you, Arizona, that don't match at all.'

'Yes, well, that's me,' she tried to say flippantly and moved restlessly.

'Tell me some more about your mother.' He stretched his long legs out and clasped his hands behind his head.

'No.'

He raised his eyebrows quizzically. 'I can always find out.'

A glint of anger lit her grey eyes. 'How despicable,' she taunted.

'Not if there's some deep dark mystery—'

'There's not. She was simply a...rather foolish woman, and I have no ambition to follow in her footsteps,' Arizona said abruptly.

'Do you mean she threw everything up for love and suffered accordingly?' he hazarded. 'Is that why you thought you'd do things the other way around?'

'Now why would I imagine you'd believe anything else?' she marvelled.

'Well, until you tell me otherwise, what am I supposed to believe?' he drawled.

'All right, yes,' she said moodily.

'So you hate your mother,' he said after a pause.

'No, I don't.'

'Do you keep in touch with her?'

'Yes, I do. But, thank heavens, she's somewhere even you would have difficulty finding—look, how are we going to go on?' she asked curtly.

'I don't have any change of plan in mind. Do you?' he queried politely.

'You seem to forget, I'm the one with little choice, Declan,' she replied with considerable irony.

'So you are, Arizona, so you are.'

'Oh, this is impossible.' She jumped up and was horrified to discover she had tears on her lashes.

He got up smoothly. 'Then let me make another suggestion.' He took her hand and forced her to face him.

'You're hurting me,' she said proudly, despite those suspicious tears.

'Only because you're asking for it,' he countered coolly, 'so just stand still and listen to me for a change.'

'Aye, aye, sir!'

His mouth hardened for a moment then he relaxed and laughed softly. 'Anyone would think I was about to attack you,' he said lazily. 'I can assure you I'm not. I'm equally sure after last night that it will never have to come to that—but it was nothing,' he said as she gasped, 'along those lines at all, Arizona.' His blue eyes mocked her. 'I was merely going to suggest,' he continued smoothly, 'that while you had your hands full with Daisy, I go back to Sydney this afternoon, pick Ben up and spend a few days with him.'

'Ben!' Arizona said huskily and put her free hand to her brow, a bit dazed. 'I haven't even had time to think about him today. But—what would you do with him?'

'Take him to see the school I have in mind and—' he shrugged '—just do a few of the things fifteen-year-old boys might enjoy.'

'Would...would you?' she said uncertainly.

'Contrary to your opinion of me, Arizona,' he drawled, 'I'm not a monster.'

'I didn't think you were in that respect,' she said irritably. 'But you are a super, high-powered businessman—or aren't you?'

'I'm on holiday,' he reminded her softly and stared into her eyes deliberately.

'Well—' she had the grace to colour faintly '—I'm sorry...but that would be—I'd be very grateful if you would.'

'Thank you. For the apology,' he murmured.

The colour in her cheeks grew and she tried to turn away but he wouldn't let her. 'There's just one thing I'd like you to do while I'm away, Arizona,' he went on. 'And that's to make up your mind about yourself.'

'What do you mean?' She frowned at him.

'You see,' he explained gravely, 'I'm getting these confused signals. Last night you went out of your way to be a fortune-huntress and a vamp, although for a while you kissed me like a girl who was rather overcome, even a little in love... I find that strange, Arizona, don't you?'

She stared into his eyes and felt like a butterfly

pinned to a cloth. She licked her lips and opened her mouth to speak, but he smiled, unamused, and released her hand to put a finger on her lips. 'No. I'd rather you thought about it instead of launching into a tirade of some kind. And of course, for my part, there'll be the sense of anticipation, while we're apart, as to what you'll be when I return. The vamp?' he mused. 'The cold-hearted gold-digger? Or simply an angry and confused young woman but at least an honest one?'

CHAPTER FOUR

HE WAS away for four days.

Days of inner turmoil for Arizona, which she would have loved to try to combat by being furiously busy but spent mostly with Daisy. The result was that at night, with Daisy tucked up and sleeping peacefully, she wasn't physically tired herself and had plenty of time to ponder on the nature of her dilemma, and Declan Holmes's acuteness... *Not that I'm in love with him,* she told herself repeatedly, *but there's no doubt I was a bit overcome.* She shivered in sudden remembrance. *There's no doubt he intrigues me as no man ever has, but at the same time he engenders this raging hostility in me! The thing is—who's to blame for that? I haven't been honest with him for a very good reason, but why should I? He certainly started out believing the worst of me. Why does he really want to marry me, then? It has to be revenge because I wouldn't look at him when Pete was alive or—afterwards, he as good as said so that awful night. But what does that make him?*

'I don't know,' she said aloud to herself in the dark, in bed one night. 'That's the thing, I don't know. What kind of a man goes to these lengths over a wife of a friend, a wife who did the right thing? Is it because *afterwards*, I was still determined to have nothing to do with him? How could he know that in spite of the way I was, it was there, this...curiosity, this... Will it never leave me?' she wondered still aloud and

67

desolately, and turned to hide her suddenly hot face in the pillow. *But then he can be nice,* she thought, some minutes later, *and good with the kids but all the same he's using them...*

How can I leave them? she asked herself another night. *Especially Daisy. I'd never forgive myself, I've promised...so I've got to work something out but it's unbelievable all the same. Or is it, Arizona,* she asked herself bleakly, and lay quite still thinking of how he'd kissed her, how it had overcome her, and wondering what it would be like to be married to a man you didn't understand, a man who you knew wanted you but had no idea how he would use you...

They came back on a Thursday afternoon, catching Arizona unawares. Daisy was up and having some fresh air, wearing a pair of sunglasses and looking much better. They were on the veranda doing a jigsaw puzzle. As soon as she saw the car and then Ben getting out, Daisy jumped up ecstatically, knocking the puzzle off the table, and dashed down the steps, calling his name.

'Ben, Ben, I've been sick and very important but I'm better now. Oh, Ben, you did come back— Arizona told me not to lecture you any more so I won't!'

Ben grinned and picked her up. 'Believe it or not, I missed you, Bubbles,' he said affectionately, using his pet name for her, and Arizona relaxed a bit because this was more like the old Ben. But she thought she detected a slight constraint as he came up the steps with his eyes not quite meeting hers as he still carried Daisy, and she breathed deeply.

'Ben,' she said with a grin of her own, 'I hope

you've had measles in case it's still lingering. Did you have a good time? We missed you, too.'

And she thought she must have pulled it off, that it must have come out easily and naturally because she saw Ben visibly relax, and he said enthusiastically, 'I had a ball!'

Then the twins streaked round the corner of the house and they flowed inside together in one noisy, happy group. Arizona bent to gather up the puzzle.

'Here, let me give you a hand.'

'Thanks,' she said to Declan as he knelt beside her, and that was all they said until every last piece of puzzle had been retrieved.

'How are you?' he queried when they stood up at last.

'Fine, thanks,' she answered but didn't know if it was true because she was still curiously affected by the accidental touching of his hand on hers as they'd sought for the same piece.

'You don't altogether look it,' he murmured, his brows drawn together in a faint frown.

'Well, I am, really,' she tried to say lightly. And because she felt she needed to emphasize that it was nothing to do with him, she added, 'Just a bit house-bound at present, that's all.'

'Would you let me take you out to dinner tonight then?'

'Oh, no.' She smiled perfunctorily. 'Daisy's much better, I'll be able to get out and about soon, and Ben looks so much better, too, thank you for that!' She was aware as soon as she stopped speaking, that she'd sounded stilted and harassed, and bit her lip.

'Would dinner out alone with me be so much worse than dinner here with me?'

'I didn't mean that—'

'Yes, you did, Arizona,' he contradicted coolly.

Her shoulders slumped suddenly. 'All right, so what if I did,' she murmured, barely audibly. 'Anyway, Daisy is still—'

'Daisy's much better, you said so yourself, she's got Ben, the twins and Cloris. And much as I appreciate your concern for her, we shouldn't allow this fear she has of being deserted to get out of hand.'

Of course he's right about that, she thought dismally, *and anyway I did decide to level with him, didn't I? Is there any point in trying to put it off?*

'You've won,' she said with an odd little sigh. 'What time shall we go?'

'About seven,' he said slowly, his eyes narrowed. 'I thought we might try Zena's in the village.' The village was the nearest town in the area, about ten miles away. 'Rosemary gave it quite a wrap the other night, if you recall.'

'Rosemary should know!'

'I thought you liked Rosemary,' he murmured.

'I do.' Arizona grimaced wryly. 'That doesn't blind me to the fact that Rosemary has an uncanny knack of always finding the most exclusive and *expensive* places around.'

His lips twisted. 'Exclusive?'

She shrugged. 'The kind of places you're liable to meet all the best people, of the same social calibre, same old schools, similar financial standing—that kind of thing. Although not necessarily the best food.'

He looked amused. 'Are you really objecting to that, or is it the thought of being seen with me by people who may recognize us?'

'Not at all.' She stared at him scornfully.

'That's more my Arizona,' he reflected. 'Do you have a better suggestion, then?'

She tried to contain her irritation but knew she was on her mettle as she said carefully, 'There's an old pub on the edge of town with a garden that overlooks the sea. A lot of the local fishermen patronize it because they serve the best and freshest lobster, oysters and prawns around, and you can eat outside, but it has absolutely no social pretensions whatever—a lot of its patrons barely made high school.'

'Well, you win this time, my dear,' he drawled, but as she stiffened he added, 'as a matter of fact it sounds much better.'

'You won't find any fancy French wines there,' she warned. 'More like cheap plonk.'

'Who cares?' he replied. 'It's the food that counts.'

She was astounded by the difference in her when they left, and more so when they entered the pub. She hadn't dressed up, although she did wear beautifully tailored jeans, flat navy suede shoes and a white top with padded shoulders made from a bubble-knit material that was at the same time simple, stylish and warm. She had also washed her hair and tied it back, dark, gold-streaked and shining, at her nape, with a navy blue scarf, and touched mascara to her lashes and a deep bronze colour to her lips.

Her sense of well-being had started as they left, when Declan had firmly but kindly told all and sundry he was taking her out to dinner but they'd be back in a couple of hours. Daisy had not so much as blinked an eyelid, and Ben had looked quite unaffected. Arizona had had to admit that this *had* caused her a mental raising of her eyebrows along the lines of how some men simply had this habit of command and how annoyingly effective it was, but she couldn't hold the cynicism of the thought for long. Not as they left the house behind, drove beyond Scawfell's fences and on to the moonlight-washed road. *Perhaps I do need a break,* she thought ruefully.

Then, as she walked through the pub and a sudden, stunned silence fell as all in the place took in her shining hair, her clear pale skin, her figure, she suddenly felt tall, lithe, elegant—and confident.

'Well,' Declan Holmes said with a curious little smile playing on his lips as he found them a table in the garden and drew out a chair for her, 'you certainly cut a swathe through that lot.'

'Didn't mean to,' she said wryly.

'But you enjoyed it?' he suggested, sitting down himself.

'I cannot tell a lie.' She smiled faintly. 'It worked wonders for my ego.' She sobered and started to look for hidden meanings in his words. 'If that makes me a vamp or—'

'Not at all—just refreshingly human and honestly female.'

'Do you mean that?' she asked abruptly.

'Yes,' he said simply.

Arizona sat back a bit stumped.

'What I'd like to know now,' he said after a pause, and she tensed slightly, which he saw and acknowledged with a twist of his lips, 'is whether someone will come to serve us or whether I have to go inside to order our meal, leaving you out here alone, which is something I'm not altogether keen to do—I'm sure there are at least fifty men around who would be only too happy to take my place.'

She relaxed and grinned. 'Someone will come for our order, I'm only too happy to tell you.'

'At least—' he paused '—you feel safe with me, Arizona. That has to mean something—no, don't tense up, let's enjoy this meal in some sort of friendship.'

So they ate delicous, plump little oysters *naturel*, and mouth-watering lobster grilled with butter on a bed of rice and accompanied by a crisp side salad. Declan ordered a carafe of house wine, probably out of a cask, she warned, but it turned out to be quite a pleasant moselle. And once again they were assailed by a variety of perfumes from the garden around them and the sound of waves on the shore not far away.

'Thanks,' she said pushing her lobster plate away at last and touching a paper napkin to her lips, whereas Zena's would have had fine linen, 'that was not only delicious, but I really think I did need to get away for a while.'

'It was your expertise that brought us here.'

'I was your—something that persuaded me to come.'

'Does that make us quits?' he speculated idly.

She didn't answer immediately. Then she said, gathering her resources, 'You told me to do something while you were away. I think I've done it.'

'What?' he asked quietly.

'Decided to tell you some things. I'm not a vamp, and I'm not really a fortune-huntress. I married Peter because I trusted him, and I don't usually trust men. I—married him because it was what he wanted rather desperately, but I would have been quite happy to stay on as the governess—only once he fell in love with me, I couldn't have. But I was always honest with him, I told him from the beginning that I didn't, couldn't love him the same way, that it didn't seem possible for me to fall in love like that...and I hoped it never would.'

'Did you tell him why?' Declan asked after a long pause.

'Yes. Well, he'd begun to guess anyway because of—as he put it—the way I so determinedly froze men off.'

'Are you going to tell me, Arizona?'

'I would rather not,' she said straightly. 'It can't change anything. Could we just leave it at that?'

'I don't think so,' he murmured. 'That's asking a bit much of me, don't you think?'

'All right,' she said abruptly. 'My mother had a few men in her life. Every last one of them deserted her, including my father, throwing her into the depths of despair. I think I was about sixteen when I made a vow no man would do that to me. And I'm sorry to say but there's nothing about you, Declan, that has made me change my mind.'

He smiled slightly. 'Point taken, but let's not jump the gun. Did it never occur to you that your mother may have been at fault at all?'

'Of course it did,' Arizona said briefly then added, 'I'm very much like my mother, to look at, that is.'

'Ah, so it's yourself you don't trust, Arizona?'

'No. But there was something in her that seemed to bring out a fatal urge in men to dominate and discard her, not to mention milk her dry. I...' She hesitated. 'I would be foolish to allow that to happen to me, don't you agree?'

'And that's why you opted for a loveless marriage?'

'It wasn't loveless,' she said very quietly. 'I was happy and comfortable with Peter, and because I like to pay my debts, I went out of my way to make him happy,' she added proudly.

'In bed as well as out of it?'

'Yes,' she said after a long pause, during which she studied her hands.

'It was pretty obvious that you fulfilled him—did he do the same for you, Arizona?'

There was a long silence, then she raised her eyes to him at last, and they were expressionless. 'Yes.'

They stared at each other. 'And will you go out of your way to make me happy in that particular way, Arizona?' he said softly but with a wealth of meaning in his tone and the way his eyes roamed over her then.

She shivered and couldn't quite hide it. But she said evenly enough, 'That's the other thing we should discuss. I don't owe you anything, Declan—'

'I agree.'

'So—' She stopped and stared at him. 'What did you say?'

'I agree.'

'Then?' Her eyes were wide and stunned. 'I don't understand what you...why we're...' She couldn't go on.

He sat up and moved his glass on the table. 'I thought we might approach this a bit differently now. On the premise that you *don't* owe me anything, Arizona, but we are caught up in a difficult situation to which the most logical solution is to get married.'

She gazed at him, her lips parted, her eyes bewildered.

'Well, it is, isn't it?' he murmured wryly.

'I don't—'

'You don't see why? Let me tell you,' he drawled. 'You find you can't leave the kids or bear the thought of them being deprived of Scawfell.' He narrowed his eyes then shrugged. 'I've had the evidence of my own eyes,' he said in a different voice, 'as to how genuine you are in these matters, not to mention what a wrench it would be for them. Whereas I—' he paused and grimaced '—find myself in the position, ironically similar to Pete's, as it happens, of not being able to just hand you the place and the kids. That's why there really is only one solution for us,' he said simply.

'I...' Once again she got stuck.

'You?'

'Don't know what to say...'

'Well, look at it this way.' He sat back and clasped his hands behind his head, 'It would be another marriage of convenience for you. It would have most of the ingredients that made you happy and comfortable before. And has it never occurred to you, Arizona, that you have me as much of a hostage as I may have you?'

'No,' she said dryly.

'Then think about it now,' he suggested. 'Unless you seriously believe I don't have their interests at heart?'

'But—' she licked her lips '—would you be happy with a...total marriage of convenience?'

Their gazes caught and held, and she saw a little glint of amusement in his as he said softly, 'Oh, no, but it would lack all the elements of me wanting to dominate and discard you, because of the nature of our—obligations.'

'So—what would it be like?'

'You here, pursuing what you've told me means most to you, me being here when I can, us sleeping together on those occasions and, I hope, fulfilling each other as little or as much as it's in us to do so. You know—' he lowered his arms and grimaced again '—for a girl like you, determined not to fall in love, I would have thought it would have been fairly ideal. You would also have the protection of my name against all the men you have to freeze off so determinedly,' he said gently.

Arizona shivered again but couldn't quite understand why and moved her shoulders restlessly.

'The other thing,' he said evenly, 'is the fact that I do arouse you, my dear. Despite being a despised member of the sex you so mistrust. Are you afraid it will—get out of hand for you?'

Yes, something in her cried, but she could only stare at him bitterly, with images of her mother and other, worse images passing through her mind.

'Then again—' he smiled unexpectedly '—I wouldn't expect our life to be all passing sex and nothing else. I'd like to think once you relaxed a bit about it all there could be some fun and laughter, some happy, good times, too.'

And she was shaken to find no evidence of irony or mockery in his eyes or voice at all.

'What happens—' she cleared her throat '—what happens when they've all grown up and left?'

He stared beyond her for a moment. 'Who knows?'

It was like a blow, she discovered, and might even have flinched unknowingly because he added, 'We might even find we've become a habit with each other.'

Arizona blinked several times, which he watched

narrowly. Then he said quietly, 'So, what's it to be, my dear?'

She didn't realize that her shoulders slumped fractionally as she looked away and said, barely audibly, 'Yes...'

He said nothing for so long, she was forced to look at him again, and then all he said was, 'Let's go—I've something to show you.'

He drove them to a spot where the road rounded a headland and there was a viewing verge where he pulled the car up.

'I've seen this view quite often,' Arizona murmured, more for something to say as she stared out over a wrinkled, silver-foil sea beneath a bright moon.

'But you haven't seen this.' He switched on the overhead light and pulled something out of his jacket pocket. A little, midnight-blue velvet box.

Arizona stared at it, knowing immediately what was to come, then switched her gaze to the plain gold wedding ring on her left hand. 'I—'

'Now is the time to take it off, Arizona. Now is the time to lay Pete to rest, finally. After all, if nothing else, we're two people who loved and admired him, two people who have the welfare of his children at heart.'

'I suppose so, when you put it like that...' But a teardrop fell on her hand as she hesitated then slipped the gold band off.

And Declan Holmes flicked the blue velvet box open, drew a sunburst of diamonds out of it, and taking her nerveless left hand, slid the ring onto her finger.

'Thanks,' she said foolishly, examining it with one

half of her mind, seeing that it was delicate and exquisite and unusual, three diamonds along the band
with two sets of two smaller ones separating them,
noting that it was probably priceless and fitted perfectly—and with the other half of her mind curiously
numb. 'I'll…look after it.'

'Is that all?' he said wryly.

'Well, what do you want me to say?' Her voice
was husky and uncertain.

'I thought there was something we might do.'

She looked across at him swiftly. 'Another moonlight kiss?' she hazarded but without the derision the
words were meant to imply. And she closed her eyes,
frustrated.

'Why not?' he mocked. 'You didn't mind the last
one, once we got going. But let's step outside for a
minute or two.'

She got out after him because she couldn't think
of what else to do, and they stood side by side against
the bonnet of the car and watched as a huge container
ship out to sea slid its dark bulk through the water
like a wraith but for its lights. 'Red to port, green to
starboard,' she murmured.

'You know something about shipping?'

'Not a lot,' she answered. 'It was just something to
say. Do you?'

'Yes. I was in the Navy once.'

Surprise caused Arizona to look at him. 'Why?'

'Why?' He grimaced. 'Why not?'

She thought for a moment. 'I don't know. But one
sort of thinks of people in the Navy as being dedi-
cated to the sea.'

'I didn't sail ships, I flew helicopters for them. My
father thought it would be a good way to combine a

love of flying, a bit of fascination for the sea—with some character building. He was probably right.'

'I can't imagine…' Arizona said slowly and stopped. 'I mean—' she tried again '—it's difficult to think of you being dictated to by anyone, even a father—you said that,' she added by way of explanation, 'as if you didn't really agree with him.'

'You're right,' he murmured amusedly, 'there wasn't a lot I agreed with him about—the way he treated my mother and the way he ran the business being the principal disagreements we had. So any of his suggestions were generally anathema to me, but in hindsight,' he mused, 'he was right about the Navy. In so far as it gave me the toughness and maturity to take control eventually and…avert bankruptcy.'

'What did he do?'

'He retired. Not exactly graciously but not exactly broke, either, after I'd pulled things together.'

'And your mother?'

'She departed this life a few years ago in an alcohol-induced haze, which was the only way she could cope with him.'

Arizona gazed at his profile, which was like a rock, and shivered.

He turned to her. 'Cold?'

'No…yes…I don't know.' But she was cold inside, she knew, at this glimpse of the cold, hard core of Declan Holmes, and it crossed her mind to wonder what chance she ever had or would have of fighting him and beating him.

'What does that mean?' he queried quietly.

That I'm attracted to you and scared of you and still mystified by you, she thought, but did not say because it was not her nature to confess things like that, but more, because some intuition warned her it would be fatal. *Why?* she wondered, dazed. *I don't understand…*

'How about a little warmth, then, of the mutual variety,' he said very quietly and drew her into his arms, but he did no more, and for an age she stood in the circle of his arms trembling then quieting as things, strangely, turned full circle, and it was a bit like being sheltered by a rock…

She closed her eyes and told herself that just for a moment she would rest and be reassured. It wasn't much longer before he lowered his head and sought her lips, and she breathed anxiously, but he lifted a hand and stroked the smooth skin of her throat down to the satiny hollows at the base of it with two fingers, lightly, until she calmed. Then he claimed her lips again, and she allowed herself to be drawn into a deep, intimate kiss before he broke it gently, held her closer and started to kiss her again.

If anyone had told her, she thought once, that she could be kissed for as long as Declan did it, she wouldn't have believed them, but it was also the feel of him against her, the strength of his legs against her thighs, the long muscles of his back beneath his jacket where her hands now were… His hands on her hips, slipping under her top and exploring her back, her slender waist, the twin mounds of her breasts, then withdrawing to stroke the nape of her neck beneath her hair. Until finally they stopped kissing and she laid her head on his shoulder, breathing deeply and shakily and feeling an unknown sensation at the pit of her stomach, an intimation of a kind of pleasure that might bind her to Declan Holmes so that she could never break free. And a warning bell struck in her brain....

She lifted her head and swallowed. 'Is that thanks enough?' But she sounded husky and unsure.

He narrowed his eyes. 'It wasn't thanks I had in mind, Arizona. Rather a celebration of our pact.'

'Well—' she licked her lips '—enough celebration then?'

'What do you think?' His voice was dry.

Her eyes widened. 'I...I—' But she couldn't go on, and patches of heat rose up her throat because she knew what he meant.

'You think we should leave that until our wedding night?' he supplied with a sardonically raised eyebrow. 'Is that what you're trying to say?'

'No—well, yes. I...it hadn't actually occurred to me until a few moments ago—I mean,' she said desperately, 'that you, that... Oh hell,' she said hollowly, 'sorry, I'm carrying on like a—child, probably. Sorry,' she repeated, but drew away.

He let her go and she turned away and hugged herself as she stared disbelievingly over the sea.

'A child, Arizona?'

'What do you mean?'

'You said, carrying on like a child, but I wondered if you meant—something else?'

'No.' She said it quietly but quite definitely.

Declan walked round her, took her chin in his hands and tilted her head so that he could look steadily into her eyes. But he didn't tell her what he saw, nor could she read it in his eyes, then he let her go but reached for her hand.

'What now?' she asked nervously.

'Home. And bed. Alone. I think we might have achieved enough for one day, don't you?'

Arizona didn't reply. But she lay in bed, alone, that night and wondered what had been achieved.

She awoke with images in her mind of how pliant and vibrant her body had been in his arms, and the sight, before her eyes, of his arm in a dark blue jacket sleeve over a paler blue shirt bearing a plain gold cufflink carved with the initials DH, putting a cup of tea on her bedside table.

She stared at the dark hairs on the back of his hand wondering if she was dreaming then said groggily, 'It's not Saturday, is it?' I mean—' she bit her lip, confused '—have you taken over from Cloris or something?'

He straightened and she followed the movement with her eyes until they met his. He was shaved, she saw, his hair was brushed and he wore a green and blue tie with his suit. 'No. But an urgent fax was waiting for me when we got home last night. I have to go up to town for a few days. I thought you might appreciate hearing it from me rather than Cloris. It's only—' he glanced at his watch '—six o'clock again.'

Arizona sat up, rubbed her face then pushed her hair back. 'Oh.'

'I could be gone for a week—will you be all right?'

She blinked. 'Of course.'

'I thought you might say that,' he murmured with a faint smile twisting his lips and walked over to open her curtains. She saw then, after adjusting to the light, that he'd brought a cup of tea for himself. It was on her dressing table. 'I meant—' he turned back and picked up his cup '—you'll have Ben to cope with for a few more weeks until the end of this term, you'll still be housebound with Daisy for a day or two, you'll still be at the twins' beck and call—are your nerves up to it, Arizona?'

'Yes,' she said steadily then grimaced as her hair slipped forward and added, before she could stop herself, 'I wish you wouldn't keep catching me like this. Could you pass me my brush and that scrunchie on the dressing table?'

He paused and looked her over before reaching for her brush and the brightly coloured elasticised ribbon. 'I've told you before, you always look—delectable.'

'Thanks,' she said dryly as he handed them over and started to brush her hair with vigorous strokes then holding it in a swathe over one shoulder so she could brush the ends before, with a sigh of relief, she slipped the scrunchie on to hold it at her nape. 'That's better, but you don't have to pay me extravagant compliments.'

He said nothing but sat down in a green velvet armchair and finished his tea. He kept his eyes on her, though, on her watermark white silk, tailored pyjamas with a narrow maroon piping, until finally with a wryly raised eyebrow, he remarked, 'I see you've given away the teddy bears.'

'I haven't,' she replied but with a tinge of colour creeping into her cheeks. 'The kids gave me that nightshirt for my birthday so I wear it as often as possible, but I can't wear it all the time.'

'No,' he agreed. 'Now that's devotion.'

'Not really, it's comfortable.' She turned away and picked up her tea.

'I have a suggestion to make, Arizona.'

'Regarding my nightwear?' she retorted b
stopped to think.

He smiled. 'Well, that, too, eventually, or rathe.
regarding the *not* wearing of it, but not, naturally,
until we're married.'

'Definitely not.'

They stared at each other, Arizona with hostility in
her eyes, he with amusement. He also said, 'I didn't
come here to fight you this morning, my dear.'

'Then don't bait me,' she replied. 'What did you
come to suggest?'

'That at the end of the week, you come up to town
for a couple of days. You can stay in a hotel before
you get your hackles up any further.'

'I...why?'

'So that we can arrange our nuptials. You might
like to shop, you might even be interested to see
where I live,' he said with irony.

'The children—'

'I appreciate and share your concern for the children, Arizona, but I've made some arrangements that
I think might be in *their* best interests while we sort
out a few of our own.'

'What do you mean?' she queried after a suspicious
pause.

'Rosemary will be delighted to take them and
Cloris for the time you're away.'

Arizona stared at him. 'When did you organize
this?'

'Last night. I'll also, before I leave this morning,
speak to the kids and let them know what's happening—I don't think you'll have a problem. Amongst
other things, Rosemary told me that although she's
never been able to have kids, she adores them, she

will delight in laying on all sorts of fun for them, she's quite certain you need a bit of a break—and if Daisy does get distraught, she'll get straight in touch. It is only a couple of hours drive away. It's less, as a matter of fact, since I decided to invest in a helicopter.'

'You what?'

'Bought a helicopter, Arizona,' he said with a sort of mocking patience. 'I told you I flew them in the Navy.'

'So you did,' Arizona said, a little dazed.

'As a matter of fact it's coming to pick me up this morning— I could have you picked up on Friday if you like.'

'No,' she said hastily. 'If I come I'll drive.'

His eyes told her what he thought of that, but instead of taking issue with it, he said, 'Getting back to the kids, you must know I would never suggest anything that I thought would harm them. But this way they'll be with someone they know, in familiar territory and having fun.'

'Rosemary *is* really good with them,' Arizona said grudgingly.

'Then you'll come?'

Arizona put her cup down carefully and lay back against the pillows. 'Why not?' she said eventually and added, barely audibly, 'As you so often say to me.'

'I did have another thought.' He got up abruptly.

'Oh?'

'Yes, that we get it over and done with at the same time.'

'You mean—get getting married over and done with?' Arizona asked after a long pause.

'Why not?' he parodied with a mocking glint in his blue eyes, and something more, a hint of steel.

'I think I might let you know how I feel about that, Declan,' she said coolly but angrily, 'but I wouldn't hold your breath.'

'All the same, I'd come prepared if I were you, Arizona,' he countered.

'I don't even know where to come!' she protested, and immediately hated herself for such a feeble protest.

He took a card out of his inner jacket pocket and laid it on the dressing table, next to, as it happened, the little crystal bowl that held his engagement ring. 'Check into the Hilton on Friday, I'll make a reservation for you. Give me a call when you arrive and we'll take things from there. Don't,' he warned coolly, 'even think of not coming, Arizona, because I shouldn't be at all amused if you do.' He strode out, closing the door audibly behind him.

I really made him angry, Arizona thought, as she stared, transfixed, at the door. *Did I bring this on myself by being—obstructive? He can't seriously believe I'd marry him like that...*

She looked away at last and felt a curious prickling of her skin as it struck her that perhaps she did wield some power over Declan Holmes, but the kind of power she had no desire to wield over any man....

CHAPTER FIVE

'AH, MRS. Adams, I'm Mr. Holmes's secretary. How do you do? Did you have a good trip up?' a cultured, well-modulated female voice asked down the telephone line.

'Yes, it was fine, thanks,' Arizona replied. 'Is—'

'I'm afraid Mr. Holmes is in a conference, but he asked me to let you know that he'll meet you at the hotel, in your suite, at six-thirty this evening. Did you get the packet when you checked in, Mrs. Adams?'

Arizona glanced at the contents of the packet she'd been presented with by the ultra-attentive Hilton receptionist and closed her eyes briefly. 'Yes, I did. Thank you.'

'Well, if there's anything you need at all, please do give me a call, Mrs. Adams. I made a list for you of the appropriate shops in the area you might like to patronize, and of course, may I offer you my congratulations and very best wishes, Mrs. Adams. Mr. Holmes was kind enough to take me into his confidence, although I gather he wants the wedding to be very private, but you can rely on me to be most discreet....'

Arizona put the phone down moments later, clenched her teeth and thought, *All right, if this is how he wants it, this is how he'll get it,* and she glared at the contents of the packet spread across the desk. A gold Mastercard in the name of Arizona Holmes, five hundred dollars in cash, his secretary's list of the most suitable places to shop for a trousseau and the briefest note from Declan himself to the effect that they would be married at noon the following day.

'I'm so angry I can't see straight,' Arizona said to herself. 'I came up here to try to defuse things, I suppose, and because I've got no choice, anyway, but this kind of treatment deserves—worse! So be it....'

And she shovelled the card and the cash into her purse, left the list of shops on the desk and stalked out of the suite.

Four hours later, she returned, accompanied by a bell-boy and a lot of stylish carrier bags. She tipped the bellboy generously, so generously that he bowed out of the suite backwards, and she sat down abruptly, buried her head in her hands and wondered miserably if she hadn't walked right into Declan Holmes's trap.

You should never do things when you're furiously angry, Arizona, she told herself, *you should know that by now!*

She laid her head back with a sigh and thought, *But it's done now so I guess I'll have to live with it,* and glanced at her watch to see that she had an hour and a half before he came, and got up to run herself a bath.

She soaked for half an hour and felt some of her spirit returning. So she opened all her purchases and laid them out on the huge double bed, quite artistically, she thought. Then she dressed, did her hair and made up her face carefully, tidied up and was walking to the lounge when, on the dot of six-thirty, the bell rang. She took a deep breath and went to open the door.

'Arizona,' Declan Holmes murmured by way of

greeting, his eyes still the cold, hard blue she remembered from their last encounter in her bedroom at Scawfell, and walked past her into the suite.

She closed the door and after a brief hesitation followed him, saying nothing. And it was like two implacable enemies that they eyed each other across the lounge when he stopped and turned to her.

Until he drawled, as his gaze roamed up and down her, 'Well, well, Arizona—new?'

She looked at the beautiful black cocktail dress she wore, then raised her eyes proudly to his. 'New from the skin out, Declan.'

'I have to say I approve.' The dress had a Thai silk short fitted skirt and strapless bodice, and the gossamer cobweb lace overblouse that tied at her waist had a stand-up collar and puffed sleeves. It was unrelieved black, and the skin of her shoulders gleamed through the exquisite lace, as did her legs, clad in the sheerest black nylons. Her medium-heel suede shoes had pearls embroidered on the heels. Her hair was loose and smooth to her shoulders.

'I'm so glad,' she answered sweetly, 'because there's a lot more for you to approve of. Would you care to take a look?' She held out her hand towards the bedroom.

His lips twisted, but he inclined his head and gestured for her to lead the way. Nor did he say anything immediately once there but scanned the bed and the armchairs all draped with clothes. There was a sensuous collection of underwear and nightwear, silk and lace in gleaming white, French blue, black and one long slim nightgown with tiny straps in a deep ruby. There were several casual outfits, shorts or slacks and jackets or blouses, two pairs of colourful leggings with fabulous printed polyester overdresses. There was a chic linen suit in the palest violet with a grey silk blouse, a long crushed velvet skirt in a colour that reminded one of blue steel with a sheer, fine metal mesh T-shirt to go with it—and beside most of the outfits, a pair of shoes or a handbag, beside some a scarf for her hair or a piece of costume jewellery, a lovely raffia hat or a pair of sunglasses. It was a dazzling collection.

'What do you think?' she asked at last when he'd said nothing for what seemed like an inordinately long time.

'I'm impressed,' he drawled turning to her at last. 'And you did it all in an afternoon, Arizona!' he marvelled. He added, 'Did you take my secretary's kind advice?'

'I did it in four hours, Declan. Just imagine what I could do in a lifetime.' She raised her eyebrows ingenuously at him. 'And no, I did not. I don't need anyone's help to buy clothes, but particularly not your secretary's.'

'So it would seem,' he murmured. 'The one thing I can't seem to find is anything resembling a wedding dress.'

'You're right, there isn't anything that's especially a wedding dress,' she said tautly as his blue gaze, which was suddenly lazy, gave her the oddest feeling of a paralysed prey about to be captured, but she soldiered on. 'For one thing, you probably need a bit more time to choose something like that, and for another, if it's going to be such a rushed wedding, why bother?' She stressed the *if*.

'Well, you certainly have made your statement, Arizona.' But he stopped as she turned away suddenly from his now horribly mocking, insolent eyes, and a visible shudder went through her.

'What now?' he said.

'I'm kicking myself, if you must know,' she said through her teeth.

'Care to tell me why?'

'Because I did all that in a blaze of anger.' She gestured vaguely towards the clothes. 'Because I feel cheap and…I don't know what. Because I walked right into the trap I suspect you laid for me, Declan, *that's* why, but the one thing I don't regret is the lack of a wedding dress.' She turned back, and her eyes were grey and haunted but curiously stubborn.

'You know what's wrong with us, don't you, Arizona?' he said after an age during which she could have cut the atmosphere between them with a knife.

'Yes, probably every last syllable of it,' she retorted.

'Tell me then.'

'I've told you so many times, *surely* I don't have to go through it all again.'

'I don't think we're talking about the same thing at all,' he said dryly. 'Particularly as it's the one thing you refuse to talk about—the mutual hunger that's making our lives quite tormented, Arizona. I don't think you would be making extravagant and hostile gestures otherwise—why bother? And I know I—' he paused '—am getting impatient and frustrated, particularly when I remember how you kissed me.'

'Well then,' she said with an effort, 'why don't I slip into something more comfortable? So we can get this…momentous event over and done with.' She walked past him to pick up the ruby nightgown. 'How about this—'

'Stop it, Arizona,' he said curtly and caught her wrist. 'Anyone would think it was fright motivating you.'

'Oh, but it is, Declan, you scare me and mystify me, but don't imagine I won't overcome it somehow—' She broke off suddenly, her eyes widening as she realized what she'd confessed. 'I mean—'

'You little fool,' he said roughly. 'I'm not going to hurt you.' He gathered her wrists in one hand and drew her right up to him. 'If you stopped fighting me for a while I'd be able to prove that to you.'

Arizona tilted her head so she could look straight into his eyes and said intensely, 'It doesn't seem *right*.'

'Well, what would you like?' he countered. 'That we declare undying love for each other? I thought that kind of thing was anathema to you.' His hand ground into her wrists and she sagged suddenly against him. He released her immediately but caught her around the waist, saying after a long moment, 'Just give up, Arizona.'

'I'm not that kind of person,' she whispered.

'Why don't you wait and see what kind of person emerges? You might get a surprise.'

She closed her eyes, frustrated, and flinched as he started to kiss her eyelids, but he ignored it and continued to kiss her until she shivered, but this time undeniably with pleasure.

She stirred about half an hour later, and laid her head on Declan's shoulder with a little sigh.

'All right?' he asked quietly.

'Yes…'

They were in the lounge with only one lamp on

and the fabulous lights of Sydney stretching down to the harbour below them from the Hilton tower. She was in his arms, sitting on his lap, with her legs stretched along the settee, her shoes on the floor beside them and, temporarily at least, all the fight in her smothered beneath a tide of exquisite sensuality, evoked and aroused by his hands and lips. What was worse, she thought, was that this was only a brief respite because he was leading them down a path from which there was no return and she didn't, couldn't care.

It was doubly ironic when he said very quietly, 'Do you want to go on—or stop?'

'Don't...stop,' she murmured and added with absolute honesty, 'I don't think I could bear it.'

He traced the outline of her lips and watched the sudden wariness that came to her eyes. He'd discarded his jacket and tie, and she could see the springing black hairs where his shirt was opened. She resisted an almost overwhelming temptation, as she waited and wondered what his response would be, to touch them.

He said at last, 'You look as if you're expecting me to crow with triumph.'

'Do you want to?'

He laid his head back and fiddled with her hair with the hand that was around her shoulders while his other one lay possessively on her waist. 'I can't deny a certain feeling of that kind—' he smiled a ghost of a smile '—but for the most part I'm almost overwhelmed with relief.'

Arizona moved and he looked into her widened eyes. 'I've wanted you for over two years, Arizona,' he said quietly. 'That's a long time. Will you come to bed with me now?'

'Yes.'

'I forgot,' she said huskily as they surveyed the bed, still strewn with her purchases.

'If you take one half, I'll take the other,' he said with a grin and let go of her hand. It only took them five minutes to clear the bed, and he pulled off the cover, but it was long enough for Arizona to be attacked by guilt and a sudden sense of shyness, so that when he held out his hand to her again, she hesitated.

He watched her briefly then came round to her side of the bed. 'You could return them all tomorrow and we could start again, from scratch,' he said gravely.

She grimaced and coloured faintly. 'I made them cut all the price tags off.'

'Did you now—were you that angry?'

'Yes,' she whispered.

'Then will you accept my apologies for doing that to you?'

'Declan—'

'No—' he put a finger to her lips '—let's just concentrate on this—have you any idea how lovely you are? Should we examine that aspect of it and the effect it's had on me?' he said wryly.

'What do you mean?' she said uncertainly.

'Sit down and I'll tell you.'

So she sat on the bed after a moment's thought, and he sat beside her, close although not touching her. 'I think it all started with your eyes,' he mused. 'So clear and piercing at times, then so totally noncommittal at others or—worse. Such as the day, I think it was the second time we met, that you looked across the lounge at Scawfell at me and virtually told me with your eyes to do my damnedest. I can even remember what you wore, a black blouse and a long skirt that rustled as you walked. I can remember cursing that skirt, in fact, because it hid your legs. I still have the same problem whenever you wear anything long.' Arizona couldn't help smiling faintly.

He took her hand in his but did no more. 'Then there was your temperament,' he went on, surprising her. 'You were so positive in everything you said or did, so constructive. You also, even in your governess days, got around, when I was there at least, as if I was of absolutely no consequence, as if I was quite beneath you and always would be. I admired that,' he said but added with a wicked glint as he looked into her eyes, 'when it didn't invoke a sense of—we'll see about that, Arizona—in me. So what have we got now, your eyes, your temperament—ah, yes,' he murmured, 'your body. Now that was quite another matter,' he said and said it so soberly she frowned.

But he went on in quite a different, much lighter tone before she could say anything. 'So you see, I've rather been like the beggar at the feast all this time. And that's why I haven't always been—quite rational, and that's why having you sit here next to me with the perfume of your skin and hair tantalizing me, the thought of taking your beautiful dress off you all but driving me crazy, not to mention the thought that you might have changed your mind—all those things are particularly hard to bear,' he finished gravely.

'You…I…don't know whether to believe you,' Arizona said with another smile curving her lips.

'Believe me, lady!' he replied laconically.

'But I didn't know you could be like this,' she persisted, although she was still smiling.

'No?' He raised a rueful eyebrow at her. 'Well, you have sometimes given me the impression you imagine I'm the grab-them-by-the-hair-and-yank-them-into-your-cave kind of man. I must say you do look at me with just that kind of suspicion in your eyes, Arizona,' he said reproachfully.

'Sorry,' she murmured, and the part of her that was incurably honest made her add, 'I just didn't expect this, though.'

'Well, I hope it's been a nice surprise—if not, I could always go back to being a strong silent type if you like. I did tell you,' he said suddenly with no amusement, 'that you might not know what you were fighting so dedicatedly.'

'I know. The thing is,' she said slowly because she was in fact thinking deeply, 'I've never seen you with a woman before, one of your own, I mean.' She grimaced awkwardly but continued. 'You never brought anyone like that to Scawfell, did you? So—' she'd been studying her hand in his but she glanced at him now '—perhaps that's why I didn't know what to expect, but there must have been…women in your life.'

'Some,' he agreed.

'None that you wanted to marry?'

He paused and considered. 'When I was twenty-two I was madly in love with a very voluptuous blonde, and I can recall being quite desperate to marry her—for the space of about three weeks.'

'Seriously,' she said quietly.

'Seriously, Arizona?' He lifted a wry eyebrow at

her then said soberly, 'Yes, I've thought about it once or twice before, once particularly, a few years back.'

'Will you tell me who she was? I mean, what she was like and why—you didn't.'

'She was—' he paused and looked straight ahead with his eyes narrowed '—a very well-known businesswoman, very independent, very intelligent. There was no way,' he said deliberately, 'despite what we felt for each other, that we could live together, as we discovered to our mutual cost. It's been over for nearly five years now.'

'Was she younger or…?'

He looked at her. 'A couple of years younger— why do you ask?'

'I was wondering whether she had the maturity or whatever it takes not to be sort of flattened by you,' Arizona murmured.

Declan grinned and glanced pointedly at the array of clothes around the room.

'That's different. You goaded me into doing that,' Arizona protested.

'I did apologize,' he reminded her and added, 'should we try to stick to the lighter side of things, though? I actually made you smile a couple of times earlier.'

Arizona flinched.

'What's that supposed to mean?' he said softly.

'I feel ridiculous now, that's all. As if I'm making heavy weather of things for no good reason.' She shrugged a touch desolately.

'On the contrary, when you were kissing me, things were electrifying. Should we try that again? But could I make a request first?'

'What?'

'This beautiful lace blouse—is it a separate entity?'

She frowned. 'From the dress, do you mean?'

'Uh-huh. Because if it is, I thought we might take it off. I'm dying to get closer to your skin.'

Arizona hesitated then undid it at the waist and he helped her to slip it off. 'Mmm,' he murmured, sliding his hands down her arms, 'that's what I meant. How about the dress?'

She tensed, then forced herself to relax. 'It unzips down the back.'

But he made no move to reach the zip. He took her in his arms instead, saying, 'On the other hand, why hurry?'

'Why, indeed,' she murmured, somewhat dazed.

But it was only a few minutes later, during which time he'd merely stroked her skin while she'd laid her head against his chest and listened to the beat of his heart, that she reached behind her and pulled down the zip herself.

She also said huskily as he tilted her chin and looked enquiringly into her eyes, 'I'm being positive, I guess. As I used to be once. I'd sort of forgotten that.'

He kissed her lips. 'I'm delighted.'

She smiled a wry little smile. 'The only thing is— I don't quite know where to go from here.'

'Could I take over then?'

'If you would, Mr. Holmes…'

She woke to a total feeling of disorientation. Then it started to come back to her and she groped across the bed but she was alone, so she pulled a pillow into her arms then realized a shaft of light was coming from the bathroom, and a dark shadow was standing in the doorway.

She blinked several times, adjusting to the gloom, and saw that it was Declan with a towel tied around his waist, his shoulders propped against the doorframe as he watched her. Then he straightened, turned on an overhead light and came over to sit on the bed.

They said nothing for a long moment, just stared at each other, and Arizona drank in the way his wet hair fell over his forehead, the still damp skin of his shoulders and chest, and remembered the feel of his body on hers, the strength of it and the way he'd held her and made love to her until she'd felt as if she was spinning off the planet like a singing top as she experienced the first climax of her life. Remembered how stunned she'd been afterwards, lost for words, incredulous—and helpless. For that matter how she felt now, only a couple of hours later, but all the same as if she might never leave this bed, but not only because she was tired—because she really felt like luxuriating between the sheets and feeling as if he was still there with her.

Then she thought she should say *something*, so she murmured huskily, 'You're dynamite, Declan.' But her eyes were completely serious as she added very quietly, 'Thanks.'

He smiled faintly and cupped her cheek. 'Don't thank me, Arizona. You had the same effect on me.' He paused and narrowed his eyes as he added, 'It didn't seem to me as if it had ever happened for you quite like that before.'

'No,' she said after the slightest hesitation.

'How do you feel about it?'

'Like…Alice? In wonderland?' she suggested after

a moment. 'I seem to remember reacting a bit like that.'

'You reacted wonderfully, you were exquisite. It's just a pity I have to leave you,' he said slowly and took her hand.

She tightened her fingers around his and said with a frown, 'Why?'

'I have an urgent meeting this evening—I know, it seems a strange time for business but it affects what goes into tomorrow's paper. There's a political crisis looming about which we have to be very careful what we say. Besides, it's supposed to be unlucky for prospective brides and grooms to spend the night before their wedding together, or something like that.'

Arizona grimaced. 'So they say—will we still be doing it tomorrow?'

His eyes locked with hers. 'Oh, yes. Did you doubt it after what's just happened?'

'No...'

The door chimes rang.

She tensed and her eyes widened.

'Stay there,' he murmured. 'I ordered some food, I'll get it.' He disappeared into the bathroom, came out wearing a towelling robe and walked into the lounge. A few minutes later he reappeared pushing a trolley with the most visible things on it being a silver bucket with a bottle of champagne—and a bouquet of red roses. 'For you,' he said and put the cellophane-wrapped flowers into her arms. 'And for us.' He picked up the frosted bottle.

Arizona stared at the perfect red blooms and was curiously touched. 'I've started a rose garden at Scawfell, I love roses. Thank you.' She lifted her eyes to his and they were suddenly wet.

'Here,' he said softly and put a glass of champagne into her hand. 'Drink it. It will help.'

It did. So that when he removed the flowers she was able to ask him to pass her the ruby nightgown and her brush and once she'd slipped into the nightgown, she sat up and brushed her hair, rearranged the pillows behind her and smiled at him ruefully. 'Sorry, I don't often get emotional.'

'If you think I mind making you a bit emotional, I don't at all. What would you like? There are oysters or fresh prawns, there's smoked salmon, a couple of slices of hot quiche and a salad—I didn't think you'd feel like a huge meal so I ordered a bit of this and that,' he said humorously.

'I would love some smoked salmon then some quiche.'

'Done, I'm yours to command!' And he served her food then drew a chair up beside the bed for himself. And they ate companionably, talking desultorily and sipping champagne.

Until Arizona lay back with a sigh of contentment. 'I feel wonderful,' she said, a bit surprised.

'Tell me,' he murmured with a wicked little glint in his blue eyes.

'Well, I feel as if I could go back to sleep, a beautiful sound sleep.'

'Good,' he commented. 'Because much as I regret this, I have to leave shortly.' And he got up, stacked the trolley, poured her the last of the champagne and started to dress.

Arizona watched him and knew that he'd organized things so she would feel this way, but a little part of her mind wondered if he knew that above all, she would still fall asleep preferring not to be on her own for the rest of the night.

Nor was it a help, as she sipped champagne, to have to watch him dressing economically and methodically, to watch him buttoning up his blue shirt and remembering how wide his shoulders were and how they'd felt beneath her hands, how she'd twined her fingers gently in the springy dark hair of his chest…

He came back to the bed with his tie in his hand. 'About tomorrow—would you trust me to take care of it all?'

'What do you mean?' she said after a moment.

'Well, I'd rather you didn't leave the hotel, or indeed the suite, until I send a car for you.'

Her eyes widened.

'Only—' he pauscd '—because if anyone gets wind of this they're liable to hound you to death.'

'The media, do you mean?'

'Uh-huh. So, say I send a car at ten-thirty?'

'And all I'll have to do is bring myself? And my new clothes?'

'Yes.'

'I…' She hesitated, dazed. 'I suppose so.'

'You could relax,' he suggested with a suddenly crooked little grin.

'Do I look as if I need to?'

'You look—' his gaze travelled down the beautiful nightgown and back again to faint blue shadows beneath her eyes '—utterly lovely.'

She closed her eyes suddenly and said, 'Don't go.' Then her lashes swept up and there was a faintly horrified expression in her eyes. 'I mean…'

'Arizona, I have to,' he said evenly. 'I'm sorry. But nothing will tear me away tomorrow, after noon.'

She blinked, then smiled. 'Okay. Sorry. I'm fine really. And I won't so much as venture outside the door.'

'Good girl.' He stood up and dropped a light kiss on her hair. 'I'm also only a phone call away, you know. Why don't you ring Rosemary, incidentally?'

'I'd already rung Rosemary twice before you came,' she said wryly. 'They're all fine. But—' She stopped and frowned.

'Glory be!' He tied his tie and slipped his jacket on and she saw him do a check of his pockets and all of a sudden he was Declan Holmes again, media magnate, not the man who had lain beside her with his strong, beautifully proportioned body naked and who had made stunning love to her.

And to distract herself, she said, 'So! Until noon tomorrow.'

'Until noon, Arizona.' And their gazes locked and it was as if by some mysterious force, she was in his arms again, helpless with pleasure… And after what seemed like an age, he turned away and walked out.

She woke the next morning with the children on her mind, but each time she reached for the phone something held her back. She was still undecided and worried about them by nine o'clock when her doorbell chimed. It was a bellboy with a suitcase and a note for her.

She took them, somewhat dazed, and opened the note first. It was from Declan and it said simply, 'The rest of my night was as lonely as hell. Don't wear the dress until you get to the house, you'll be able to change there. P.S. I chose it myself.'

She turned to the suitcase and opened it with unsteady hands. There was a dress box inside, and from the tissue paper within she drew a dream of a dress. It was in a pearl-coloured delicate crepe with a three-tiered slim skirt, a sleeveless round-necked bodice and a short jacket embroidered with tiny seed pearls to form little flowers. Just the elegance and grace of the outfit as well as the beautiful workmanship caused her lips to curve into a smile, and she held the dress to her cheek for a moment. Then she noticed two smaller parcels in the case, which turned out to be a pair of kid shoes that matched the dress and the much smaller one, another velvet box from which she drew, with a gasp, a river of flawless pearls with a ruby clasp.

The house turned out to be a two-storied mansion on Point Piper above the harbour with a fabulous view. A housekeeper met her as the car drew up and showed her to a bedroom that was obviously the master bedroom with French doors that opened on to a veranda, and another note from Declan to the effect that the ceremony would be in the garden and he would meet her there at noon. In the meantime, she was to do as she liked and ask for whatever she wanted.

Arizona asked the housekeeper for some tea, which came in a silver pot with some macaroons, and sat down as the door closed behind the polite housekeeper with a sigh and a feeling, definitely this time, of Alice in Wonderland.

And to distract herself, she looked around then got up to inspect the lovely bedroom. It had a velvety,

close-pile pewter blue carpet, a king-size bed covered
with a quilted ivory silk spread with a trim that
matched the pillowcases in shadowy hyacinth pinks
and greys. The windows were dressed similarly, ivory
silk curtains with hyacinth and grey pelmets and tie
backs. There was a breakfast table and two chairs set
at one window and two deep armchairs set in front
of a fireplace. The walls were papered in a thick matt
slate blue with an ivory trim, and there were crystal
and silver ornaments on the mantelpiece and occasional tables dotted about. There was also a full-size
dressing room leading off the bedroom and into an
ensuite bathroom, a symphony of blue and silver. She
lingered in the dressing room, touching one of
Declan's suits almost as if she could imbibe some of
his spirit to give her courage. Then she looked at her
watch and realized she only had three-quarters of an
hour before she became Mrs. Declan Holmes. And
was touched by a moment of panic, unreality and the
feeling that she shouldn't be doing this without having warned the children it was happening. She returned to her dress, laid out across the bed, and fin-
gered her engagement ring, and there was a soft
knock on the door, which revealed the housekeeper
again but not only that, Sarah, Daisy, Rosemary and
Cloris.

'Oh!' Arizona gazed at them for a moment, taking
in the girls' new lovely matching blue silk dresses,
Cloris in matronly mauve, Rosemary in a stunning
green décolleté outfit, and then they were all kissing
and hugging each other, Arizona with some tears of
happiness in her eyes.

'It was Declan's idea,' Daisy told her, sitting on

the bed while the others helped Arizona to dress. 'He said he wanted it to be a surprise for you.'

'We all flew up in his new helicopter!' Sarah contributed enthusiastically. 'Do you think the boys aren't wrapped in it?'

'They're here, too?'

'Sure are, but Declan reckons the boys stay together and out of the girls' way on wedding days. You should see them. They've got new suits just like proper men!'

'And where did all these lovely new clothes come from?'

'That was my doing, darling,' Rosemary said, not without a certain smug air as she urged Arizona to sit down so she could attend to her hair. 'Got a call from Declan yesterday morning asking me if I could rustle up the goods, so I rang David Jones with all the details, and they came down on the helicopter this morning.'

'And I brought these,' Cloris said proudly. She opened her purse and withdrew two handkerchiefs, a beautiful old handmade-linen and crochet-trimmed one with tiny blue forget-me-nots embroidered in the corners and an obviously new one trimmed with lace. 'You know what they say, something old, something new, something borrowed, something blue? Well, this belonged to my mother and I'll lend it to you for today, so it's old, it's borrowed, it's got some blue and the other—'

'You're an absolute darling,' Arizona said huskily and hugged her.

'How was that?'

Arizona looked at the new gold wedding band on

her left hand and up into Declan Holmes's eyes and was curiously speechless. They were alone for the moment in a small latticework gazebo where they'd been married by a marriage celebrant in a simple ceremony with the children, Rosemary and Cloris as witnesses. It was a clear, sparkling day, and the waters of Sydney Harbour were like pale blue stretched silk. The gazebo was beautifully decorated with flowers and ribbons, and the white wrought-iron table they'd stood before had been clothed with an exquisite linen cloth embroidered with silver thread. The celebrant, an elegant woman in her fifties, had spoken quietly but wisely on the joys and pitfalls of married life, calling on some of her own experiences as a wife of twenty-five years and the mother of four children with touches of humour. Arizona, during the ceremony, had found herself more moved than she'd expected to be, more relaxed with the children about them obviously feeling happy, excited and important.

'It was,' she said, 'fine. You're an excellent organizer, Declan.' She looked around and added genuinely, 'It's all lovely. Thank you so much for bringing them up. I was—worried about doing it behind their backs.'

'So was I. It didn't feel right. They don't seem to have any problems with it, do they?'

'No.'

'And how does it feel to be my wife?' he murmured with a slight smile quirking his lips.

'I'll have to let you know about that. It's only been ten minutes.'

'Do you think ten minutes is long enough for me to kiss you? Properly, that is.'

Arizona hesitated and looked towards the house through the latticework.

'We're alone,' he said, following her gaze.

'I know, but they—'

'There's a feast set out up there. I doubt we'll be interrupted for a minute or two.'

'In that case, you may,' Arizona said.

CHAPTER SIX

THEIR wedding feast was laid out in a lovely long veranda room with huge glass windows facing the view. There was a table for eight set with silver and crystal, decorated with flowers and ribbons—and if the bride looked a little bemused it was because she had just been very comprehensively kissed. The bridegroom, however, looked completely at home, and it was a gay meal as they ate asparagus vinaigrette, roast turkey with pine nut stuffing and Cointreau ice-cream. And after it, he made a little speech to the effect that he was 'borrowing' Arizona for a short honeymoon right here in Sydney, but that they'd both be back at Scawfell in a few days, and in the meantime Rosemary and Cloris had a few surprises planned for good children.

Daisy looked vaguely mutinous for a moment, but when she discovered they were to fly back in the helicopter, she brightened immediately. It seemed she'd taken to it like a duck to water, although Sarah did say in an aside to Arizona that she'd probably be unbearable at school boasting about it. But it was a happy, contented band they waved off a little later.

Then Declan led her inside, saying wryly, 'Alone at last—I hope you liked my choice of a dress. As soon as I saw it I could visualize you in it, looking unapproachably lovely.'

Arizona blinked then glanced at her outfit. 'I love

it, but it doesn't seem to have made me unapproach-able.'

'Yes, it did,' he contradicted. 'For the first few minutes when we met in the gazebo, you were just that.'

'Well,' she confessed with a faint smile, 'that's be-cause I really felt like Alice in Wonderland. Why—' she hesitated '—did you want me to look unapproach-able?'

'A purely masculine whim. I wanted to contrast that in my mind with how you might look later. Sit down,' he invited and poured two glasses of cham-pagne. They were in the room overlooking the har-bour, but the remains of the feast had been magically cleared. He took his glass and said gravely, 'May I toast the bride?'

'Thank you,' Arizona responded. 'May I toast—us?' she added very quietly.

'With great pleasure, my dear.' They clinked their glasses together and stared into each other's eyes. Then he dropped a light kiss on her hair. 'Do you know, we're absolutely alone now.'

'Oh?'

'Mmm—I gave the staff some time off. I thought you might prefer it that way. For a while.'

'Thanks, I would.'

He looked into her eyes then said lightly, 'Would you like a tour of the house?'

'Yes, please.'

So he showed her around and told her a bit of its history. It was grander than Scawfell, filled with beau-tiful old furniture and paintings, and in one of the most prestigious suburbs of Sydney, the view alone guaranteeing that, but what surprised her was that he'd bought it for his mother.

'Why?' she asked as they got back to the veranda room.

He shrugged. 'I thought she deserved something like this. She didn't have long to enjoy it, unfortunately.'

'And your father?'

'He moved out after she died. In fact he moved out of the country. He lives in London now.'

'Does he know about us?'

Declan looked at her. 'No.'

'Wouldn't he approve?'

'I've no idea. Does your mother know about us, Arizona?'

'I wrote to her this morning.'

'Will *she* approve?'

'I don't know.'

He went to say something then seemed to change his mind. She looked at him enquiringly.

'It just occurred to me I was in no position to lecture you on parental relationships—what would you like to do now?' he asked, changing the subject completely.

Arizona hesitated then was unable to stop herself from yawning, but he only laughed as she grimaced. And said, 'Why not? After a meal like that it's entirely sensible.'

'What about you?'

'I'm going to join you—but only for a nap at this stage,' he said gravely. 'It is my wedding day, too, you know.'

'Well, that's what I wondered,' she said honestly.

'Whether I was going to leap on you straight away?'

'Yes—no…Declan, you're teasing me. But I didn't think you were the napping type, nor that you would have been consumed by nerves this morning.'

'Ah, but I was, of a kind,' he said. 'You could have run away.'

Arizona's eyes widened, and he smiled slightly then said simply, 'Come.'

She changed out of her wedding dress in the privacy of the ensuite dressing room and put on a long T-shirt, and she fell asleep in his arms and slept deeply and dreamlessly for nearly an hour. By which time long shadows were stretching across the garden and the pool. But she was alone when she woke, and after a few moments of reorientating herself, she got up and padded over to the window where she saw him, sitting beside the pool in bathers with a mobile phone on the table beside him, reading through what looked like a pile of documents. She grimaced then searched through her new clothes for the swimsuit she'd bought, plain white and one-piece, but low-cut at the top and high-cut at the legs.

And she grimaced again as she eyed herself in the mirror. It was deliberately sexy, this swimsuit, and clung to her figure like a second skin. There was a white voile shirt that went with it, but it was so sheer it didn't hide much, either. She put it on all the same, tied her hair back, and with an odd little breath, went to join her husband.

He wasn't there when she got to the pool, although the phone was. She shrugged and looked around. The pool was in a walled garden with flowering creepers growing riotously over the mellow, old pink bricks. There was thick smooth grass on three sides of it then a paved area that led out of a side veranda and some dark green garden furniture. There were small statues dotted about that were also plant holders with flowering shrubs growing out of them. There was a bower, smothered in climbing roses, and a small waterfall at one end of the pool. It was a lovely, peaceful, scented and very private area.

She took her blouse off and was just testing the water with her toes when she heard a low whistle. She straightened and turned to see Declan with a tray in his hands, walking towards her.

'Oh. I wondered where you were,' she said a little breathlessly.

'I went to see where you were and to bring us some drinks,' he replied, putting the tray down without taking his eyes off her. 'We must have just missed each other.'

'The water looks so inviting.'

'So do you. That costume is quite stunning.'

Arizona laughed a little then said ruefully, 'It's not exactly my usual style.'

'No? So it was one of your heat-of-the-moment purchases? Designed to teach me a thing or two, one way or another?'

'Yes, but I'm not sure what,' she replied.

'In that mood, perhaps an eat your heart out, Mr. Holmes type of message?' he suggested with the wickedest glint in his blue eyes.

Arizona blushed but couldn't deny it. 'Perhaps.'

'Thank God things have turned out the way they have, then,' he murmured wryly. 'I'd be an absolute case, otherwise. Would you like a swim first or a drink first?' He gestured to the tray. 'It's not alcoholic, just very cold and refreshing fruit juice.'

'I think I'll have a swim first.' And so saying, Arizona dived into the water. It was heavenly, also refreshing, and she swam quite a few laps energetically before she pulled herself out and accepted the dark green towel he handed her.

'Feel better?'

'A whole heap better!' She rubbed herself down and wrung out her hair. 'Thanks,' she added, sinking into a chair.

'I—hell,' he said as the phone rang. 'Sorry about this, but it will be the last one today, I promise.'

It was a fairly long conversation, and she couldn't help divining it was to do with the current political crisis, something she'd normally have been very interested in. She grimaced as she thought that nothing outside her immediate situation seemed to have the power to interest her or hold her attention, and as she sipped her drink her mind wandered to the night before, what had happened and how it had happened— and when it was likely to happen again. So that it was out of quite a considerable reverie he brought her when he said her name.

She coloured faintly because she hadn't even realized his phone call had ended. 'I was miles away.'

'Where, I wonder?' he murmured.

She coloured more brightly this time but said honestly, 'I was thinking of last night.'

'So have I been, all day—could this be the right time to relive last night?'

'I don't know. I mean—' her lips twisted into a wry little smile and her eyes were suddenly mischievous '—we could wait until we go to bed tonight.'

'That might be harder than you think,' he responded.

'But...' She hesitated and looked at her hands then shrugged. 'I don't know how to begin, I guess.'

'May I make a suggestion?'

She grinned. 'You always do, and, much as it has pained me on occasions, they're nearly always good ones.'

'Thank you! That might even spur me to greater heights. Let's see. Had you noticed that the sun has just set?'

'Uh-huh.' Arizona looked around. The garden was now a mysterious place of rose-tinted shadows, and the sky was reflected on the pool in streaks of orange and lemon amidst the glassy blue surface of the water. 'I've also noticed,' she said impishly, 'that you never rush into your suggestions. You often set the scene first, so to speak.'

He raised a wry eyebrow at her. 'Any guesses?'

'No—well, only a very general idea.'

'Good. I like surprising you. Uh—the air is warm and balmy, would you also agree?'

Arizona eyed him through her lashes. 'Yes.'

'How was the water?'

'Lovely,' she said slowly.

'Ever swum without your clothes?'

A little jolt of breath escaped, but she took time to say thoughtfully, 'As a matter of fact, no.'

He sat forward and picked up her hand. 'Would you like to try it?'

Arizona felt a tremor run through her and, foolishly, looked around and up at the sky.

'They'd need a helicopter,' he said amusedly. 'I assure you, no-one would see, other than me.'

'All right.' But she bit her lip, then on an impulse, freed her hand, stood up, stripped her costume off and dived into the pool. When she surfaced, though, he was right beside her and he was laughing at her, his teeth glinting whitely, his dark hair plastered to his head, and he resisted the sudden rush of embarrassment that made her try to twist away by gathering her slim, satiny body in his arms and holding her against the length of his as he trod water then moved them to a shallower area where he could stand. 'Don't,' he said as she made another effort.

'Don't laugh at me, then,' she retorted.

'If you knew what I'd really like to do to you,' he replied, 'you'd know it was no laughing matter at all. But,' he continued, overriding her, 'don't you like this?'

Arizona quietened suddenly and thought about it. Or felt it, would have been more to the point, she reflected, and in the sudden gesture of freedom it seemed to generate she wound her legs around his thighs and lay back against the circle of his arms, murmuring, 'I hope this speaks for itself!'

'It does,' he agreed, his gaze intent on the water lapping around her breasts, the chill of which but not only that had caused her nipples to unfold and stand erect. 'Most eloquently, my lovely mermaid. Did you know you were a symphony of rose and ivory and the most tantalizing curves?' His hands moved down to her buttocks, and she floated on her back, still with her legs twined round him and a dreamy sense of delight in her heart. But he hadn't finished, it seemed. 'Then there's this lovely slender waist—' he moved his hands upwards, and her skin felt slippery and satiny '—and a veil of darkness here.'

She gasped and shuddered as he traced his finger-tips through the mound of curls that guarded the core of her most secret, sensitive area.

'No good?' he said, barely audibly.

'Too good,' she whispered, and pulled herself up-right, slipped her arms around him and laid her cheek on his shoulder, her breasts against his chest. 'If you see what I mean,' she added with a tremor in her voice. 'Is it any good for you?'

'So good, my dear,' he answered, 'I'm going to get you out of here before it's...too late.'

'Not very far away, I hope.'

'No...'

In fact he carried her out of the pool and laid her on the grass beside it and it felt wonderful beneath her, thick and cool, and he knelt over her for a while, running his hands up and down her body, tasting her skin and her nipples while she stroked his back and moved with ever growing desire until she said his name urgently, and he parted her legs and claimed her powerfully and equally urgently so that they were united in a burst of white-hot passionate delight.

'How...does it always happen like this?' Arizona said shakily, many minutes later but still cradled in his arms.

'There's certainly something about us that's— highly combustible,' he said. 'How do you feel?'

She considered and moved against him for reas-surance, warmth and the pure pleasure that the grace and strength of his body brought her. 'I feel...very womanly,' she said at last.

'Do you mind?' he asked quizzically.

'Right now, no. I love it. But if you'd ever asked me whether I would enjoy making love on a lawn beside a pool in the dark, I think I might have been quite scornful,' she confessed.

He kissed her hair lightly and grinned. 'Then I'm honoured, Mrs. Holmes, to be the one to bring you to this state. Talking of the dark, though, and the possibility of getting chilled, would it be terribly mundane if I suggested we should go inside, have a shower and put some clothes on?'

'No, as usual, Mr. Holmes, it's an excellent suggestion!'

They showered together, and it was while she was drying her rose and ivory body with a huge, snowy white towel before a wall of mirrors, and studying it quite openly and with some curiosity, that she was struck by a sudden thought.

She turned to Declan, who was towelling himself off also, and said, 'Is that what you meant?'

He raised an eyebrow at her, hung up his towel and came to take hers from her. 'Meant?'

'I mean—did you plan that all in advance?' Her eyes were very grey and serious.

'I planned to make love to you some time today,' he said gravely and put his hands on her waist. 'But, no, I did not say to myself, we'll do it by the pool at six-thirty on the dot after an unclothed interlude in the pool. Why do you ask?'

'What I really meant was, when you said earlier that you wanted me to look unapproachable so you could contrast in your mind—' She stopped abruptly.

'Ah, that,' he drawled. 'Yes, the contrast is quite stunning.' And his blue gaze swept up and down her body, from the top of her head to the tips of her toes and all the flushed, silken, curved and slender spots in between. 'Does it bother you?'

'No,' Arizona said slowly, but it did. For no reason she could put her finger on, though.

He narrowed his eyes. 'You don't sound too sure.'

She moved, but he kept his hands on her waist. Then he surprised her—he turned her around so they were both facing the mirror, she standing in front of him, he looking at her inscrutably.

'What?' she whispered after a long, tense moment.

His eyes met hers in the mirror and he brought his hands up and cupped her breasts. 'It's mutual, Arizona. We do this to each other, don't we?'

'I…yes,' she said uncertainly then closed her eyes and laid her head back against him as those long fingers plucked her nipples almost absently. 'But again? I mean…so soon?' Her voice cracked a little.

'We've a bit of lost time to make up for,' he said, rather dryly she thought, but before she could take issue, he added, 'I'm afraid it can't be soon enough for me at the moment.' And without waiting for her permission, he picked her up and took her to the vast bed in the master bedroom. But what surprised her most, perhaps, was the corresponding hunger he was able to arouse in her, again, so soon and despite her better judgment for another, obscure reason.

But there was no doubting that he did arouse her, and as their limbs mingled and his hands sought and stroked and teased, her breathing grew ragged and she stretched her arms above her head and pointed her toes and made an odd little sound in her throat as she grew warm and wet, and ached for him to commit the final act. Which she participated in with growing boldness that secretly amazed her but seemed only to please him until they were breathing as one and the pleasure ran through them at the same moment.

Minutes later, he rolled onto his side, taking her with him in his arms, and said into her hair with a tinge of amusement, 'For a second time, and so soon, how was that?'

'It was—I can't actually describe it,' she whispered. 'But I do know I'll be good for absolutely nothing for a while. You've worn me out, Mr. Holmes, although I must say you did it beautifully.'

He laughed and hugged her. 'Go to sleep then.'

And she did.

She woke alone, saw drowsily on the bedside clock that it was ten o'clock at night, and for a few minutes simply lay with her hands at her sides wondering where he was. Wondering if millionaires had separate bedrooms. Wondering if it was common amongst them to spend the first night of their marriages in separate beds and rooms. Then she realized she was hungry and thirsty, and she shook off her odd feeling of foreboding, had a quick shower, pulled on the dark blue towelling robe that hung behind the door and padded to the kitchen.

The light was on and Declan was there in shorts and a T-shirt with a percolator of coffee bubbling aromatically on the gleaming range. The kitchen was tidy but the remains of their turkey was on a platter on the table. He looked up as she stood in the doorway and simply held out his hand.

Arizona hesitated then slipped into a chair beside him. 'I wondered where you were,' she said quietly.

'I was starving but I didn't want to wake you. Like some?'

'Yes, please.' She looked around.

He carved her some cold turkey and buttered her some bread. 'Coffee?' She nodded and he got up to pour it.

'So you're fairly domesticated,' she reflected between mouthfuls of turkey.

He glanced at her quizzically. 'Well, the Navy teaches one all sorts of useful things. How to open a tin of baked beans, for example.'

'Seriously,' Arizona said.

'Seriously?' He raised a wry eyebrow at her. 'Did you have me pictured as some dangerous beast you might have to house-train?'

'No, of course not.' Arizona grimaced. 'I just don't know, well, those kind of things about you. Some men are great cooks. Pete was, for example.' She stopped abruptly.

Their eyes met, and she tingled curiously, not only because as soon as she'd said it she'd wished fervently she hadn't mentioned Pete's name, but also because of the sudden little glint of steel she thought she saw in the blue depths of his eyes.

'I know,' he said at last. 'No, I'm not in Pete's class cooking-wise, although I mightn't starve if left to my own devices. How did you cope with Pete's uninspiring lovemaking, incidentally?'

Arizona went cold and her eyes widened. 'What do you mean?' she said with difficulty.

'Did you fake it?' he suggested.

'No.'

'He must have wondered what he was doing wrong.'

'He knew…he—' She pushed her plate away suddenly and stood up. 'Why are you asking me this, Declan?'

'You brought his name up, Arizona,' he said with irony.

'I'm sorry about that,' she said evenly. 'It just—' she paused '—came out in the context of what we were talking about. It wasn't because I'd been thinking of him or anything like that.'

'How kind of you,' he said dryly and put two mugs of coffee on the table. 'Going somewhere?' he added coolly.

'I…it crossed my mind to wonder whether the honeymoon was over,' she said tautly. 'If so, I might as well go back to bed, alone.'

'Sit down, Arizona,' he ordered. 'Let's not get all dramatic.'

'You started this,' she countered.

'Perhaps I have an unusual sensitivity on the subject. It is, after all, our wedding night.'

Arizona stared at him because the way he'd said it didn't seem to match up with what he'd said. In fact there'd been a flat sort of indifference in his voice that made her blood run cold and made it very hard for her to believe that she'd genuinely touched a nerve even though she knew it was not in the best taste, if nothing else, to mention one's previous husband to one's very new husband.

'Is—' her voice shook slightly 'something else wrong, Declan?'

'Such as?' He raised an eyebrow at her.

'I don't know. I'm only guessing. Perhaps I didn't altogether please you last time round.'

'Not at all, Arizona,' he drawled. 'You please me exceedingly. But *you* were the one who came into this room with something on your mind, then brought Pete up.'

It was true, of course, only she'd forgotten that in the last few minutes. But it struck her suddenly, so that she bit her lip as the words formulated in her mind—*yes, I always seem to wake up alone and it bothers me!* But the implication of that sentiment suddenly hit her with a force that made her close her eyes briefly and then sit down as she swallowed unexpectedly. *Have I fallen that much in love?* she wondered.

'Arizona?'

She swallowed again then lifted her coffee mug. 'Not really—I mean there wasn't much on my mind. I—'

The telephone rang.

Declan swore then lifted the wall receiver, and his voice was hard as he said hello. But it was Rosemary, worried because Daisy kept waking up with nightmares and asking for Arizona.

'You better talk to her,' Declan said and handed her the phone.

She got Rosemary first, who said, 'Darling, the last thing I wanted to do was interrupt your honeymoon but she seems quite upset and I just can't get her to stay asleep. None of us can! I think she might have had just a bit too much excitement today.'

'Let me say hello, Rosemary.' And a moment later, 'Daisy, is that you, pet?'

'Arizona,' Daisy wept down the line, 'I don't want to stay here any more. I want to go home and I want to see you and I can't sleep because there's cars smashing and crashing and—'

'Daisy.' Arizona tried to stem the flow. 'Darling,

I'm coming home first thing in the morning, I promise you! Now I'll tell you what I want you to do. You know your Christopher Robin book? Well, get it out and let Cloris read it to you, it's your favourite book, remember? Tell you what, why don't I say some of it to you now?'

'But I've got the book here.'

'I know it off by heart, we both do, don't we?' Arizona said gently. 'So what shall we start with? You choose…'

Fifteen minutes later she put the phone down and rubbed her brow wearily, feeling drained and tense.

Declan watched her for a moment then walked over to her, put his hands on her shoulders and started to massage them. He also said with a strange little smile, 'I can see we are going to be hard put to get much more of a honeymoon. It was probably my fault—too big a day today.' He grimaced. 'But I did want them to be here for you—for their sakes and yours.'

Arizona searched his eyes but that steely glint was gone. So was the indifference, but at the same time his blue gaze was entirely enigmatic. She moistened her lips and thought that she'd never felt more at sea with Declan Holmes than she did now. 'I know, and I'm grateful, but I did say I'd go back tomorrow…'

'I heard. Does she get these nightmares often?'

'Not for ages.' His long fingers were working a minor miracle. '

'It's just going to take a bit more time, I guess. You look exhausted. Come back to bed.' And he released her to take her hand. *Just like that,* she thought, dazed, as she went with him obediently. *Did I imagine the rest?*

And she stood compliantly while he slipped the

blue robe off and slid the ruby nightgown on over her head.

'Did you leave the teddies behind?'

She blinked. 'Oh—yes.'

He smiled. 'I'm glad in a way. You look about nineteen in it. Certainly not both a wife and a widow. Hop in,' he invited and pulled the bedclothes back.

But Arizona stared at him, her eyes dark and shadowed, and seemed unable to move. So he picked her up and laid her down as if she was a child, then he got in beside her, turned her on her side so she was facing away from him and took her in his arms.

She moved once, but he slid his hand slowly down her flank and said into her hair, 'Go to sleep, Arizona. It's been a big day all round.'

She did, after a while, thinking that it might have been too big a day for her as well as Daisy, because she didn't seem to understand anything any more, and certainly not why she should be falling under the soothing spell of what this man was doing to her, a man who was her husband but in some respects a complete stranger. Nor why he should be doing it after the things he'd said.

And she woke in the morning with the same thoughts on her mind, and reached across the bed suddenly—but she was alone.

CHAPTER SEVEN

'WELL, I won't go looking for him this time.'

Her words seemed to echo and she sighed, laid her cheek on the pillow and wondered if she was being childish or ridiculous or particularly fanciful. *But for some reason it does make me uneasy,* she mused, *and it probably was just that uneasiness that led me into committing the solecism of mentioning Pete on our wedding night, although it wasn't really such a solecism, did he but know it...*

The thing is, she thought, *I've got the oddest feeling that he expects it to be all or nothing for me, which doesn't quite fit in with our mutual concept of this marriage and might not be what I'll get from him. Then again, the real thing is, does the fact that always waking up alone upsets me mean I'm going to want more than I'm going to get from Declan Holmes? And if that's the case, I'm in trouble...*

She stared unseeingly across the room then closed her eyes briefly. Five minutes later she got up and started to pack. Then she showered and dressed in a shorts suit outfit made from silky crepe in thyme green with a tiny beige dot, a beige blouse to go beneath the jacket and thyme flat shoes. It was one of her purchases and was cool, elegant and uncrushable for travelling.

She was just closing her last case when the door opened and Declan came in with a tray.

'Ah,' he murmured after one long moment when

they stared at each other, 'you're up. I was hoping to bring you breakfast in bed.'

'Thank you. But I'm up, as you see,' she replied evenly.

'And still annoyed with me.' He crossed over to the table by the window, put the tray down and pulled out one of the chairs with a polite gesture. He added with a wry lift of an eyebrow, 'Why don't you sit down and tell me all about it?'

Oh, no, you don't! Arizona thought, and sat down, composed. 'I didn't say that, Declan.'

'Everything points to it, however.' He sat down opposite, removed some covers and revealed two perfect herb omelettes. There was also fresh orange juice and toast.

'I don't see why,' she answered calmly. 'This is a fair jump from opening a can of baked beans,' she added quizzically.

'Would that it were—the staff are back.'

'I see.' Arizona said and refrained from saying, *so the honeymoon is over.* He was also dressed, in a grey and white striped shirt, maroon tie and charcoal trousers.

'Well, I guess as soon as I've finished this I can head for home.' She paused. 'The only thing is that my car is still at the Hilton, but perhaps you wouldn't mind giving me a lift into town? I gather you won't be coming down with me.'

'As it happens, I'm going to give you a lift to Scawfell, although I won't be able to stay,' he said and continued to eat his omelette imperturbably.

'You don't have to drive all that way, Declan, I'll be fine.'

'I'm sure you will,' he murmured, 'but I'm not driving you, I'm flying you.'

'And how will I get my car back?' Arizona enquired.

'I'll have someone return it for you. It may interest you to know that one of the reasons I acquired a helicopter, apart from not wasting my Navy training and because I do have to hop about the place such a lot, was that I thought it would bring me back to your side much more quickly than any other means.' He caught and held her gaze and raised his orange juice to her.

'Ah, but I imagine it will do the opposite just as speedily,' Arizona commented with considerable irony.

His blue gaze hardened and he put the glass down. 'My dear, I don't know if you have any idea what the country is going through at the moment or how peculiarly it affects my business—'

'I do, I do,' Arizona interrupted. 'I realize all sorts of things. That Daisy is waiting anxiously, for another, that this is how we decided our marriage would be—I'm not complaining, Declan.' She glanced at her packed bags, at her purse and sunglasses set neatly ready and waiting on the bed. 'I'm being if anything most cooperative, I would have thought,' she finished gently.

'At the same time as you'd like to scratch my eyes out,' he said after a tense little pause.

Arizona sipped some juice and slipped the stem of the glass between her fingers before she said dryly, 'Dear me, Declan, do you really think I'd be so uncouth?'

'Not uncouth at all,' he corrected her as dryly. 'But

I really think that were we to go to bed now, you'd
fight me every inch of the way, and enjoy every minute of it.'

Arizona stood up and slammed her knife and fork
together beside her unfinished omelette. 'Don't count
on it, and don't dare to lay even a finger on me,' she
warned him furiously.

'Sit down, Arizona,' he recommended, not angrily
nor even particularly coldly, but something in his eyes
warned her to obey him or suffer the consequences.

She tightened her mouth and sat down.

He waited a moment then said evenly, 'What are
we fighting about, Arizona? If it's still to do with you
being forced to marry me, let me ask you this. Do
you regret sleeping with me at the Hilton, do you
regret me making love to you beside the pool or here
in this very bed? If you do I have to tell you you're
a sensational actress. Do you regret being able to go
back to Scawfell and starting to do all the things
you've been wanting to do for ages?'

'I…' She clenched her fists in her lap. 'No.'

'So?' He gazed at her narrowly.

'I think you better take me back to Scawfell,
Declan,' she said very quietly. 'It's just possible that
new brides are a bit emotionally unstable,' she added
and wondered if he knew the effort it cost her to smile
slightly. 'Sorry.'

'In that case I think there's something else I ought
to do.'

Her lips parted as she suddenly recognized the way
he was looking at her. And she trembled inwardly.

'But only to—warm and reassure you,' he said.
'Not fight you.'

'You really don't have to, Declan,' she said, barely

audibly. 'I'm all right.' *And I now know exactly what I'm up against,* she thought, but again, did not say.

'On the other hand, would you like me to?' he asked.

'Like you to?' She hesitated.

'Make love to you.'

She stared at him helplessly.

They landed on the lawn in front of the house a couple of hours later, and everyone was there to meet them, Cloris, the children and Rosemary.

'I'm so, so sorry,' Rosemary whispered to Arizona, but Declan immediately took charge of things as he picked Daisy up and hugged her then handed her to Arizona, saying, 'If anyone's interested in a joy flight over the ocean I've got a bit of time.'

He didn't have to make a second offer. Richard and Ben raced for the machine, as well as Sarah, although Daisy elected to stay with Arizona. And Rosemary urged those staying on the ground inside, saying she had a surprise, which took the form of a wedding present.

'Oh, Rosemary!' Arizona gasped.

'Like it?'

'It's stunning!'

It was, in fact, a full-size, black-faced, woolly, extremely lifelike sheep. 'Not that easy to choose gifts for the very wealthy,' Rosemary said wryly, 'but it's beautifully made by a little man who lives down the coast, and his work is starting to be highly sought. I'll leave it up to you to find a spot for it,' she added with a lurking grin.

'Thanks, pal.' Arizona kissed her warmly. 'I think he's beautiful. Why don't we put him in the hall?

Then he can greet everyone who comes to Scawfell. Daisy, darling, would you like to think of a name for him?'

Daisy brightened and let go of Arizona's hand for the first time. 'Bendigo,' she said promptly. 'Can I have a ride on him?'

'Bendigo,' Rosemary and Arizona said together, and laughed.

'Couldn't have done better myself,' Rosemary remarked.

A little later, Cloris waylaid Arizona as she came in alone from farewelling Rosemary. Declan had been duly introduced to Bendigo then dragged off to the stables by the kids. And once Cloris had said again that she was so happy for Arizona, how right it all was, and so sorry she hadn't been able to calm Daisy down the night before, she asked Arizona which bedroom she'd like her to prepare.

Arizona frowned. 'I don't understand—anyway, Declan can't stay tonight.'

'I know, but Mr. Holmes told me that you—you and he—that is—' Cloris blushed '—would be using a different bedroom. He brought down a bag of clothes and things and I just wondered where to put them.'

'Oh, I see! Just leave them where they are for the time being, Cloris, until I have a moment to think about it,' Arizona said brightly but feeling foolish underneath and thinking, *Why does he do this to me?*

She was in her own bedroom when he came back from the stables, starting to unpack. He closed the door, looked at her profile then came over, wrested the bundle of clothes from her hands and took her in his arms. 'Remember me?' he queried quietly.

'Declan—'

'The man you slept with this morning?' he persisted.

'Declan, of course—'

'And the way it was?'

She quietened abruptly in his arms and felt a tide of colour creep up her throat. 'Yes,' she said huskily, and laid her brow on his shoulder as she was shaken by the most intimate memories.

'But you're angry with me again.' He said it as a statement, not a question.

She breathed in the heady masculine essence that went to make up Declan Holmes, felt the strength and hardness of his body even through his suit and said a little wearily, 'No. I'm not.'

'Arizona.'

She raised her head and looked into his eyes and knew she would have to come up with some explanation because he could read her too well. 'Cloris told me you wanted us to share another room.'

He swore beneath his breath but said straightly, 'Yes, I do. I didn't expect her to tell you, though.'

Arizona smiled sketchily. 'I thought you might have known Cloris better than that by now.'

He grimaced. 'I will from now on. But I thought that that's at least what you would want to do yourself—'

'Declan,' she interrupted, 'Pete and I never used this room. It was to be my—retreat, and that's what it was.'

He frowned faintly, and she could see the ramifications of what she'd said going through his mind.

She opened her mouth to add something, but a wariness that not even their magnificent lovemaking of that morning could altogether dispel made her stop and bite her lip.

'Then there's no problem, is there, Arizona?' he said slowly. 'So why are you upset?'

'Because I can't help wondering whether the shadow of Pete isn't going to hang over us all the time.'

He searched her eyes intently. 'Because *I* didn't want to use a bedroom you and he had used? I would have thought that was perfectly natural—'

'Because it was his house, because—' She broke off. 'Do you really think I would have done that to you?'

'I'll tell you what I think,' he murmured after a moment and cupped her face gently. 'That we're at cross-purposes for no good reason at the moment. Tell me something, would you mind me sharing your retreat with you?'

'Oh…no.'

'Then that's resolved that,' he said and kissed her.

And she stood in the circle of his arms for a while longer until he took her hand and said, 'I have to go. Coming to see me off?'

'Yes. But not because I want to.'

'I'll be back as soon as I can, I promise you.'

'Thanks.'

'So, tell me all about married life,' Rosemary said chattily on the veranda at Scawfell a fortnight later over a cup of coffee. The children were at school— Ben at his new school now—and Cloris could be heard humming in the kitchen. The old house drowsed in the sunlight and bees hummed in the flower-beds below the veranda. The sea was an inky blue, and you could hear the surf below the cliff. Rosemary had called in on her way back from the village.

Declan had been home four times in the past fortnight, but only for a night each time.

'Married life?' Arizona said, and added unguardedly, 'well, we certainly don't live in each other's pockets.'

Rosemary said after a moment, 'He's a very busy man, no doubt. It's just a pity, I expect, that the kids depend so much on you, but that could improve.'

'Oh, I don't mind.' Arizona recognized as soon as the words left her lips that she was trying to back-pedal, and a glance at Rosemary revealed that she, too, thought the same.

Damn, Arizona thought. *Well, there's only one thing to do and that's soldier on.* 'I mean I don't really think I'm cut out to be a tycoon's wife, and I'd just as soon be here instead of jet-setting around the place.'

'Besides which,' Rosemary said energetically, 'when you get to be married as long as I have, you don't want to be living in each other's pockets. How is Daisy?'

'She's fine. In fact they're all benefiting from Declan even though he's not here such a lot. But he seems to leave a presence behind him, of law and order—' she grimaced '—and growing confidence that their lives aren't going to be torn apart again.'

'There you are then!' Rosemary looked triumphant. 'Before long you might be able to go on a delayed honeymoon. I was really so sorry I couldn't calm Daisy that night, your wedding night of all nights, but she was just inconsolable, absolutely distraught. You know, Arizona,' she continued thoughtfully, 'I don't think any of us realized what you've had to cope with or just how marvellous you've been, and I have to tell you, with my famed delicacy, that a lot of us thought Pete might be doing the wrong thing when he married you.'

'Thanks,' Arizona said with irony.

'Don't hate me, darling.'

'Rosemary, I don't,' Arizona said with a cross between a grin and a sigh.

'Are you in love with Declan?'

'Now, Rosemary, your famed delicacy has gone a little too far—'

'It's just that it's a bit hard to tell with you, my pet.'

Arizona paused, considered then said barely audibly, 'A little too much perhaps.'

'Do you think you can ever be too much in love with a man…who is also your husband?' Rosemary queried after a long pause.

'Yes, I'm afraid I do, but look—' Arizona smiled with genuine humour then '—I'm probably a bit strange in these respects. Rosemary, seeing as you're so well-named, would you like to see my rose garden? Declan sent me down *twenty* new varieties the other day.'

Indeed, she thought as she worked in her rose garden that afternoon, Declan, who might only grace her bed from time to time, was certainly providing her with plenty to think about and plenty to do. Not only twenty new rosebushes to plant and plan for but plans for a glass-roofed conservatory to be added to the house, which he'd thought they might be able to use as a summer dining room as well and in which, he'd said, she could grow all sorts of exotic plants. It had been impossible to hide the quickening of interest this had aroused in her. He'd also taken her up on a chance remark that the cliff path down to the beach was a bit dangerous and sent a team of workmen down to cut some steps out and erect a handrail. And he'd asked her if she'd like the inside of the house repainted, and when she'd agreed that it did need it, had left the choosing of colour schemes, if she wanted to change anything, up to her. Added to this he'd insisted on hiring a gardener for her, to do all the heavy work and help her to implement all the ideas she had, and to occupy a vacant cottage in the grounds. A man who didn't seem to have much feel for growing things, she thought once, but did have a passion for neatness and order and was extremely self-effacing. With the net result that the estate of Scawfell was starting to look its best.

Whereas I, she thought as she sat back on her heels, *feel as if I'm in a state of limbo, despite having all this to do and think about, not to mention Christmas, not that far away, to plan for. Why can't I just be happy, or if not that, content? Because every minute I'm away from Declan Holmes is extraordinarily hard to bear,* she answered herself. *If only I hadn't been so righteous, so sure I couldn't fall in love like this. How did it happen to me so quickly and completely? Is it the sex? This passionate attraction that I might even be confusing with love? Am I more like my mother than I ever dreamt possible?*

Strangely enough, she got a letter from her mother the next morning, in reply to her letter telling her she was getting married.

'Dear Arizona,' she read. 'Your news came as a bit of a shock. I had hoped that by now you would have forgiven me enough for all I put you through to have confided in me earlier about this second marriage, but I do hope with all my heart that you'll be happy, darling. Is it a love match? You didn't say so, in fact you said so little I don't know what to think and all I can tell you is that you're in my heart and my prayers constantly. Yes, I had heard of Declan Holmes, although not lately....'

Arizona stopped reading because tears were blurring her vision and she whispered, 'Oh, Mum...'

She took the kids for a swim about a week later on a Thursday, a week or so during which she'd seen nothing of Declan. It was a searingly hot day, and the surf was delicious. But it was a tiring exercise nevertheless because Daisy was still a very novice swimmer, and even Sarah and Richard had to be watched all the time in the waves. They, however, were still full of energy after their swim and they bounded up the now safe cliff path and disappeared from view while she was still gathering together towels.

And knowing they could come to no harm, she lingered a little, slipping her togs off beneath her towel and putting her button-through dress on, then discarding the towel, shaking them all then simply standing staring out to sea with the bundle in her arms. Until she began to get hot again and with a strange little shrug turned towards the path. Declan was waiting for her at the top. Declan, casually dressed in jeans and a sports shirt, looking big, fit and entirely enigmatic.

She gasped and grabbed the handrail. 'I didn't hear the helicopter! I didn't expect you...how long have you been here?'

He took his time answering as his blue gaze roamed over her, her wayward damp hair blowing about her face, her pretty floral dress with a heart-shaped neckline and its line of buttons down the front, her bare legs and feet and said finally, 'I drove. I've been *here* for the last few minutes.'

'Why didn't you come down?' she asked and wondered why she sounded, and felt, nervous.

'You looked oddly deep in thought.'

'I...' She stopped and grimaced.

'You also look tired,' he added and took the towels from her.

'I'm fine! Did you see the kids?'

'Yes. I've given them a treat.'

'Such as?'

'Cloris is taking them into town for a movie and then a hamburger dinner.'

'Declan!' she protested. 'It's a school night.'

'I can guarantee that once every Pancake Day, it won't hurt them.'

'I suppose not,' she said ruefully. 'It will be nice and peaceful for a while.'

'That's also what I thought,' he murmured and took her hand.

But he didn't seem to have any more to say to her, and they walked up to the house in silence, although hand in hand, and he simply dropped the towels on the kitchen floor and led her upstairs to the cool green bedroom where he not only closed the door but locked it.

'Just in case they come back early,' he said and crossed the carpet to stand in front of her. 'May I?' He looked at the top button of her dress then into her eyes. Arizona started and coloured.

'What?' he queried quietly.

'I've just remembered I've got nothing on underneath,' she said self-consciously and wondered what she could have been thinking of on the beach.

'I know.'

'How?'

'I saw you change very modestly beneath your towel. There was no evidence of any underclothes, but I really don't think it matters at this point. Do you, Arizona?'

She grimaced. 'No. All the same, it was an odd thing to have done.'

'As I mentioned, you did look oddly preoccupied.' And there was a query in his blue eyes.

She coloured again but said, 'There's a lot to think about at the moment. The conservatory, the new colour schemes, the garden, Christmas—all those things.'

'I wondered if you were missing me.' He put out a hand and touched the top button then slipped it free of the buttonhole.

Arizona looked down as his fingers moved to the next button and it met the same fate. 'Well, yes,' she tried to say lightly. 'It's been a while, I guess.' It had in fact been exactly a week and two days, she knew, almost to the hour.

He smiled, but not with his eyes, and she shivered suddenly as the last button gave way and her dress fell open. 'Not too long?' he said, making no move to touch her.

'Declan…' Her voice sounded strangely hoarse. 'Is something wrong?'

'Why do you say that?'

'I don't know. I—don't know.'

'No, nothing that this won't cure,' he said after an age and raised his hands to slide the dress further apart and cup her breasts.

She took an unsteady breath, and he moved his hands down to her waist and the curve of her hips, and the dress slipped off her shoulders so she was exposed, the whole slim, curved, salty length of her. And he studied her body minutely, as if renewing his acquaintance with it, studied the delicate ruffled pink of her areolae, the paler satin of her skin that the sun didn't see, moving his hands again and drawing his fingers very lightly up the curve of her breasts then lingering slowly on a path down to her thighs.

'Declan,' she whispered, trembling finely not only with exquisite pleasure but some strange sense of unease, 'don't…'

'Don't you like it?' he said looking into her eyes but never for a moment ceasing to move those fingers over her skin. She looked away and stood for a moment with her hands clenched into fists at her sides, her head bent, her dress caught only on her upper arms now. Then she raised her eyes to his and said honestly, 'I'd prefer it if I didn't feel like an object somehow.'

'Then why don't you tell me you were thinking of me on the beach, Arizona?'

Her lips parted and her eyes widened and she turned away, or tried to, but she stumbled, and he caught her wrist and steadied her, and brought her right back in front of him where she'd been, saying only with a cool smile chiselling his lips, 'Arizona?'

'All right, if that's what you want to hear, I was,' she answered tautly.

'But not that happily?'

'If you're trying to make me say I missed you, yes, I did,' she replied but tossed her hair in a suddenly defiant gesture.

'And you take exception to that?'

'What would be the point? And I suppose now you're here I might as well make the best of you—is that what you'd also like me to say, Declan?'

'In fact it was something else I had in mind,' he murmured.

She blinked. *What?*

'Oh, something along the lines of welcome home,' he drawled. She opened her mouth to say that this was no more home to him than the moon, just a temporary stopping off place where there was a convenient bed and a bedmate, but stopped herself with her eyes darkening as if she'd received a blow because, of course, these conditions were as much her choice as his, or had been...

'Welcome home then,' she said in an oddly choked voice and brushed a tear away. 'Sorry. I seem to be making a habit of saying that to you. But I didn't expect you and I suppose I got a bit of a shock.' She swallowed. 'And I didn't think you were particularly welcoming, either, so perhaps we should—both start again?'

He released her wrist and she gathered her dress about her.

He watched her then said only one dry word. 'How?'

She attempted to smile and attempted to be honest. 'If you'd like to take me to bed I think I'd need to be held for a bit and possibly talked to, not for long, just a while. And I think you know,' she said slowly, 'that another habit I've acquired is to respond most favourably to you in bed—that hasn't changed. When—' her voice shook '—I don't feel I'm being...when I'm...' She stopped and swallowed again.

'Being treated as an object,' he supplied. 'That's what you said.'

'Yes, well—yes.'

'It would be strange if we had the same problem, wouldn't it?'

She licked her lips. 'What do you mean?'

'Oh—' he frowned faintly then shrugged. 'One day you might work it out. In the meantime, of course, I'm quite happy to bow to your preferences.' And without warning he picked her up and laid her on the bed, lay down beside her on his stomach with his chin propped on his hands, and said, 'What shall we talk about?'

Arizona sat bolt upright and said through her teeth, 'I could hit you, Declan Holmes!'

'Okay,' he said obligingly and sat up, possessing himself of her fist, 'but let me show you how. Most women go for the good old slap, whereas a punch in the mouth is probably doubly effective and doesn't leave you with a ringing hand. But then again—' he looked into her flashing eyes with the corners of his mouth twisting '—I think I'd rather be kissed.' And he dropped her fist, pulled her into his arms, said into her hair, 'For what it's worth, Arizona, I've missed *you* and I'm sorry I've been gone for so long.'

'Oh…'

'I know,' he agreed and buried his head in the curve of her shoulder some time later. 'This certainly hasn't changed.' And she felt his long body shuddering on hers.

'The really strange thing,' Arizona said later when they were lying in each other's arms beneath the sheet, and stopped.

'Go on,' he prompted.

'No. It's rather embarrassing.'

'Look, you have to tell me now,' he said with a crooked grin. 'Or I'll start imagining heaven knows what.'

'Well, it's this,' she said ruefully and couldn't stop herself from running her fingers through the thick dark hair that lay in his eyes. 'I feel incredibly calm.'

He kissed her palm and said, amused, 'It may be strange to you, but I can assure you it's a great boost to my ego.'

'I don't believe that for one moment,' Arizona said, equally amused.

'Then you don't know me as well as you think.'

She was silent for a long time, revelling in being nestled against him, in the calm and serenity that lay on her spirit like a balm, not able to care that this might be a very temporary state.

'How long do you think this will last?'

'This calm or the calm of having no kids pounding around the place?'

'Well, both, I guess.' She looked at him wryly.

He kissed her brow and smoothed some strands of hair from her cheek. '*This* calm for a few days, because I'm staying down over the weekend. Kids calm, I regret to say, for another hour at the most, but you don't have to get up—'

'Yes, I will. A whole weekend,' she added and bit her lip.

'There's a downside, unfortunately. I have to go to the States for about a fortnight on Monday.'

Arizona was silent then she moved against him and said, 'Never mind.' Her lips twisted mischievously. 'I'll make the most of my weekend.'

'Good girl.' He kissed her again.

If she was delighted to have him for the weekend, so were the kids, and supremely, so was Cloris. The weather held and they swam, rode together, not Cloris, but she was in her element cooking up magnificent meals, and on Sunday she packed a gourmet picnic lunch and they drove to Ben's school, which was having an open day and a gymkhana.

Ben seemed happy and contented and rode Daintry well enough to be presented with a rosette. It was, for Arizona, a happy though different experience—the first time she was introduced, in this case to the headmaster, as Mrs. Declan Holmes, the first time she was out in public as such.

She said to Declan that night when they were alone in the green bedroom getting ready for bed, 'Despite your fears, the press has shown no tendency to hound me. For which I'm duly grateful, but all the same.'

'It's funny you should say that, Arizona.' He raised a wry eyebrow at her. 'Because I was about to mention it to you.'

'Oh?'

'Mmm… It can't remain a secret forever, so I thought it would be a good idea if we gave one interview when I get back, as unrevealing as possible, but enough to satisfy them and not have our marriage seen amidst all sorts of speculation.'

She stirred. She was sitting in bed against the pillows with her knees drawn up, watching him pack, taking pleasure in his economical movements and his brown body in a white T-shirt and shorts. She was wearing her ruby nightgown, her hair was brushed and shining and her beautiful diamond ring shone in the lamplight on her finger. 'Here?' she said.

'No. In Sydney. Nor do I plan to mention Scawfell.'

Arizona twisted her ring.

'They might know about me, anyway.'

'Because of Pete? They probably will, but they'll be working for me, you see.'

'I see.'

'Don't look so concerned, it's the best way, I promise you. I've also upped the security here.'

Arizona blinked. 'It must be very unobtrusive.'

'It is. Did you never suspect—' he grinned at her '—your new gardener?'

'No.'

'Well, now you know. You get on well with him, don't you?'

'Yes, I do,' she said slowly, thinking of the tough, weather-beaten man in his late forties she'd quite come to like. 'But why couldn't you have told me?'

'I didn't want you to feel—hemmed in or whatever. And resent him in consequence. Now that you *do* know, though, he's here to protect your privacy and the kids', as well as your persons and the property. By the way—' he dug down into his bag and brought out a parcel '—I forgot to give you these.'

Arizona, who was frowning anyway, frowned at the parcel he placed in her lap, but didn't open it as she said slowly, 'He must be very versatile.'

'He is. We were in the Navy at the same time, and I had the opportunity to save his life once. He's been rather devoted ever since. He's also been at a bit of a loose end ever since he got out. He's a loner, no wife or kids, so this job, so he tells me, suits him down to the ground.'

'Oh,' She still didn't start to open the parcel.

'What are you thinking?'

She registered the slight change in the tone of his voice and wondered whether to tell him that what she resented was not being taken into his confidence, being treated like a child, in fact, then decided against it. She looked up with a brief smile instead, and said, 'I'm thinking that you're managing my—our—life very competently.' And tore the brown paper to gasp at what she saw. A photo of them on their wedding day in a beautiful silver frame.

'Oh, it's lovely.' She lifted it to the light and studied herself in the dress of his choosing, unsmiling but looking oddly uplifted whilst he was looking at her enigmatically.

'Glad you like it.' He took it from her and put it on the bedside table. 'There's a smaller one, too, which I thought we might give to Cloris.' He lifted the other one out.

'She'll be thrilled,' Arizona said wryly then sobered suddenly. 'Are there any more prints?'

'Yes. Why?' He handed her a photo envelope.

'I thought I might send one to my mother.'

'Have you heard from her?'

'Yes.' She hesitated. 'It occurred to me I should stop—feuding with her.'

'Why not?' he said as he so often did. He added, 'What brought that on?' And sat down on the side of the bed.

Arizona shrugged and avoided looking at him. 'Nothing special, but it's been a long time, and she is my mother, I guess.'

The silence stretched until she was forced to look into his eyes and was slightly disturbed to see the narrow, rather intent look she was on the receiving end of. So she said, 'Will you send one to your father?'

He continued to look at her narrowly for a few moments more then said, 'I hadn't thought of it, no. But why don't you ask your mother to come down and stay for a while?'

'Oh, she wouldn't do that,' Arizona said hastily. 'But this is a start, I guess.'

'I guess,' he repeated. Then he seemed almost deliberately to change tack as he picked up the silver-framed photo again. 'Remember what happened later, on this day?'

Arizona thought of the walled pool garden in Sydney and swallowed unexpectedly. 'Quite accurately, as it happens,' she said huskily.

'Well, I was wondering if you would consider taking your beautiful nightgown off for me now, and while I'm not suggesting we seek a pool or anything like that, we could try to recreate other aspects of that—happening.'

A faint flush rose to her cheeks, but her eyes were

grey and steady as they held his, although her voice was not quite steady as she said, 'I would…like to do that, Declan,' And did it.

He remained as still as a statue as her hair sank about her shoulders and the lamplight played on her breasts, then he took her in his arms in an oddly convulsive movement and his voice was curiously unsteady as he said, 'Arizona, I wonder if you know what you really do to me?'

He was up, dressed and ready to go when she woke the next morning but, for once, she didn't care. Because she still had those words on her mind and in her heart, and they seemed to sustain her without his presence beside her to wake up to.

CHAPTER EIGHT

SHE was sustained, a little to her surprise, nearly all of the time he was away, and when she made herself analyse it, she discovered it was because he was out of the country that she didn't seem to mind being alone so much.

So what does that mean? she wondered and decided, after more thought, that it meant she believed there were absences he couldn't avoid, such as this one—and those he probably could in this day and age of fax machines, mobile phones and so on.

The disturbing nature of these thoughts prompted her to resolutely try to banish them from her mind. The other thing that intruded now and then was the idea of going public about their marriage, and she realized that she was uneasy about that.

But his homecoming saw a passionate reunion between them, plus his insistence that she spend a few days in Sydney with him, although he made no mention of an interview. He also decided against relocating the children to Rosemary's, vetoed her idea of taking them to Sydney, as well, and took Daisy for a walk on her own. From which Daisy returned bursting with pride but would not be drawn on the subject.

'What did you say to her?' Arizona asked curiously, later that evening.

'We discussed,' he said with a wry little smile, 'her importance in the scheme of things, how it upset you to know she was unhappy, especially when it was for no real reason—and for good measure I threw in a bribe.'

'Declan?'

'My dear Arizona, look at it as an incentive system, then. Kids thrive on incentives.'

'And just what incentive did you *bribe* Daisy with?' she asked ominously.

'I told her that if she showed us she was grown-up enough to spend a few days with Cloris, without you, I would consider her grown-up enough to start riding lessons on her own pony. I also told her it was our secret, just between the two of us.'

Arizona tried to maintain her expression of severity but failed. And said through her laughter, 'Oh, God, if *that* works I'll—I don't know what I'll do!'

He laughed, too, then said, 'You know that pale violet suit you bought when you were—planning to show me a thing or two?'

'Yes. Why?' Arizona asked ruefully.

'I've never seen you in it.'

'You haven't seen me in a lot of those clothes. But why now? I mean, it's ten o'clock at night.'

'Would you humour me and try it on, though?'

She looked at him him strangely then shrugged. 'Come up in about five minutes.'

Five minutes later she stood in the middle of their bedroom wearing the lovely linen suit with its pale grey blouse and a very high-heeled pair of grey kid shoes.

'Mmm,' he said, walking around her. 'Yes, that will be excellent. You have great taste in clothes, Arizona. Even when you're spitting mad,' he added with a wicked little glint in his eye.

'Thank you,' she replied. 'Would you mind telling me what all this is about, though?'

'I think this will be the perfect outfit to be interviewed in tomorrow, that's all.'

She stilled and eyed him narrowly then said coolly, 'I wish you wouldn't spring these things on me, Declan. I am old enough to be consulted.'

'I told you before I went away that we'd be doing this, Arizona,' he said mildly.

'You may have—you did,' she corrected herself as he looked at her a little mockingly, 'but you've said nothing since you got back, and, well—' she gestured then said exasperatedly '—is that why you want me to come to Sydney?'

'One of the reasons, yes. But it will take an hour of our time, at the most.'

She swung away from him and went to sit by the window. And heard herself say rather desolately, 'I don't want to do it.'

'How would you like to handle it then?' he queried dryly.

'I have no idea. I'd rather it didn't have to be handled at all.'

'Arizona,' he said impatiently, 'this is only a magazine interview—'

'I don't want to be splashed over the pages of a magazine, in my violet suit or out of it—'

'I'm sure you'd cause a sensation out of it, but it's not that kind of magazine.'

'You know what I mean,' she said tautly. 'But I particularly don't want to be parcelled up to look like an appropriate wife for a millionaire or to be seen holding hands with you, looking coy or whatever.'

'How about simply looking as if you're in love with me?'

Some heat rose up her throat, but she said bleakly, 'I'm surprised you want this, Declan, I really am. I thought you valued your privacy.'

'It's exactly because I do value my privacy that I'm doing this, I thought I'd explained that to you. Don't you want people to know we're married, and if so, why?' he asked curtly.

'It's not that,' she answered slowly. 'You've managed to keep it pretty private until now.'

'That's mainly because you've been incarcerated at Scawfell most of the time,' he said impatiently. 'Arizona, trust me on this.'

'All right.' But she said it stonily.

He stared at her bent head and the way her hands were clasped in her lap, then swung on his heel and walked out.

Nor did he share her bed that night, and they drove to Sydney the next morning in a chilly sort of silence for the most part. Until Arizona said abruptly, 'Don't treat me like this, Declan. And all because I expressed some very natural reservations about being exposed to about seventeen million people.'

He glanced at her briefly but long enough for her to see the glint of steel in his blue eyes. 'Nevertheless it's what we'll be doing this morning, my dear.'

'I'm surprised you didn't add something along the lines of—so you might as well make the best of it,' she said contemptuously.

'Those were your words, not mine.'

'On another occasion when I felt I was being taken advantage of. You're right.'

He swore beneath his breath and then, taking her

by surprise, pulled the car off the road. They had not reached the outskirts of Sydney, and it was on a grassy verge beside a huge, open paddock that he switched the engine off.

'What are you doing?' she asked evenly.

'I'm going to have this out with you here and now, my beautiful but unreasonably stubborn *wife*.'

'Declan,' she said through her teeth, 'you may call me what you like, but the fact that you were able to force me to marry you should not lead you to imagine I am going to be like putty in your hands!'

'No?' he drawled.

'No,' she snapped back.

'Of course there are times when you're not exactly putty in my hands but—'

'Don't,' she said coldly but with a sudden flush staining her cheeks.

'I suppose it is a bit embarrassing to be reminded of how you sleep with me in light of this rebellion,' he mused and touched an idle finger to her hot cheek. 'All right, you win.'

Her eyes widened and flew to his.

'Unfortunately, it's going to delay Daisy's pony, not to mention her opportunity to prove something to us, but be that as it may.' And he switched the key on, glanced in the mirror and swung the car into a U-turn so they were going back the way they'd come.

'You!' Arizona whispered, going quite pale with rage.

'It's up to you, my dear,' he said grimly.

'Turn around then,' she commanded. 'But while I may do this interview, don't expect me to be anything like putty in your hands for…the rest of my life, probably!'

He laughed softly as he did another U-turn and said, 'Now that is throwing down the gauntlet, Arizona.'

'Well, you didn't even have to look coy.'

Arizona breathed deeply and stopped what she was doing. Which was changing out of her violet suit. The bedroom of the Sydney house was bathed in sunlight. It was a very hot day, and Declan had just come in, closed the door and leant his broad shoulders against it.

'No,' she said turning her back on him to hang her jacket up carefully.

'How about a swim?' he suggested lazily. 'Seeing as we've got that out of the way. Incidentally—' he straightened and strolled over to her '—you were very good, Arizona. Cool, beautiful, poised—definitely an asset.'

'Good. You can send me back to Scawfell now.'

'I thought you'd decided Daisy deserved her chance. But anyway,' he murmured, his blue gaze drifting down her body, 'I have other plans for you at the moment.'

'No,' she whispered through a suddenly dry throat. 'You can't do this to me.'

'What, as a matter of interest, do you think I'm about to do?'

'Something along the putty in your hands line?' She was only able to say it barely audibly but she was able to add, 'You won't enjoy it unless you have a preference for overpowering women.'

'Look, Arizona,' he said abruptly and took her hands. 'I think we can deal better than this. I'm sorry you felt so much against going public, and I'm still not sure what your reasons were, but it was for the best, believe me. You know, you yourself told me only a couple of weeks ago that I was managing our lives very capably.'

'I didn't altogether mean that.' She stopped and bit her lip.

'Tell me what you meant, then.'

She grimaced, but it was too late. 'I suppose I feel—you said just now that I was an asset, that's how I feel. As if I'm a parcel of shares, or something inanimate that you can move around at will. I...' She stopped and shrugged.

'On the other hand, didn't we agree that for two people not in love although greatly attracted to each other,' he asked gently, 'you would live your life and I would live mine?'

She couldn't answer, only stare at him.

'And, when you think about it,' he continued with that same deadly gentleness, 'it's only where our lives have collided that I've made arrangements, which I consider are in all our best interests. For the rest of the time, you're free to go your own road. You're free to do what you once told me you liked doing best. You have the means now, moreover, to do it in great style. Or—' he paused and searched her eyes in a manner that made her wish devoutly she could run away and hide from him '—are you trying to tell me that those things you once liked to do best are beginning to pall?'

Yes, she answered, but in her mind. *Because I don't want to spend ninety per cent of my life doing my own thing, because I want to be loved and be able to love you openly. Why can't I just tell you? Is it pride,*

*stupid vaunted pride? Or am I still afraid I'll end up
like my mother?*

'Arizona?' He waited with courteous attention for
her to speak, but when she didn't, said, 'Or is it a
desire to be able to queen it over all and sundry as
my wife, and spend my money in a much more public
way?'

For a moment, she thought she was going to faint,
so great was the hurt. But a moment later, she merely
freed her hands and said quietly, 'No. None of those,
Declan. I'm quite happy to continue our…purely
business affair—with a dash of physical attraction
thrown in, let's not forget that.' She managed to smile
a queer tense little smile at him. 'And if you don't
mind, I think I will go for a swim.'

'You think that will solve this—impasse?'

'I have no idea,' she whispered.

'Then let me make another suggestion.'

She broke then. 'Please,' she said in sudden desperation, 'that's like asking me to prostitute myself in
your bed unless—' tears, foolish tears started to slip
down her cheeks '—that's what you believe I've been
doing all along?'

He stood like a rock for a full minute, watching
the way she attempted to stem the flow, how her
shoulders shook, his eyes unreadable, his mouth set
in a hard line. Then he sighed, put an arm round her
shoulders and pulled her against him, which she had
not the composure to resist, and said against her hair,
'No, but I think we may be two of a kind. I'm sorry.
Would you consider coming to bed with me because
I rather desperately need you?'

*   *   *

Three days later, he said to her, 'Do you think we should take pity on Daisy?'

They were in bed, it was very early and raining heavily. Arizona moved her cheek on his chest and smiled faintly. 'You must be a mind-reader. I woke up thinking about her.'

'Then we'll go home this morning. How do you feel?'

'Fine. Don't I look it?' she asked whimsically.

'I can't see that much of you at the moment,' he murmured and drew aside the sheet that covered them. 'That's better.'

'Is that a way to tell how fine a person is—'

'In your case you're looking exceptionally fine, but then, you always do like this.' He moved his hand down her back to her hips.

'I was going to say—'

'However,' he interrupted, 'as you were probably going to say, I also need to look into your eyes and there's one *particularly* fine way to do that. Let me show you.'

'Declan,' she said on a breath, moments later, when he'd sat her up and guided her to sit astride him while he lay back with the pillows heaped up behind him.

'Arizona?' He put his hands under her arms and drew them down the outline of her body from her armpits to the swell of her breasts that lay like pale, pink-tipped orbs to the slenderness of her waist then the curve of her hips and finally, her thighs. 'You were saying?'

'Nothing—of great moment,' she said with an effort. 'Just that I don't believe it's my eyes you're concentrating on, particularly.'

'You're wrong, you know,' he said wryly, stroking

the tender skin of her inner thighs. 'I love looking into your eyes when I'm doing something like this. Don't you like it?'

She put her hands on his chest and considered. 'If I could be allowed to—come down to your level, eventually,' she said gravely.

'Be my guest.'

She smiled gently. 'All in good time, Mr. Holmes.' And slipped her fingers through the springy black hair on his chest with concentration, her lashes veiling her eyes.

'Arizona,' he said suddenly and differently.

She looked up and didn't know it but with a tinge of wariness.

'Don't…hide from me,' he said, not quite evenly. 'Nor is there anything to be afraid of.'

Isn't there? she wondered but said, 'I'm not.'

'Good. Come here then,' he commanded softly.

'This was your idea,' she murmured with a genuine flicker of humour curving her lips.

'For my sins,' he agreed and cupped her breasts until a tremor ran through her. 'That's better,' he added lazily and with a wicked glint.

'I have to wonder why,' she murmured ruefully as her nipples flowered beneath his fingers and a tide of living desire flowed through her.

'I'd hate to think I was alone in—experiencing this.'

'Well, you're not,' she said on a little jolt of breath but was able to add with composure—but only just— 'I'm coming down, Declan, be warned.'

Then she was in his arms, lying on the length of him, and they were laughing at the same time as they climaxed in a way that was new to them, stunning

but with warmth and…tenderness? she wondered. Of
a kind they'd not known before?

Daisy was fine when they got home but thrilled to
see them, as were Sarah and Richard, and a mood of
excitement gripped the house when the subject of the
new pony was brought out into the open.

'Where, er, does one acquire new ponies at very
short notice?' Declan asked Arizona rather ruefully.

'Rosemary,' she replied promptly.

He raised a wry eyebrow at her. 'What would we
do without Rosemary—but how come?'

'Rosemary is very into horses and president of the
local pony club. If anyone can dig up a suitable pony
for Daisy, she can. She also gives riding lessons.'

'Then I think we ought to pay a call on Rosemary
right now.'

'Well, I'm sure Daisy will understand if we leave
it until tomorrow.'

He looked at her steadily for a moment then said
quietly, 'I won't be here tomorrow, unfortunately.
And I do feel I should keep faith with Daisy, having
instigated this, by at least looking over some ponies
with her.'

Arizona hid her sudden inner pang by saying with
a grin, 'Well, I'm sure Rosemary will be delighted to
see you! Do you mind if I stay here and unpack? I
would imagine Daisy will feel doubly important and
grown-up if you two go alone.'

He looked at her searchingly but said nothing and
that's how the rest of the day was organized.

When they got home Daisy was almost speechless
with happiness and succumbed finally to a storm of
tears brought about by overexcitement.

'Sorry,' Declan said when they were alone at last, after Arizona had finally managed to get Daisy to sleep. 'Here.' He handed her a glass of wine.

Arizona sank into a chair beside the fireplace. 'Thanks! I'm going to enjoy this.'

He sat down opposite and told her about the pony, which was due to arrive in a few days, and passed on Rosemary's good wishes. Then he said slowly, 'I'm sorry about this, but it's another trip to the States. I've—acquired a television station and there's a lot to bone up on.' He smiled briefly. 'Pay television, cable television and the like.'

Her eyes widened. 'That sounds like…really big time.'

'Hopefully.'

'How long?'

'Three weeks.' He gestured. 'Maybe a bit longer, but I'll definitely be home for Christmas.'

'Christmas,' she murmured. 'That's not that far away now, I'll have to start making plans.'

'You don't mind?'

Arizona looked across at him and said honestly, 'Yes, of course, but I'll have plenty to occupy me.'

'Good girl,' he said almost absently.

Arizona sipped her wine and laid her head back, mainly, she thought, so that he couldn't see her eyes.

It surprised her, therefore, when he came, gently prised the glass from her fingers and pulled her to her feet, and said, 'It's going to be a hell of a long three weeks.'

She trembled suddenly and he felt it through his hands and frowned. He said, 'What is it?'

'Nothing,' she said huskily. 'I think I'm a bit like Daisy. Just in need of a good night's sleep.'

He paused, watched her narrowly, then dropped a light kiss on her hair. He also said gravely, 'I would offer to come with you but I have an incredibly early start so I'm flying back to town this evening.'

'Now?'

'In about half an hour. Think you can keep your eyes open long enough to wave me off?'

She did, and went inside, hugging herself, and went straight to bed. It was not such a simple matter to get to sleep, however, although she kept telling herself to hold onto those minutes of warmth and tenderness that had happened only that morning, and to use them to combat not only the loneliness but the lack of understanding as to why she couldn't be told of his plans sometimes, why she always had to find out at the last minute… Why?

In fact he came home early from his trip, only two and a half weeks after he'd left, and he drove down, so she didn't even have the whir and roar of the helicopter to forewarn her. She was also in her beloved rose garden, on her knees, digging and watering with her hands dirty, a streak of mud on her chin, wearing her old dungarees when she heard a car and decided to ignore it, until she heard Daisy.

'Declan, Declan—you're home!' Daisy called joyfully. 'I've called my pony Pippa and I can nearly sit on her on my own!'

Arizona stilled, her eyes widening.

'Well, you are a clever girl!' Declan's deep tones came quite clearly round the corner of the house. 'Where is everyone?'

'Sarah and Richard are playing with friends, Ben is staying with one of his new school friends and

Cloris is cooking. It's Christmas soon, did you know? And we're all on holiday!'

'Indeed, I do. What about Arizona?'

'I don't know where she is. In the garden prob'ly. She does a lot of gardening because she's cross.'

Arizona froze in the act of getting up off her knees.

'Cross?' Declan's voice expressed quizzical surprise.

'Yes,' Daisy confided.

'Why is she cross, do you think?'

'I don't know but she *is*,' Daisy insisted. 'Maybe it's because you're not here,' she added ingenuously.

Arizona groaned quite silently, got up swiftly and took flight. It did her little good, because he found her not five minutes later in the toolshed.

'Declan!' she said without having to simulate surprise as she turned and discovered him leaning against the doorway, and dropped a trowel.

'Arizona,' he answered amusedly. 'Sorry, I didn't mean to give you a fright.'

'But—it's not three weeks yet,' she protested, totally foolishly, she knew.

'Well, I'm sorry about that, too—would you like me to go away for another half week?'

'No. I mean, no. I…was surprised, that's all. Welcome home!'

'Thanks,' he said but didn't move. 'What's this I hear about you being cross?' he added, his blue gaze quite grave now, but it didn't fool her for a moment. She knew he was laughing at her.

'Cross?' She raised an eyebrow. 'I don't know what you mean.'

'I have it on the best authority.'

Arizona closed her eyes and wished fervently that

she didn't blush so easily because she could feel the heat pouring into her cheeks and knew it was useless to dissemble any further. She could also think of absolutely nothing to say.

He straightened. 'So were you?'

'No,' she said a little bleakly. 'Well, if so I didn't realize—and Daisy could be exaggerating.'

He laughed softly. 'You heard?'

'I heard,' she agreed.

'And ran away?' he suggested.

'And ran away.'

'Do you think she's right about the cause of it?'

Arizona sighed, examined her dirty hands then looked into his eyes. 'Possibly.'

'That's very gratifying,' he murmured.

'I'm sure it is,' Arizona returned a shade tartly.

'Because I have to tell you,' he continued, 'that I have been singularly, er, cross over these past two and a half weeks, as well. What do you think that means?'

The corners of her mouth started to twitch. 'You… missed my home cooking?'

They laughed together then he said, 'Come here.'

'I'm filthy.'

'I don't mind in the slightest.'

She came. And a little later she indicated she'd like to be released, which he did immediately, but it was only so she could wind her arms round his neck with a queer little sigh.

'Better?' he said gently.

'Much better,' she whispered. But it was only a couple of days later that they had a row, the contents of which she found unbelievable…

*   *   *

It started after breakfast when he said casually, 'Arizona, I think you should invite your mother down for Christmas.'

'What?' She blinked at him and stopped what she was doing, which was wrapping Christmas presents on the floor in her study with the door firmly closed against any spying children. Then she said flatly, 'No, I don't think I should, but why?'

'Why not?' he said with some irony.

'Look, I don't understand,' she persisted.

'You said yourself a little while ago that it was about time you stopped feuding with her.'

'I know but—have you stopped feuding with your father?' she asked with a frown.

'No, but there is no mystery about my father.'

Arizona sat back on her heels. 'What do you mean?'

'Put simply—' he paused '—I'd like to meet your mother. But for some reason or another, it would appear as if you're hiding her from me.'

Arizona gasped. 'I…hesitate to repeat myself but what do you mean, Declan?'

'That she is not to be found, Arizona. Want to tell me why?'

'Not to be found,' Arizona repeated and then, as full implication of this hit her, 'have you…been looking for her?'

He said quite simply and coolly, 'Yes.'

She swallowed. 'How dare you, Declan Holmes. How—I don't believe this—'

'Well, before you get too dramatic, Arizona, is there any reason I *shouldn't* meet your mother? Such as her being a criminal or a—' But he stopped as

Arizona picked up a box of games that were to be a Christmas present for Richard, and flung it at him.

The result of this was that the box missed him as he dodged, but they were showered with dice, little chessmen, ludo markers and the like.

'You're unbelievably childish at times, Arizona,' he said grimly and hauled her to her feet unceremoniously.

'No, I'm *not*,' she said, panting. '*You* are unbelievably underhand and conniving, you have no right— and all the money in the world, all the television stations in the world don't give you the right to hound my mother or me like this and—'

'On the contrary, I have every right to protect what is mine.'

She stared at him disbelievingly and with an almost paralysing sense of shock. 'Do you seriously believe that, Declan? That my mother and I have concocted a devious plan to milk you dry? Well, you're right, of course,' she heard herself say. 'I'm only sorry I didn't get you in for a bit longer, but all the same, I'm still your wife and it's going to cost you an awful lot of money to—get rid of me.'

'There's only one problem with that, Arizona,' he said roughly. 'I have no intention of getting rid of you.'

CHAPTER NINE

THE silence was electric. Until she broke it.

'You can't keep me against my will, Declan.'

'Try me, Arizona,' he said grimly.

'That's ridiculous. Do you plan to lock me up?'

'Oh, I don't think I'll have to go that far, not before Christmas, at least—would you run out on the kids now? That *would* be utterly conclusive, wouldn't it?'

'Damn you,' she said angrily.

'And once you've had time for some sober reflection,' he drawled, 'you may see things my way, after all. I'm going up to town now. I'll be back on Christmas Eve. Don't do anything rash, Arizona, will you?'

But although he waited with polite insolence, she was speechless with rage, and he left her, closing the door gently behind him.

'When is Declan coming back?' Daisy said fretfully a few days later. They were decorating the Christmas tree.

'When it suits him,' Sarah said pertly. 'You can't pin a man like Declan down, Daisy.'

'Sarah,' Arizona said, frowning, 'that's an...odd thing to say.'

'She heard it said,' Richard contributed. 'Didn't you, Sarah?'

Sarah threw a tinsel bauble at him. 'Don't tell!' she commanded.

'Why not? You said it,' Richard reasoned, and threw the bauble back, whereupon Sarah reached for some tiny bells.

'Stop it,' Arizona warned. 'And I think you better tell me what you heard said, Sarah.'

Sarah sighed theatrically, glared at her twin then shrugged. 'It's what Maddy Mason's mum said, that's all.'

'When did she say this?' Arizona went on hanging things on the tree and contrived to keep her voice calm, although not to be brooked.

'When I went to play with Maddy the other day. She's very nosy, Mrs. Mason. She was asking me all sorts of questions about you and Declan, she had that magazine, too.'

'What kind of questions?'

'How much time he spends here at Scawfell, how much time you spend with him. It was when I said not a lot that she said he's a hard man to pin down and it might not be a real marriage anyway, she was sort of talking to herself then but I—'

'Sarah, I don't think you should discuss those kind of things with other people,' Arizona broke in.

'If you'd let me finish,' Sarah said with ten-year-old hauteur, '*that* was when I told her it was really none of her business. I don't think I'll be invited to play with Maddy Mason again,' she added with a giggle. 'But it's true, you don't spend a lot of time together, do you, Arizona? I mean, it's not really like having a mother and father again. Not that it bothers us,' she added with the absolute honesty that reinforced Arizona's opinion that Sarah was going to be one of those uncomfortable people who always called a spade a spade, 'but there's always our baby,' she finished and rolled her eyes in Daisy's direction.

'If you're calling me a baby, Sarah,' Daisy said hotly, 'I am not! Declan himself told me I was very grown-up. That's why I want to *show* him how well I can ride now,' she added, but with a distinct break in her voice.

'See what I mean?' Sarah said out of the corner of her mouth with a worldly little sigh. But she went on, 'Listen, Daisy, Ben will be home tomorrow, you can show him!'

Daisy brightened and they finished the tree amicably.

It was Cloris who completed another difficult day for Arizona by saying to her after the children were in bed, 'You don't look well, pet. I'm tempted to call Mr. Holmes and let him know you need a break.'

'Cloris.' Arizona swallowed irritation, disbelief and horror. 'Don't. I'm fine.'

'Well, he did say to me once if I thought you needed anything just to let him know.'

Arizona blinked at her. '*When?*'

'I can't remember exactly,' Cloris said airily and added, 'you know, I'm sure he'd be here if he could.'

'He'll be here on Christmas Eve, Cloris,' Arizona said and bit her lip in case any of her prejudice on the subject had shown through.

'Oh, well, that's less than a week away now, and then I'm sure we'll all be happy and more comfortable.'

All Arizona could do was walk out, as normally as possible, she hoped, but instead of taking herself to bed she went for a walk down to the cliff edge and sat on the turf with her knees drawn up, her chin resting on them—and the leaden heart within her breast feeling even worse than usual as she contemplated the fact that she couldn't go on much longer under this intolerable strain, could no longer reconcile sleeping with a man who believed the things Declan Holmes believed of her. And contemplated the bitter sense of failure in her heart, because although she had slept with him and laughed with him and thought there was a new, unique and growing sense of tenderness between them, she couldn't have been more wrong. Nothing had changed his doubts of her, apparently, nothing.

But what to do about the children? she mused painfully. *In the long run is it going to help them to have me as tormented as I am? Did Sarah not demonstrate today that the imperfections of our marriage are becoming obvious to all and sundry? Has Daisy not flowered under his care as much as mine?*

She shivered suddenly, dropped her face into her hands and came to a decision. And the next morning saw her driving away from Scawfell on the pretext of a last-minute Christmas shopping spree, having mentioned the possibility that she might spend the night in Sydney with Declan, having reassured Daisy that Ben would be home today, and having left with a heart almost breaking because she had no idea whether she would return.

She made one call in the village, which took her about half an hour, and then about ten miles south of Sydney she pulled into a garage to fill up with petrol and got the surprise of her life when her new gardener peered in through the offside window, cleared his throat and said, 'Sorry about this, Mrs. Holmes, but

Declan asked me to, well, let him know if you made any surprise moves.'

'*What?*'

'*Are* you going to see him, Mrs. Holmes? If so, there's no problem but—'

A red mist of rage swam before Arizona's eyes but she pulled herself out of it with a Herculean effort and said sweetly, 'But if not you'd like to know where I'm going? Look, why don't I save you a lot of trouble? Where's your car?'

'Uh—over there.' He pointed and Arizona recognized the car parked neatly off the driveway, could not imagine how she'd missed that it was following her but didn't care either.

'Is it locked?'

'Well, yes—'

'Good, then hop in.'

'Mrs. Holmes—'

'Do as I say,' Arizona commanded with such a blaze of anger in her grey eyes that the ex-naval man cum gardener did just that, although not precisely happily.

'Where are we going?' he asked tentatively as Arizona paid for her petrol and drove off.

'You'll see.' And she spoke not another word to him as she drove fast and furiously right into the heart of Sydney Town, parked illegally at the base of a tall building and commanded him to accompany her inside.

The foyer of the building was extremely impressive, and she had to pause for a moment to study the direction board, but she soon saw what she was looking for and with an imperious wave of her hand dictated to the poor man to follow her. They got out on the twentieth floor, and she swept into the reception office she sought, didn't even blink at its magnificence nor at three men all conservatively dressed and apparently standing in conference as she approached the desk.

Where she said in clear, crisp tones, 'I'm Mrs. Declan Holmes and I would like to see my husband *immediately*.'

You could have heard a pin drop for about half a minute before the clearly flustered receptionist said, 'I…I'm afraid he's in a meeting, Mrs. Holmes, but his secretary—'

'Then you better get him out of the meeting, unless he wishes to be confronted by an extremely angry wife in front of whoever he's meeting with!'

'Yes, Mrs. Holmes,' the poor young woman whispered and grabbed a phone while the three men blinked and gaped, and the gardener looked as if he wished the floor would open up and swallow him.

A minute later Declan strolled into the reception area looking dark, inscrutable but curiously relaxed, unless you happened to know that glint of steel in his eyes. And he drawled, 'Ah, Arizona. Come to see me, I believe. Will you come through?'

'No, I will not, nor did I come to see *you* particularly, Declan, merely to drop your watchdog off! In fact you're the last person I'm desirous of seeing at the moment, although since I'm here I might as well tell you how utterly contemptible I find you—'

'And that's enough, my dear,' he murmured, and closing on her, took her elbow in a vice-like grip and forced her to walk beside him out into the corridor. Nor did he relax his grip as he summoned a lift and they rode down to the basement garage swiftly and silently, with Arizona, now that the magnificence of her rage had spent itself although not the cold outward manifestation of it, inwardly shaking a little.

'Get in,' he said as they came up to the Saab.

'No.'

'Don't make me have to force you, Arizona,' he recommended through his teeth.

She looked around but there was not a soul in sight, and got in.

He drove her to the Point Piper house, which gave her a little time to collect her nerves, and she got out proudly and walked inside in front of him, her head held high while she murmured a formal greeting to the housekeeper who opened the door. But when she turned to go into what she knew was his study, he took her elbow again and directed her upstairs to the master bedroom. And although he shoved his hands in his trouser pockets after he'd closed the door firmly, there was menace in every line of his tall figure and something so cold in his eyes, she shivered involuntarily.

'Well?' he said but only after subjecting her to the coolest, most insolent stripping her of her clothes with his eyes imaginable, so that she looked at her stylish, sleeveless, camellia pink linen dress with its slim lines and long skirt as if to assure herself it was still there—and then clench her hands into fists.

'Don't ever have me followed again, Declan,' she said clearly, her anger refuelling itself, 'in case I'm tempted to embarrass you even more. And while we're on the subject, I might as well tell you, we're finished, you and I, nor is there *any* way you can stop me leaving you, and don't even mention the children because I have it on good authority this time that they're well aware our marriage is a sham and I can only see it hurting them now if I stay to fight on. But let me tell you, perhaps most importantly, since I know how you doubt me on these matters, that I went to see a solicitor this morning and I signed a waiver to all your worldly goods, or even half of them.' And she stripped her shoulder purse off, opened it to extract a document from it, which she dropped on the floor between them. 'I want nothing from you, Declan,' she added proudly. 'Not a single thing. Nor does my mother, because, since she's a nun in a closed order these days, you see, there's not a lot she could do with a single cent.'

But if she'd hoped to shock him, he merely narrowed his eyes and didn't even glance at the paper on the floor. And he said, 'Why did you wait to leave me to tell me all this, Arizona?'

She took a breath, turned away abruptly and strode over to the French window overlooking the pool, to see with some surprise that the day had clouded over heavily and that there was lightning in the sky. Then she said in a suddenly toneless, weary voice, 'You married me, not my mother. Anyway, I did tell you about her. Why didn't you believe me, Declan?'

The room was very quiet, apart from the rumble of thunder in the distance. Until he said, 'Arizona, have you any idea what simply the sheen of your hair, the curve of your cheek, the line of your lips have done to me over the past nearly three years?'

She turned slowly, as if she couldn't believe what she was hearing, and her lips parted. Then she shook her head, dazed, as if to say, *No, this can't be for real—*

And he hadn't moved from the door and it seemed

to her as if there was an acre of pewter blue velvet carpet between them. 'I...' She licked her lips. 'I don't know what you mean. You don't trust me, you—'

'Do you trust me?' he broke in. 'But no, I haven't been able to trust—or rather believe that you love me. For one thing, you've never told me, never reversed those views you told me you held of yourself nor told me I might have restored your faith in men—or even just one man. To this day,' he said very quietly, 'I have no idea whether I mean more to you than Pete, who you married for the sake of convenience.'

To her horror, Arizona discovered that her legs were no longer steady and she sank to the carpet on her knees then sat back on her heels. 'But I showed you, I *must* have shown you that,' she said hoarsely.

'Did you?'

She had to tilt her head back as he towered over her for a moment then sat down on the end of the bed beside her.

'Did you sleep with him the way you sleep with me, for instance?' he went on. 'I have no way of knowing how to differentiate.'

'You do—you know I'd never—that it had never happened that way for me before... Didn't that tell you...anything?'

He shrugged slightly. 'It gave me hope at times. And there were times when you indicated you weren't happy with the way things were, but on every last opportunity I presented you with to tell me why, you—slipped away from me.'

'And it means so much to you?' she whispered, shaken suddenly to her core.

'It means,' he said quietly, 'that until you tell me
these things, I can't know whether you love me.'

'And it's never occurred to you,' she said barely,
'that I might have the same problem?'

'Such as?'

'Declan,' she whispered, 'I have no way of knowing whether you love me. In fact I have a lot of evidence to the contrary. You're hardly ever with me,
you…force me to do everything your way, you use
the kids to hold me—'

'Did you never stop to wonder why?'

'Because you mistrust me,' she said distraughtly.
'Because you can't ever forget Pete—'

'Only you can do that for me, Arizona.'

Their eyes locked then he added, 'If it means anything to you, the fact that I will never let you go, if
it means anything that possibly the worst year of my
life was the year you were married to Pete, but it has
to be closely followed by these months when I've
waited to hear you say just three words, or at least
explain better why you couldn't. If it means *anything*
that the reason I've stayed away from you as much
as I have was that I was seeking a form of protection
against falling more and more in love with you, if
that was possible.'

Arizona stared at him with stunned eyes. Then she
said uncertainly, as if she couldn't trust her voice,
'Can I…can I start at the beginning?'

He nodded.

It took her a few minutes to compose her thoughts,
and she plucked at the carpet before lifting her eyes
to his. 'I've told you about my mother already, or
most of it, but it was only when she began to see, in
my late teens, how much I despised her for the way

she was that *she*, I suppose, stopped and tried to take stock. It was too late for me, though, I—' she paused and sighed '—rejected her. By that time I'd left school and was living on campus at teacher's college. She hung on for a year or so, trying to make a home for me that I didn't want, trying to show me that she'd not reformed so much but was a different person now, but I didn't believe it, and then one day she came and told me that she was going into this convent. I…I'm afraid I laughed. I can only say in my defence that I'd never known my father, that I'd been to twelve schools in every state of the country and I'd lived through four…men, none of them bad men particularly, none of them who didn't try at times to treat me like a daughter, but all the same, *all* of them walking out on her. I…now know I can never forgive myself for laughing at her, for not trying to support her because she is my mother, and she went into every last one of those relationships believing this was *it*. Even believing, I think, that it would create a better life for me.'

'Go on,' Declan said gently after a long pause.

'But the truth of the matter was that I felt betrayed even though I'd done all that rejecting. Strange, isn't it?'

'Not in the circumstances, and if you were only nineteen or so,' he said quietly.

Arizona shrugged. 'I also, at nineteen, wondered if I might have fallen in love with a fellow student. He, well, at times he used to make my heart go bang and make me feel quite breathless and weak at the knees.' She grimaced. 'But, although everyone else seeemd to be experimenting with sex, I began to dislike the proprietorial way he started to treat me and I couldn't be persuaded to go to bed with him, probably because I had my mother at the back of my mind all the time, and it turned into a rather unpleasant fiasco.'

'He got nasty?' Declan suggested.

'He—' Arizona paused and sighed. 'I gained a reputation for being—well, there were two versions, a tease or frigid.'

Declan smiled slightly and said, 'We men have very fragile egos, I'm afraid. But if nothing else, didn't that convince you you weren't about to follow in your mother's footsteps?'

It was Arizona's turn to smile, unamused. 'Yes although I came to doubt that later,' she said barely audibly. 'Uh…what it did leave me with was the feeling that I might have inherited her…poor judgment, but there was something else, I began to sympathise with her then, in a mostly subconscious way, but I did think, well, I convinced myself I'd be better leaving the whole tribe of men alone. It just…wasn't that easy, though,' she said with a sigh.

'Not with your looks and your figure, I imagine it wasn't.'

She looked at him suddenly. 'The funny thing was the more I froze them off the more…' She stopped and bit her lip.

'That's something you don't have to tell me about, Arizona,' he said, not without irony.

'Anyway,' she continued after a moment, 'then I got the job at Scawfell. And it was a revelation,' she said with a little, oddly helpless gesture.

'Tell me why.'

'I fell in love with the house, with the country, with the kids. I felt for the first time as if I had a *place* in, well, in the scheme of things. I discovered talents I didn't know I possessed. I was needed, really needed—and I knew by then that my mother only needed God. I went up to see her once, you see, and she was a different person, serene, confident, loving yes, but...' She shrugged. 'So that's how it was, Declan.' She studied her hands then looked into his eyes to see if he understood.

'My dear, I think I've always understood that,' he said and reached out a hand. She put hers into it after a moment. 'One only had to see you with the kids, to see that. So, tell me about Pete now.'

She swallowed. 'Pete...put a proposition to me after I'd been there for nearly a year. He told me he'd fallen in love with me but he knew I didn't reciprocate. He told me, no, he asked me to tell him a little of why I was the way I was and I did. He then... Declan...' She stopped.

'Go on.' The pressure of his hand on hers increased, but as if to give her courage.

'He told me he had a disability, quite a complicated rare condition.' She paused. 'One...of the side effects of it was that he was impotent, and he told me that apart from losing his wife, it was the most shattering thing that had ever happened to him. That it had knocked his self-esteem about to the extent that it had seriously affected his creativity. It amazed and horrified him, he said, to discover that although it was a side effect of his condition, that although no-one need know other than himself and his doctor, yet he was getting around like half a man and couldn't help living his life as if it was written all over him. And so, he said, while he couldn't consummate a marriage, if I needed a home and security, if I needed some respite from my own problems, it was possible that we could help each other out. That it would be a way for him no longer to feel as if everyone could guess that he had this awful problem, a way for him to get back to work, he hoped.'

'And you believed that?' Declan said after a long silence.

She glanced at him but couldn't tell much from his expression. 'I had lots of doubts,' she confessed. 'But I had seen him all but tearing his hair out trying to get the genius that had made him such a wonderful architect flowing. He was, by then, a friend I trusted and a confidante and we were—comfortable with each other. On the other hand, I couldn't help wondering what would happen if he got better and I said that to him. *He* said it would always be up to me. So I looked at the options, which seemed to me to be pretty bleak, and I took the plunge.' She stopped and swallowed.

'Did he ever get better, Arizona?'

'No,' she whispered. 'At least, I don't think so. Because he never tried to sleep with me, he never even brought the subject up in the year we were married. But if I did do one thing for him, if I was ever able to repay him for all that I gained, it was to see him working again with all his old flair and to know that I must have been able to alter his perception of his self-esteem as seen through the eyes of others. Nor would I ever have told a soul this, Declan, I would have kept faith with him, for everything he did for me, for ever, if it hadn't been for you.'

'My dear,' Declan said, in curiously strained voice, 'forgive me.' And then he stood up and pulled her to her feet and was cupping her face gently, kissing the tears that had at last started to flow. 'There's only one thing I need to know now,' he said at last. 'If *I've* been able to alter your perception of yourself, the one that told you you couldn't fall in love, and never with me.'

'Oh, that.' The tears fell faster and she kissed the inside of his wrist and tasted them salty on her lips. 'If only you knew how many times I wanted to say it, or knew how lonely and miserable I've felt without you, and wondered and tormented myself with the thought that the rest of our lives were going to be like this, and tortured myself wondering if I did tell you, whether I'd be like my mother, so…somehow *vulnerable* so as to invite desertion and all the rest, but if it means anything to you, Declan, I love you so much that every time you leave me, every time I wake up without you beside me from the very first time we made love, *all* the time I haven't known how you felt, I've died and die a little inside. Sorry…'

'Don't,' he said harshly and held her in his arms so that she could barely breathe. 'Don't apologize for loving me. I should be the one—'

'No,' she said softly. 'Perhaps we should concentrate on how much we love each other?'

'Where were you going today?' he said later.

They were still clothed but lying on the bed in each other's arms.

'Oh!' Arizona started guiltily as memories of the earlier part of the day came back to her. 'Oh, no. I feel terrible.'

'Why?' he asked quizzically and kissed her hair.

'I…the things I did. And said, in front of heaven knows who, but your receptionist for one, and the gardener. I feel *really* terrible now. On top of which—' she sat up with real perturbation '—my car has probably been clamped or towed away—'

'Come back here,' Declan interposed with a laugh in his voice and took her in his arms again. 'You were magnificent,' he added.

'I was awful— Do you mean that? How—'

He put a finger to her lips. 'My dear Arizona, don't you know that that's why I love you so much? For your total refusal ever to be intimidated by me. For fighting me every inch of the way—'

'That's not quite true.'

'Yes, it is. But also for—' he paused and threaded his fingers through hers '—making love to me like no other, with a mixture of joy, honesty and rapture, making me aware of your likes and dislikes at times,' he said gravely.

'I haven't done much of that.'

'You have. You definitely ticked me off for treating you like an object once,' he reminded her.

'Well, was I wrong, though?'

'No,' he conceded. 'What you may not have realized at the time was that I was nearly at the end of my tether. Because I'd almost convinced myself you'd come up from the beach that day after looking so lonely and somehow lost, and beg me not to leave you again because you couldn't live without me.'

Arizona caught her breath. 'I…I'm doing that now, Declan,' she said unsteadily. 'I mean, I know you'll have to go away from time to time but—'

'Don't cry,' he said into her hair. 'You won't be able to prise me away with a crowbar now—'

'But I'm trying to tell you I do understand that there will have to be times—'

'Times, yes, but the absolute minimum now, my

darling. You still haven't told me, though. Where you were going today?'

'Oh, that. I *was* coming to see you. I was going to try to tell you all this and then, if I couldn't sort of prove it to you, I was also going to go…away, but I hadn't worked out where, other than to see my mother first. That's how I knew where to come,' she added. 'I had your card in my purse—do you remember giving it to me?'

'Only too well, unfortunately. Arizona…' He stopped, sighed and said simply, 'Thank God.'

'For coming to your office? And creating all that mayhem—your poor ex-naval friend must be…I don't know.'

'Wondering what he's done to deserve being treated like a loose cannon between us?' he supplied with a crooked little grin.

'Yes.' She smiled ruefully.

'I love you,' he said, his grin fading.

'Would you like to know what I love about you?' she answered huskily.

'Yes…'

She told him, and presently he helped her out of her dress and made love to her in a way that caused her to give thanks rather fervently.

'Tell me,' he said gently.

'I wondered once, not so long ago,' she said, 'whether there was something new between us, something incredibly lovely and tender that—made me want to die for you. Then I thought I must have imagined it.'

'And now?'

'Now I know I didn't imagine it.'

He kissed her and held her very close. And later

he said, 'Would it be possible for us both to go and see your mother?'

'Yes, I think so.' Arizona sighed with pure happiness.

A year later, Christmas Day dawned bright and clear at Scawfell and began with a squabble. 'It's *my* turn to give him his bath,' Daisy said. 'I'm nearly seven and a half now, and I know all about babies, so you can just go away, Sarah!'

'Daisy, darling—'

'Well, it's true, isn't it, Arizona?' Daisy turned to her heatedly. 'You've shown me how, and anyway, I'm not the baby any longer, am I? He is.'

'Oh, definitely. Why don't you bath him and let Sarah dress him?'

'And I'm taking him for a walk in his pram,' Richard contributed. 'It's his first Christmas, after all, and we are both boys. There'll probably be lots of times when he'll need to get away from you two, not to mention Cloris!' he added to his sisters.

'Well, I'll have to be content with taking his picture,' Ben said wryly, looking interestedly at the new camera he'd just received. 'I know—I'll make a pictorial record of how baby mania has overtaken this family!'

'Baby mania?' Declan said some time later when he'd firmly closed the door of the green suite so that Arizona could rest before they embarked on the rigours of Christmas dinner. 'How long is this going to last, do you think?'

Arizona glanced down at her son, who was barely six weeks old but was appearing to thrive on all the attention. 'I don't know, but we do truly feel like a family now, and they're really very sweet, aren't they? But there's something I wanted to tell you, Declan.'

'Oh?' He sat down on the bed beside her and also glanced at his sleeping son in the crib beside the bed. 'That sounds a bit ominous. Have I done something to displease you, Mrs. Holmes? I must say it's quite a while since you cast me that autocratic, do-your-damnedest-Declan, pure grey gaze.'

'I didn't!' Arizona protested laughingly.

'Do you know something, I think, on the odd occasion, you always will.' A wicked little glint lit his eyes.

'This is not one of those—extremely rare occasions,' Arizona said, trying not to smile.

'Ah. What is it then?'

'Well, it's to do with my Christmas present. Not the one that was under the tree this morning,' she said as he raised an eyebrow, and she blushed faintly.

He started to frown. 'You have another one? I—'

'Yes, yes, I do. It's time to—well, it would be all right now to resume—I don't know why this should be so difficult,' she said with sudden exasperation.

'Resume relations do you mean?'

'Yes, which I thought might make rather a nice, if not to say, special sort of present and—'

'I agree, wholeheartedly,' he said gravely.

'But I did also want to,' Arizona went on determinedly, 'say thank you for your patience and the way you were when I was…anyway, thanks,' she said huskily and blinked suspiciously. 'You've been great.'

'Arizona.' He took her hand and with his other hand cupped her cheek. 'You do know why, if that's so, don't you? I thought I might have convinced you that you're not only my wife but the partner of my thoughts, and that anything to do with your welfare is my top priority.'

'Partner of your thoughts,' she said softly. 'That's lovely. Thanks again.'

'These—relations you were talking about,' he said a few minutes later. 'Would it be too decadent to resume them at eleven o'clock in the morning? It looks as if this young man is having an excellent sleep and could be returned to his nursery with impunity.'

'Decadent?' Arizona returned. 'If so, deliciously so, Declan.' And some minutes later, she settled into his arms with a sigh of pure pleasure, but not only that, almost overwhelming love that she now knew was returned in full measure.

Modern Romance™
...seduction and
passion guaranteed

Tender Romance™
...love affairs that
last a lifetime

Sensual Romance™
...sassy, sexy and
seductive

Blaze
...sultry days and
steamy nights

Medical Romance™
...medical drama on
the pulse

Historical Romance™
...rich, vivid and
passionate

27 new titles every month.

*With all kinds of Romance for
every kind of mood...*

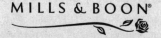

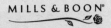

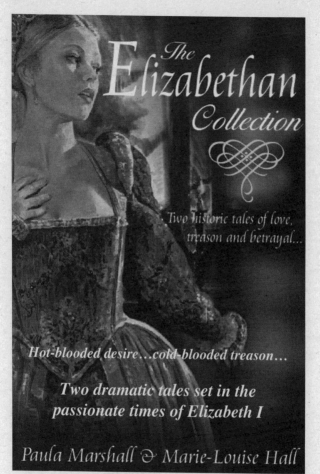

CHRISTMAS
SECRETS

Three Festive Romances

CAROLE MORTIMER   CATHERINE SPENCER
DIANA HAMILTON

Available from 15th November 2002

Available at most branches of WH Smith,
Tesco, Martins, Borders, Eason, Sainsbury's
and all good paperback bookshops.

1202/59/MB50

Don't miss *Book Five* of this BRAND-NEW 12 book collection 'Bachelor Auction'.

Who says money can't buy love?

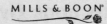

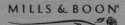

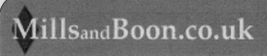